The

Gatsby
Gambit

The

Gatsby Gambit

Claire Anderson-Wheeler

RENEGADE BOOKS

First published in the United States in 2025 by Viking Books,
an imprint of Penguin, a division of Penguin Random House LLC, New York
This edition published in Great Britain in 2025 by Renegade Books

1 3 5 7 9 10 8 6 4 2

Copyright © Claire Anderson Wheeler 2025

The moral right of the author has been asserted.

*All characters and events in this publication, other than those
clearly in the public domain, are fictitious and any resemblance
to real persons, living or dead, is purely coincidental.*

All rights reserved.
No part of this publication may be reproduced, stored in a
retrieval system, or transmitted, in any form or by any means, without
the prior permission in writing of the publisher, nor be otherwise circulated
in any form of binding or cover other than that in which it is published
and without a similar condition including this condition being
imposed on the subsequent purchaser.

A CIP catalogue record for this book is available from the British Library.

Hardback ISBN 978-1-408-74851-0
C-format ISBN 978-1-408-74850-3

Printed and bound in Great Britain by Clays Ltd, Elcograf S.p.A

Papers used by Renegade Books are from well-managed forests
and other responsible sources.

Renegade Books
An imprint of
Dialogue
Carmelite House
50 Victoria Embankment
London EC4Y 0DZ

The authorised representative
in the EEA is
Hachette Ireland
8 Castlecourt Centre
Dublin 15, D15 XTP3, Ireland
(email: info@hbgi.ie)

www.dialoguebooks.co.uk

Dialogue, part of Little, Brown Book Group Limited,
an Hachette UK company.

For Mum and Dad
And for Pavol

"If we could only learn to look on evil as evil, whether it's clothed in filth or monotony or magnificence."

F. SCOTT FITZGERALD, *THIS SIDE OF PARADISE*

The
Gatsby Gambit

Chapter One

The train gathered speed as the sea finally blazed into view, and Greta Gatsby fiddled with the crumpled letter in her lap.

"Next stop, Great Neck. Great Neck!"

The conductor strode through the corridor, knocking on compartment doors. Great Neck was the first stop on Long Island; though the train would continue through a smattering of resort towns all the way to Port Washington, Greta would not be on it. She was bound for West Egg, the secluded little haven some four miles north of here where her brother, Jay, had made his home. *Their* home: seven years younger than her brother, Greta had lived under Jay's guardianship since their parents had died fifteen years ago.

You couldn't deny it was a remarkable turnaround of fate. They'd been born poor and orphaned early. All she'd had was Jay, and then he'd gone off to the front, and Greta, to live with their dour Aunt Ida. Lonely years, indeed. But Jay had always said everything would change once he was rich, and though others might have thought him a dreamer, he'd been right. He had a head for strategy, it turned out. Though he didn't much use the marble chess set in the library, he knew its rules. Greta had noticed how people never expected her brother to be shrewd in business—he had the soul of a dreamer, and therefore they underestimated him—but since childhood Greta had known her brother was special. Even so, she'd never expected him to be *quite* so successful.

"The art of the gambit," he'd told her once, years ago. She'd been confused; chess was hardly gambling.

"Gam*bit*," he'd corrected her. "It's a tactic. In chess it means sacrifice: you lose something to gain something."

At the time, she hadn't thought much about the sacrifice part. But sometimes now she wondered exactly what Jay had lost—what they had both lost, perhaps—in order to get where they were.

"Going somewhere nice?"

A young man had entered the compartment shortly after Grand Central. He was the sole other occupant of the enclosed space and the hint of impropriety in this was faintly thrilling, even if the same could not be said for the young man himself, who had been sniffing energetically the whole way from Manhattan, and on whose lapel a souvenir of lunch was prominently displayed. He looked at Greta expectantly, awaiting her answer.

"Home," she obliged. Somewhere she'd longed to be many times these past few years.

As soon as he'd had the money for it, Jay had sent her off to a fancy boarding school stocked with Mayflower types, and then to an even fancier "finishing school" for a couple of years. Jay wasn't a snob, but he detested being looked down on, and was determined that Greta would escape the stain of New Money. For her part, Greta had begged him, if further learning was to be involved, to send her to a *real* university, one where she might learn something about the world besides the art of watercolor and how to recite poetry, but to no avail. She'd done her best to learn about the world all the same, burying her head in a science book or a newspaper as often as in her beloved mystery novels. Her father had been something of an amateur scientist, and her mother a pragmatic woman who made balancing the household accounts look like child's play. They had always agreed on one thing above all, which was that a mind was a terrible thing to waste.

Greta wholeheartedly agreed, but she also felt that *life* was a terrible thing to waste. Happily, this summer, at the grand old age of twenty-one, Greta Gatsby had finished her education for good and was coming home to stay. It was absolutely thrilling and a little intimidating. She hoped for freedom, and feared for a new set of restrictions—the world Jay had bought them entry into had already shown itself to be heavy with codes and rules—but escaping from the Academy was an incontrovertible joy. Whatever the real world held for her, she decided, it had to be more invigorating than how she'd spent these last years of her life.

The young man opposite gave another protracted sniff—he really was exerting himself with this one—and for both their sakes, Greta felt moved to offer him her handkerchief.

"I'm all right." He waved. "You dropped your letter."

She demurely retrieved the crumpled paper from the floor and tucked it away. She knew all its news by now anyway. Chiefly, Jay had wanted to alert her that his friends Tom and Daisy Buchanan would be at the house upon Greta's return—apparently, they had been staying there for some weeks while their own stately pile, in the tonier locale of East Egg, underwent some repairs.

The Buchanans had been a fixture in Jay's life for years now, which was not an alliance Greta particularly rejoiced in. She was used to them traipsing in and out of Jay's house during the summer when they weren't on the Côte d'Azur or in Monte Carlo or up in Newport or the Cape, and Greta knew her brother considered Daisy to be the epitome of graceful womanhood and a perfect role model for Greta. She supposed Daisy didn't care much either way about Jay's mostly absent little sister, and certainly Greta had never considered Daisy and herself to have much in common. Jay, however, persisted in thinking that the two held a high sisterly regard for each other, and Greta had long learned that when Jay believed something, he'd believe it in the face of all evidence to the contrary.

"Great Neck!" the conductor called again, now with an air of finality, and the train began to slow. Greta stuffed the letter back in her bag and gathered her things, holding on to her new cloche on the seat beside her as it made a bid for freedom. The hat was a beautiful pale green shade, newly purchased upon Greta's graduation from the Academy, and she thought it looked rather dashing with the brand-new bob she'd just had done. Jay would hate the bob, of course—*It's rather unfeminine, Gigi, isn't it?*—but Greta thrilled every time she ran her hand through her hair and felt that blunt, shorn edge. Like everything else today, it seemed to hold a promise of freedom.

There was a hiss and a final lurch, and the train came at last to a standstill. Her nasally companion tipped his hat to her, and Greta dismounted in the churn of slammed doors and raised voices.

"Miss Gatsby? Miss Gatsby!"

A young man was making his way across the platform toward her, clad in the smart, gold-trimmed livery of the Gatsby house, but Greta didn't recognize his face.

"Miss Gatsby? I'm the new chauffeur. Bill Richardson."

She frowned. Jay had sent the chauffeur? And what had happened to Silas, the old one? She'd rather hoped her brother would be here to greet her in person.

"Here, miss—a note from Mr. Gatsby." Bill Richardson fished a paper out of his pocket and passed it over.

Terribly sorry, Gigi, it read, in Jay's familiar scrawl. *I came in to get you with Daisy, but the train was so delayed and she was expiring with the heat, I had to ferry her home. Bill here is the new chap.*

Bill smiled at her. Under the peaked cap, he had sandy hair and a freckled, narrow face.

"Your brother showed me a photograph so I'd be sure to recognize you. And if I may say, you've not changed much, miss, except for the hair."

Greta allowed herself a small grin.

"Yes, it's rather a new feature. I'm not sure that it will be terribly well received back home."

Bill nodded.

"Part of the appeal, miss?"

Greta smiled. Bill was a wit, evidently.

The station master's whistle blew. The train pulled out, and Greta let Bill relieve her of the small valise she carried.

"That's it?" he said.

"There's an awfully large trunk coming on the slow train in a few days," Greta admitted, and Bill chuckled.

"A lady never travels light, so I hear."

Perhaps Jay hadn't *entirely* failed to make a lady of her, then.

In the parking bay, she was greeted by the sight of Jay's beloved automobile, that primrose-colored Rolls Phantom he'd bought in a particularly indulgent spree. Subtlety had never been her brother's strong suit, Greta reflected. The heavily muddied undercarriage was a surprise, though: usually Jay insisted on it being kept pristine.

"Had a lot of rain?" she asked, as Bill hoisted up the valise.

"Pouring nonstop the last few days. Your brother and his guests have been feeling quite housebound. But it's cleared up nicely for your arrival." Bill swung open the Phantom's heavy door for her, and Greta stepped inside with a feeling of giddiness. Buchanans or no Buchanans, nothing was going to interfere with her pleasure at being back on the island. Jay had chosen well, making his home here. Greta had once thought that her brother would return to North Dakota once he'd made his fortune, and settle there. After the war, though, it was clear he'd set his sights on the East Coast. The world was fresher up here, the air as crisp as dollar bills. The people were crisp, too, Greta had noticed: brisk and cliquish and often frosty. But Jay seemed either not to notice that part, or not to care.

Bill installed himself in the front seat and the Phantom purred to life. They chugged out of the station onto a road busy with automobiles and bicycles, men in golf caps or trilbies, women carrying baskets . . . but soon the narrow streets with shops and houses gave way to roads with trees and ditches, and sun coming through a canopy of leaves overhead.

"Are you a fast driver, Bill?" Greta called from the back. "You rather look as though you might be."

He didn't seem to mind the goading. "If you're eager to be home, Miss Gatsby, I'll endeavor to oblige."

He was as good as his word, and as he fearlessly took the corners on the country road, Greta put her head out the window, and let the wind rush through her newly shorn hair and tickle her scalp. They passed a brick schoolhouse, a white-painted church, a corner where a small boy chased a dog. Greta thought she could already feel that fresh, bright air of Manhasset Bay, the glory of West Egg. She pictured it now: the long lawns that led down to the water and to the Gatsbys' private dock where their boat, the *Marguerite*, bobbed gently in the waves. The summer nights when fireflies would congregate and the green light from the Buchanans' dock winked at them from across Manhasset Bay. The window seat in the living room where she'd passed many summer hours ensconced, deep in one of her mystery novels. She'd ordered that new Agatha Christie book only last week from Dauber & Pine, that lovely little place just off Manhattan's Book Row; perhaps it would have arrived by now.

And perhaps this summer might give her an opportunity to spend some real time with Jay. Maybe it was the gap in years between them that made him seem so . . . distant, sometimes. Or perhaps the rupture he'd made with their past? He was always so immersed in his world of parties and friends, being the man *they* had come to know instead of the boy Greta remembered him being. He was as kind as ever, as generous as ever, but he was so determined not to look backward . . . and sometimes Greta wondered if she, too, might be part of that *backward*.

Bill tooted the horn, rounded the bend, and there were the tall black gates rising up in front of them. Bill unlocked them, then got back in and coaxed the Phantom gently up the incline. One more corner, and the Gatsby mansion emerged out of the trees. Excess reigned in every room of that house, but nothing could spoil its stately simplicity as it rose up before her now, the glorious white stone bathed in the afternoon light, the leaded windows reflecting fiery gold. Greta felt a small bubble of joy rise up in her chest.

Home.

The door was opened by a woman with steely hair gathered into a bun, who looked at Greta with a faint air of suspicion.

"Miss Gatsby—you're here! Your train was *quite* delayed, you know."

Mrs. Dantry had a particular skill for inflecting almost everything she said with an air of reproach; it was really a considerable talent. Greta smiled demurely at the housekeeper.

"Alas, Mrs. Dantry, my eagerness to be home bore little weight with the train driver."

Dantry turned her humorless stare on Greta, who had shrugged off her light travel cloak, and was now divesting herself of the green cloche. At the sight of what lay beneath, Dantry emitted a faint, strangled sound.

"Miss Gatsby—your hair . . ."

"Yes, it's all the rage now." Greta patted the blunt cut at the back. "Do you like it?"

The housekeeper managed a choked sort of *hmph*, but beyond that seemed quite lost for words. She blinked, then recovered herself sufficiently to address the chauffeur: "Take Miss Gatsby's valise around the back, Bill, and Molly will bring it up. No need to dawdle."

Greta stepped into the hall, relishing the familiar surroundings: those double-height ceilings and the enormous French Empire chandelier, designed to awe visitors on sight, as was the gilded wood staircase at the end of the hall whose dual branches curved magnificently up to the second floor. But Dantry's words echoed, distracting, and Greta brought her gaze back to the housekeeper.

"Who is Molly?" Surely Jay hadn't hired a *third* housemaid? That would be rather profligate, even for him.

Mrs. Dantry frowned.

"Why, Molly—the new maid. Nora Sweeney's replacement. Didn't Mr. Gatsby write you?"

Replacement! Greta felt momentarily crestfallen. Nora had been only a few years older than Greta, and had worked at the Gatsby house in one capacity or another since Greta was sixteen. *Friends* was hardly the right word for it, but they'd been something *like* friends. At least, Greta thought they had been. And now she'd left—and Greta had heard nothing of it until this moment.

"Why did—when did she leave?" What was Jay doing wrong, to be shedding staff like this? First the new chauffeur, now this.

"Oh, I don't know." Mrs. Dantry waved a hand. "A month ago, or three weeks. We have a new girl now, Molly Riggs. Perhaps she'll prove less flighty."

But Nora hadn't been *flighty*. She'd been lively and fun. And she hadn't said goodbye.

"Why, Miss Gatsby!" An imposing figure of a man with a tremendous gray mustache emerged from the passageway at the far side of the hall. "You're safely arrived! Welcome home."

"Thank you, Beecham." Greta felt her spirits lift at the greeting. "It's good to be back."

Beecham was the Gatsbys' butler and the longest-serving member of staff—a lofty, formal sort of man who, behind his rather prim facade, Greta suspected was quite fond of her and Jay. He was a butler of the most old-fashioned sort, loyal and punctilious and terribly proud. Jay had been most fortunate to secure his services and retain them all these years.

"Your brother and his guests are in the garden, Miss Gatsby," Dantry informed her, and then, with a slight wrinkle of the nose: "Playing a *game*, I believe."

Her tone left no doubt as to her views on such behavior. Greta briefly wondered what sort of a child Dantry had been, but was forced to abandon the exercise; one simply couldn't conjure such a vision.

"Then I shall change out of my traveling things and join them."

Greta made her way across the marble tile and took the stairs two at a time, hearing a faint *tsk* from Dantry behind her. It *was* wonderful to be free! And though it really was too bad about Nora, one couldn't let that spoil the pleasure of a homecoming. No doubt working under Dantry all this time must have been a rather joyless endeavor. It had been a strained relationship, with Dantry frequently lamenting that Nora's Irish brogue lowered the tone of the household, and Nora returning, sotto voce, that she'd rather have the voice of a Mick than the mind of a shrew. Upstairs, Greta ran a damp washcloth over her dusty skin, then flung open her wardrobe and wriggled out of the tired traveling clothes, letting them fall in a heap at her feet.

Greta's bedroom was a girlish confection of pink and white, picked out by Jay for her many years ago. She hadn't felt quite right in it then nor did she now—it had always felt rather like sleeping inside a large slice of cake—but it was home, and that was what mattered. She rifled through her wardrobe, and found the harem pants Jay so hated, but which she found so comfortable, and donned a fresh blouse. Finally, she wrapped a headband around her temples to hold back the copper-tinted locks already curling in the humidity, and glanced in the mirror. How wonderfully modern her new hair looked! And rather dashing, with the boyish trousers.

Trousers! Just a few years ago it would have seemed impossible that a woman should wear them. Greta cast a glance at the small celluloid print she kept framed on her bedside table. What would her mother and father say if they could see her now? She imagined her father would be rather shocked by the new fashions, but her mother would approve, and would surely talk him around.

Smiling a little wistfully, Greta gave herself a last approving glance in the mirror before turning to run back downstairs.

In the dining room, the French doors were flung wide, but there was no one in view—they must be around the side of the house. Daisy's laugh drifted in on the warm air, with its top note of indolent amusement. Daisy Buchanan did have a way of making herself heard first.

Greta stepped out onto the lawn, following the silvery trill. She was almost at the corner of the house when a sound cut through the silence that made her stumble and her heart race. Had that been . . . had she just heard a *gunshot?*

Chapter Two

Greta burst around the corner, then almost laughed with relief at the sight before her: a great bull's-eye set up in the middle of the lawns and four clearly uninjured figures standing in a line before it. So her brother had brought his guests out for a little target practice.

Jay had always fancied himself rather a keen shot, and enjoyed showing it off. It was fortuitous indeed that the Gatsby mansion sat on its own thirty acres, given her brother's special penchant for pastimes of the noisier variety.

They still had their backs to her—with all the noise they were making, they hadn't heard her approach—and as her heart steadied, Greta took in the sight. They cut such fine figures, glowing in the afternoon sun. On the left, Jay, golden-haired and slight—from the back, you might think him twenty still; then Daisy, her pale-blue dress aflutter in the breeze; and Tom, that bearlike frame instantly recognizable. And there was another man next to Tom. Could it be . . . ?

Nick Carraway didn't visit quite as often as the Buchanans did, which Greta considered a crying shame. Daisy liked to say Nick was taciturn, but Greta thought he must only seem that way because the rest of them were such relentless talkers.

"Gigi!" Jay turned at last, as if feeling her stare. "You're home!"

The others turned. So it *was* Nick Carraway. Greta smiled back at her brother.

"Home indeed."

"Darling, how splendid to see you," Daisy said brightly. "But, goodness, what *have* you done to your hair? And those trousers. So . . . bohemian!"

"Just the ticket, I say," Tom said, eyeing the trousers—and the rest of Greta's figure—in a most off-putting way.

Nick shot her one of his quick, elusive smiles as Jay crossed the lawn and wrapped her briefly in his arms.

"I'm sorry I wasn't there to greet your train. Daisy wanted to come into town with me, but then there was the delay and we were simply melting on the platform . . ."

Greta knew how persuadable Jay was when it came to Daisy, although she didn't believe for a moment that Daisy was as fragile as Jay seemed to think.

"Are you going to join in our bit of target practice?" Daisy waved her rifle around in a frankly unnerving manner. "It's tremendous fun."

"Despite your not having hit within ten feet of the target," Tom said in quashing tones.

"Well, *you're* no William Tell, you thick-fingered brute," Daisy retorted.

Tom's eyes flashed.

"Shall we put an apple on your head and find out, my dear?"

Greta caught Nick's eye. She was used to the Buchanans carping at each other—everybody was—but they might have waited until she was here five minutes before launching in.

Nick cleared his throat.

"I've another suggestion: How about we pack this in and call it cocktail hour?"

"All right." Daisy's rancor disappeared as quickly as it had arrived. It was part of her charm, the way her moods hurried along like scudding clouds, but Greta sometimes wondered if things didn't lodge there more deeply than they seemed to.

"I suppose Jordan and Edgar will be here soon anyway," Daisy added, as Nick led them up the lawn.

More guests? Greta supposed she oughtn't be surprised. Playing host was a compulsion for Jay.

"Who's Edgar?" she said. There was no need to ask about the other name—Greta was quite familiar with Jordan Baker, a semiprofessional golfer whose tournament schedule seemed remarkably conducive to a social life filled with cocktails and men. She was Daisy's best friend, and Greta knew there'd been an on-again, off-again "thing" with Nick Carraway for years . . . which, if she was honest, probably accounted for most of Greta's reservations about her.

"Tom's brother, Edgar," Jay supplied. "He's in New York this summer."

More Buchanans, Greta thought dismally.

"A rotten idea of yours, Jay," Tom groused. "I don't know what you want to suck up to that dry old shrub for."

"Well, he *is* your brother, old sport. I thought it would be nice," Jay said with one of the benign smiles he seemed to reserve for Tom's more ill-humored remarks.

"So much for a quiet night," Greta said. Behind her, Daisy gave a warm burble of laughter.

"My dear, have you *met* Jay Gatsby? Less than thirty people *is* a quiet night."

Jay had just finished pouring out the gimlets when Beecham announced Miss Baker's arrival.

"Hullo, chaps!" Jordan hardly let the butler finish before strolling onto the porch. She certainly cut a striking figure in her silver moiré tabard-cut, the square neck draped elegantly against her narrow collarbones, and showing her tall, thin frame to perfection. Anyone else in her outfit might have looked overdressed, but it was doubtful whether Jordan knew the meaning of the word. Her nails were lacquered, her chestnut hair waved tightly against her head, and she wore that cherry-red lipstick Greta had rarely seen her without.

"Jord!" Daisy put out her cheek to be kissed.

"Good to see you, old girl," Jay said. "You look smashing."

Jordan *did* look smashing, and Greta wondered if Nick Carraway was thinking the same. Meanwhile, Tom's eyes passed over her with that slow appraisal that seemed to happen anytime a woman crossed his field of vision. But Jordan, clearly desensitized by now to Tom's ways, moved on to the last person left to greet.

"Why, it's Greta!" She laughed, turning to their host. "You do rather hide her away, Jay—I think I sometimes forget you *have* a sister."

It wasn't unkindly meant, but the comment stung all the same. Jordan surely wasn't alone in forgetting that the great Jay Gatsby had a sister. Greta had been quietly tucked away all these years, summoned back only for annual summer and winter holidays when her progress on becoming *a lady* was monitored and charted. Her life, for the most part, had been kept quite separate from her brother's. In recent summers, she'd been allowed down to some of the annual parties, but the experience had left her with a strange ambivalence. She'd determined it was best not to tell people who she was, otherwise all they had wanted to ask her about was Jay.

"I haven't been *hiding* her, Jord, I've been *educating* her," Jay said, a little irritably. "And in any case, she's home for good now, so I dare say you may see as much of each other as you like."

"Home for good!" Jordan raised her eyebrows. "I suppose you'll be planning more parties, then. Introducing her to some eligible bachelors."

Jay glanced dubiously toward his sister.

"Oh, *yes!*" Daisy looked animated at the thought.

It wasn't that Greta minded parties. Nor indeed did she mind eligible bachelors, in principle. But Daisy's enthusiasm made her uncomfortable. Perhaps Daisy was just playing a part—after all, women like her were *supposed* to love matchmaking and gossip and weddings. But Greta had noticed how it was often the women who endured their own marriages with the greatest discomfort who were most eager to propel others into unions of their own.

There had been talk of Tom Buchanan's liaisons over the years, everywhere from dancehalls and bars to shopgirls in department stores. There was even a rumor that one of the gas stations on the Manhattan road had been shuttered due to a dalliance of his—something to do with the owner's wife. The humiliated husband had finally dragged them back to New Jersey, leaving the denizens of Long Island to find alternative pit stops on their route into the city. That particular rumor had come direct from Jordan last summer, so Greta supposed it was true. Then again, with Jordan, one never could be quite sure.

"Speaking of romance"—Jordan's voice pulled Greta back to the present—"what of *you*, Jay? All these parties and still no paramour! It's really too bad."

Tom snorted in a most unpleasant manner, but Jay only laughed.

"Oh, I'm a lost cause, you know that. After all, Tom here has married the only woman worth having." He smiled. "No offense, Jord, old thing."

Daisy smiled bashfully.

"Oh, Jay, you *are* too much."

Jay smiled, pleased with his flattery. He was prone to schoolboy crushes, and had never felt a need to hide them. What's more, he seemed habitually drawn to women who were either hard to please or hopelessly unavailable; Greta suspected that in Daisy, he had managed to unite both ideals.

Oh well. Nobody minded a little gallantry on an evening like this, when the air held the scent of summer grass and, more faintly, of roses. The sun was low, the water twinkling like the beading on Jordan's dress.

Just then, the sound of tires on gravel drifted through to the porch, and Jay, closest to the front of the house, craned his head to see.

"I expect that's your brother now, Tom."

"Bloody bore." Tom scowled. "You'll regret this, Jay."

Edgar Buchanan, despite his well-tailored pinstripe and immaculately shined shoes, did not cut a very impressive figure. A head shorter than his brother and half Tom's width, he lacked the same impression of ruddy good health. Still, the two were recognizably brothers, with the same dark hair and pale skin, unpleasant downturn at the corner of the mouth, and what would have been the same sharp nose had Tom's college football career not adjusted its native shape. Their manners, too, while similarly unpleasant, showed some divergence, Edgar's being of the more introverted variety: evidently, he preferred to scorn them privately rather than mock everyone publicly as was his brother's way. He troubled himself only to say, "Gatsby, is it?" when Jay introduced himself, and then delivered a monotone "how'd you do" to Greta, Jordan, and Nick. Daisy, however, he leaned in to kiss, and his eyes lingered on her when he drew back. Dusk was falling now. A string of lanterns had been lit, and the green light of the Buchanans' dock was visible across the water. There were the soft caws of birds, and a few white boats drifting on the sound, catching the last light. Really, it was exquisite. Greta tried not to feel resentful that she wasn't able to enjoy it in peaceful solitude.

"Edgar," Daisy said. "It *has* been a while."

Edgar half smiled. "Too long." His voice was a lighter timbre than Tom's, smoother, colder.

"Has it?" Tom said, between the olives he'd just stuffed in his mouth. "Can't say that I noticed."

Greta saw Edgar's face stiffen, but no retort came. The brothers eyed each other, Tom smirking. Did no one but Greta see it? Something was up between these two, some acrimony that ran deep, and seemed recent.

A well-timed cough came from the door.

"Dinner, sir," Beecham announced.

Candelabras had been lit on the dining table and sideboard, their small flames reflecting in the cut-glass goblets and tumblers like so many diamonds. As the guests found their places, wonderful aromas, buttery and herbal, drifted along the passage from the kitchen.

Jay took his seat at the head of the table, and pulled out the chair to his right as Daisy approached.

"I may claim your company for dinner, I hope?" He turned to the others. "I've dug up a rather nice claret for us to drink. It should go nicely with the chateaubriand. You like a claret, don't you, old sport?" This last was addressed to Tom, who only grunted in return, but was nevertheless rewarded with Jay's blithe smile.

Greta's brother was an enigma to her sometimes. At times, he seemed so tremendously astute. At others, a dreamer determined to live in his own reality. Did he really not notice Tom's slights? Or did he simply cover his feelings that well? Nick had said that it was part of Jay's peculiar charisma that he never seemed to pass judgment on anyone or anything—or if he did, he kept his opinions inscrutably private.

"May I?" Edgar said, with no great enthusiasm, and pulled out the seat to Greta's left. He had little choice, since Jordan had seated herself with alacrity, and Daisy, too, was already spoken for. To Greta's dismay, Tom descended on her other side. Sandwiched between the Buchanan brothers—some luck! But Nick had the seat across from her, which was some consolation, and soon the wine was poured, which was another.

"I thought we might take the boat out tomorrow." Jay turned to the table at large. "A little adventure on the Sound."

"Ooh! We could bring a picnic." Jordan looked pleased. "How is Mrs. Smith at deviled eggs?"

"A genius, no doubt," Nick said, eyeing the smoked trout pâté appreciatively. "As she is at everything."

"Sounds divine," Daisy said. "Doesn't it, Tom?" She looked at her husband, who ignored her and reached for the bottle of claret.

"Me, too, while you're at it." Jordan waved her glass at him. "Now tell us, Jay, what's the plan for the Fourth this year? Daise, you're staying for the bash, aren't you?"

The Fourth was usually the centerpiece of the summer at the Gatsby mansion, although between last year's sunstroke and the equestrian camp Jay had packed her off to the year before, Greta had now missed the party two years running.

"Not us." Tom maneuvered a large piece of pâté into his mouth. Daisy looked down at her plate.

"Not this year, I'm afraid." She glanced apologetically at Jay. "We're leaving for Newport the day after tomorrow."

"I may have to miss it, too, unfortunately." Nick glanced up. "It's busy at the firm these days. I can't stay past the weekend."

The flicker of disappointment Greta felt was foolish. It was only that Nick had always been so pleasant to her. Greta never felt lonely in this house when it was empty—on the contrary, it was a magical place to be with a little solitude—but on those occasions when Jay stuffed it full of revelers, she *did* feel lonely. Perhaps Nick had noticed it: she had always appreciated how he was wont to find her on those evening, and always had a thoughtful question or two to ask. To be sure, he was quieter than Jay and the others and less prone to smiling, which at first might give him the affect of being standoffish, but Greta was sure he wasn't, not really.

"That's right—back to your bean counting in the city, eh, Nicky?" Tom said in patronizing tones. Nick sold bonds in an office in Manhattan, and he was the only one at the table who worked for a living. Tom's family had never *not* been rich—they'd owned, and still owned, acres upon acres of farmland in Illinois, and the fruits of it had doubtless been multiplying in various Wall Street accounts for decades. And then there was Jordan, who came from old money, too, though a more modest amount of it. Greta wasn't sure exactly how Jordan kept pace with Daisy's lifestyle, but being wined and dined for free by the likes of Jay Gatsby and others presumably helped. Greta thought Nick ought to be admired for his industry, but no one else seemed to see it that way.

"Well, the beans won't count themselves, I suppose." Nick shrugged. "And I rather like being busy."

"Well, if it helps you afford a decent suit." Tom smirked. "Did yours shrink in the wash, Nicky?"

Daisy's yawn cut across the barb.

"Oh, let's not talk about work, it's so *boring!*"

Boring for some. It was fortuitous, Greta reflected, that the future of women's liberation did not depend solely on Daisy Buchanan. One had to admit, though, that Daisy looked quite resplendent in her evening wear, diaphanous in the candlelight, much like the white roses arrayed the length of the table. Pearl drop earrings winked prettily from each lobe, and her matching necklace was set off to perfection. It was the famous one Tom had given her as a wedding present, over which half the East Coast had murmured at the time. Three hundred and fifty thousand dollars' worth of Tahitian saltwater pearls, with an emerald and diamond clasp!

"So—Edgar," Jordan said, turning the full beam of her attention on the dour guest. "Tell us more about what *you've* been doing in New York. Here for a jaunt?" She winked slyly across the table at Greta. "Or perhaps there's a lady you're courting?"

Greta sensed the irritation emanating off the man in the seat beside her. Clearly, Edgar wasn't used to being teased.

"I'm here on business," he said curtly.

"Indeed! What kind?"

"Various kinds," Edgar answered, then glanced at Tom. "Unlike some people, I prefer to make money than spend it."

"Oh, don't be such a drip, Edgar," Tom said impatiently. "Nobody cares."

Edgar sat up straighter, and Greta could fairly feel the sparks coming off him now. But he didn't get the chance to say whatever he was planning: an almighty crash echoed through the dining-room doorway, causing all of them to turn toward the hall.

"Oh dear," Jordan said. "Is that remarkable chef of yours throwing a tantrum, Jay?"

Daisy looked up with startled blue eyes. "I do hope no one's done themselves an injury."

It *had* been quite a crash.

"Had someone better see if everything's all right?" Daisy added, as raised voices rang out from down the hall.

Greta hurried down the service passage that led off the hall, following the rich scents toward Mrs. Smith's domain. She'd been more than ready to escape the latest Buchanan contretemps. What her brother saw in that bunch—excepting Nick, of course—was beyond her.

Mrs. Smith's gifts in the kitchen were legendary but so was her temper, and Greta had the distinct impression that her entrance had interrupted a vigorous tongue-lashing. A quick glance told her that although a beautiful cut-glass punch bowl had seen the end of its days, no one was otherwise harmed.

"Everything all right, Mrs. Smith? We heard a bit of a crash."

"I should think you heard it!" Mrs. Smith was a tall woman with a thick Bostonian accent and hands like ham hocks.

"Nearly brought the house down, Molly did!" She glanced toward the oven. "I was sure she'd gone and collapsed my soufflés. Soufflés are ever so temperamental, you know," she said sternly to Greta. "*Very* delicate."

Greta kept a straight face. "But *your* soufflés could never collapse, Mrs. Smith. They wouldn't dare."

Mrs. Smith eyed her narrowly.

"All right, you'll have your fun. But Molly here is going to have to get a grip on herself—you mark me, Molly Riggs!" She turned to the unhappy-looking young woman beside her.

So this was Nora's replacement. Poor thing, she seemed a timid sort. No doubt she'd be perfectly fine at taking over Nora's duties, but she'd be no replacement for the jokes and chatter that Greta had counted on Nora for. Nora had always had a pleasing sense of irreverence, which Mrs. Dantry had put down to her seditious, Papist upbringing.

"Oh well." Greta tried to catch the maid's eye to show her that all was well. "A heavy bowl like that, it's easy to drop. Jay won't mind."

"*I* was the one who dropped it, Miss Gatsby," Mrs. Smith looked aggrieved. "But only because of the shriek *she* let out."

Greta frowned.

"Why, did something happen? Are you all right, Molly?"

"Quite all right, thank you, miss." The girl spoke stiffly, eyes averted.

Mrs. Smith sighed.

"She thought she saw someone in the garden."

Greta glanced out the window. Nothing but trees, grass, and water. Still, there *had* been some burglaries last summer at the big houses.

"Perhaps we ought to—"

"There wasn't a soul in sight," Mrs. Smith said firmly. "Ada even ran out to have a look. Not a soul. Isn't that right, Ada?"

"Quite right," said Ada, a buxom brunette whom Mrs. Smith had on past occasions denounced as a giddy-headed flibbertigibbet. The cook must be quite fed up with poor Molly to have chosen Ada as her ally now.

"What exactly did you think you saw, Molly?" Greta said, keeping her voice gentle.

"I . . ." Molly blushed now. "I could hardly say. It was only for a moment. I just, I thought I saw a person there. Outside the window. I took a fright only because it was so unexpected." She looked at the glowering Mrs. Smith, and swallowed. "But perhaps I was mistaken."

"*Certainly* you were mistaken," Mrs. Smith said in dangerous tones. "And you'd better not be telling us it was a ghost you saw neither."

Molly looked down at her shoes. "I don't believe in ghosts, ma'am."

The garden could be a lively place in the twilight: deer sometimes, or rabbits, flashes of white in the dusk that could startle a person, and glimpsed out of the corner of one's eye, it might be easy to imagine something more. But what if there was truth to Molly's account? The gates would have been opened earlier for the guests to enter. Might some dubious character have also found their way inside? Greta felt a strange, prickling feeling, as if of foreboding. Which was silly, really, on a beautiful night such as this.

"Well, it's done now." Mrs. Smith sighed. "You might as well head upstairs, Molly—Mrs. Dantry needs someone to do the turndowns. Only try not to let the sheets spook you," she said tartly. "And when you've done that, go and find Mr. Beecham. He'll want to log the breakage for replacement."

Greta hesitated.

"While you're at it, Molly, perhaps you'd ask him to make an inspection of the grounds? I'm sure it was nothing, just as Mrs. Smith says. But perhaps we'd all rest easier, having him verify it."

The cook looked nonplussed.

"Say it's at my behest," Greta added. "I'm afraid I'm guilty of reading too many ghost stories myself, Mrs. Smith."

Chapter Three

Jay Gatsby had always loved beautiful things.

In the opulent, lamplit drawing room, letting the others' voices drift over her, Greta stood by the window, thinking of then and now.

Even as a boy, when there'd been no money for anything beyond necessities: when their mother sent Jay out on errands, he was as like as not to come back late with a bouquet of handpicked wildflowers for the kitchen table, causing anxiety to their mother but delight to Greta. And he had loved to delight her, then. She remembered the sketchbooks he'd make, assembled from scraps of old paper. He tore pictures from catalogues and newspapers, too—anything that spoke of luxury or elegance or beauty. Greta had barely seen an automobile in those days other than in the collection of Jay's scrap pages. Once he'd started making a little money of his own, he'd been able to afford a small indulgence or two, like the pomade in a beautiful gold tin he started using for his hair. He hadn't cared that he was teased and even beaten in the schoolyard for it; he'd kept wearing it.

You couldn't fault a person like that for their love of beauty. You couldn't say it was just superficial. Sometimes Greta thought beauty was what had kept her brother alive all these years. It was what had nourished him after their parents were gone.

"Here. You look like you mightn't mind another one of these." Nick appeared beside her, proffering a martini. Greta glanced into those dark eyes. Unlike Jay, who ran a campaign of charm with most anyone he met, Nick struck her as deeply self-contained, and something about his attention felt precious.

"I mightn't. Thank you."

The cool, clean taste of gin hit her palate. Nearby, the mantel clock ticked comfortably on its marble surround, but she and Nick were surely the only ones to hear it, with Tom's voice drowning the rest of the room in talk of Chicago, and a friend from "the League" who was running for office, and Tom's thoughts of doing the same.

Greta glanced in Tom's direction.

"You don't think he really means it about running for office? What's this 'League' he keeps talking about?"

Nick made a face.

"Oh, Wilson disbanded them after the war, but Tom still has notions he was some sort of solider. The American Protective League, you know."

Greta had heard of them vaguely: a self-appointed group of vigilantes who had organized "slacker raids" during the war, rounding up other civilians they suspected of draft dodging. Unlike Nick or Jay, Tom hadn't served during the war—some poor-health excuse had been drummed up. Naturally, someone like Tom *would* compensate for it by going around terrorizing others.

She glanced at Tom now, ensconced on his chaise longue, feet up on a marble coffee table, a modern-day Emperor Nero in the making. Nick followed her eyes, then turned back to the window. The sound was dark and still, picked out by moonlight.

"Quite glorious," he observed.

Greta ran a hand over the silk-upholstered window seat, thinking of the hours she'd spent in exactly this spot with her nose in a book, glancing up from time to time to admire the view over the bay and dream.

"I've always loved this view. Though Tom and Daisy's is better, I suppose, being west facing." All the houses on East Egg were deemed slightly better than those on West Egg for just this reason. Of course, the Buchanans had to have the best of the best.

Nick smiled. "I envy you, you know—able to look out on this all summer long. Indeed, longer," he added, "now that you are home for good."

Some doubts must have crept onto her face; he frowned.

"What is it? You're not glad to be back?"

"Oh, I am," she said. She had perhaps not spoken quite so frankly to Nick Carraway before. "I truly am. It's just that, well, one doesn't want the same exact view for the rest of one's life—does one?"

He looked curiously at her.

"And is there a particular view you're in search of?"

"I'm not sure I know," she confessed. She just couldn't help but feel there ought to be something *more* in her life besides the marriage and children everyone seemed to assume for her. Surely, she wasn't wrong to hope for fulfillment from some other quarter, too? Greta thought it would be rather fine to have a profession, but being a woman—and a woman of her social standing to boot—that was simply off the table.

She thought of some of her heroines, the Nelly Blys and Annie Lauries of today's press, traveling to faraway places or even journeying around the world. And not just for giddy adventure, either: they were changing the world, pushing for justice in places that sorely needed it.

The world was large, and time was short. What was one to do with it?

"I suppose I'd just like to see as much as I can of life," she said, looking out at the moonlit glow over the water—it was easier than looking directly at Nick, whose eyes she could feel on her. "And to be of some use, perhaps," she added.

"Then I'm sure you shall be," Nick said quietly.

A burst of music erupted from the gramophone then, one of those slow, swaying Al Jolson numbers.

> *Down by the Swanee*
> *The folks up North will see me no more*
> *When I go to that Swanee shore . . .*

The girls at school had liked that one. Greta did, too—there was something about its lilting, playful melody and the melancholy underneath.

"Dreadful caterwauling."

Tom rose to his feet, extracted a cigarette from his pocket, and left the room, which immediately felt lighter without him. But Greta was surprised to see Edgar rise from his seat a moment later, and follow Tom out the door.

"I rather like this song."

Nick's words cut across Greta's train of thought. His eyes were on the window, but she thought he sensed her glance. It was rare to hear Nick announce a like or dislike; he didn't tend to give much of himself away.

"So do I," Greta said.

"Do you?" Nick turned from the window. "Then . . ." He hesitated. "Perhaps a dance?"

Greta flushed, but before she had time to answer, Jordan ambled up, cocktail in hand.

"I don't know what your brother was thinking, inviting that Edgar fellow. Even liquored up, he's no fun."

Greta sighed inwardly; a bubble had burst. There would be no dance now. But Nick didn't seem particularly dismayed at the interruption.

"I thought it was Daisy's idea to invite him." He shrugged. "But then you know Jay, always pouring oil on troubled waters. No doubt he liked the idea of a *rapprochement*."

Jordan raised her eyebrows, then turned to Greta.

"Well, as long as it wasn't for *your* benefit, my dear. I should think you could do much better. Besides, he's not as rich as Tom—or at least he won't be. Curse of the younger brother and all that."

Nick looked amused. "Well, I should say neither of them is very hard up."

"They got a tidy chunk when they came of age," Jordan conceded. "Set them up nicely all right. But the real thing is the inheritance." She looked meditative. "I shouldn't be surprised if old lady Buchanan is sitting on a cool half million, all things considered. And when she shuffles off her mortal whatsit, I gather it's Tom who'll get the land. Although"—she glanced back at Greta—"I suppose the rest of her estate will be split evenly, so it's not as though Edgar doesn't have *something* going for him."

Greta winced. She was quite sure that no amount of money could induce her to marry a man like Edgar Buchanan even had he taken the slightest interest in her.

Jordan chuckled.

"Oh, I know what you're thinking, my dear—and I can't help but agree."

Greta felt her neck warm. Jordan had a terrific knack for making her uncomfortable—an effect she probably had on most people, if not, apparently, on Nick. Despite Nick's essential seriousness, he appeared to have a gift for not being drawn into things. Greta rather envied him that.

"Why don't they get along, anyway?" Greta blurted. "Tom and Edgar, I mean."

Jordan nudged an olive to the side of her glass, and tipped back the last of her gin.

"Money, darling. What else? And, of course," she went on. "Edgar knew Daisy before Tom did." She nodded, seeing Greta's surprise. "*He* introduced her to Tom, in fact. Of course it was long ago now. The brothers came down from Chicago one summer for a flutter on the Kentucky horses. The summer ended, Edgar went home, Tom didn't." Jordan shrugged. "Not that

Edgar ever had a real shot with Daisy himself—he always did have that runt-of-the-litter look to him." Jordan put her glass down on the mantelpiece, a little unsteadily. "Goodness, I absolutely can*not* drive home tonight," she declared. "I do hope Jay has one of the spare rooms made up."

"I should think so," Nick said. "He didn't meet you yesterday, Jord."

Jordan pouted, her red lipstick still miraculously intact, then turned to Greta. "I fear your brother's hospitality brings out the worst in me. Or is it the best in me? Oh well." She picked up her empty glass. "Seeing as that's resolved, I suppose I *ought* to have another drink. Nicky, dance with me, will you, there's a lamb! I do so love this record."

Jordan wheeled Nick over toward the music even as he shook his head at her. Greta wasn't sure what she read there—exasperation, amusement, affection? Once again, she wondered what exactly had happened—and what, if anything, persisted—between Nick Carraway and Jordan Baker.

With her back to the window now, Greta felt the touch of cool air on her neck. The candelabra on the mantel flickered faintly, reflected in the great mirror above the fireplace. The teardrop chandelier sparkled. A play of light and shadow everywhere. Across the room, two tall lamps framed the doorway to the hall, two obsidian nymphs holding their golden orbs aloft. They seemed to gaze out at Greta, their expressions mischievous and knowing.

She found herself thinking about the new maid and the stranger that had allegedly been sighted. The cold air from the window whispered across Greta's neck, and she shivered. Perhaps she'd go and find Beecham just to reassure herself.

She was out in the hall when she heard the voices drifting in from outside—the Buchanan brothers. Greta was not an eavesdropper by nature, but there was something about the intensity of the voices, the urgency of them.

"You may think you can cheat me," one of them was saying—Tom or Edgar, she wasn't quite sure. "But you can't. You won't!"

Greta waited a moment longer, but they must have moved away from the doorway, and if more was said, it was lost to the night air.

Beecham's door was ajar. She knocked, and the butler looked up, then stood. Greta felt a flash of comfort at the sight of him, his craggy features, the faintly drooping eyes that never failed to make her think of an English bulldog. He was their most long-standing member of staff, and beneath the rather crusty and formal exterior, she was sure he was the kindest. While Greta would readily admit to teasing the irascible Mrs. Smith on occasion, and wrong-footing Dantry, that joyless old lemon, when she got the chance, she'd never been tempted to visit any mischief on Beecham.

"Bill and I both took a turn about the premises, Miss Gatsby," he reassured her, when she asked about Molly's sighting. "Nothing amiss at all." His eyes met Greta's and he gave a discreet cough.

"I believe the consensus is that Molly may have a somewhat . . . nervous temperament."

"Yes, Mrs. Smith seemed to think that might be the case." Molly hadn't struck Greta as the silly or histrionic type, but timid, certainly, and still rather out of her depth. A person's mind could jump to false conclusions under stress. Greta swallowed a smile.

"I suppose I might be rather jittery, too, if I were working under Dantry and Mrs. Smith—especially on a soufflé night."

The mustache twitched.

"No doubt the household takes some getting used to," Beecham said graciously. "I expect the young woman's nerves will settle down soon enough."

If Mrs. Smith doesn't bite her head off first.

"I suppose Dantry had to hire someone in a bit of a hurry." Greta paused. "Beecham—did Nora give any reason for her departure? I gather it was rather sudden."

The eyebrows furrowed.

"Indeed, it was regrettably abrupt. No proper notice. Not well done, I'm afraid."

"It just doesn't seem like her."

Nora had been strong-willed but not, Greta thought, impulsive. And it stung a bit that she hadn't even left her a note. Nora was the only member of the household who'd been something like a friend, trading backstairs gossip for Greta's stories of the more outrageous or objectionable characters she'd met at boarding school. In the end, Nora would laugh and say, *Rather you than me, stuck in a convent like that.*

Greta wasn't sure how much Jay paid—ought she to know these things?—but he was very generous with money, almost apologetically so sometimes, so it was hard to think Nora had moved on for a better wage. Perhaps she'd gone off to be a telephone operator! Nora had always been rather enamored with the phone ever since they'd got it installed. She'd observed to Greta more than once what fun it must be to listen in on all those conversations. Greta had wholeheartedly agreed.

At least, Greta hoped it was a reason like that. Sometimes she felt—oh, it was such a tricky thing to put into words!—this suspicion that the world was not quite the world she read about. That she was still being . . . protected from things. Not by Jay exactly, not by anyone in particular, but by some invisible, insidious buffer.

Greta shook her head. What a silly, ominous way to think! Staff moved on; households turned over; people complained about it all the time. And that sort of thing was contagious: probably all it had taken was for Silas to announce his departure, and Nora had started dreaming of new horizons of her own.

Greta made her way back down the corridor. The ceilings were lower here than in the rest of the house, and her footsteps made a flat sound against the rough floorboards. She passed the door to the housemaids' room and then the kitchen—empty now and dark, but still aromatic—and back down the service passageway to the hall.

"What do you think you're doing?"

It was Tom's voice, the voice of a bully amused by his own power. And the person he was speaking to was Edgar.

What *was* Edgar doing on the stairs? He was three steps from the bottom—going up or coming down? But what on earth for? He saw Greta now, and flushed; Tom laughed unpleasantly.

"You're making a fool of yourself, Ed. But I suppose you're used to that."

"Miss Gatsby." Edgar descended the steps, and yet it was not embarrassment Greta saw in his eyes but irritation. If she had been a different sort of woman—a woman of the "right" pedigree, a woman like Daisy or even Jordan—he would have had the decency to be embarrassed. What had he wanted to go upstairs for anyway? To make fun of the house, of Jay's taste; to rifle through what was private?

She kept her voice cool.

"Was there something you needed?"

Tom smirked.

"My brother was just leaving. Weren't you, Edgar?"

Edgar flashed his brother a hateful look, and then his eyes met Greta's. There really was something deeply unpleasant about the man—those cold eyes, that face that gave away nothing.

And then, in an instant, he was gone. No goodbyes, no attempt at niceties, no fetching of his coat. The door banged, and Greta saw the lazy, satisfied look that bloomed across Tom Buchanan's face in the wake of it.

"Poor show," Jordan commented. "You *did* feed him a very nice supper, Jay."

Point made, she collapsed back onto the chaise in a flutter of sequins, but the screech of car tires and spinning gravel from Edgar's abrupt departure still seemed to linger in the air.

"Tom, what did you say?" Daisy whirled around as her husband entered the room. "I expect you were a beast as usual."

Tom's grin froze; his eyes narrowed.

"You're just sore because he was acting moony over you. Don't you get enough of that from your friend Gatsby?"

Daisy's pretty mouth fell open.

"Now look here, Tom." Jay sounded disoriented. He was unused to defending himself, or to overt aggression, but his voice grew firmer as he spoke. "There's no call to speak to her that way. And I haven't the foggiest—"

"Don't, Jay. There's no point when he's like this." Daisy moved toward the door, and paused, waiting. "Jordan, are you coming?"

Jordan evidently didn't like the tone of Daisy's summons, but she got to her feet nonetheless. Daisy's gaze swung back to her husband.

"Sometimes I truly do wish I'd never married you."

Greta blinked. Those were startling words coming from Daisy, who was not one to let the cracks show. But Tom evinced only a momentary discomfort. If the words had caused any puncture, his smirk quickly plastered over it.

"You keep telling yourself that, princess."

Daisy stalked out the door, her cheeks bright pink, like a porcelain doll stirred to fury.

"For heaven's sake," Jordan muttered, and followed behind. Greta and the three men were left in sharpened silence, Jay's fists clenched by his sides. Everyone was used to seeing Tom and Daisy trade barbs, but this had been worse than usual, closer to the edge somehow. It made Greta wonder what would happen if they ever reached that edge, if they ever stepped over it.

"Let's all retire for the night," Nick said, with an air of calm authority. "It's late, and I think we can all consider the party over."

"Yes—come on, Jay." Greta placed a hand on her brother's arm.

With an effort, Jay tore his eyes from Tom, and for a brief moment, when his gaze landed on her, Greta glimpsed the boy she remembered, with eyes of wild, turbulent blue. The eyes she'd looked into that long-ago day when he'd told her their parents would not be coming home from work. Eyes that had held hers as he stood on a train platform, enlistment papers in hand. Eyes that still didn't know how to hide their emotion.

Tom shook his head and waggled his half-full glass.

"I'll stay down here and finish my drink. Not to worry—I'll put myself to bed, nanny." He grinned.

"Have some water, Tom," Nick said sharply.

The door slammed closed as the grandfather clock rang midnight.

Chapter Four

Greta sat up in bed with a sigh. She'd been tossing and turning, unable to find sleep despite the day's exhaustion. Perhaps it was the night's events, or perhaps it was being home again and feeling so surrounded by . . . what was it? Memories? Anticipation?

Shadows crisscrossed the room, and the armoire made a great black shape against the wall. Greta reached out to her nightstand and picked up the silver-framed photograph that stood there always. Her parents had had it taken in a studio a couple of years before Jay was born. Henrik and Rosa Gatz: Gatz had been the family name before Jay adapted it to sound more "Anglo." Their mother had looked like Jay—the same fine hair, the same slight build, and in repose Jay's face often wore the same guarded expression that hers showed in the picture. Greta, on the other hand, took after their father. He had had the same undisciplined hair she had, curling in all directions with a coppery tint to it. When she was younger, she'd been told she had his eyes—she remembered his still, those quizzical, often merry eyes—but now there was no one left to tell her those things. Jay never really wanted to talk about their parents. Perhaps because being the son of an immigrant shopkeeper didn't fit the persona he'd carved out for himself . . . or perhaps he just missed them too much.

They'd come here on a boat and never gone back. Not on the same boat: Henrik had come over with his brother; Rosa, already motherless, some years before with her widowed father and cousins. Having found their way west, respectively to Racine, Wisconsin, and to Minneapolis, they were eventually to meet in Duluth, Minnesota. Henrik had been an enterprising type, and shortly after Greta was born, he'd moved the family farther west still, away from the iron ranges and urban life, to open a general store in what was still farming country. English had been her father's third language and her mother's fourth. They had, none of them, been easy years, and her parents had poured everything into their work. *Freedom*: that had been the dream at all costs, the one they'd sought to pass down to their children.

And then had come the accident. A fire in the neighboring store; everything was wood, and it had spread fast.

All that was long ago now. An old story, grieved often, but no longer fresh. Greta just wished her brother was open to talking about it all more.

The room felt overheated. Some cool night air, that was what she needed. Outside, a soft rain had started. There was a light patter on the eaves as she lifted the sill, and below her, the tree-lined driveway up which Bill had driven them only hours ago. Now, in the darkness of their isolated acreage, the black shapes were witchlike and spindly. Really, Greta reprimanded herself, there was no call for this unsettled feeling that flickered around her. They'd all go sailing tomorrow as Jay had suggested, and that would blow the cobwebs away. Everything would be all right.

Greta paused. Had there been a noise in the corridor? She held her breath: she thought someone had knocked, very faintly, on her door.

She crossed the room and cracked the door open noiselessly.

Oh.

The knock had not been on her door at all. It had been for Daisy. Greta saw the slippered heel of a man's foot disappearing from view before the door closed again.

So it appeared Tom and Daisy had made up their fight already. Greta felt a little repelled, then reminded herself that it was none of her business. Quietly, she drew her door closed and climbed back into bed. And this time, sinking between the crisp sheets, she was carried off at last to a truly dreamless sleep.

"Miss Gatsby?"

Groggily, Greta rolled over, then remembered all in a rush where she was.

Home. She nudged her sleeping mask onto her forehead and blinked her eyes open to the pink-and-white room—and Molly's thin face appearing around the side of the bedroom door.

"Miss Gatsby?" Molly nudged the door farther open. "Your coffee."

Greta stifled a yawn.

"Thank you, Molly. What time is it?"

"Ten o'clock, miss," Molly said, hesitant, as though guessing the answer would be unwelcome.

"Ten? Already?" After all that tossing and turning, she'd slept the morning half away! And Jay wanted to go sailing! "Tell the others I'll be right down, will you?"

The girl nodded.

"Molly." The young woman turned.

"I hope Mrs. Smith wasn't too hard on you about that silly bowl last night. Nora, who used to work here, she always said Mrs. Smith's bark was worse than her bite."

Molly's face seemed to close over.

"I'm not complaining, miss."

"No, of course not," Greta said hastily. She hadn't meant to get Molly's guard up. For all that the girl seemed fragile, she clearly had pride.

After a few swigs of coffee, Greta selected a seaworthy outfit, quickly fixed her hair, splashed her face, then stepped out onto the landing. Across the hallway, Daisy's door was wide open, displaying an unmade bed with rumpled sheets. Greta felt her cheeks warm, thinking of the accidental glimpse she'd had last night of Tom disappearing inside. How grotesque, to share one's bed with such a man. She put the idea from her mind, focusing instead on the smell of bacon and poached eggs that drifted up the stairway.

"Sorry I'm late," she blurted as she hurried through the dining-room doors. At least they hadn't all set off without her.

Jordan looked up from her coffee.

"One down, one to go."

"No rush," Nick explained. "We're still waiting for Tom."

Greta looked around, seeing the vacant chair.

"Nicky already knocked on his door." Daisy tapped her cigarette and exhaled, carefully directing the smoke away from Nick beside her. "He's not in bed—the silly chump's gone out for a walk or something. Honestly! He knows we're supposed to be starting early. I'm sure he's doing it just to be difficult." She blew another plume of smoke over her shoulder. Daisy Buchanan was a curious creature. There seemed to Greta something positively performative about her—and yet, now and again, her theatrical ways were shot through with flashes of what seemed like real earnestness.

Jay glanced at his watch, and Greta wondered how the general mood lay as regards Tom. Daisy showed no signs of tension as she spoke of him—she was either a woman who bore no grudges or a wonderfully breezy actress. Nick seemed slightly more touched by the night's martinis, his collar askew and hair unbrushed, which Greta thought gave him a rather rakish look. Jordan was sipping coffee, perfectly fresh-faced, having stayed the night as promised—and having obviously packed with that very intention, given the morning robe of Chinese silk she was now sporting.

"That came for you." Jay indicated a parcel that was lying with the morning's mail. His voice was terse, but that wasn't intended for Greta. He just loved sailing, and hated to miss a morning of it.

Greta picked up the brown paper package with the Dauber & Pine label.

She considered slicing open the pages of a freshly bound new novel to be one of life's particular pleasures; it was much nicer than the new way, where books arrived already trimmed by the publisher. She was looking forward to a period of peace and quiet once the guests were gone, with time to catch up on her reading and dream a little of the future. She wondered if Mrs. Christie ever answered letters from her readers. Greta was sure the authoress must be a tremendous explorer who had traveled to a great many interesting places; her stories did have such wonderfully exotic locales.

"Crumpet?" Jordan proffered the silver dish. "Gird the loins and all that." She paused. "Unless the waters are very choppy, in which case I suppose an empty stomach would be advisable. Oh well. Too late for me now."

Greta put a crumpet on her plate, then got back to unwrapping her parcel and cutting the pages. Even if the others couldn't, Greta could feel her brother was stewing over Tom's delay, and she was glad have an activity to busy herself with. The letter opener doubled readily for her task—it was an antique Jay had bought a while ago, a sharp little jade-handled knife, and besides being very handsome, it was devilishly keen: it slid along the paper much faster than she'd reckoned, and made a neat cut in her palm.

"Oh *dear*," Daisy said, "are you all right, Greta?"

The cut stung, but it wasn't deep. Greta prided herself on being more robust in such matters than her sex was alleged to be, but even so, the sight of one's own blood did tend to dismay.

Jay pushed past Jordan.

"Are you all right, Gigi? Someone ring the bell!"

"May I?" Nick leaned across the table and inspected the cut. His tone was soft, his touch cool. Greta looked down. It was the sight of blood, she decided, that had made her heart quicken like that.

"Here, take my napkin. Have Beecham bring some ice and a bit of gauze."

"She might want a dab of whiskey on it," Jordan added. "Maybe a swig of the stuff, too."

Nick turned. "Is that your answer to *everything*, Jord?"

She shrugged.

"I say, Jay, do your friends *really* use card stock so thick you need a dagger to go through it? What fearful snobs they must be."

Soon the wound was neatly bandaged, and Jay was urging Greta to eat as though bacon and eggs were the prescribed antidote to her new ailment.

"It doesn't even hurt now," Greta assured him. Jay had better not insist she stay behind, not over such a little thing as this. "I mightn't be hoisting any jibs today, but other than that, I'm as right as rain."

But just the mention of sailing made him grimace.

"We probably won't get out at all. The morning's all but gone, and we're liable to hit a calm spell in the afternoon."

Daisy frowned, took a last inhale, then stubbed her cigarette out decisively.

"Let's go," she said. "We can't wait around all day. If he comes back and finds us gone, it's his own rotten fault."

Jay perked up.

"Are you sure, Daise?"

She nodded.

"All right! Then let's get a move on, shall we?"

"Oh, very good." Jordan bounded out of her chair. "I'll just throw on some duds."

"Nicky, you'd better come out to the kitchen with me," Jay said. "Mrs. Smith's packed a *most* abundant picnic and I shall need some help."

"And the champagne." Daisy laughed. "Don't forget the champagne, or

Jordan will be most chagrined." She turned to Greta. "That leaves you and me, dear—shall we get a head start?"

Outside, the sky was utterly cloudless, the air still fragrant after the overnight showers, a summer breeze rustling the lawns that sloped down to the water. And yet, beneath the breeze, it was as if some greater stillness lurked . . . Greta supposed it was the residue of last night. Everyone seemed to have moved on, but she had to wonder; such ugly things had been said. Well, it was only one more night with the Buchanans. Nick was the only one she'd be sorry to see go. And more than a little sorry, truth be told, even though she knew it was foolish to think such things. Doubtless Nick saw her the way they all saw her: as the great Jay Gatsby's little sister.

Still—Greta inhaled the fresh, grassy scent, and let the sun wash over her bare arms—the day was exquisite, one of Nature's late-summer marvels. She resolved to rid herself of that silly feeling of foreboding; there really was no cause for it.

"Isn't it delicious, that sun?" Daisy sighed luxuriously, and slipped an arm through hers. The gesture of intimacy was unexpected, and rather warmed her. Daisy flashed her a bright smile. It wasn't hard to see what drew men to Daisy Buchanan, Greta reflected. There was her obvious physical beauty, of course—the perfect, petite frame, which childbirth seemed not to have touched at all; the porcelain skin and fine hair, a blonde shade usually left behind in childhood. Her eyes were a darker blue than one might have expected, and lent an unexpected gravity to her otherwise dolllike features. But the appeal of Daisy Buchanan was more than her striking looks. A few moments in her company let you know that Daisy was someone who enjoyed life; one sensed in her a great appetite for adventure, for delight. And whatever faults she might have, the buoyancy of her good moods was contagious.

No, it was not hard to see why Tom had chosen Daisy. What was more surprising, really, was that Daisy had chosen Tom, when by all accounts she'd had a deluge of suitors back in Louisville. People ascribed it to Tom's immense fortune, of course, and surely that had been part of it. But perhaps the attraction had been genuine, too. A surprising number of women, it seemed, felt a strange lure to that pugnacious, boorish type. Tom believed himself to be king of the jungle, and Greta supposed he made others believe that, too. He exuded power, and if you were on the right side of it, power made people feel safe. Daisy had probably been on the right side of it when she married him. Whether she still was or not, Greta couldn't say.

The young women walked on through the grass, beads of dew brushing against their ankles. Ahead of them, the water shone, and at the end of the dock, Jay's boat, the *Marguerite*, bobbed gently. Greta was briefly put in mind of Nora, who had detested the mere sight of a bobbing boat. The two-week passage across the Atlantic would do that to a person, she'd explained—certainly if they were in steerage.

"It looks so *crystalline*, doesn't it?"

Daisy slipped off her shoes and sat on the dock, immersing her feet with a squeal.

Greta remained standing. She was looking down the dock to where the *Marguerite* sat waiting.

That was odd.

It looked as if the door to the captain's cabin was swinging open. But Jay was as punctilious about his boat as he was about his Phantom; he'd never risk leaving it open to the elements like that. The cabin was so beautifully upholstered. Had that door been open all night through the rain? Greta took a couple of steps along the dock. The door was *definitely* ajar.

"Greta?" Daisy asked from behind her. "What is it?"

There was an uncomfortable sort of feeling in the back of Greta's head, like a high, faint ringing.

"Oh," Daisy said, noticing. "That door—it oughtn't be open like that, ought it?"

Greta stepped farther along the dock. A large wave broke and the boat bobbed, lurched, and a low beam of sunlight hit the deck. Greta froze. She'd thought . . . she'd thought she'd seen something just inside the cabin. Something dark on the floor, like an oil stain. The ringing grew in the back of her skull.

The wooden planks creaked, and Daisy was beside Greta.

"It wasn't *very* heavy rain," she said, her voice bright. "I'm sure there won't be any real damage."

Greta shook her head; Daisy's voice seemed to be coming from far away. She was waiting for the boat to bob and tip again, for the light to catch the inside of the cabin once more. She felt a need to go closer, but she didn't want Daisy to follow.

Distant, merry voices called down from the lawns behind them. The others were coming.

A wave came, the boat tipped, the oil stain flashed again.

But it was not oil. Where it caught the sun, it was red.

Beside Greta, Daisy grew still, standing now as if hypnotized.

"Is that . . ." She stepped forward.

"Daisy, no!" Greta tried to grab her arm, but it was too late. She could only hurry behind Daisy to the end of the dock. The boat listed as Daisy stepped onto it.

"Daisy, wait, don't—" The ringing in Greta's ears was now a sharp buzz. She clambered onto the boat, and as the hull rocked beneath them, she stood with Daisy in the doorway of the cabin.

The scream that followed, Greta knew, was a sound she would remember for the rest of her days.

Chapter Five

The body was slumped in the captain's chair, tilted drunkenly to one side. Blood lay dark on the ground, a thin pool that had trickled as far as the door. Even from where she stood in the doorway, Greta could make out the terrible dark wound near Tom's temple.

A gun, black and glinting, lay beside him.

A hurricane lamp rolled gently on the floor, a mesmeric back-and-forth.

Daisy had stopped straining under Greta's grip. At the first sight of the body, she had gone quite limp.

Tom Buchanan was dead.

Greta's mind repeated the words, and yet they failed to make any sense. Tom was not the sort of man who died. Tom was the sort of man who was brutish, unpleasant, and vividly, vigorously *alive*.

"But I—" Daisy murmured, "he can't—I don't—"

Voices, clamor, the boat swaying as the others boarded. Greta felt the need to turn to warn them, but every muscle was frozen in place. Behind her, Jordan screamed.

"Dear God," Jay's voice said.

It was as though his words woke Daisy from her stupor. She let out a faint whimper, then stumbled from Greta's grasp. Jay pushed forward to keep her from falling; he locked his arms around her like a brace.

"I'm here," he said. "You're all right. I'm here."

Daisy made a small desperate noise, and buried her head in Jay's chest. Greta looked at her brother over Daisy's small frame. His eyes were dazed and staring.

She turned back to the dreadful sight in front of them. Tom was wearing last night's suit, and the pomade glinted in his lush dark hair. He looked like what he was: a wealthy, well-dressed man in his prime. A former football captain, a polo player, muscle-bound, tan, powerful. And yet, that awful dark spot at his temple...

It seemed so incongruous. Not just incongruous: impossible. Why would a man like Tom Buchanan shoot himself? A man who had everything? And moreover, a man who seemed impervious to guilt or shame, or even self-doubt.

"Greta, Jordan." Jay's voice shook. "Come with me. We'll take Daisy back to the house. Nicky—can you stay? We'll need to telephone for an ambulance."

Nick nodded, ashen. Jordan moved mechanically to Jay's side, speechless for once. Daisy whimpered, and Jay gathered her in his arms.

"Greta," he repeated. "Come."

But she couldn't. It was a terrible sight, and yet she could not leave it. She could not pretend it away.

"I'll stay with Nick," she said.

"This is no place for a woman," Jay said. But then Daisy let out another moan, and he dropped his eyes from Greta's, shook his head. "Do as you please."

He left them, half carrying Daisy up the lawn while Jordan hurried beside them.

Greta felt her breath in her chest. She turned back toward the body. It was so still. Only the hurricane lamp on the floor continued its quiet motion, rolling a steady back-and-forth.

"I can't believe it," Nick said quietly. "Tom, of all people."

Greta remembered Tom's face as he'd come into the room last night after Edgar's abrupt departure. How pleased with himself he had looked, that unpleasant expression of satisfaction. How had his mood changed so much in a matter of mere hours?

Or had the despair been there, hidden, all along? The inside of another's mind was always a mystery no matter how well you thought you knew them—but even so, it was all just so unthinkable.

"We ought to check his pulse," she heard herself say. "Just to . . . just to be quite sure."

The idea that Tom Buchanan might still have any life left in him seemed preposterous when you looked at that body in the captain's chair. But what if he *was* still breathing? She stepped into the cabin, but Nick held her back.

"I'll go."

He stepped inside, skirting the pool of blood on the floor. Greta watched him put his hand to the base of Tom's neck.

"Nothing." He stepped back, his voice forced. "He's cold, Greta."

Greta's other senses seemed to be waking now. She smelled the warm mineral tang of blood, and heard, almost obscenely loud, the twittering of nearby birds.

It wasn't that she had remotely expected Tom to be alive. And yet, the finality of Nick's words . . .

She drew small breaths, and tried to look on the scene without fear. *It is only death*, she told herself. *It comes to us all.*

But not like this, a voice inside answered.

She'd have expected Nick to retreat out of there as quickly as he could, but instead, he seemed to be lingering: his hand reached out carefully past

Tom's slumped form, and plucked something from the desk. A sheet of paper, folded. Greta and Nick stared at each other.

So he'd left a note.

Nick hesitated. "Should I open it?"

Greta nodded. "I suppose so. There's no name?"

Nick shook his head, and carefully unfolded the paper. Greta watched his eyes: the frown, the faint incredulity.

"What?" she said. "What is it?"

"Almost better to have left nothing at all," he said, and then, as if just noticing: "Good God, it smells vile in here." Greta stood back as he stumbled from the cabin.

"Here." He held out the paper. "See for yourself. It's only a line long."

Old Girl, Greta read. *I'm terribly sorry about all this.*

That was it. That was all. Greta stared. It was so terribly meager, insulting even. Nick was right, it would almost have been better to have left no word for Daisy at all. How was this casual little note supposed to offer any comfort? But it was in character, she had to admit—that essential callousness at the heart of Tom Buchanan. Even in death, he could manage only a token regard for other people's feelings.

It was a reminder that even though Tom's life had been cut unduly short, those years that ought to have lain ahead of him were unlikely to have brought the world much benefit, or brought Tom himself much increase in either grace or wisdom. Greta let out a breath, and felt a shiver travel down her back.

And yet, she thought, *it does not make the horror any less.*

The living-room windows were open; the gauze panels flapped in the breeze, but the sight seemed grim now, where an hour ago it had been buoyant. Through the window, Greta could see the *Marguerite* still bobbing gently on the water, and standing outside it like two sentries, Beecham and Bill Richardson, the driver. Jay had sent them down to relieve Nick and Greta; somehow no one could face leaving Tom's body alone and unattended.

Although it's not as though he'd know the difference now.

Greta rubbed her eyes, and leaned back into the armchair and its bed of silk cushions. The room seemed too sumptuous, the day too beautiful; everything felt so *wrong*.

The rest of the staff aside from Bill and Beecham hadn't been told yet, but they would have to be, and soon; no doubt they were already wondering. Greta could almost feel it in the air already, that new alertness, fear-tinged. A doctor had been called and, having administered a sedative to Daisy, had now departed, leaving Jordan upstairs in Daisy's room. And the police would be arriving soon—the doctor had certified Tom's death, but had informed Jay that given the nature of the death, the authorities would have to be called before the body could be removed.

Removed. The logistics of it all were so horribly surreal.

Nick stood by the window, arms folded, staring out at the water.

"It's so *senseless*."

Greta felt the truth of that. No matter how she added it up, it was hard to see Tom Buchanan doing something like this. For what reason, what motive?

They turned as one at the sound of the door. Jay had been using the hall telephone to call Edgar. He came in looking pale.

"That was ghastly." He looked at them blankly, and dropped his weight onto the sofa. With the color drained from his face, Jay's features stood out sharply, absent their usual glow—a prince who'd lost his kingdom.

"I don't think he believed me at first, you know. I think he thought it was some kind of sick joke." Jay shook his head. "Damn me, it *feels* like some sort of sick joke. Tom Buchanan, *dead*. I can't get my head around it."

Greta wondered how much of what Edgar Buchanan was feeling right now was grief as opposed to simply shock. There had seemed so little love lost between Tom and him. Still, a bereavement was a bereavement.

"I think you could use a stiffener, Jay. Perhaps we all could." Nick rose and poured them each a whiskey, planting one in Jay's hand and passing the other to Greta.

"And now Edgar will have to break it to his mother. And then I suppose *she'll* have to break it to the child."

That's right—the child, Pammy, had been staying with her grandmother. Greta felt sick. What could a child of such a tender age possibly understand of death, let alone *this* sort of death? Greta had been only four years older than Pammy was now when she'd been schooled in her own awful lesson in mortality. Surely whatever sort of a monster Tom had been, his young daughter hadn't seen him as one.

Jay grasped the tumbler without acknowledgment, and shivered as he stared out the window. Between heavy silk drapes, the gauze curtains still fluttered. The bay view had always been the room's most glorious feature, but when she looked out the window now, Greta found her eyes drawn against her will to that one spot: the dock, the moored boat, and the two somber figures standing guard outside.

Nick had shown Jay the suicide note, and like Nick, Jay had shaken his head at it, a flicker of anger passing over his face.

It's like him, though, isn't it, he'd said.

Now, from outside the front window, came the sound of wheels crunching on the driveway. Jay stood up as two policemen exited the vehicle, and moved smartly toward the front of the house. He went into the hall, and Nick and Greta waited wordlessly. It seemed more real, even, than when the doctor had come. There was no going back now. Greta caught Nick's eye as they heard parts of the exchange drift in from the hallway—words like *gun* and *missing* and *terribly shocking*—but no one came into the living room.

Soon the front door closed again, and from the window, they watched Jay leading the two policemen down toward the boat.

"Well." Jordan appeared in the doorway, looking uncharacteristically shaken. "Daisy's out for the count." She glanced down at the whiskey in Greta's hand.

"I think I'll be needing one of those myself."

The inspector turned out to be a pink-faced man of considerable stature, with yellowish hair cropped close to his head: Inspector Francis, he introduced himself as. Installed now in the living room, he seemed to dwarf all the furniture around him, his knees rising like cricket bats above the marble coffee table, incongruous among the potted ferns and polished onyx statuettes. Molly had brought in coffee for them all, but had been so nervous that she'd almost poured a cup all over the inspector. Now five cups sat untouched on the table, growing cold.

"A bad business," the inspector said. "A bad business indeed—although not so rare, unfortunately, as one might think."

"I'm sure people say this all the time, Inspector," Jay said, looking at the rest of them for affirmation. "But it does seem especially shocking that Tom Buchanan would have done such a thing. He was a very—well, a very *robust* sort of man. And he didn't seem to be acting any differently than usual."

The inspector nodded sagely.

"Often you wouldn't think it to look at them. And they do say, you know, that this sort of thing can come on sudden. Particularly if a fellow was in the war. Shell shock and all that. A fellow can seem just fine, and then something or other sets him off, brings it all right back."

Nick and Jay glanced at each other.

"Well, but Tom wasn't in the war."

"Ah." The inspector's lips tightened a little.

"A medical issue," Jay said.

The bronchial condition Tom had regretfully hinted at whenever anyone brought up the war had surely fooled no one. Honest pacifism Greta could readily respect: wishing to avoid the slaughter of one's fellow man was perfectly comprehensible. But Tom had been such a disgusting hypocrite about the whole thing. He'd been perfectly happy to ride out on horseback and terrorize anyone *he* suspected of draft evasion, and meanwhile, he'd taken it as his birthright that he should never be sent anywhere near the battlefields.

No, Greta acknowledged: the world had not lost much when it lost Tom Buchanan.

"In that case." The inspector cleared his throat. "Does his wife—ahem, widow—did she suggest what might have led to such an act?" Informed about Daisy's sedated sleep upstairs, the inspector had consented not to trouble her for the time being. "Marital difficulties?" he went on. "Money troubles?"

"Money troubles!" Jordan scoffed. The inspector looked at her askance. Next to the inspector's cheap uniform and unforgiving haircut, Jordan, even in Greta's rather more restrained clothes, managed to look as if she were attending a Parisian salon rather than a police briefing. Her cigarette holder dangled loosely between two fingers, and when she exhaled, her smoke narrowly missed the inspector's nostrils.

"No money troubles, then," he said with a flinty look.

"The Buchanans were terribly rich, Inspector." Jay said. "As for the other thing..."

Greta shot him a look. Jay might be tempted to tell the inspector all about Tom's deficiencies as a husband, but Daisy wouldn't thank him for airing that dirty laundry in public.

Jay caught Greta's glance, which seemed to do its job.

"Just... the usual, Inspector," he finished blandly. "A typical marriage, you know."

The policeman nodded. He made a quick entry in his notebook, and glanced up again.

"I understand there was a suicide note?"

Nick slid it across the coffee table.

"Rather brief, all right," the inspector observed. "Mr. Buchanan didn't sign his name to it, I see. You can confirm it's his handwriting?"

Nick gave a quick nod.

"Yes, Tom had rather a distinctive scrawl. I've known it for years."

"So have I," Jay said.

Greta wished suddenly she could take another look at the letter. She couldn't say quite why—only that she felt somehow it deserved a second look. But that was silly, surely. She was getting overwhelmed, that was all, by the shock and tragedy.

The inspector nodded. "Have to ask, you know. Part of procedure and all that. Well, it certainly rules out any idea of accidental death. Not that the placement of the head wound left much doubt." He slid the note into his pocket.

"Now, this boat," he continued. "Any particular reason Mr. Buchanan would have been on it?"

Jay didn't take great pains to disguise his impatience.

"Well, of course—he went out there for privacy, or decency, or whatever you want to call it."

Bad manners to do oneself in in the guest suite.

"Yes," Nick said in his level way. "I should think he didn't want the gunshot to rouse his wife in the middle of the night, Inspector."

"Mm." The inspector made a note. "And who was last to see him alive?"

They looked at one another.

"Miss Baker here, and Mrs. Buchanan, they retired first. The rest of us—my sister, Mr. Carraway, and I—went up some moments later," Jay said. "Tom stayed behind to finish his, er, nightcap."

"I see. And did anyone hear Mr. Buchanan actually go upstairs?"

They glanced around again.

"Well, I shouldn't think so. You see, Inspector, he wouldn't have had to pass by any of our rooms. His was right by the stairs. Your room's the nearest, Gigi." Jay turned. "I don't suppose you heard anything?"

"No." Greta felt her cheeks color. She hadn't heard Tom go upstairs, but she *had* seen him after that—she'd seen him disappearing into Daisy's room. But that hardly mattered, she reasoned. This was all bad enough already without quizzing Daisy about a final encounter that surely was deserving of some privacy—and Greta certainly wasn't going to send the inspector up to interrogate the poor woman about it now. *But how dreadful,* she thought afresh: to welcome one's husband to one's bed for what would turn out to be the last time, only for him to leave it a few hours later and put a bullet through his head. Had it been Tom's twisted idea of goodbye?

"Something to add, young lady?"

The inspector was looking at her; she shook her head.

"Very good." Inspector Francis cleared his throat in a pointed way, and turned back to Jay and Nick.

"Now, gentlemen. You discovered the deceased at about ten thirty this morning, yes?"

Gentlemen! Greta's color rose farther. They had all of them been present; and her powers of recall were just as good as anyone's.

"That's right, Inspector," Jay said.

"And did anyone touch or move the body or adjust the room in which he was found in any way?"

Nick frowned.

"Well, I took his pulse—or tried to. Ought I not to have done that?"

The inspector waved his hand reassuringly.

"Just procedure, sir. I simply have to ask. So you went into the cabin. Step on anything? Move anything?"

"I was careful not to. I"—Nick swallowed—"I touched his neck. It was cold. And then I suppose I stood there a moment. And then," he continued, "I saw that note on the desk. I picked it up and read it. And then I came back out of the cabin. I didn't touch anything else." He looked over. "Greta, am I missing anything?"

"That's perfectly clear, Mr. Carraway, thank you," the inspector said breezily, and looked back at his notes. "Ah, yes. And the gun the deceased used—that was his own revolver, I take it?"

There was a hesitation throughout the room as they looked at one another.

"I suppose so—" Nick said, but Jay was already clearing his throat.

"As a matter of fact, Inspector—"

They all turned to look at him, but if he felt their stares, he didn't show it. His voice was calm, his face opaque.

"As a matter of fact, Inspector," he continued. "The gun is mine."

Chapter Six

*J*ay's gun? Greta blinked.

"Yours, Mr. Gatsby?" Inspector Francis looked concerned. "Were you aware that he had borrowed it?"

"Not at all." Jay cleared his throat. "It's usually kept in the gun room. That is, just a small room off the hallway, there—a sort of mud room, really, but it's where I keep my little collection. My Enfield from the war; a few antique pieces; some shooting rifles and a few revolvers—including that particular Smith & Wesson, I'm sorry to say."

"You don't keep the room locked, Mr. Gatsby?" The inspector's mouth curled a little, and Jay looked uncomfortable.

"Well, yes. But it seems I must have forgotten on this occasion. You see, we took some rifles out yesterday—the four of us"—he gestured—"Mr. Carraway and I, and Mr. and Mrs. Buchanan. We were doing a little target practice out on the lawns—just a bit of sport, you know. And then my sister arrived at the house, and then our guests were en route . . . I suppose, in all the excitement, I forgot to lock up." He paused. "Inspector, my staff are very trustworthy—they have to be, you know, considering some of the objects in this house. I can't keep everything of value under lock and key. Beecham and Dantry are *most* rigorous with our applicants on account of that. So you see, perhaps I'm not in the habit of locking things up as much as I ought."

"I see." Inspector Francis still looked unimpressed. "And the Smith & Wesson Mr. Buchanan used last night—was this the gun he had used earlier in the day? For this 'target practice'?"

Jay shook his head.

"We were using rifles in the afternoon. I shouldn't think anyone's touched that little revolver in ages, Inspector. Presumably, Tom went back into the gun room and took it out late last night; I suppose it was just the first thing that came to hand."

"So one might suppose. Although, since you're not particularly assiduous about keeping the room locked, Mr. Gatsby, he could have taken it at some other point during his stay. There's no telling how long he'd been planning this."

It was a sobering thought, and the room fell silent.

"Inspector," Jay began. "The Buchanans, you know, are quite a prominent family. I should think they may be quite, ah, sensitive, to the nature of the death. I imagine they may count on your discretion?"

A beat passed.

"I'm sure I should never want to offend a family like the Buchanans, sir," the inspector said smoothly.

There was another silence, longer this time, and the inspector patted his knees with an air of finality, and rose. "Well, I should think I've all I need to turn in the report to the coroner. If Sergeant Stanhope has finished up on the boat, we can be out of your hair."

Although she hadn't warmed to the man, Greta felt oddly reluctant to see him leave. It seemed premature somehow, and she couldn't help wondering if there was something they were forgetting.

"Inspector." There *was* something. "Perhaps you ought to be aware . . . one of the maids thought she saw a stranger about the gardens yesterday. I wonder if before you go, you might not want to question her or any of the other staff."

Inspector Francis turned from the doorway, and slowly raised his eyebrows. He looked, Greta thought, quite displeased with her.

"A stranger about the gardens?" Jay frowned. "I never heard anything about that."

"It was at dinnertime." Greta turned. "You remember that crash? That new housemaid was coming out of the pantry, and thought she saw someone out the kitchen window. Beecham went to see if there'd been any disturbance."

Jay gave her a look that almost mirrored the inspector's. His handsome face looked quite leonine when displeased.

"And had there been a disturbance?"

"Of course not," Greta said. "You'd have been told of it."

Jay gave her a look that said, *You see?* Greta's irritation rose again. Did he really have to take the inspector's side like that? Perhaps it *was* all down to Molly's strained nerves, and if it wasn't, Greta couldn't fathom the connection either. But surely it was worth at least mentioning.

"Inspector," Jay turned. "Molly Riggs is that jumpy little thing who almost upset the coffeepot on you. She's new here. Hasn't quite settled in yet, I'm afraid."

"That trembling leaf of a girl?" The inspector coughed. "I'm not sure we need take *her* too seriously. Besides, young lady"—he turned to Greta—"even if she did spot some wandering vagrant or Peeping Tom, I can't say I see the relevance. This is an open-and-shut suicide, if you'll forgive my bluntness."

Greta folded her arms. They needn't act as if *she* were guilty of a nervous imagination.

"Well, but what if—what if there *was* a man, and he was blackmailing Tom?" she blurted. "Or came to threaten him? What if he had something to do with *why* Tom shot himself last night?"

Frankly, neither seemed a particularly likely scenario to her, either. She just couldn't shake the uncomfortable feeling that perhaps there might be something they were all overlooking. Something they were forgetting to notice. Her father had always said a methodical mind was the solution to most things. She was only trying to consider all the particulars.

"Greta," Nick said reasonably, "Tom was with us all night apart from when he went for a smoke with Edgar. Even if some mysterious blackguard *had* tried to show up here and threaten him for some reason—and I don't see why they would—I can't see how they'd have managed it."

He was right; of course he was right. Except there was that episode when Greta had found Edgar in the hall before he'd gone back out to join his brother. That meant Tom had been outside by himself for at least a few minutes, maybe more. But did that mean anything? Probably the others were right: she was giving too much credit to Molly's strange account.

"Gigi," Jay said, "this is no sensationalist ladies' novel."

"I *know* that," she said. "I'm merely pointing out—"

"Your brother is quite right," the inspector chimed in. "You must not let lurid fantasies run away with you." He paused, and said with condescending grace: "Still, I suppose I may have a word with the staff before I return to the precinct."

Jay glanced at Greta.

"Very well, Inspector. I shall take you to them."

The silence in the room seemed to pulse once they had left. Nick stood, and went over to the window. Jordan lit another cigarette. For a while, no one spoke.

"I say," Jordan broke the silence first. "Do you think Tom *was* planning it? Do you think that was why he stayed behind after the rest of you went to bed?" Her eyes widened. "I *say*. You don't think he picked that fight with Daisy just to make us all go upstairs and leave him?"

"I shouldn't think so," Nick said without turning. "Not if those were going to be his last words to Daisy."

Jordan frowned, and took another drag on her cigarette. Sunlight bathed the room in a midafternoon glow, brightening the black-and-gold upholstery, making the potted plants glow emerald. It seemed wrong that the day should be so beautiful.

It was a while before Jay came back into the room. He glanced at Greta again, and the look on his face was unreadable. Was there a hint of apology there?

"Well, whatever Molly told you last night, she's quite disavowed it now. Seems rather embarrassed about it all. But there *was* something." He paused. "Ada says she saw a light on in the boat last night."

At that, everyone turned.

The staff all had accommodations on the premises apart from Bill, the driver, who had an apartment over the garage a little ways from the house. The housemaids shared a room a few steps from the kitchen at the back of the house; the windows there would have a side view onto the water.

"At one in the morning, she said," Jay continued. "And Molly corroborates it. What's more," he hesitated. "It seems they saw the light go *out* again."

Out? That was unexpected. Tom would hardly have shot himself in the dark.

"Ada was in the middle of wondering whether it might be a trespasser, whether she ought to wake Beecham, and then, as she was looking at it, the light just"—Jay paused uncomfortably—"went out. So I suppose, in conjunction with what the doctor told us about time of death, we must infer this was, well—the fatal moment."

"You mean he knocked over the lantern when he . . ." Nick cleared his throat. "With the ricochet."

Everyone went silent, trying not to picture Tom's flailing arm, the final throes. Greta recalled the bloodied floor of the *Marguerite* and the hurricane lamp rolling gently side to side, and shivered. She was glad she had not witnessed what Ada and Molly had.

"They didn't hear it?" she said. "The sound of the shot?"

Jay frowned. "I suppose not. The windows were closed, and it was raining—that would have dampened the sound."

The room felt colder than it had before. It was so unthinkable, and this new little piece of information only brought it home afresh: What the deuce had made Tom do it? And how was Daisy going to cope with it all?

Jordan, looking toward the driveway, suddenly sat up straight.

"Oh dear. I think Edgar's here."

Greta felt dread creep through the room. What on earth were they supposed to say to the man?

Of course it wasn't the Gatsbys' fault that Tom had chosen their home for the tragic deed . . . and yet she did feel a grim sense of responsibility, and saw in Jay's eyes that he felt the same. Jordan stepped back from the window, and Greta had a strange reminder of Tom in the same stance last night, the same expression of foreboding and displeasure on his face, as he'd watched Edgar pull into the driveway. Could that really be less than twenty-four hours ago?

They heard Beecham's sonorous voice as he opened the front door, and it seemed to rouse them all from paralysis. Jay took a breath, and they followed him into the hall.

"My dear fellow," Jay said somberly.

Edgar turned. He was even more gaunt than last night, Greta thought, and his gray eyes looked even flatter and deader.

"You should have telephoned me first," he said. "First thing, d'you hear? You had no call getting the police involved; it's a family matter."

If Jay found Edgar's priorities as distasteful as Greta did, he showed no sign.

"I assure you, Edgar," he said gently, "we had no other desire. But you see, a doctor had to be called right away, and he explained that the precinct simply must be called in. He said we weren't to move him—that no one was to touch him—until the police had come. It's very unfortunate, you know, but with—with this sort of death, the police will have their say. Of course," he added, "it's an open-and-shut case; the inspector said so himself." He paused; his gaze met Edgar's. "I'm afraid there's no question of its having been an accident, old sport."

Edgar scowled, and cast a furious look over his shoulder to where Beecham stood.

"Don't talk like that in front of the staff, damn you!" he said, and stalked past them into the living room.

Greta exchanged a glance with her brother. Jay went over to where Edgar stood by the coffee table. The cold cups of coffee sat there still; everything was surely too topsy-turvy downstairs for the staff to even think of removing them.

"Edgar, I assure you: Beecham is the soul of discretion. It's not my staff you shall have to worry about." Jay's tone was polite, but his meaning was clear. A family like the Buchanans was too much in the public eye not to attract attention. There would be talk.

Edgar's eyes dropped from Jay's, then moved searchingly toward the window.

"Where is he?" he demanded. "I must see him. And where's Daisy?"

"Daisy's upstairs. The doctor gave her a sedative. She's sleeping. Tom remains where we found him, as advised. I can take you to him now if you wish."

Edgar stared. He seemed to think Jay was tricking him with his unflappable, polite tone; abruptly, he turned to where Nick stood by the door.

"What exactly did the police say?"

"The inspector was quite by the book." Nick spoke quietly. "An open-and-shut case of death by self-harm."

Edgar stared at them for a moment, his face opaque, then he began to pace the room.

"But it doesn't make sense," he said. "Tom always said he despised suicides. You know—cowardice and being ungodly and that sort of thing..." He pinched the bridge of his nose. "I tell you, I don't understand it. Mother's a wreck, an utter wreck. He was her favorite, you know."

He took a steadying breath, and looked to Nick again.

"Very well," he said. "Take me to him."

After the two men left, the others sat uncomfortably in the half-empty room, the silence interrupted only by Beecham asking if Mrs. Smith might go ahead and send up lunch.

Beecham, Greta thought, looked exhausted. This whole horrid business must be taking its toll on him, too—that marvelous mustache was positively sagging.

"Yes, I suppose so," Jay said distractedly. "Buffet-style, Beecham, can you tell them? I don't think any of us want to sit looking at that empty chair."

"Very good, sir." Beecham withdrew, and Jordan crossed to the window. She was fidgeting, Greta thought, which was unlike her. But none of them were themselves right now.

"Where do you suppose they'll have the funeral?" Jordan said. "Chicago?"

"Perhaps," Jay murmured.

"I shall have to write to my manager, I suppose. I'm expected in Florida on Tuesday." She lit another cigarette. "May I stay here, Jay? Until we know what's going on with the arrangements?"

"Of course," Jay said, distracted: Nick and Edgar were walking back across the lawns.

When the two men came back into the room, Edgar looked more shaken than before.

"He was perfectly himself last night," he said. "There was nothing to suggest..."

"I suppose there must have been something, all the same," Nick said quietly. "Something under the surface that none of us saw."

Greta watched Edgar's face. She'd have liked to ask him there and then about the business he'd wanted to discuss with Tom. About the angry words she'd overheard from the hall. But then the door opened, and they all turned.

"Daisy!" Jay rushed to her. "You ought to be in bed."

Her fine blonde hair was wisping loose from its chignon as if she'd been tossing and turning; her sorrowful blue eyes seemed larger than ever. She turned her lovely face on him.

"I'm a widow, Jay, not an invalid."

"Daisy..."

Edgar crossed the room and pressed both her hands in his.

"My very deepest condolences."

She blinked, then dropped her eyes.

"And I offer you mine, Edgar," she murmured.

He seemed softened by the sight of her; Greta supposed even he wasn't immune to the tragic beauty before him. He released her hands as Beecham entered the room, clearing his throat apologetically.

"We've laid out a cold lunch in the dining room as requested, sir."

Edgar shot Jay a look.

"*Lunch?*" he said, as though someone had suggested cocktails.

"We must see to it," Jay said, with a meaningful glance in Daisy's direction, "that everyone keeps their strength up."

But Daisy had drifted toward the window, and put her hand softly against the glass.

"Is he—is he still out there?" she asked in a small voice.

Jay hesitated.

"Yes. They're coming for him soon."

She gave a small sniff, and nodded.

In the end, nobody could stomach much lunch, and most of the dishes went back to the kitchen untouched. As the undertaker arrived, Greta heard Mrs. Smith's voice carrying loudly up the kitchen passage. She watched as the man and his assistant carried Tom's body solemnly across the lawn wrapped in a white sheet.

"A curse on the house," Mrs. Smith was declaiming. "It's foul luck, it is—a curse on us all, you mark my words!"

Chapter Seven

In some ways, Greta thought, the second day was worse than the first. There was the freshness of the morning and the few seconds upon waking before the grim remembrance sank in, and then after that, there was no getting out from under it. Everyone in the household was terribly on edge, of course, the staff as much as anyone. Greta had tried to show some solicitousness to the new maid when she came in with Greta's coffee.

"And how are you, Molly? And how is everyone downstairs?"

But Molly, though she looked quite pale and underslept, clearly thought it would be inappropriate to disclose any weakness.

"Fine, miss." The hint of defensiveness—or was it anxiety?—stirred once more. "We're all fine. It's very tragic of course, what happened, but it's over now, isn't it?"

If only Greta could find the conviction that it really *was* all over.

"Molly . . ." She hesitated. "I hope nobody told you to keep mum over that incident the other night. When you thought you saw someone at the window, I mean. If you really think you did see something, I hope you wouldn't let anyone talk you out of it—the inspector, or Mrs. Smith, or anyone."

Molly flushed, and looked at the carpet.

"No, miss. But the truth is, I . . . well, I think Mrs. Smith was right. It was stress, what with the dinner party and the new menu and all—I'd not done soufflé before, nor duchesse potatoes. And me being a bit nervy, my eyes must have played that trick on me. I never meant to cause a fuss." She glanced up; the flush deepened. "Mrs. Smith says it's the result of an oversensitive imagination, and I expect she's right. I'm afraid I've never worked in such a big house before. All the creaking and noises at night . . . it can take a moment to get used to."

Greta regarded her closely. It wasn't obvious to her if the girl was lying. Then again, a person could persuade themselves that all manner of things were true if it felt risky to admit otherwise.

"And Ada's story?" she said gently. "About the light in the boat?"

Molly's eyes widened.

"Yes, miss."

"Was she right to tell my brother that you saw it, too? She didn't just . . . persuade you that she saw it?"

"I saw it, miss. With my own eyes."

Molly was unhesitating now. Greta had to believe her.

"And you're sure of the time? One in the morning? I wouldn't have expected anyone to remember so precisely. And then, it's a rather strange time to be awake."

Molly looked back at the carpet as though wishing for it to swallow her whole.

"I get nightmares sometimes, miss. And when I cry out, I suppose it wakes Ada; she doesn't like it much. I must have woken her that night, and then she woke *me* to shut me up. But then she saw the light. I looked at the alarm clock, so I know it was one o'clock, like you said." She paused, face furrowed. "Is the time important, miss?"

"No, I'm sure it's not," Greta said hurriedly. She had no wish to lay a new burden on this young woman's shoulders. If Molly had had a nervous temperament before, then a violent death in the house surely wasn't helping.

"Forgive me," she said, "for bothering you about it. I'm sure it's best for us all to put such unpleasant recollections behind us. Only . . ." She waited for the girl to meet her gaze. "Only if anything *were* to trouble you, Molly, I hope you'd feel at liberty to voice it."

The stiff look returned.

"Of course, miss." Molly bobbed her head, and left the room.

Funeral plans were put in place, not by Daisy, but by Tom's mother, a widowed matriarch by the name of Rosemary Buchanan. Jordan was the only one besides Daisy to have met her, and spoke of her with muted apprehension as an "absolute Valkyrie of a creature." Daisy didn't seem at all offended by having the funeral taken out of her hands; practical details were too ghastly to contemplate.

It seemed to Greta she'd barely seen her brother since she got back—seen him alone, at any rate. He'd knocked on her door yesterday evening after dinner as the surreal day finally began to slow to its close.

"Hardly the homecoming you were supposed to have." He'd pressed her hand, and neither of them had mentioned the inspector.

"How is Daisy?" she'd asked, because it seemed the only thing to say, or at least the only thing Jay seemed to want to talk about. Greta could hardly blame Daisy for being the center of everyone's focus, but it had certainly put paid to any hopes she'd had of having a different kind of conversation with Jay this summer, of having her brother to herself for a while.

Daisy had spent yesterday and today variously in bed or downstairs on the chaise longue, speaking little and refusing to eat. Tragedy hung over her like a mantle, lending her a new air of nobility. Reclining on the chaise, she stared out the window toward the water, one white wrist pressed against her brow. Grief became her. Indeed, if one were being uncharitable, one might even say there was a slight theatrical air to it—and yet, Greta couldn't really blame Daisy for that. Daisy was used to doing what was appropriate, to giving the reaction society expected. Probably, she was still too much in shock to feel anything but numb—but it wouldn't do to admit that. She had to *look* desolate; it was what a loving wife ought to be. And perhaps she really believed, now, that she had been devotedly in love with Tom.

Jay's attempts to get Daisy to eat only became more desperate as the day went on.

"Mrs. Smith has roasted a chicken," he tried, as the afternoon waned into evening, "and made some broth to strengthen you. At least a little broth? You must have *something*, Daisy."

It had been decided that Daisy would stay at the house until after the funeral, which was to be held not in Chicago but in New Haven: there was a cathedral there that Tom had allegedly attended during college, although Nick confessed that he had no memory of Tom's ever going to Mass at all. But it seemed Rosemary Buchanan had donated amply toward the construction of the new cathedral, which presumably had helped the family secure a funeral there, and a traditional Catholic burial, despite the murky circumstances of Tom's death. *A tragic accident* was how it had been described in the death notice Mrs. Buchanan had placed in the *Times*.

After the funeral, little Pammy would be released back to her mother's care, and the two would travel to the summer house in Newport for a period of rest and recovery. Jordan would stay in West Egg until Daisy's departure, and Nick, too, had arranged to stay until after the funeral, delaying his return to the office in Manhattan.

When Greta left her room again, it was approaching dinner hour. There was a light on in Jay's study, the first room at the top of the stairs. That was where he seemed to have retreated when he wasn't trying to coax Daisy to eat. She walked quietly past Daisy's closed bedroom door, and on downstairs to the living room. But it was not empty as she had thought.

"Oh!" she said.

Nick glanced up from the decanter, his frown settling into something gentler at the sight of her.

"I'm having a bourbon. Shall I pour you one?"

Greta nodded. She did not think she had been alone in a room with Nick before. She supposed it was not the sort of thing that mattered when a man had just been found dead in one's home, but she couldn't help thinking of it just a little bit all the same. The arrival of the whiskey tumbler was doubly welcome; it saved her from having to think about what to do with her hands.

He poured himself a glass, and both of them stood there for a moment, their drinks awkwardly aloft as if debating whether there was anything appropriate left to drink to.

"To hope," Nick said at last.

It was well chosen. Greta knew the kind of hope he meant: that last bastion against despair, the thing that saved men's lives from ending as Tom's had. And yet there had been something in the shape of Nick's mouth as he spoke it, something in the quiet look he gave her, that made the word go around in her head.

Hope.

Greta tilted her glass, and they drank.

"Is your hand all right?" Nick said after a moment.

"Oh—yes, entirely." Greta had almost forgotten the little cut with the letter opener. It seemed such a silly thing now.

"And—are *you* all right?" He frowned. "I mean, I suppose we're all dreadfully shocked. But you seem particularly . . . distracted?"

Greta looked down at her drink. It was true: she certainly wasn't grieving, and while she *was* shocked, she didn't think she was shocked in the same way the others were. What she felt was something different. She just couldn't shake the feeling that all this . . . it didn't add up. It didn't make *sense*.

"I suppose people say this all the time, but I just don't understand it, Nick."

He nodded.

"I know. I keep half expecting him to walk in here any minute."

"Yes, but . . ." Greta shook her head. "I can't pretend to have known Tom well, but *suicide!* It just doesn't seem like a thought that would ever have entered his head."

Nick frowned, and gave her a heavy look.

"I suspect there may be more to come, Greta. Something we don't yet know."

"He had a secret, you mean?"

Nick sipped from his tumbler.

"I wouldn't be surprised."

What kind of secret, Greta wondered, could drive a man like Tom Buchanan to such an act? Nick seemed to think that whatever it was, it would come to light soon enough. She rather hoped it would. However unpleasant such an explanation might be, at least it would relieve her from all this wondering, this senseless fixation.

"You know." Nick took another sip from his tumbler. "I think your brother would do well to speak to the staff. It's a great shock to the household, and I should think it's put them all on tilt."

He was right: Dantry was scowling even more than usual, perhaps because she sensed the scandal would taint her prospects of future employment, and Mrs. Smith hadn't stopped her doom-laden murmurings. When Greta had gone out to clear her head with a walk around the shrubberies, she'd overheard Ada by the back door, regaling Bill the chauffeur with tales of Molly's night terrors; in the wake of Tom's death, Ada seemed to have ascribed to these the status of prophetic dreams.

More leadership and assurances from Jay did indeed seem like a good idea, but Jay evidently had no thought right now for anyone other than Daisy. And it was hard to fault him on that, of course, but . . .

"Nick, do you think—" Greta flushed. "Do you think his attentions to Daisy right now might be seen as . . . well, excessive?" She cleared her throat. "Of course, Daisy deserves all of our care, it's just . . ."

It wasn't only the pained attendance outside Daisy's door. Greta hadn't been able to help but notice how Jay's eyes followed Daisy since the disaster, and it was the *way* they had followed her: the way he stroked her hand, touched her hair—more than a comforting touch. It was so very tender—intimate, even. It didn't seem to have offended Daisy, but Greta suspected that was only because Daisy was too distracted to truly notice or rebuke him for it. Greta knew he'd always had a soft spot for Daisy, but speaking of staff morale, Greta thought some of them might question its appropriateness.

Nick looked away at her question. He was loyal, Greta knew, and didn't like speaking against Jay. And yet he was a pragmatist—and observant.

"No doubt the tragedy has aroused his most chivalrous instincts, but perhaps he could stand to show a little more restraint."

"If he keeps it up, people will talk, and he won't like that," Greta said. "And Daisy *certainly* won't like it."

Nick glanced at her.

"I'll have a word." He paused. "But you know Jay—he tends not to hear anything he doesn't want to."

Dinnertime was an awkward affair. As she sat down, Greta found herself suddenly ravenous, and yet even in the face of Mrs. Smith's leek velouté and garlic-roasted chicken, it seemed inappropriate to do more than pick at the food. Jay seemed distracted, Nick withdrawn, and Jordan almost sulky.

"What a joyless bunch we are," she said, stabbing into a glazed carrot. "I do *hate* being so dull and miserable; it's not fair."

Nick drew Greta into the library after dinner to tell her that he'd had a word with Jay. But whether her brother's behavior to Daisy showed more restraint, Greta was less sure. The following day, she found him outside Daisy's room again, with a tray of sherry consommé.

"She won't let me in," he complained to Greta. "She let Jordan in."

"Perhaps she needs to be alone," Greta offered. Her brother could be so all-or-nothing. He ardently wanted to do what he thought best for his friends—regardless, sometimes, of what they thought best for themselves.

"You don't know Daisy," he said instead, shifting away from Greta as though she'd said something unkind. "Daisy doesn't do well alone."

Greta only hoped that if Molly or Ada noticed the amount of time the master of the house was spending in the young widow's bedroom, they would choose not to interpret it amiss.

The night before the funeral, Greta sat by her bedroom window watching the evening darken and a low mist roll in from the sound, trailing its gray fingers over the lawns. Just the thought of the day that lay ahead sent her heart quickening. A funeral was a day for bringing peace to both the grieving and the dead . . . and yet, she sensed peace was not going to be on the table for anybody tomorrow.

She glanced down at the celluloid image of her parents, wished them a silent goodnight as she always did, then rose to pull the curtains. She blinked then, squinting at the figure she'd spotted out on the lawn, only half-visible in the light. What on earth was Ada doing out there? Greta stepped closer to the cold windowpane, nose to the glass. She watched the distant figure come closer, walking up the lawns toward the kitchen entrance until she disappeared from view. Had Ada been down at the waterfront? What ghoulish impulse had brought her there?

Greta shivered, and pulled the curtains closed. Tomorrow would be here all too soon, and she was going to need all the rest she could get.

But eight hours later, Greta was bolt upright, swatting the sleep mask off her face, her heart skittering. Someone had just screamed outside her bedroom door.

Chapter Eight

She leaped to her feet, and hurried into the corridor. The door to Daisy's bedroom was ajar, and there was Daisy in front of her closet, a look of frantic disbelief on her face. Even as Greta reached the doorway, Daisy began to manically rip out drawers, upending their contents on the floor—gold jewelry, silk slips, stockings.

"Daisy? What is it?"

There was the sound of drawers squealing as Daisy dragged them from their rails.

She turned, staring wide-eyed at Greta.

"My necklace. My pearl necklace. It's *gone*."

"Daisy?" The others had arrived now, a bleary-eyed Jordan with her chestnut hair askew, and from the other end of the corridor, Nick and Jay, both half-dressed for the funeral, Nick in pajama pants and a pressed white shirt, and Jay in his gold dressing robe with a pair of pleated black suit trousers poking out below.

"My pearls!" Daisy's voice rose an octave. "My pearls, someone's *taken* them!" She threw a despairing look back at the closet she'd just ransacked. "They were in that box, there, on that shelf, and I just opened it and they're *gone!*"

Greta now saw the empty case Daisy had flung onto the vanity—a large case lined with royal-blue velvet, the kind that only a particularly magnificent piece of jewelry would rest in—which now sat open and utterly empty, with only a thick semicircular groove in the velvet to show where the pearls had once lain.

Greta knew those pearls. *Everyone* knew those pearls. They were the famous wedding-gift pearls, the ones Daisy had worn the other night . . . the night of Tom's death.

"Tom gave them to me!" Daisy went on, her voice rising. "They *can't* be gone. They can't be!"

She went back to the closet drawers, opening and shutting them senselessly. There was no self-conscious performance about any of it: Greta could tell that the other woman's shock was totally and utterly genuine.

"Daisy . . . you are *quite* sure you put them back in that box the other night?" Nick said.

"Yes, of course! Of course I'm sure. I put them in that box like I always do! Jordan, you remember, don't you?"

Jordan gave a slow nod.

"See? Jordan saw them." Daisy stopped in the middle of the room, quivering. "You see, don't you? Someone's gone and stolen them!"

"Let's just be absolutely sure, all right?" Jay said. "Let's just . . . let's have a look around the room in case they . . . in case they fell anywhere."

It seemed a thin hope, but of course he was as appalled as Greta was at the thought of any of the staff being responsible. And it *would* seem an outrageous thing for any of them to do. Not to mention they'd all been here for years except for Molly—and it was rather hard to imagine Molly having the temerity to pull this off.

Greta followed Jay's lead, and dropped down to search under the bed while Jay glanced around the vanity, then behind the curtains. Daisy stood in the middle of the room, pink-faced, staring from one to the other.

"This is troubling indeed," Nick said slowly, "but perhaps best dealt with on our return? I'm afraid we don't have all that much time before Edgar and his mother arrive."

He was right, but Greta was distracted. Under the bed—Ada had really been doing a second-rate job of dusting down here—something promising had caught her eye. A glimmer of something round and lustrous and white. She reached, and felt a leap of anticipation when her fingers touched the smooth surface, but in the next instant realized she'd been mistaken: what rolled into her hand was just one little orb, a mother-of-pearl cuff link.

One of the pair she'd given Jay for his birthday last year. She recognized it easily.

"Gigi?" Jay was looking at her, hopeful. "Find something?"

Oh, Jay. Oh, Jay, you fool.

She kept her face innocent of all emotion, hard as it was.

"I'm afraid not," she said, standing and surreptitiously pocketing the item in her silk robe. A small rock seemed to have settled in the pit of her stomach. There might have been innocuous reasons for Jay to come into Daisy's bedroom of late . . . but there was absolutely no good reason he would have been *unbuttoning his shirt* in here, and right by the bed, too! Besides, Greta knew when he'd last worn those cuff links. He liked to wear them when she was visiting. She'd seen them in his sleeves the night of her homecoming. The night of Tom's death.

Suddenly everything realigned in a rather dreadful way.

That night: the noise in the corridor, that knock at the door at one in the morning. The slippered foot disappearing through Daisy's doorway. It had been too dark to make out the man—Greta had assumed it was Tom. *How very awful*, she'd thought later. *How very macabre.* A last conjugal visit mere hours before taking a gun to his head.

But what if that slippered foot hadn't been Tom's at all? What if . . . ?

Greta hoped against hope that she was wrong.

Downstairs in the hall, they all stood assembled near the door while Daisy fidgeted in front of the mirror. She would be riding in the hearse with Edgar and his mother—the formidable Rosemary Buchanan. The rest of them would go separately in Jay's car.

"How do I look?" she said anxiously, and glanced around at them. "Tom would want me to look my best, you know."

In her tightly bodiced and heavily beaded black lace dress, Daisy was by far the most glamorous widow Greta had ever seen. It might look a little vain, the way she fussed and primped before the mirror, but Greta supposed what Daisy had said was true enough. Tom had married a trophy, and he'd wanted the world to see her that way.

"You look very well," Nick said reassuringly.

"Perfect," Jay amended, his voice hoarse, and Greta felt a renewed sense of gloom. Seeing the way her brother's eyes were fixed on Daisy now, she realized she had underestimated it completely, this schoolboy crush of his. It was more than that, wasn't it? He was utterly in love with Daisy Buchanan. The way he looked at her, the devotion in his eyes. Whatever might have happened in Daisy's bed that night hadn't been just some frivolous dalliance, not for Jay.

But was Daisy in love with *him*? If she was, it certainly wasn't so obvious—but perhaps she was just more inscrutable. Greta wasn't sure which prospect was worse: if Daisy had only been toying with Jay, there was heartbreak to come. But if she *did* love him, the union couldn't be more ill-timed.

Now Daisy angled that cool, angelic face toward the mirror again, and swept her palms down the front of her dress in a final, agitated gesture. Small diamond earrings glinted in her ears; without the pearl necklace, she'd resorted to a small gold chain with a solitary diamond at the center.

They'd endeavored to put the fiasco of the missing necklace to one side for now, but Jay had quietly informed Beecham of the disappearance, and the butler was going to have the staff perform a search while they were gone. The intention, of course, was to give anyone who might have stolen the pearls an elegant opportunity to "find" them again without further repercussions. The pearls would not be "found" in Daisy's room, though—she had insisted on locking her door before they left, lest any other objects of value start to disappear.

There was the sound of wheels on gravel, and slowly a black hearse swept into the driveway. They watched as Edgar dismounted and shut the door.

"We'll see you at the church," Nick said, and pressed Daisy's hand. She nodded; each of them kissed her, then she stepped outside, meeting Edgar before he reached the house. He kissed her hand and drew her around to the door of the hearse. He was standing very close to her, Greta thought. There was something quite proprietary about it.

Rosemary Buchanan did not get out of the vehicle; instead, Daisy walked around to the window and spoke to her from there. Her body language was deferential as she lowered herself to speak through the window—Daisy Buchanan, who bowed to no one. Greta thought Tom's mother must be an impressive character indeed.

Driving to a funeral in Jay's bright-yellow Rolls did seem a little inappropriate—the whole impression it gave was so very *jaunty*. Inside the car, though, it was a subdued place: each of them seemed lost in thought, although Greta was surely the only one whose mind was on a single mother-of-pearl cuff link hanging in the pocket of her dressing robe back at the house. Should she tell someone—Nick, perhaps? On the one hand, the fewer people who knew about her brother's ill-timed liaison, the better. On the other hand, if anyone could talk sense into Jay, it was Nick. Nick and Jay were quite opposite in character—Nick sober, Jay full of emotion; Nick practical and cerebral, Jay an ardent dreamer led by instinct—but the two men had a deep respect for each other. Jay might listen to Nick.

Or perhaps she ought to confront Jay herself—but heavens, what words to use?

Whatever had happened had not been simply a one-night thing, Greta was realizing. It couldn't be. Jay wouldn't have knocked on Daisy's door unless he had every reason to believe she'd let him in, and he'd been admitted without a word, without even a murmur of surprise.

Jordan broke the silence. "I'm sure it's just a storm in a teacup, you know—those pearls. Daisy's got too many nice things; she's always putting them in the wrong places. They're bound to turn up."

Nick frowned.

"You didn't actually see her put them away, then?"

Jordan flushed.

"Well, I *thought* I had, but honestly, Nicky, I can't remember. I was rather smashed that night, you know."

Jay rolled down the window. It was hot in the car, and the breeze that flowed in was hot, too. He rolled it up again as they reached the industrial wasteland that stood at the border of Queens, full of factories and gas stations, belching chimneys and warehouses with piles of car tires lined outside.

"For dust you are and to dust you will return," Greta heard him murmur as he looked out at the desolate land, and she wondered if he was thinking of Tom or of himself.

But soon they reached the highway, and then the greener lands around New Haven, and then the town proper, with its tram tracks and white columns and Woolworths stores. Greta looked up, and inadvertently caught Bill Richardson's eye in the rearview mirror. He had sharp eyes set in a sharp face, and it seemed to Greta that he was watching them all with some curiosity. It *was* a curious occurrence, she supposed: a funeral of pomp and circumstance that followed a violent death at your new employer's home. Greta wondered what he thought about it all. He must hear all sorts of things up there. People forgot to be private in a car the way they were at home.

Nick looked out the window as the car slowed.

"Looks like we're here."

"Quite a turnout," Jordan said, as they stepped down. She, too, was dressed rather glamorously, though by Jordan Baker's standards, Greta supposed one could consider it demure. The slash of scarlet lipstick certainly set off the black dress at any rate.

A steady trickle of well-dressed people in black climbed the church steps ahead of them.

Society funerals were like weddings: it was all about decorum, who attended, who was invited, and who sat where. Greta wondered how many of the mourners filing into the church today knew, or speculated as to, the real circumstances of Tom's death. Well—no matter if they did: everyone would do their part and keep up the pretense.

Jay offered Jordan his arm as they walked up the steps. Nick turned to Greta and did the same, but he must have seen something in her face to trouble him.

"Are you all right, Greta?"

She hesitated.

"May I speak to you about something?" She kept her voice low, as Jay was only a few feet away. "Later?"

Nick glanced at her, then followed her eyes and slowed his pace.

"Of course." He frowned. "Anything."

Despite all that was on her mind, Greta's heart faltered a little. She knew she should not set much store by that *anything*; it was just a turn of phrase. But it became harder, then, to meet his eyes.

They entered the church, leaving the summer air behind. Inside, it was high-ceilinged and cavernous, and smelled of incense; Greta shivered, and Nick looked at her, concerned. But she could not continue the conversation now: they were halfway up the nave, and Jay was already guiding Jordan into a pew.

"Later," she said again, and Nick nodded.

The atmosphere was heavy. Stained-glass windows cast lozenges of light across the pews and their inhabitants, but their slight flicker seemed the only movement in the vast, still space. The coffin—a closed casket—stood beneath the altar.

Greta had spent little time in churches. The lands her parents had sailed here from had been lands of prayer, but America had been a land of work. For them, the work had become the prayer: the prayer was in the work. Aside from that, religion had mostly been a form of nostalgia, slumbering for seasons at a time, only to awake once or twice a year, suddenly acute: days when candles were lit, and her parents would, each in their way, turn inward.

Jay had long ago declared disinterest in bending the knee to any god who had so conspicuously failed to save them. Greta took his point, but it didn't stop her from offering up a prayer from time to time to a vague, amorphous God inside her head. She reasoned that if she hoped to receive the benefit of His doubt, it behooved her to afford Him the same.

The organ music swelled; the priest appeared. He spent only a brief amount of time talking about Tom, whom he obviously had not known at all, but he had plenty to say about God and God's will. In God's plan, he asserted, there were no accidents. It was up to those left behind to draw upon faith, and sustain themselves through the working of His mystery.

Greta understood that it was supposed to be a comforting thought: that tragedy was never random, pain never senseless. But sometimes it seemed that everyone was always telling her to accept "what was" rather than question it. Ladies, certainly, were not supposed to question things. *Ladylike* meant gracious, and gracious meant accepting.

Greta could accept that Tom Buchanan was dead. And she could accept the sad truth that people sometimes chose to take their own lives. So why couldn't she seem to accept what everyone else—the inspector, Jay, even Nick—all seemed to accept: that the events of the recent past were as simple, sad, and straightforward as they seemed? Nick reckoned Tom had a secret of some kind that had pushed him to it. But there was no sign of any such secret, let alone one terrible enough to account for *this*.

"And in His infinite wisdom and mercy," the priest intoned, "He has chosen to call home His beloved son, Thomas Ignatius Buchanan III . . ."

Greta looked over at Nick, who seemed absorbed by the sermon. Jay, on her other side, had his gaze locked on the front of the church. Greta followed its direction: there in the front pew was Daisy's coiffed, golden head, the shapely neck held high. Nearby was a broad-shouldered woman with lead-colored hair. No doubt this was Tom's mother, the Valkyrie. And between her and Daisy . . . Greta's heart constricted. A small blonde head, barely visible above the pew. What did the child make of all this? What *could* she make of it? Greta wondered, as she had wondered before, whether there had been any blessing in losing her parents when she was still too young to fully understand death, the finality of it or its subtler cruelties. Jay had been older; no detail had escaped him. But he'd had them, he'd had the benefit of them, for all those extra years.

All the memories.

The small blonde head swiveled toward Daisy, questioning, and Greta blinked hard and looked away.

Edgar approached the pulpit then and began to speak, drawing her thoughts in a different direction. Greta felt a strange wave of discomfort as she watched him. Did other people feel it, too, this . . . coldness? It was as though the man sucked light from the room.

Greta shook off the feeling, and tried to pay attention as Edgar spoke. His voice was cool and steady, but to Greta's ear, it sounded more emotionless than stoic.

Tom had been such an unpleasant man—and yet, Greta thought, he had not *unnerved* her the way his brother did.

At the funeral reception, in a quiet corner of the hotel—an establishment of subdued opulence—Nick drew her aside with a look that made Greta's skin warm.

"Well? Are you going to tell me what's the matter?"

Greta wondered if she'd been wise to bring him into this at all. She'd been too impulsive, perhaps. The news would shock him. And what if she was wrong?

But she wasn't wrong—she knew she wasn't.

She drew a breath, and divested herself of the morning's discovery.

"Nick—I found something in Daisy's room when we were looking for the pearls." She felt the flush spread across her cheeks. She'd already been accused once of having a mind like a "sensationalist ladies' novel."

"It was one of Jay's cuff links," she went on, her eyes on the floor. "And I know when he last wore it. I hate to leap to any conclusions," she said hurriedly. "It's just, I can't think how it would have got there unless . . . well, I never imagined there was anything, you know . . ."

Even as she spoke the words aloud, she felt her doubts renew. *Had* she jumped to conclusions? But when she looked up at Nick, he wasn't looking askance. On the contrary, he looked . . .

A stone turned over in the pit of her stomach. That expression. He *knew*.

"Oh, Greta. I did think Jay would have told you the truth by now. The truth is"—he looked at her—"the truth is, you see . . . well, it's been going on for years."

Chapter Nine

Years?

Greta stared at him, dazed.

"But... Tom! You don't mean they were carrying on right under his nose?" She shook her head. "Since *when*?"

An affair? Between Daisy and Jay—for years?

She felt stupid—and yet, she could not be the only stupid one. Tom certainly hadn't known, or even suspected—there'd have been hell to pay if he had.

"But *Daisy*," she said.

Really, it was astonishing. That Daisy, never mind Jay, should be so reckless. Perhaps that in itself *was* evidence that she loved him.

"Is she in love with him, Nick? She doesn't seem like she is, you know."

Nick looked away.

"Well, she certainly hasn't confided her heart to me. But perhaps she's just more... guarded than your brother. She's rather a good actress, you know. Perhaps she's hiding much more than she shows."

Greta frowned.

Perhaps. After all, if Daisy had behaved toward Jay as Jay had toward her, Tom would never have stood for it.

"Nick, can you imagine what people will say if this gets out? It would have stained their reputations before. But *now*, after all this with Tom . . ."

She looked across the room to where Edgar Buchanan, his mother, and Daisy all stood in a line, receiving the condolences of the funeral-goers. Despite all the black garments, there was so much opulence in the room—everywhere Greta looked there was the flash of gold, of silver, of diamonds. But in the center of it, Daisy stood out like a pure thing. Her skin, devoid since Tom's death of the heavier makeup she had used to apply, only looked younger and more radiant. Her hair reflected the light through the window like a second sun. There was no doubt about it; she was magnetic.

And it was obvious others thought so, too. Greta didn't have to look hard to see where the bulk of the room's energy was directed and where the longest line of condolence-givers was. She also couldn't help but notice that many of those approaching the young widow to offer their respects were men—young men and not-so-young—all of them giving off that same well-fed air of establishment money that Tom had had in spades.

"Who else knows?" she said quietly.

Nick cleared his throat.

"I should think hardly anyone does." Like Greta, he kept his gaze on the opposite side of the room, and spoke in an undertone. "I know Jordan suspects, but Daisy's never let on. And if Daisy hasn't told Jordan, she surely hasn't told anyone else. As for Jay . . ." He looked apologetic. "I suppose I'm the only one."

Greta shook her head, still a little dazed by the discovery. That Tom should never have suspected . . . she supposed that he, like her, had been fooled by the sheer obviousness of Jay's crush. Everyone knew he had a sweet spot for Daisy; he'd worn it all on his sleeve in that earnest way of his. In a sense, they had been hiding the affair in plain sight.

"With Daisy, it's different, Greta—even I can see that. There've been other women before, but it was never like this." Nick glanced over to where Daisy stood now, receiving her long line of well-wishers. "Whatever Daisy feels for *him*, though . . . I wonder if it can survive this. It's one thing to betray Tom when he's alive, but another to do it when he's dead."

Greta wondered if that was why Jay hovered so close to Daisy now—because he feared Tom's death would be what cost him her love.

Greta sighed. It didn't honestly surprise her that he'd never entrusted her with a confession of the truth. But it saddened her—they were each other's only family, and yet they knew so little of each other's hearts. What she did know was that her brother had a habit of charging forward with eyes for nothing but the goal ahead.

"I just hope he won't get himself into trouble."

"I'll speak to him," Nick said eventually. "I promise, Greta."

It was as much as she could ask. They lapsed into silence until Nick glanced across the room to where the Buchanans stood.

"We should pay our respects, I suppose."

The line of people waiting to speak to Daisy had not abated. Edgar stood next to her, as pale-faced as ever, and to her other side was the formidable Rosemary Buchanan: a statuesque woman whose force of personality seemed chiefly concentrated in her chin. The little girl, Pammy, had been there for a few minutes, but had been carried off since by a nanny.

"Mrs. Buchanan." Nick stepped forward. "Nick Carraway—a college friend of Tom's. Really, it's the most shocking thing."

Rosemary Buchanan nodded slightly, accepting the offering.

Nick put a hand on Greta's arm by way of introduction.

"And this is Greta, Jay Gatsby's sister—Tom's friend Jay."

The effect was instant; the woman's face darkened thunderously. Her gray eyes grew narrow, her nostrils flaring.

"You dare show your face here." She spoke under her breath, but the rage was perfectly evident.

"I beg your pardon?" Greta thought for a moment the woman had mistaken her for someone else. But Rosemary Buchanan carried on.

"Your brother and his disgusting, dissolute ways. Dragging my son into the gutter with him." She fixed her furious eyes on Greta. "That obscene place of his, drowning my son in liquor and drugs," she hissed. "*He* did this. He did this to us!"

Her voice was rising, and Edgar, beside her, put a hand on her arm. "Mother."

Greta's mouth was hanging open. She closed it, and took a step forward. "Mrs. Buchanan—if you think for one moment—"

But Nick's hand was firmly on her arm, steering her backward.

"Leave it, Greta," he hissed. "You won't help Jay this way."

Other funeralgoers swallowed her place in the line as Nick urged her away. If they had heard any of the exchange, they were putting up a good front. Meanwhile, Nick pulled her around so that his dark eyes were on hers.

"Greta, Rosemary Buchanan is a pillar of society. You pick a fight with her at her son's funeral, of all places, and it'll just cement everything she's accusing you of. I thought you wanted to keep Jay *out* of the spotlight."

Greta seethed; her skin was hot, and her limbs trembled with unspent energy. How satisfying it would have been to tell Rosemary Buchanan exactly what kind of a son she'd had in Tom. But Nick was right. Greta had more urgent matters to deal with today.

The drive home was quiet. Jay was sullen, Nick pensive, and without anyone to share in her repartee, Jordan had ceased to bother. Daisy wasn't with them; a separate car would take her back later.

Greta glanced over to where her brother sat by the window. He'd lowered it a little, and now a light wind ruffled his hair, showing off its fine gold hue. He frowned, his noble features drawn tight. Most likely, he was thinking about Daisy—or about that long line of high-society men so eager to offer their condolences.

Greta wondered briefly about the necklace, and whether it would have turned up by the time they returned. She still had a hard time believing any member of the Gatsbys' staff could have taken it. She'd much rather Jordan was right, and Daisy had just misplaced it. Although that felt equally difficult to believe.

Really, it was such a sordid thing to happen, and right on the day of Tom's funeral.

Beecham opened the door for them, his heavy brows full of concern. Greta noticed again the toll the last days had taken on him. He seemed to have aged years since the night of Tom's death. The poor man, he took the household's troubles greatly to heart.

"Sir," he said in a low aside that Greta nonetheless heard, "I regret to inform you, the item in question . . . it has not materialized, despite a concerted search by all the household."

Jay sighed.

"I'm most sorry to hear it. I'm afraid we shall have to deal with another unpleasant visit from the police department."

"Sir," Beecham bowed, but he looked as uncomfortable as Jay did at the prospect.

"I'm sure the pearls will turn up, you know," Jordan observed, as they made their way into the living room. "I shouldn't think it's really necessary to have the police back out here."

Jay looked at her grimly.

"I should think Daisy's insurance firm may feel differently. Nick, pour us all a drink, would you, old sport?"

The conversation returned once more to the funeral. Greta could see Nick was looking at her, probably to dissuade her from unburdening herself about Rosemary Buchanan's vicious words, but the way Greta saw it, Jay ought to know what he was up against. She relayed what had been said to her in the receiving line. Jay stared in disbelief; Jordan's eyebrows shot up.

"Oh, I see—she thinks you were shoveling cocaine into poor Tom, I suppose—or something that made him go off his rocker. So *that's* why she insisted on the autopsy. She's quite adamant there'll be an inquest, you know."

Greta stared.

"Jordan..." Had she heard correctly? "Did you say... an *inquest?*"

Chapter Ten

"I suppose the autopsy results will take a while," Jordan said. "It was all hush-hush, naturally. The Buchanans don't want anybody to know."

"An *inquest?*" Jay had recovered his powers of speech. "But that's absurd."

"Well . . . but might she have a point?" Nick frowned. "Despicable as her accusations were, of course. Maybe he *did* pop some pill that scrambled his brain that night. Perhaps it would help explain why he'd do something so . . . so very out of character." He glanced at Greta.

Jordan crossed her feet on the coffee table and stretched her thin arms in a sigh of dramatic proportions.

"Tom wasn't *on* anything, Nicky. And besides, if he was, what sort of a drug would have an effect like *that?*"

The rest of them looked down into their glasses of bourbon, as short of answers, Greta suspected, as she felt herself.

Greta was sitting on the porch swing overlooking the water, where gray clouds banded across the horizon. Her hands turned over the cuff link she'd found this morning as she thought back to the events of the day.

How dreadful Rosemary Buchanan had been! And how troubling Nick's disclosure about Jay and Daisy. *Someone* had to talk to Jay about it, but perhaps such words were better coming from Nick? Jay hadn't wanted Greta to know of the affair in the first place, and she feared getting his guard up if she tackled him about it now. And on top of that, there was still this nasty business with the necklace.

Greta had hoped that once the funeral was behind them, they might at least feel a kind of relief. But if anything, Tom's ghost seemed stronger today, as if his hold on them all were growing. Or maybe it was just these gray, turgid skies that made her feel so claustrophobic, even anxious. It felt as though a storm were brewing; somewhere, rabbits waited in their dens with flattened ears. The only noise that pierced the spell was the sound of Bill hosing down the Phantom over near the garage: she could see the glint of the yellow paintwork and the intermittent spray of water from here. The noise was soothing, distant but pleasant. It had been a frequent sound when Silas had worked here; he'd been absolutely meticulous about keeping the car pristine.

The churn of wheels on gravel interrupted her thoughts, and Greta glanced down the driveway. Daisy had returned in a taxicab, and Greta watched the petite, black-clad figure hurry indoors.

Even had Daisy been widowed in less garish circumstances, even had an appropriate amount of time passed since Tom's death; even then, Greta would not have rejoiced at the idea of Jay's falling for her.

"Out for some air?"

It was Jordan, holding a pack of her favored Turkish cigarettes. She had changed out of her funeral garb and back into the silk kimono she'd been wearing as a morning robe, where sinuous dragons twisted their way through gold-embroidered clouds. She drew out a cigarette and extended the pack toward Greta.

"Have a gasper?"

"No, thanks."

Jordan shrugged and lit up, exhaled toward the overcast sky.

"Was that Daisy's cab I heard?"

Greta nodded, and Jordan sighed.

"Better fortify myself before I go in, then."

Greta hadn't thought Daisy's company was something Jordan would have to "fortify" herself for, considering the two were such close friends. But she suspected Jordan's empathy was of the tough-love variety, and probably it *was* rather draining having to provide the kind of unstinting support Daisy sought right now.

"Bet you'll be glad to have us out of your hair soon, won't you?" Jordan rested her chin thoughtfully on her smoking hand, and gave the ash a tap. "It's too bad, though, isn't it—you won't really be able to get rid of what happened. It'll always stay with the house in a way."

Was she right? Daisy would leave, as would Jordan and Nick—but Greta and Jay might *never* be rid of Tom's ghost.

"You're going to Florida after this?" Greta glanced out at the water.

"That's the idea. I suppose we'll all leave tomorrow if Daisy can manage it." Jordan sighed. "Poor little Pammy, did you see her at the funeral? At least she has her nanny with her." Jordan shook her head, and exhaled a stream of cigarette smoke. "It's the nanny who's raised her, really. Daisy's awfully fond of the little moppet, but she doesn't know the first thing about mothering—why should she, when *she* was raised by a nanny herself. Daisy's mother was a bit of a cold fish, you know. I don't think they even speak anymore."

Greta, who hadn't had the benefit of much mothering herself, felt an unexpected flash of sympathy for Daisy. Daisy didn't seem like a lonely sort of person, but her life was certainly beginning to sound that way.

"The first time Tom cheated on her—and mind you, it was all quite public and humiliating—she went back to Louisville." Jordan glanced over.

"Her mamma met her at the door, heard her story, then refused to let her in. Told Daisy to go back to her husband and make things right. *Don't come crying to me* was about the size of it; not very fair when you consider they just about propelled her into Tom's arms in the first place."

They sat in silence for a while as Greta wondered what *her* mother might have said had Greta ever come home with a man like Tom Buchanan. Rosa Gatz had been a very practical woman, but the right kind of practical, Greta thought. The kind who would consider wealth bought at the cost of misery to be horribly *im*practical.

Jordan drew down another drag of her cigarette.

"You and Nick seemed to be having a nice little tête-à-tête earlier."

Greta flushed.

"I had something I . . . wanted his advice about."

Jordan gave her a wry glance.

"Wise of you. I never was very good at getting advice. Or giving it, either." She plucked a thread of tobacco from her tongue, and idly inspected it. "I did try, sometimes," she said. "When Tom started courting Daisy, for example. I told her he couldn't possibly make her happy no matter what her mother said or how filthy rich he was." She glanced at Greta. "But you know, I'm not sure if Daisy even *wanted* to be happy."

Greta took her eyes from the horizon.

"What do you mean?"

Jordan shrugged.

"She wanted everyone to *think* she was happy; she wanted to *look* happy. That was something she knew how to do much better than actually *being* happy. Poor old Daise has been told how to look and what to feel for so long, I think sometimes she hardly knows how to locate a feeling of her own. I suspect it's why she was such a marvelous little actress—she's always performing feelings in order to try to find 'em."

Jordan took another drag of her cigarette, and it struck Greta, not for the first time, that there was an uncanny shrewdness about Jordan Baker. She had a way of looking at you that made you feel she knew the things you hid from yourself. She was observant, Greta thought, and more than a little ruthless.

"And now here she is, still a young woman; more beautiful, if anything, than she was at nineteen, and suddenly one of the wealthiest women in New York. She won't need to marry again—but if she ever *does* want to, well." Jordan shrugged. "I think we all saw today that she'd have her pick."

Greta studied her companion.

"You're saying Tom's death was to her advantage."

Jordan looked amused.

"I think what I'm *really* saying," she said, and tapped out more ash, "is that it's starting to sink in for Daisy. It would have been indecent of her to show it, but if you ask me, underneath it all, she's starting to understand just how different her life might be now if she chooses.

"I think she was realizing, *really* realizing, that for the first time, she can do anything she wants. I shouldn't be surprised if it was a little bit intoxicating." She glanced over. "Have I shocked you?"

"Not at all," Greta began to say—but she stopped as a voice traveled toward them from inside the house: the library window was directly above them, and ajar.

"But Daisy, it would be a tremendous insult." It was Jay's voice, sharper than usual. "Some of them have been here for years. Can you imagine old Beecham having his room searched?"

"Well, *he* didn't do it!" It was Daisy now, and her nerves sounded just as frayed as Jay's. "It was that skinny little one with the mousy hair, I'd put money on it. I've seen how she goggles at my jewelry, Jay! And you *said* she was the only one who's new. Of *course* it's her. You can ring for her right now, and have her take me down to her room. It's probably right there, buried in her socks."

Jay's voice came again.

"I don't think it would be very fitting for you to be rooting around the poor girl's underthings, Daisy."

Greta wondered how much of the conversation was really about the pearls. Daisy *was* upset, that was clear—but Greta suspected the emotion in both voices had a lot more to do with the day they'd just been through. She glanced over at Jordan, who seemed to have perked up considerably at the prospect of drama. It would be wise, really, to get Jordan out of here; Nick said Jordan had her suspicions about Daisy and Jay, and there was no telling what terrain this conversation might stray toward.

"Well, if it's not fitting for me to do it, Dantry can. I'll just watch. And if it doesn't turn up there, we're calling the police. I'm not waiting till tomorrow, Jay—for all we know, the little devil's about to cycle into town and flog it!"

"Don't you think it's rather unseemly, Daisy?" Jay must have come to the window now; his voice was perfectly audible suddenly, and it sounded sharp. Not the usual, soft way he talked to Daisy. Perhaps that, too, was due to the eager line of men at the funeral earlier.

"Unseemly?" Daisy's voice was brittle, daring him to say more.

"Calling in the police about a necklace on the same day as your husband's funeral."

"It was *Tom's* necklace, Jay!" Daisy snapped.

"Of course. The monument to your happy marriage."

"How vulgar of you, Jay! How horribly vulgar." Daisy sounded quite furious now.

Jordan caught Greta's eye. *My goodness, what an interesting conversation we've stumbled into,* the look said.

"Vulgar?" Jay said then. "*I* wasn't the one receiving admirers at a funeral as if it were a debutante ball!"

Daisy let out a small shriek of outrage. Even Greta had to admit that had been rather unnecessary of Jay. But she knew how he hated being called vulgar. It was something Old Money liked to call New Money, and it was his greatest sensitivity.

A door slammed, and from inside the library, there was silence, and then a shattering sound.

Chapter Eleven

She found Jay in the library, blood on his trembling fingers as he collected the shards of a broken blue-and-gold Sèvres vase, one of a Louis Philippe pair Greta knew he'd always been fond of.

"Oh, Jay."

He didn't look up.

"I'm all right. No need for a fuss." But he was searching his pockets for a handkerchief to no avail.

"You'll get blood on your shirt." Greta rang the service bell, and took off the silk scarf she'd tied around her neck for the funeral. "Here, just hold that against it."

He stood back, inspecting the damage. The porcelain shards stood out brightly against the Persian rug, their tones a perfectly complement to the bleu de France curtains.

"I did like those vases."

"Well, at least you didn't throw both of them."

Jay looked at her, unsure whether to begrudge her the attempt at humor.

"Mr. Gatsby?" Molly appeared in the doorway, and blinked when she saw the remains of the shattered vase. "Oh—I'll just get the dustpan."

Daisy was right, Greta conceded: Poor Molly Riggs did rather have a way of goggling. No doubt she *had* been staring at Daisy's jewels, but the idea of her stealing them was rather harder to believe. It was hard to imagine her getting up the nerve to actually steal anything. But Greta remembered, too, that flash of defensive dignity when Greta had volunteered too much sympathy that first morning. Molly had pride, a moral code that seemed unlikely to allow for thievery. And yet, the girl was nervous; there was no denying that. *Was* she hiding something? Something she'd seen, perhaps; something she knew that they didn't?

"I was reaching for a book," Jay explained, gesturing vaguely at the bookshelves. "Knocked it over, I'm afraid."

"Of course, Mr. Gatsby." If Molly found his explanation unconvincing, she betrayed no sign of it. Her face remained carefully opaque, and she bobbed a diligent little curtsy before scurrying off. Jay turned back to Greta, and frowned.

"What are you looking at me like that for?"

Greta hesitated, closed the window, then took a seat in the Jacquard-print fauteuil by the fireplace. The library smelled, as it always did, of teak paneling and old books and just a hint of tobacco, and Greta had always considered it one of the most restful spaces in the house. But not today.

So be it. Greta had told Nick that very first evening, by the window, that she wanted to be of use. And she was *going* to be of use whether Jay welcomed it or not, whether he saw he needed it or not. Almost all her life, Jay had been in charge. In charge, alone. Leaning on nobody, asking for nothing. Always the self-made man. Never mind he'd been just a boy when it all began.

Tom's death would have put anyone on tilt. But it wasn't just that, was it? Greta thought of the indiscretions with Daisy, Jay's willed blindness, his raised temper, his recklessness, his failure to understand the leadership his household needed, and his obliviousness to Molly's pinched face or Ada's red eyes or even Mrs. Dantry's newfound pallor.

He'd simply been doing it all by himself for too long—to the point that he was at risk of disappearing into his own little world. And maybe Greta wasn't the best person to pull him out of it; maybe he wouldn't welcome her efforts, but she was damn well going to try.

"I know." Greta folded her hands in her lap. "About Daisy."

For Jay's sake, she kept her eyes from his, but even so, she saw him freeze.

"What do you mean?"

"I know about you and Daisy. Nick told me."

"Confound him." Jay scowled. His temper didn't surface often, but when it did, it burned like a swift and righteous fire. Well, let it burn if it must. Greta found, suddenly, she was not afraid of it. Why *had* she been afraid before?

"What'd he go and say that for!" Her brother's eyes snapped.

"I didn't leave him much choice. He was only confirming what I already knew." Greta took the cuff link from her pocket, having retrieved it from her morning robe earlier. "I found this. In Daisy's room—this morning."

Jay turned away, his hands on his desk, staring out the window. She could see the tendons in the back of his neck. Out the window, in the distance, she saw the flash of yellow from the Phantom by the garage; Bill would be toweling the car dry by now.

"It's no use," Jay said eventually. "I do realize it's not *wise* to love her, but I can't help it. I always have."

Always?

Greta heard Jay's words from that fateful night once more: *Tom has married the only woman worth having.* Greta knew Jay hadn't been entirely single all these years, but it was true, there'd never been anyone serious. She'd thought perhaps he was afraid of love, which didn't strike her as foolish; *she* was a little afraid of it. It seemed so . . . all-encompassing. Both she and Jay had lost the people who loved them most at a tender age, and that sort of thing taught you a lot about life. About the dangers of relying on anyone else too much; about expecting what was beautiful to also be permanent.

"It certainly feels like always," Jay added. "I knew her during the war, you know."

Greta stared. Had they been lovers even then?

Jay looked up at Greta, his green eyes wide. "I don't know what it is about her, you know. I'm just mad for the girl—always have been, ever since that summer night in Louisville." He smiled faintly. "She had a dress the color of a snow peach, and a jasmine flower behind her ear. I still remember that first sight of her. Like a jolt to the heart, like I'd walked into an electrical storm.

"And then Tom came along while I was at the front. And that was that." There was bitterness in his voice now, and Greta felt for her brother who would never quite get what he wanted. Because what he wanted, she saw, was more than to win Daisy for today. He wanted those lost years. He wanted a world where Tom Buchanan had never existed.

They were quiet a minute.

"She should have waited for you."

Jay looked at her, surprised. Then his eyes moved back toward the window.

"Yes," he said. "She should have." He paused. "But I've always been good at waiting, and Daisy never was."

The silence grew.

"Tom was not a good man," Jay said at last.

"No," Greta agreed. "He wasn't."

Jay looked at her.

"There was a sort of honesty to him, I suppose, but really that's the best that can be said, isn't it? He wasn't generous; he wasn't kind. He had no sense of beauty, no sense of the sacred." Jay stopped. "He never really knew what it was to be *alive*, if you ask me. But Daisy does."

His words settled around them, and after a while, Greta glanced up.

"It's no coincidence that you found her again, is it?"

Jay shook his head.

"No, but it did seem like fate, I suppose. When I heard this site was for sale, just across the water. She was right *there*, Gigi." He nodded. "Right across the water."

Oh, Jay. Her brother had such a power of belief—there was something fearless about it, as though disappointment were something he had never known. His conviction could carry him—and others—like a tide. It always had. Until now, perhaps.

"She'd have left him in time. I was sure of it." He stared out at the water. "But, after *this* . . . It's a damned messy business, Gigi. It's far more confusing than if the rotter had just divorced her. I know she loves me." He turned and looked at Greta fiercely, as though to forbid her countenancing any other thought. "But everything's just . . . out of focus now. She needs some time to recover, that's all."

If that was all, then "all" was still asking a lot, Greta felt. But Nick was right: Jay was not apt to listen to what he didn't want to hear.

Outside the window, at the end of the lawns, waves lapped mutely against stone. Her mind, turning slowly on its axis, rotated back to the uneasy thought that had been nudging at her throughout the funeral service.

"Jay . . . do you *really* think Tom could have killed himself?"

Jay turned, irritable now.

"I'm no expert in bullet wounds, Gigi, but I should say his were rather categorical."

"Well, of course! I just meant . . ."

But what *did* she mean? Even in her own head, she couldn't quite find the words. Suicide might seem improbable, but any other attempt at explanation was far *more* improbable. Greta frowned, studying the clouds that had drawn in across the bay.

"Is Daisy still going to Newport tomorrow?" she said at last. Jay sighed, and dropped into the matching chair on the other side of the fireplace.

"I suppose this necklace business will have to be resolved first."

Greta looked down at the porcelain chips. Molly would be back to clean up the vase any minute. Poor goggle-eyed Molly Riggs, whom Daisy now had such a vendetta against.

"I don't think you should let Daisy inspect the rooms, Jay. She's liable to tear the poor girl to shreds."

"Well, but if I have Dantry do it, Daisy's bound to say the search wasn't thorough enough." He glanced at Greta. Enraged as he'd been at Daisy, he still couldn't bear to let her down, to be less than her champion. "I'd go myself, only it wouldn't be appropriate, would it—me rummaging around in the poor girl's personals?"

Greta narrowed her eyes. On another day, she might have been amused by this attempt at subtle coercion. But she had to admit: this was progress. In his own, awkward way, he was asking for her assistance.

"Fine, then." She glanced toward the hallway, hearing Molly's quick, nervous tread.

"I'll supervise."

The housemaids' room was down the corridor from the kitchen, sparely furnished, with one large window looking out onto the back gardens and, at an angle, the dock. Molly and Ada stood by their beds, Molly with her hands balled anxiously, and Ada with a look on her face as if she couldn't decide whether to be offended or afraid. The twin beds were neatly made, Molly's a little more so than Ada's, and beside each bed stood a locker with a crocheted cover on top. Molly's locker held a couple of threadbare books and a family snapshot, serious Midwestern faces outside a brick farmhouse. Ada's held a water glass and a plaster-of-Paris model of a child cuddling a lamb.

"I'm very sorry about all this," Greta said. She was changing her mind: Jay really shouldn't have agreed to the search. Better to have just telephoned the police and let them do what they must.

"It's you two that will be sorry," Dantry said grimly, turning to the young women, "if either of you are found to have anything to do with this, d'you hear? Never in all my days have I had a housemaid stealing! I'm the one who had you hired. I won't forget this."

Greta was struck by the different expressions on the young women's faces: the fear on Molly's and the crystallizing resentment on Ada's. There was a strength of purpose in that girl, Greta thought. Not someone you wanted to make an adversary of. Mrs. Smith might call Ada flighty, but there was a strength of purpose in that girl, Greta thought. She was grateful, at least, that Nora wasn't to be part of this. Ada's pique would have been as nothing compared to Nora's contempt and scorn; Greta doubted whether she would have been able to meet the former housemaid's eyes.

Dantry proceeded to search the room, drawer by drawer, cubby by cubby, meticulously. "Whose is this?" she would bark at intervals, and Molly or Ada would step in, laying claim to the shoebox or locked drawer that Dantry was demanding access to. Daisy needn't have worried about the housekeeper being thorough.

Greta found her gaze moving toward the window—the one through which the girls had seen the light on the boat on the night of Tom's death. She couldn't help imagining that eerie moment when the light had suddenly gone out. It was odd, she thought, that they'd heard no sound—she remembered how loud the shots had been that same afternoon when Jay and his friends had been at their target practice. She calculated the boat to be a similar distance. Yes, it was odd.

Something jangled then as Dantry pulled open one of Ada's closet drawers.

"What's this!" she said. Greta could hear the grim note of triumph in her voice. Dantry closed her fingers around whatever it was and brought it out dangling by a chain: a golden locket.

"Ada?" The housekeeper's voice was sharp.

"Yes, it's mine," Ada said sullenly. Beneath the sullenness, though, Greta was sure she heard a note of fear.

"A *gold* locket? Yours?" Dantry said. "An heiress, are we, Ada?"

Ada stood her ground. "It's mine, I tell you."

"Mrs. Dantry," Greta said quickly. "Let us remember, no such locket has gone missing from this house."

Gruffly, Dantry put it back, but continued her search with renewed vigor. No other necklace, however, was found.

The room had been searched top to bottom—and Greta could testify, Dantry's hawk eyes had been thorough—yet the pearls were not there.

Greta took on the unpleasant news of informing Jay, who dutifully but with evident dismay, went to place the call to the police station. Greta left him in the hall, having no particular desire to hear one-half of another conversation with Inspector Francis.

But when she opened the living room door, there was Nick, a silhouette at the window, his hands clasped behind his back. He turned at the sound of her, his frown ebbing just a little, leaving only that soft divot between his brows.

"Jay's calling the police about the pearls," she informed him, and he gave her a rueful look.

"As if the rest of it weren't enough to be getting on with." He glanced briefly at the floor. "I'm very sorry, you know. Leaving you here like this. I feel I oughtn't to be taking the train tomorrow, but the firm's so busy right now . . ."

"Of course you must go." She looked down, nudged a gold curlicue in the carpet pile. They were silent for a moment. Some words fluttered through her mind, but they were not words she might say, so she turned, instead, to words she might. "Nick . . . do you really think we'll get to the bottom of this? Of what could have made a man like Tom do this to himself?"

His frown returned.

"I hardly know, Greta. I hardly know what to think about anything right now."

Instead of Inspector Francis, the courteous young officer by the name of Stanhope was sent out to take the report, his eyes bulging slightly when he learned the value of the necklace. He took the particulars and said an alert would be sent out, and particular attention would be paid to all the pawnshops in the surrounding area. It was indeed too distinctive an item to be easily disposed of.

"Nice young specimen, wasn't he?" Jordan commented, once he'd left. "Not like that jowly inspector—so horribly brusque, and no chin to speak of at all. I can't abide a man with a weak chin, you know."

Nick poured out a whiskey from the decanter.

"You may disapprove of the inspector's chin, Jord," he said, "but I can only assume the Great Neck police force deems it quite satisfactory."

"Well, more fool them," Jordan said blithely.

Daisy had taken to her room again, whether spurred by the fight with Jay or the more significant events of the day. Without her there, Jay seemed turned inward, his green eyes dark and distracted. He was still the attentive host, pulling out Jordan's chair and ensuring all glasses were full, but he was absent from the conversation and there was no light in his face. Jordan was back in her dropped-neck flapper dress, explaining with a shrug that she would have packed differently in hindsight, had she only known.

"Yes," Nick said tartly. "I imagine we might each have done things rather differently, had we known."

They would all be leaving tomorrow—Nick, Jordan, and Daisy—even if Daisy seemed to be planning to stay in her room until their departure. Greta couldn't shake the feeling that none of this was really over—that it wasn't even close to over—and thinking of them all going their separate ways made her feel anxious, as though something important had been forgotten.

That night she tossed and turned; a strange half-dream kept disturbing her. It floated around her mind in a most unaccountable way. It was that note—that absurdly abbreviated suicide note Tom had left behind. When she shut her eyes, the spiderish scrawl hovered there, the blue ink violent on the white paper.

When Molly knocked on the door with coffee, Greta roused herself with a heavy feeling. After a haunted sleep, some feeling of evil, of the unnatural, pressed down on her.

When she dressed and left her room, Nick was across the landing, closing his bedroom door as she closed hers.

"Oh!"

"Good morning," he greeted her.

The smell of breakfast drifted up from the dining room, and morning light filtered onto the grand double staircase and the marble tile below.

"I do hope you and your brother can put all this behind you soon," Nick said. "Jay's got plenty to be getting on with, and you . . . well, things are supposed to be just beginning for you." He glanced at her.

Greta found she could not quite look him in the eye just then.

"I don't suppose you'll find your way into Manhattan very often this summer," he said after a while. "But if you should . . ."

Another door on the landing slammed, and Jordan was sauntering toward them, fresh-faced as ever.

"I say—I promised Daisy I'd go over to the house and pick up some things for her. Do either of you want to come?" She grimaced. "It does rather give me the willies, the idea of going there by myself."

"Sorry, Jord, I've got my own packing to do, and I want to have a talk with Jay this morning."

Greta wondered briefly what about, but Jordan's gaze had already swiveled her way.

"Greta? Want to come?"

It was an odd sort of invitation. Surely only individuals possessed of a particularly morbid curiosity would want to go for a wander around a dead man's deserted home.

"I'll get my coat," she said.

Chapter Twelve

It started to rain while they were in the car, great splattering drops that flattened themselves against the windows and trickled wide paths down the glass. The view was half-obscured, but Greta could still see flashes of the sea, leaden and dull, as they slipped down the shore road. They hugged the coastline the whole way, avoiding town to take the sharp turn out onto the East Egg peninsula, where an air of peaceful money emanated even from the more modest houses, those without sea views or turreted second and third stories. Ahead of them was a marina, its small forest of masts moving slightly in the wind, gray steel against gray water.

"So what are we picking up?" Greta turned to Jordan, who was plucking at some speck on her skirt with painted fingernails.

"Oh, Pammy's things, mostly. And some fresh clothes for Daisy. They'll need their beach wear for Newport." Jordan leaned forward and raised her voice. "Hallo! Next house on the left here."

Bill took the turn slowly, hesitantly, and Greta had plenty of time to observe the lush lawns as they drove up toward the pristine white edifice ahead. For all that the Gatsbys' home was so magnificent, this place had something theirs didn't.

The trees towered above the driveway, at least twice the height of the gracious three-story home that rose up ahead. Leafy canopies spread above, sheltering them from the downpour. Even in the rain, there was an effortlessness about the place, the kind that belongs only to those homes that have stood a long time. Nature seemed unhurried here, the trees presiding with their ancient wisdom, and the gnarled roots that broke through the lawn were not a sign of imperfection but a mark of pedigree. "It just *feels* like it's looking down its nose at you, don't you think?" Jordan turned. "I suppose people envy Pammy, growing up in a place like this, but I don't."

A startled pheasant burst from the foliage as the car crept farther up the driveway.

"Aren't any of the staff still here?"

Jordan shook her head.

"They closed the place down entirely while the renovations were underway. The roofers only finished their job a few days ago."

It *was* grim, wasn't it? The house Tom and Daisy were supposed to be returning home to. Newly renovated, everything in its place. And now Tom would never walk through that door again, and Daisy would be returning to it a widow.

Bill swung the car around in the forecourt, and fished a large black umbrella from the seat beside him. He took it around to the back door, holding the cover over their heads as the two women descended.

"Thank you, Bill."

At the door, they waited while Jordan fumbled around in her purse, finally extracting a ring of brass keys.

"I really don't see why there have to be so *many* of them."

But she found the right one eventually, and the door swung open to a large, echoing hallway paneled in dark wood. It was dark in the gray rain-light, and would have been darker still but for the tremendous white fireplace that covered one full wall, its plasterwork a wilderness of carved wreaths and garlands fringing the enormous mantel. The whole place had an *old* sort of smell, one that made Greta think of wine cellars, of red wine stored in cool, earthy places, and libraries whose curtains lay always drawn against the sun.

A burnished chandelier dangled in the middle of the room, and drew Greta's eye toward the tremendous oil painting that hung on the opposite wall. Greta blinked at the unnerving sight of a larger-than-life Tom Buchanan staring back at her from the center of a family portrait. The artist appeared to have added an extra few inches to his height, and a noble frown replaced the faint sneer that had usually hung about his face. Daisy's likeness seemed somehow distorted, too, her quick and lively prettiness transmuted here into something more stately, almost stolid.

The child looked to be barely walking age in the portrait, but already she favored her mother, with that wide-eyed, beguiling blue stare and the dimple in her left cheek.

Greta's eyes lingered over the child. At least she would be able to imagine a different version of her father for herself. One more like the man in the portrait and less like the person he'd really been.

"Greta? Are you coming?"

She pulled herself away from the portrait and followed Jordan toward the grand staircase covered in royal-blue carpet secured by golden stair rods, its pile all perfectly brushed.

"It's terribly elegant," she offered.

"Tom's mother bought it for them. Wedding gift." Jordan shivered. "It's not a *happy* place, is it?"

Greta followed her along the upstairs corridor to a room that Jordan evidently knew well. She threw open the door, and they were in a beautiful pale-green boudoir with murals all over the walls: bucolic scenes of golden-haired girls in swings, painted nosegays of daisies gathered in bunches or growing wild in the meadow.

It was utterly charming and more than a little saccharine. Greta wondered if Daisy really had such chocolate-box tastes or just found it soothing to live in a room that felt so girlish, even old-fashioned.

Jordan sighed, and moved over to the three large closets that lined the far side of the room. She flung them all open in turn, then stood back to survey the contents.

"Where the deuce does she keep her traveling cases?" She turned. "Have a poke about, would you? I think there might be a box room down the hall."

Greta did as she was bid and processed down the corridor, opening one door after another. She found a nursery, and then a sunroom, and a little upstairs parlor of some kind with a bridge table and some books, and then two guest suites. At the end of the hall was another door, and the moment Greta opened it, she balked. A scent emanated from it that she recognized instantly as Tom's: cigar-inflected, a whiff of polished leather and cologne. The room contained little furniture, just a large desk and a fat stuffed chair, the desk covered with a chaotic amount of papers. Of all the rooms, this one looked the most recently inhabited, as though it alone had escaped the housemaids' tidying endeavors before Tom and Daisy closed the house down for the summer. Or perhaps Tom didn't let the staff inside his private study.

Greta stepped gingerly inside.

The desk was cluttered with papers and receipts and uncapped pens, torn envelopes—evidently Tom Buchanan wasn't someone to bother with a letter knife—a bottle of rye, a box of cigars, and a stack of letters held down with . . . Greta stepped closer. Yes, a glass paperweight with an actual, real lizard entombed inside, gray-green and scaly. Greta's nose wrinkled, but she didn't step away, having spotted the sign-off on the uppermost letter on the pile, which stoked her curiosity.

Your fond mother, it read.

Greta inched closer, and peered down at the missive. It wasn't very proper to read a dead man's letters, but *proper is as proper does*, Greta decided; she was sure Tom would have had no compunctions about reading her private correspondence had he ever got the chance. She moved the vile paperweight to one side.

> *Your brother is in a fine pique since his last visit here. He was most offended to see your Papa's antique snuffboxes were gone, and demanded if I'd handed them off to you. He just about threw a temper tantrum right there on the floor—you remember how he was as a little boy. Not like you, Tommy. You never were the whining sort.*
>
> *I told him I wanted you to have them, as I knew the collection would look very well in your downstairs parlor—the jade will be terribly fetching against the yellow, I think. I really can't abide this fixation of his about his inheritance. I'm glad you never inherited that miserly strike, Tommy, it really is most unbecoming.*
>
> *I wish you good luck with the renovations. Poor you, having to manage it all yourself. Daisy's no help at all in such matters, I suppose. That delicate constitution sort rarely are, I find. Well, you made that bed a long time ago, I suppose. It can't be helped now.*
>
> *Tell Pammy her grandmama looks forward to her summer visit.*
>
> *Your fond mother,*
> *Rosemary Buchanan*

Greta frowned. Even Edgar's mother, it seemed, didn't hold him in high regard. But that didn't say much about her judgment of character, given the woman's starry-eyed view of her elder son. Greta wondered, briefly, what the "temper tantrum" had looked like—not pleasant, she felt sure.

Replacing the paperweight, she dislodged something else—an embossed card that had been propped against the pile. At first, all she read was the word *Esquire*. She lifted it free and turned it over.

ROBERT SINCLAIR, ESQUIRE.

WILLS. TRUSTS. DIVORCE.

Divorce?

Jordan had always said the Buchanans "were too Catholic for divorce," which certainly seemed borne out by Rosemary's barbed comment about Tom's having to lie in the bed he'd made. But what if Tom had acquired a different persuasion, enough to risk his mother's displeasure? He'd broken from plenty of *other* Catholic principles, of course—marital fidelity for one, if rampant rumors were to be believed—but affairs were a sort of hypocrisy widely tolerated by the Catholic elites. Not divorce.

It put a certain spin on things, didn't it, if Tom *had* been contemplating divorce? Daisy would have had an allowance presumably, but her standard of living would have plummeted. Seen through that lens, one might say Daisy had been very lucky indeed in the timing of Tom's death.

Greta caught herself chewing on a thumbnail, and forced herself to desist; it was a habit she was trying to break.

"Never mind!" Jordan's carrying tones drifted down the hallway just then. "I've found some!"

Greta glanced back toward the door. None of this was really so important, she told herself. Whatever matters Tom might have been consulting Robert Sinclair, Esquire, about were irrelevant now. Tom had been a rich and highly unlikable man. There was nothing unnatural about it if various people's situations were improved by his absence.

The sound of a small tumbling avalanche emanated then from down the hall, followed by a string of Jordan's colorful oaths.

Greta turned her back on the room, doing her best to shake off the prickling feeling that persisted on the back of her neck, and went to rescue Jordan.

The rain had stopped by the time they drove back.

"Got everything you needed, miss?" Bill's voice was courteously neutral, but his eyes were sharp and curious.

"What I *need*," Jordan sighed, "is a holiday. Some very understanding staff, a large sun umbrella, and a tray of mint juleps."

As Greta caught his eye, Bill coughed and looked away.

An unexpected sight awaited them, however, as they crested the driveway of the Gatsby mansion: a brown Studebaker Greta rather thought she recognized—the same one they'd all watched careening out of the driveway that unhappy night. Edgar Buchanan's car.

Jordan wrinkled her nose.

"What's *he* doing here?"

As they drew closer, Greta saw Edgar was still sitting in the car. He must have been only barely ahead of them on the roads, or else he'd been sitting here delaying his entry for some time. The arrival of the Gatsbys' car seemed to bestir him, though; he flung the door of the Studebaker wide, and marched resolutely toward the house. Jordan exchanged a glance with Greta, and they quickly dismounted.

"Edgar?" Jordan called, but he didn't turn.

"Have the cases brought up to Mrs. Buchanan's room, would you, Bill?" Greta said hurriedly, before following Jordan across the forecourt.

Beecham appeared at the door.

"Mr. Buchanan. How do you do, sir." He blinked at the unexpected assembly. "Miss Baker, Miss Gatsby."

Edgar handed his derby to Beecham; he was already two steps into the hallway.

"I must speak to Mrs. Buchanan," he said. "I have not missed her, I take it?"

Beecham's dark eyes caught Greta's, sharing her bewilderment at this abrupt entrance.

"No, sir. Her train is not scheduled to depart until this afternoon, I believe."

"Edgar, is everything all right?"

Edgar swiveled and, for the first time, spared Greta a glance—that same cold glare he'd trained on her at the funeral, his hand on his mother's arm.

The door of the dining room opened and Jay strode out, with Nick behind him.

"Edgar! I thought I heard your voice. Thank you, Beecham, that will be all."

"Sir." Beecham moved off, not quite managing his usual impassive look—whether because Edgar had spoken so offensively on his last visit or because something was so obviously amiss.

"Edgar—what can I do for you?"

"It's a matter for Daisy." Edgar spoke crisply and offered nothing more.

"What's a matter for me?"

They turned; Daisy had appeared on the landing. The air seemed to quicken; Edgar flushed. Daisy cast a suspicious look over them all as she made her way downstairs. Greta glanced at Nick, who shrugged his shoulders. Jordan looked quite agog—Jordan, Greta reflected, had an unerring nose for drama.

Edgar cleared his throat. "Daisy . . . I've come to talk to you about Tom's will." He opened the door to the living room, gesturing for her to walk through. "It's"—he glanced at the others—"rather a private matter."

"Private?" Daisy blinked. Greta felt an unexpected wave of sympathy for her. Tom's death hadn't added a single wrinkle to Daisy's beautiful face, which was as fresh as ever, but her voice betrayed how close she was to being overwhelmed.

"What is it, Edgar? You're not going to tell me he changed his will?"

"No indeed." Edgar looked down.

"Well, it can't be anything so very bad then. I know his will; I've seen it." Greta heard the relief in Daisy's voice.

She'd seen it? Greta wondered when and how that had come about.

Edgar gave the small assembly a dubious glance.

"Oh, it's all right," Daisy said, with a hint of impatience. "I'm among friends." She reached for Jordan's hand. "Speak freely."

He paused. "As you wish. The thing is, Daisy . . . Tom was in debt."

Greta felt the prickling feeling on her neck once more. She'd felt it at the sight of Edgar's car, and now it came back redoubled.

Daisy blinked, smiled.

"Oh, I'm sure he'd run up some accounts here and there."

Edgar shook his head.

"Daisy . . . Tom was—I don't know how to say this more clearly—he was *severely* in debt. He was making very significant withdrawals from his account—from *your* account—on a regular basis. You knew nothing of this?"

All Daisy's nonchalance was gone now. She stared at Edgar.

"When you say, 'severely' . . ."

"What I mean is"—Edgar pushed on, the words halting—"that once the debts are settled . . . there won't be much left, Daisy. Not much at all, by the looks of it." He drew a breath. "I supposed what I'm saying is . . . it very much seems that Tom has left you bankrupt."

Chapter Thirteen

The room seemed incredibly still. Everyone but Edgar seemed to have momentarily stopped breathing.

"And... the houses?" Daisy murmured.

"The banks have put a lien on everything."

"Good Lord," Nick said. None of the others spoke. Daisy, as usual, was the center of attention, but looking at her now was like watching a beautiful flower being trodden underfoot.

What had she to fall back on now? *Bankrupt.* Greta supposed Daisy's family might be willing to take in a widow where they had not been willing to take in a divorcée, but would Daisy's own pride allow it? How would she cope with such a drop in fortune? And there was the child to think about, too.

"I must sit down." Daisy moved toward the living room, but she was dreadfully white, and had barely gone two paces before she was swaying dangerously on her feet. Jay dashed toward her but Edgar was nearer, and it was he who caught her before she hit the floor.

There were too many bodies in the room, Greta decided. The air felt close in there: Daisy on the chaise longue, and neither Edgar nor Jay willing to leave her side. Both of them seemed to be competing to rescue her, each saying bold things about hiring lawyers to fight off the banks and creditors, insisting that Daisy would be "taken care of."

Greta quietly extracted herself and retreated to the library. There was so much to think about; every day, more unexpected news seemed to arrive. The version of Daisy's future that Jordan had been outlining only yesterday was already disappearing like a mirage. She would be a young and beautiful widow still, but not a wealthy one, not by a long shot. To marry her now would be to marry into debt. Greta wondered what that meant for the line of ardent, well-groomed men at yesterday's funeral, all so eager to kiss Daisy's hand. What would become of them?

Nick's departure time came and went, but it seemed Manhattan would have to do without him for another day. Eventually, he and Jordan found Greta in the library where she'd retreated.

"I wish that vile Edgar would shove off." Jordan wrinkled her nose. "I can't help feeling this is all *his* fault."

Nick raised his eyebrows. "And how do you reckon that, Jord?"

"Oh, I don't know," she said impatiently. "It's just he's got all the money now, hasn't he? I mean, when that banshee of a mother of his kicks the bucket, he'll really have *all* of it."

Greta looked up.

"What about Pammy? Won't half the estate go to her?"

Jordan looked dubious. "I shouldn't think so. I suppose it would be different if Tom and Daisy had had boys, but the Buchanans are rather traditional. Pammy will come into a trust fund when she's of age, and no doubt Rosemary will make sure she's taken care of. But she'll be expected to marry and live on her husband's income principally."

"But Daisy?" Greta insisted. "Rosemary would hardly let her son's widow starve."

"Well, not *starve*." Jordan shrugged. "But there's no love lost between them. She'll keep Daisy on a tight leash now, I should think." She paused. "And I shouldn't think Daisy's parents will be stepping in, either. What with the tobacco farms going bust, they're barely getting by these days." She looked meaningfully at Greta and Nick. "And the truth is, they were stretched pretty thin as it was. All that pomp and spectacle just to get the girls married. They never had as much as they put on."

They were all silent for a moment, thinking of Daisy's predicament and the repercussions, like ripples, flowing outward from Tom's terrible act. This debt, presumably, was the secret Nick had been anticipating. The clue that would render Tom's dreadful choice suddenly explicable. On paper it made sense. And yet . . .

"What do you suppose he spent it all on?" Greta said finally. Tom and Daisy had lived lavishly, to be sure, but surely still within Tom's tremendous means. A "tidy chunk" was how Jordan had referred to his current fortune—tidy indeed, when three hundred and fifty thousand dollars' worth of Tahitian pearls could be paid for without discomfort.

"Can't you guess?" Jordan raised an eyebrow. "I think the real question is whether it was only one woman or many."

Nick sighed, and went over to the bookcases. There was a globe atlas on a stand beside the shelves, and he gave it a push with his finger, sending it slowly rotating.

"Exorbitant as the sums are, I suppose it does seem the most likely answer."

There was silence again.

"I feel dreadful for her, of course," Jordan said. "I do. But in a way, perhaps it *would* do Daisy some good if she had to rely on herself for once. Start over. Daisy's clever, you know. Cleverer than me, *much* cleverer than Tom. But she's always hidden it, always felt she had to." She glanced over at them. "According to Daisy, if you're a woman, you have to pick: either looks or brains. Men will tolerate clever women, she says, but only if they're plain.

She says her great hope for Pammy is that the child grows up to be a pretty little fool."

Greta was startled. Did Daisy really feel she had to calibrate things so finely; did she really feel so restricted? And was she right?

"*You* don't mind clever women, do you, Nicky?" Jordan glanced over.

Nick flushed a little but was silent, wisely deciding it was a rhetorical question.

Jordan took a swig from the coffee cup she'd brought in with her.

"I don't know. Perhaps I'm just a hypocrite, saying I have Daisy's best interests at heart. Perhaps I'm secretly pleased to see things go wrong for her—they never have before. And I *can* be quite hideously competitive, you know."

Greta studied her. What a curious specimen Jordan Baker was.

"Are you and Daisy . . ." Greta hesitated. "Are you very good friends?"

Nick snorted.

"One can see why you'd ask."

"Don't we seem like it?" Jordan was unoffended. "We've always been friends. Friends, enemies, something like that. We've known each other since we were just girls, you know—Daisy Fay, as she was then." Jordan took a pensive swig from her cup. "She was a dreadful little beast half the time." She tipped back the last of her coffee, and set it down on Jay's desk.

"Don't hold back now, Jord," Nick said, and she shrugged and lit up a cigarette.

"Well, I was terribly tall and skinny, like a boy, in those days, and she liked to tease me about it. *Beanstalk,* she called me. She was always the princess. People never wanted to pal around with me in the way they wanted to pal around with her, but they were . . . well, they were a little bit afraid of me, I think. And Daisy liked that. *She* was never afraid of me, of course. No." Jordan switched her cigarette to her other hand, tipped the ash into the empty coffee cup. "Daisy Fay isn't afraid of much."

Greta frowned. "But do you . . . *like* her?"

Nick coughed into his fist. Jordan gave Greta an appreciative look.

"No one's ever asked me that before, you know. But I *do*. I mean, I hate her sometimes—but I miss her awfully, you know, when I don't see her for a while. And yet I'm not at all sure we bring out the best in each other."

Greta couldn't help wondering who *did* bring out the best in Daisy. Tom certainly hadn't. She wasn't sure Jay did, either.

"You see, unlike Daisy, who was breaking hearts from the age of twelve, *I* was a rather ugly little thing until I hit twenty, and when she's feeling very low, she has a way of reminding me of that, and of the fact that unlike *her* I never landed a rich husband, never mind that her rich husband only ever brought her misery." Jordan stopped. "I'm making her out to be quite dreadful, aren't I? She's not; it's just that Tom made her terribly unhappy sometimes, and anyone can say ugly things when they're miserable. Daisy would never admit to that—she's got all that Southern belle etiquette bred deep into her." Jordan dragged on the cigarette, blew a thin plume of smoke heavenward. "She can't ever afford to be ugly—it's how she was raised. 'Don't look ugly, don't act ugly, don't speak ugly, don't think ugly.' But there's ugly in all of us, and there's ugly in Daisy Fay Buchanan." She glanced at Greta. "I suppose you could say I'm the one she lets that out with. So I get to see that side of her—but then, of course, I'm liable to do or say something ugly right back. Which"—she exhaled again—"is why I say we don't bring out the best in each other. But I suppose we need each other all the same."

Jordan paused at the sound of footsteps in the hall. Someone passed very near the library door.

"Don't think you're getting your hooks into her, Gatsby." It was Edgar. "Daisy doesn't belong in a place like this."

"She *belongs*"—Jay's voice came as fierce as Greta had ever heard it—"where her friends are. Beecham, show Mr. Buchanan the door."

A moment later, the sound of its slamming echoed through the hallway.

"Miss Gatsby?"

It was Ada, knocking on Greta's bedroom door. Her pretty face was flushed; she must have taken the stairs at a pace.

"Mrs. Dantry wanted me to let you know that your case has come in on the afternoon train. Bill's driving in to pick it up in a jiffy."

It was a valiant pretense at normality, Greta thought—this idea that the arrival of her traveling case was still an event worth her attention—but it struck her as a good excuse to get some air.

"Would you mind asking Bill to wait a few minutes? I'd be grateful if he'd take me into town with him."

Greta was downstairs, just passing the library again, when she heard loud voices coming from behind the door.

"Jay, *think*, man!" Nick Carraway was discreet by nature, and did not easily give way to emotion, but these were not his usual phlegmatic tones. "Don't make a fool of yourself. You can't be serious. Tom's not dead a week!"

Greta's heart quickened and she froze where she stood.

"Perhaps in a year," Nick went on. "Six months, at the very least—try your luck then if you want. But not now, Jay, you must see that."

"But *now* is what Daisy needs, that's the point!" Jay said, impassioned. "*Now* is the time to help her."

"Then help her," Nick cut in. "But quietly, with no attachments. Too much has been speculated about the two of you already; too much would be whispered. You know the rumors are rife. I'll eat my hat if she accepts a proposal from you now."

A proposal. Greta felt her legs sag under her.

"It would be so utterly lacking in propriety—"

"Well, hang propriety!"

Nick snorted.

"*You* may have decided you no longer care about propriety, but I can assure you, Daisy cares very much. It's different for a woman, Jay. *You* may very well get by in the world by flaunting your nonchalance, but Daisy would be punished—punished roundly—for the very same transgressions. She's always worked to keep society's approval on her side, and she does that, Jay, because she *must*," Nick went on. "You know as well as I, it's how a woman survives in our world. Why expose her to scorn and censure, Jay, if you profess to love the girl?"

There was the thump of a fist on wood.

"Damn you, Nick, I don't *profess*! You know my feelings."

A silence fell.

"And if she rejects you?"

Jay's voice dropped.

"What do you want from me? It's love, I tell you." He sounded almost sulky.

Nick sighed.

"What I want, Jay, is for you to wake up before you do something you regret."

Quick footsteps were coming toward the door. Greta pulled back as Nick emerged, but he must know she'd overheard. His face showed no remonstrance, though, only regret.

"Greta. Off somewhere?"

"Just to pick up my trunk from the station." She cleared her throat. "I'm sorry you had to miss your train earlier, Nick. But . . . I can't help but feel . . ." She paused, flushed. Words that had seemed quite natural in her head sounded suddenly rather too bold for her tongue.

He looked at her.

"Yes," he said gravely. "I think for now I'm more needed here."

Chapter Fourteen

Greta's heart was still fluttering a little as Bill took them down the driveway. How she hoped Jay would listen to Nick! She wasn't concerned about the Gatsby fortune one bit—let Jay write Daisy a check if he wanted; let him write a hundred checks. But to marry her! *Now*, like this, in the middle of such chaos and scandal! If Daisy spurned him, Jay would be devastated. If she accepted, they'd be on a sinking ship together.

Would Daisy accept if Jay were to make his suit?

Jay was a taker of risks—not foolish risks, but risks nonetheless. But Daisy, though she had the airs of someone more frivolous, was in reality far more cautious. She had built a large life for herself, as Jay had, and with just as much intention and care. But while Jay had achieved his as a man might—in the upheaval and chaos of the war and all that followed—Daisy had done it in the only way a woman might. She had groomed herself into a trophy, a prize to be won. Men had been her stock market; their competition for her driving her value steadily higher. But that was the thing about prizes: they had to be desirable and stay that way, or their value would plummet.

Nick had been all too right when he'd said the world was different for women. Daisy hadn't made the rules. She was doing what she needed to survive.

She *might* love Jay, Greta conceded. She really might. But would she risk all she'd built to marry him now?

She might, to save herself from bankruptcy.

"Everything all right, Miss Gatsby?"

Greta glanced up to see Bill's astute, freckled face in the mirror, watching her. She supposed her expression had been giving her away.

"I don't know, Bill. Everything just seems such a mess."

He hesitated, and his eyes were drawn back to the road to make the turn, but they soon found her again.

"If you'll forgive my asking, miss—do they have any idea why he did it?"

It was such a blunt question, Greta was surprised. But why shouldn't he ask it?

"They might," she said at last. No doubt Rosemary Buchanan would be horrified at the idea of Greta's sharing the news of her son's bankruptcy—and with staff, no less! But Greta was growing tired of codes of conduct that she no longer believed in. Bill had as much a right to know as anyone; this was his world, too, and he did not strike her as a gossip.

"We heard this morning—it seems Mr. Buchanan was in considerable debt. But keep it to yourself, would you, Bill?"

Bill's eyes widened; he dropped his gaze back to the wheel.

"They say money is the root of all evil, don't they?" he commented after a while.

"They do," Greta said, though privately she suspected that whatever the root of all evil was, it went deeper than money.

They rolled along the roads in silence after that, past fields and hedgerows, and glimpses of the driveways that led to other grand houses artfully shielded from view. Here and there where the trees were low, there were vistas of the sound, and then a short drive over country roads, and they were in town: busy, loud, awash with pedestrians and cars. Alas, the change of scene did little to soothe Greta's mind.

The car pulled up in the forecourt of the station and Bill turned off the engine.

"I'll just go in and find the station manager."

Greta rolled the window down farther and waited, inhaling the summer breeze and the smell of steam trains. Her boot nudged something on the floor of the car, something almost obscured in the sheepskin carpeting. She prodded it free and picked it up: a matchbook. There was something written on the flap, which was bent open: an address—*112 Bowery*—and below that, the words *Swanee shore*. What sent a shiver down Greta's spine was that the writing was Tom Buchanan's. Greta might not have known his script so well, but it was written in that particular royal-blue ink just like the note they'd found on the boat.

Curious. The Bowery wasn't a place the Buchanans would have been likely to frequent. And *Swanee shore?* That was part of a song—Jordan had been playing it on the gramophone that night—a popular tune, but she wondered why Tom had written it down. Greta turned the little matchbook over, then slipped it into the front pocket of her blouse.

She looked around. Bill was taking rather a long time in the station. Perhaps the luggage room was busy today. Greta decided to get out of the car and stretch her legs—and then blinked as she saw, across the road, a seemingly familiar figure.

Was it . . . ?

She stepped toward the road. Yes, she was almost sure.

The figure turned, moving up a side street now; another second and they were lost from sight. But Greta was sure she had not been mistaken. Although she had not seen the face clearly, the hair, the figure, the gait were familiar.

She dashed across the road to what she hoped was the right street, and yes, there, down an alley to the left: the familiar silhouette once more. Her pace had quickened now, so Greta abandoned all propriety and, skirts in hand, bolted down the street, kid boots thumping. She called, but the woman didn't turn. Finally, Greta came abreast of her, and caught her by the arm.

"Nora!" She panted as the young woman spun around—for indeed, Nora Sweeney it was. But at the look in her eyes, Greta dropped her arm.

"Kindly don't manhandle me, Miss Gatsby," Nora said. "I'm no longer your servant."

Greta was startled. Such a reception as this! She had assumed Nora would be glad to see her. It hadn't occurred to her until this moment that Nora *had* seen her; had been trying to escape her while Greta had been running after her in expectation of a fond reunion.

"I don't understand. Have I offended?" She was bewildered and not a little chafed. Why did Nora's eyes, even now, stay coolly averted from hers? "Couldn't you stop to say hello?"

Nora bristled. Her warm green eyes looked colder than Greta ever remembered seeing them, and the wide mouth, so often pulled into a mischievous grin, was now pursed tightly. Her dark hair lay thickly coiled beneath her hat; she wore a dress Greta had not seen before, and altogether looked quite different. Thinking about it, Greta realized she had only ever seen Nora in her working clothes.

"I'm running errands," Nora said now, quite pointedly. "I did not think I was obliged to entertain my former employers when passing them on the street."

Greta felt the blood fly to her face.

"*Entertain*! You left our house with no proper notice, with no forwarding address. You all but disappeared! I merely wanted to hear how you were." It had stung, if she was honest, that Nora had not so much as left a note upon her departure. "And besides," she added sorely, "*I* was never your employer."

Nora folded her arms.

"My pay may have been drawn from your brother's coffers, but let's not split hairs, Miss Gatsby."

The *Miss Gatsby* landed like a slap.

"I'm well aware," Greta said sharply, "that you worked in our household for your employment, not for pleasure. But all the same, you know, I rather thought of us as friends."

Nora gave her a hard look. The brogue, which in the past had sounded so lively, now felt sharpened.

"And how can two people be friends, Miss Gatsby, if they are not equals?" She paused; her face darkened. "I have no power to decide *your* fate, and yet, my fortune may be made or broken according to your whims. Is this the basis of a friendship?"

"I..."

Greta didn't understand Nora's ire, but in truth, she could not fault the logic. She found herself embarrassed by the other girl's words. Greta had certainly considered Nora an equal in the ways that she always felt mattered most—in quickness of mind, common sense, moral judgment. *But isn't it a fine luxury,* a voice chastised now, *to decide which are the ways that matter?* She flushed. She had not *meant* to be a hypocrite. But perhaps—she felt the chastising voice dig deeper—perhaps she had not thought about all of this as hard as she might have.

Red-faced, she forced herself to meet Nora's eyes again. Nora didn't seem angry anymore; she had delivered herself of that emotion, and Greta saw something else there now: pride and... pain? It occurred to her then to wonder what Nora had meant when she spoke about whims and fortunes made and broken.

"Nora... I know very little about the circumstances of your departure from my brother's household. Dantry told me you gave notice with no particulars. I was under the impression you left of your own accord, that perhaps you had secured a better situation. Did I misunderstand?"

Nora stood still.

"That's what Dantry told you?"

Greta nodded.

They stood there in the narrow, dusty street until finally Nora shook her head.

"I think you'd better come with me," she said.

Chapter Fifteen

A construction site dominated the narrow street and its row of small brick houses. The site was deserted at present, but had left its mark on the surroundings with a thin layer of chalk dust that covered the street like flour.

Greta followed Nora inside one of the houses, where powerful smells of cooking assailed them in the hallway. On the first-floor landing, Nora turned a key and stepped inside.

"Silas! We have company."

Silas?

Greta's mind worked fast. She did her best not to show her surprise as Silas Young, the man who had been Jay's chauffeur before Bill, came out of the next room, wiping his hands on a cloth and frowning apprehensively. Seeing Greta, his eyes widened.

Nora and Silas. Suddenly, things were falling into place. But it was a most unpleasant falling into place.

It was frowned upon, in theory, for members of staff to be "carrying on" together. Everyone knew that, just as everyone knew that it happened all the time, and except in extreme circumstances, it was hardly a firing offense. But Nora and Silas were not most couples.

"Hello, Silas," Greta said. "It's good to see you again."

One corner of his mouth tugged wryly. In shirtsleeves, his arms glowed ebony in the small sunlit room. A gold ring shone brightly on his hand.

"Likewise, I'm sure." His voice was its usual smooth baritone, but he rubbed one forearm as if, despite the heat, he'd felt a touch of cold—or as if his mind had gone to the same place hers just had.

Now do you see? Nora's glance seemed to say. *Now do you understand?*

Silas rested his hands on his hips and looked from Greta to Nora. Greta suspected he was not best pleased with either of them: with Greta for being here, or Nora for having sprung her on him. He looked different now, too, the same way Nora looked different. His clothes were of cheaper, rougher fabric than the uniform he'd worn at the Gatsby house, but he wore them with flair, and he'd grown in a debonair mustache, too.

"Well, Nora. I trust whatever point you were trying to make, you've made it. Are you finished exhibiting me?"

Nora looked abashed.

"Oh, Si, I—I didn't mean it like that, really I didn't."

He sighed.

"I didn't suppose you had." He glanced at Greta, evidently unsure what to do with her.

"Please, I must know," Greta said. "Is my brother responsible for your departures?" She hoped ardently they would say no. Surely, Jay had known nothing of this.

Silas took his time before he spoke.

"Mrs. Dantry made it clear to Nora that neither of us were welcome in your brother's employ any longer."

"She found out somehow." Nora glanced at Silas. "I don't know how—and she confronted me. When I gave her the truth, she said we were both to leave, effective immediately. She said our employer"—Nora paused—"could not be expected to bear the stain on his establishment."

Greta felt sickened.

"Jay can't have known. Dantry kept it from him."

Nora and Silas exchanged a look. They thought her naive—and indeed, Greta was coming to realize, they might be right—but not *that* naive, surely.

"I'll tell Jay. It's not right—you have to come back—"

"Miss Gatsby!" Nora's voice cut across hers. "Stop, please. Do you imagine yourself to be rescuing us? We are not in despair, and we certainly would have no wish to return."

Greta glanced between them. It took some effort, but she bit back the things she was burning to say, and the indignation that these two could have no use for, which came at any rate too late. She saw how easily Nora and Silas stood within their nest, how naturally their bodies turned toward each other. They looked happy, she realized.

"I have a new job," Silas said, "at a garage. It's a good place. Decent pay."

It struck Greta once more how different they both looked than when she had last seen them. But they had not changed—not much, anyway. It was that Greta had not seen them in full relief before. She'd seen only the side they were supposed to show, not understanding how much of their personalities—of their essence—they'd felt obliged to constrain.

"Forgive me," she said. "Of course, neither of you would wish to return. But . . ." She felt her cheeks warm. "You ought to be recompensed somehow. For the loss of wages. For the insult . . ."

Silas let out a soft laugh.

"If I had a cent for every insult . . ."

Greta saw the glance Nora snuck him, its mixture of pride and guilt and love. Shame pricked at Greta, too. How familiar this must all be for Silas. How patient he was being with her own futile indignation. Greta became aware of the room again. Of the pot waiting on the stove, of the high afternoon sun outside, of Bill waiting at the station many streets from here. What would he be thinking?

"I—I must not keep you any longer. You were about to eat. Forgive my intrusion." She hesitated as she reached the door. "But perhaps—might I visit you again some other time?"

She hadn't intended to say it, and in the circumstances, perhaps it was an outrageous request to make. A quick look passed between them, an exchange so fleeting she could not read it. Warmth crept up her neck.

"You might," Silas said. "If you come for the pleasure of the visit, and not as our benefactor."

Greta flushed.

"Gladly," she said, and meant it. But she made her way downstairs and back through the streets with much food for thought. Beneath the roiling indignation and shame, she felt, well . . . stupid.

Of all the reasons she'd run through in her head for Nora to have left, she'd only ever imagined it as a choice freely made. As though the world lay as open and inviting to Nora as a new book. But now Greta wondered if she hadn't been overestimating freedom—her own, perhaps, but more important, others'—for some time.

Dantry was in the middle of some household accounting; she folded her hands over the ledger, then blinked archly at Greta from behind her wire spectacles.

"Miss Gatsby." She folded the ledger closed with a thump. "Your brother employs Mr. Beecham and me to run this household, and part of that managerial duty is to protect him from matters beneath his notice—the petty, distasteful, or time-consuming elements that he does not wish to be troubled with. I assure you, Miss Gatsby, if we did *not* take those pains, he would quickly be looking for replacements who did." Her steely eyes bored into Greta's.

So Jay *hadn't* known, then. Dantry had as good as admitted it! She'd kept the real reason behind Silas's and Nora's departures to herself. That was some relief. Greta had been almost glad when Jay hadn't been in his study upon her return. There were questions she had to ask, but in truth she hadn't been quite as sure of his answers as she'd wanted to be.

"It was my duty," Dantry continued, "to ensure that such behavior would not be comported under your brother's roof. *Especially* when he has a younger sister of a delicate age."

"You're trying to say this was on *my* account?" Greta fumed.

"And I certainly did not behave toward Nora out of *malice*, as you seem to be implying," Dantry went on seamlessly. "Her behavior was the stuff of which scandal is made, and there is not one house on the island that would welcome *that*. Moreover, she was given the opportunity to leave with dignity intact rather than be fired, which I dare say is more than she'd have got in many households. The same"—Dantry's mouth tightened—"goes for Mr. Young."

The worst of it was, what Dantry said was not ill-founded. Greta knew the households of West Egg. It didn't make what Dantry had done—so summarily and so *smugly*—any more excusable. But the problem, one had to admit, was much bigger than just her.

"Once the allegations were"—Dantry hesitated—"were brought to my attention, I gave Nora full opportunity to deny them. But she was very clear about the nature of her . . . *relations* with that man, and proceeded to call *me* some terms that were quite unacceptable."

Well, bravo, Nora. Greta was glad to know Nora had given as good as she'd got, but that crumb of satisfaction was quickly displaced as she realized what else Dantry had said. *Allegations were brought to my attention.* Nora herself had seemed puzzled over how Dantry had found out about the romance . . .

"And what can you tell me of these 'allegations,' Mrs. Dantry?"

Dantry blinked. "Beg pardon?"

"You said *allegations*," Greta repeated. "Whose?"

Dantry's mouth pursed tighter.

"I . . . received some correspondence."

"Correspondence?" Greta crossed her arms.

Dantry hesitated.

"A letter informing me of the situation. The author did not reveal themselves."

Greta stared. "You mean some sort of anonymous letter? Is this not a little beneath you, Dantry? Acting on some nasty-minded tip-off from someone who would not show their face?"

Dantry straightened, the skin under her chin trembling with indignation.

"I told you, I gave the girl every chance to deny it."

Greta put aside the distastefulness for the time being. More than distasteful, it was odd. Why *had* the accuser bothered concealing their identity? Given Dantry's disposition, she'd have thanked them, no doubt.

"Was it left by someone in this house?"

Dantry, clearly disliking the whole line of questioning, shook her head.

"Postmarked," she said shortly.

Greta frowned. Anyone could have dropped their tawdry little missive in the mail on their day off—but it did seem a lot of trouble to go to.

"And have you the letter now?"

Dantry shook her head. "Threw it out."

Convenient.

When it became clear there was no more information to be got out of the woman, Greta turned to go.

"It's unfortunate that what's done can't be undone," she said, her hand on the doorknob. "But you may be sure, Mrs. Dantry, that any future dismissals in this house will be according to my brother's and my choices, not yours."

And I shall hope for your name to be first on the list.

Greta walked slowly back toward the great hall, pondering this unpleasant little piece of information. Who was it who had found out about Nora and Silas—and had wished them ill enough to write such a note? Silas had kept largely to himself out there in the garage apartment, and both he and Nora, to the best of Greta's knowledge, had been well-liked in the house. But the note had been written nonetheless. By an outsider, then? Yet who besides other members of the household would have guessed at the affair? She went over the roster of possibilities in her mind: Ada, Mrs. Smith, Beecham . . . or Dantry herself, fabricating the story of an anonymous letter for reasons of her own.

Greta couldn't speak to Beecham's politics, but she knew he was a stickler for propriety; he'd likely have disapproved of any staff relationship, race aside. But he'd never stoop to an anonymous note. Besides, he wouldn't need to: he was the only one in the house that Dantry deferred to.

Mrs. Smith might have found out about Nora and Silas, but been reluctant to express her disapproval directly. Greta knew very little of Mrs. Smith's opinions on such matters.

And then there was Ada. She had inherited the position of head housemaid after Nora's dismissal, so it was true she'd had something to gain. And if Nora had confided in anyone, it was most likely to have been Ada. Sharing a room as they had, even a well-kept secret might readily be discovered. But Ada had *liked* Nora. They'd been friends, or seemed to be. Greta hoped it hadn't been Ada.

Her feet tapped against the boards as she got closer to the service passage that led back to the great hall. At least she was right, and Jay hadn't known about any of it . . .

Yet even as she had the thought, her mind called up an image of Nora standing on the street, her arms folded, her look impatient, slightly pitying.

And under that gaze, Greta realized she could no longer feel consoled by Jay's innocence in this matter. Not entirely.

Fond though he'd been of Silas, well-disposed though he'd been toward Nora, he'd accepted Dantry's shallow account of their departures without question or comment, like Greta, without any inkling of injustice. And there was a reason it had been so easy to satisfy him: it was what he expected. What he welcomed, even. It had not occurred to him that anything else should exist. For people like the Gatsbys, after all, it was not reassuring, not terribly comfortable, to hear that the troubles of people like Nora, like Silas, might be so complex, that one's own world might be so nearly tainted. So perhaps it was not so hard as it ought to have been for Dantry to fob them off with a perfunctory explanation.

Greta swallowed. This bolt of clarity was more than a little humiliating, more than a little dismaying.

And what if... was this happening all around her? But of course it was! Among their neighbors, at the Academy, in the newspapers: the dispersal of shallow, simple stories, so as to let those with money and influence believe that those without it led shallower, simpler lives.

And no doubt that sort of thing trickled down. People like Nora, like Silas, would in turn offer simple, easy stories of themselves—because the parameters had already been set, and to say otherwise was to be disaffected, a troublemaker. And what was to be gained from that?

Greta sighed as she emerged into the hall. These were painful reflections, indeed. But she suspected they were all too necessary.

From the billiards room there came the faint clack of wood on ivory, and she glanced through the open doorway: it was Nick, shooting billiards by himself. She watched him for a moment, his quiet face, the small frown that never left his brow. What would he make of the thoughts she'd just been having? Would he think her naive for not having realized it all before? Or would he try to placate her, tell her she was wrong?

No, she didn't think he'd do that.

And then, over Nick's shoulder, Greta saw something out the window that made her grip the door handle.

"Oh, my."

Nick looked up, and turned to follow her gaze out the window. The black Model T was instantly recognizable.

The police, it appeared, were back.

Chapter Sixteen

Inspector Francis stood, imposing and pink-faced, in the middle of the hall. He bore that same faintly resentful demeanor Greta remembered from last time—but there was something else, too. An unmistakable air of importance, of superiority even. His courtesy was stiffer this time, and failed to hide what Greta was fairly sure was becoming dislike. She couldn't think what anyone in the household had done to provoke such ire, but by the disgruntled way the man glanced around at his surroundings, perhaps he'd just been spending more time fulminating on the social evils of the nouveau riche. It wasn't just the blue bloods who disliked new money, after all.

"Inspector?" she said. "It's kind of you to come. Beecham's just gone upstairs to fetch my brother. Will you come inside?"

He nodded briskly, then strode ahead of her into the living room. Limp hair clung to his scalp where his helmet had rested.

"Inspector." Jay greeted him once he'd arrived downstairs. Nick and Jordan were there, too; only Daisy was absent. Still in bed, perhaps, after this morning's shocking news.

"We hadn't expected to see you again so soon. Is this regarding the pearls? Daisy's upstairs—it's just that she's had some rather upsetting news today."

"I'm not here to discuss missing jewelry, Mr. Gatsby. It's about the late Mr. Buchanan." He peered at them through narrow blue eyes, and continued in the most portentous tones: "There has been a development."

Greta felt a strange sensation go through her. *Here it comes,* she thought.

"The precinct," the inspector continued, "has just received the full medical report, the one requested by the deceased's mother. And a substance has been detected that rather complicates matters."

A knowing look passed among the group. So what was it, Greta wondered—opium? Cocaine? Mrs. Buchanan might try to blame Jay for that, but surely the inspector would see that Jay had no responsibility for Tom's personal habits.

"There was a considerable dose of barbiturates in Mr. Buchanan's blood," the inspector said at last.

Barbiturates?

"Sleeping pills?" Nick frowned. The anomaly was dawning on each of them.

"But . . . why on earth would a person take sleeping pills on a night they're planning to . . ." Jordan shook her head. "I don't understand, Inspector. Was it a fatal dose?" She flushed. "*Would* it have been fatal, I mean? If he hadn't gone and . . ."

The inspector's lips thinned.

"In a man of Mr. Buchanan's size . . . unlikely. It was a strong dose, but unlikely to do him permanent damage." He watched them, eyes roving over everyone in turn, waiting for their answers to this oddity. It *was* odd. Because—

"If he took them before going to bed," Nick said slowly, "they'd have knocked him out cold, wouldn't they, Inspector? It's hard to see how he would have got himself downstairs and out to the boat."

"He obviously *intended* them to be fatal," Jay said. "I suppose he went out to the boat and swallowed them there. Perhaps then he changed his mind. He'd meant to end things with the pills, but he got cold feet, decided a fast death was better than a slow one—so he got the gun." He looked at the inspector. "How quickly would the sedative effect have kicked in, Inspector?"

The inspector's eyes were steely.

"Within ten minutes, we think."

"Certainly enough time, then, for him to change his mind." Jay spoke confidently enough, but an unconvinced silence followed his words.

"Or," Jordan said slowly, "he took the pills, then realized he didn't have enough. Like you said, Inspector—it wasn't enough for a fatal dose. He realized this, and knew he had to resort to a different method."

Jordan looked to the inspector as if waiting for his approval. The blue eyes didn't give it.

"Either of those scenarios," he conceded, "is possible. And yet . . . for the most part, such indecision about one's method is rare in suicides. The act is usually well planned. Pistols are more common in men, poison more common for women—but I've never known a person to use both." He shrugged. "There's a first for everything."

The group of four sat, taking in the development in silence. Nick looked up after a while. "I suppose we had better call Daisy down to hear this."

Jay frowned.

"It's all so unpleasant, on top of everything else. Can't we just let her rest?"

"I don't think we can, Jay."

"No," said the inspector dryly. "I don't think you can."

Jordan, seeing they would leave it to her, stood from her chair.

"Fine. I'll get her. Though I don't see why it's got to be *my* job."

"Before you go, Miss Baker . . ." The inspector cleared his throat. "I would like to know if there are any barbiturates currently kept in this house—pills, powders, any sort of sedative?"

Jay flushed.

"I keep some in my bathroom, Inspector—powder form. It was prescribed for me some time ago. I do sometimes suffer from . . . interrupted sleep, you see. A shoulder injury, from the war—it plays up on occasion."

Poor Jay, he so hated to show weakness. It was as though he thought they would be disappointed if they were ever to find out he was human like the rest of them.

The inspector nodded, impassive.

"And did you ever give any to Mr. Buchanan?"

"Certainly not."

"Hm. The powder—it's clearly labeled?"

"It is."

"And this bathroom of yours, would Mr. Buchanan have had any cause to go into it?"

"Well, of course not," Nick chimed in. "It's an en suite, and Tom had his own. What would he go tramping through Jay's room for?"

"And you never noticed any missing, Mr. Gatsby?" the inspector continued.

Jay flushed. "No."

"Mr. Carraway?" The inspector turned. "Miss Baker? Miss Gatsby? Are any of you in possession of such a thing, or do you know of any other locations in this house where some might be stored?"

There was a quick chorus of *nos*, and the inspector settled back in his chair.

"In that case, since Mr. Gatsby is so sure that the barbiturates used could not have been removed from his room, we are to infer that either they were among Mr. Buchanan's own possessions at the time or, possibly, that he acquired some from Mrs. Buchanan." He glanced at Jordan. "And that latter question we can clear up, I should think—Miss Baker, if you'd be so kind as to fetch your friend?"

"But it's absurd." Daisy blinked once the question was put to her. "Tom never took sleeping tablets."

"Didn't he?" The inspector looked closely at her.

"No," Daisy insisted. "He said they were for women and the weak-minded."

Nick glanced at Jay. "Well, of course, he may have *said* that, but taken them all the same. Tom wasn't a fellow who liked to show any sort of . . . fallibility, Inspector."

"I suppose he might have had a prescription filled," Jordan suggested, "just in order to—you know." She shot Daisy an awkward look. "In order to do what he did."

Daisy's nostrils flared; her cheeks grew pink.

"We'll look into the possibility," the inspector said. "Meanwhile, Mrs. Buchanan, have you any barbiturates in your possession? Or had you on the night in question?"

"No," Daisy said, her cheeks pinker still. "I don't. And didn't."

"In that case"—the inspector looked around—"Mr. Buchanan's personal effects, are they still in this house?"

"We had my butler pack them up," Jay said. "The valises are still in his room."

The inspector inclined his head.

"If you would be so good as to take me up, Mr. Gatsby."

Jay did, and the living room became a most uncomfortable place while they waited. Greta rang for coffee just to give them all something to do. When she rang, Beecham opened the door almost instantly—he was not the type to listen at doors, but he must have suspected something from the look on his face. It seemed he'd failed to shave today—how very unlike him. The folds beneath his eyes looked bluish and deeper than usual. Everyone, Greta thought, would need some time off after all this.

Greta took her coffee to the window, and stared out at the jetty and the little pleasure craft moored there. Even now, it bobbed so innocently next to the dock, its stenciled name glinting on the hull when it rose in the swell.

Abruptly, Greta put her coffee cup back down on the saucer.

The *Marguerite*! Oh, Jay!

Greta ought to have noticed it long ago, for all the vocabulary Madame Dupont had drilled into them throughout her years at the Academy: marguerite was the French for *daisy*. Greta glanced over at Daisy, who was sitting silent and pale on the edge of the sofa. No doubt she was aware of Jay's little tribute—she'd surely studied French at school. Perhaps it had even been a little joke between Daisy and Jay. How many times had he taken her out sailing on that very boat?

Greta looked up as Nick joined her at the window.

"Strange business, isn't it? You look lost in thought—can you make anything of it?"

She shook her head. Of course Nick thought her preoccupied only with the question of the barbiturates. And, indeed, it was most troubling.

"I can't, I'm afraid. But I don't like it one bit."

The door opened; Jay and the inspector, grave-faced, reentered the room.

"Well?" Jordan said impatiently, and Jay shook his head.

"No such drugs, or receptacles that might once have contained them, were to be found among the late Mr. Buchanan's effects, ma'am." The inspector's look took in Daisy first, then the rest of them. "And Mr. Gatsby tells me the room has not been touched—nothing removed, no baskets emptied—since the day of Mr. Buchanan's death."

There was a pause.

"Well," Jordan said after a while. "I suppose he might have got rid of the bottle on the boat. You know—finished whatever was inside and thrown the empty bottle overboard."

The inspector cocked his head, and Greta was sure he did not take to Jordan Baker any more than Jordan had to him.

"Yes, Miss Baker," he said evenly. "It's possible."

"Well, goodness," Daisy said, with an artificial laugh. "You're not going to dredge the Long Island Sound looking for it, are you, Inspector?"

He indulged her with a brittle smile.

"I shouldn't think so, Mrs. Buchanan."

"Look," Nick said then, his voice matter-of-fact. "I don't really see there's any great mystery around all this. Tom procured some pills, swallowed them, and now they're gone. That's all there is to it. We don't know where he got them, but it wasn't from anyone in this house. I'm really not so sure that it matters what he did with an empty bottle."

And a glass, Greta thought. Tom would have needed a glass of water—or whiskey or whatever it was—to swallow down such a quantity of barbiturates. There had been no such glass found in the cabin—was Tom supposed to have thrown that overboard for some reason, too? Greta felt a shadow of unease creep over her.

"If the poor fellow took an overdose first and then decided a gun would do a better job—well," Nick continued, "I don't see why we should be expecting a suicidal man to be terribly *rational*."

"Mrs. Buchanan." The inspector reached into his inside jacket pocket and drew out an envelope. From it, he removed a single sheet of folded paper. Greta knew immediately what it was.

"We did not want to put you through the pain of examining this note earlier," the inspector went on, now with Daisy's full attention. "But I believe it is now of rather greater importance. May I ask you to inspect it and tell me whether or not you can confirm with confidence—with confidence, you understand—that this is your husband's hand?"

Daisy looked with dismay at the folded sheaf he held out toward her.

"Please, Mrs. Buchanan," the inspector said curtly. "If you'd be so kind."

Reluctantly, Daisy took it from him, unfolded it, and read the words. Greta saw the small crease between her brows, and something else passed over her face, quickly hidden.

She folded the note once more and handed it back. "I have no doubt, Inspector. This is my husband's handwriting."

"You are positive?"

Daisy's voice sharpened. "Positive."

Nick cleared his throat.

"Inspector! You're not suggesting . . ."

The implications were clear: the inspector was asking if the suicide note could be a forgery. But if someone had forged a suicide note . . . well, then it wasn't suicide any longer.

"I don't suggest anything, Mr. Carraway," the inspector said mildly. "Except that Mr. Buchanan's death has thrown up some anomalies—anomalies that need resolving. And I would like to assure his widow that I will be looking into them." He bowed his head to Daisy, then his eyes made one last, quick survey of them all. "While I do so, I'd advise you all to stay in the vicinity. And now, I'm afraid, I had better be on my way—I have a call to pay on the younger Mr. Buchanan."

Chapter Seventeen

Daisy's bedroom door was ajar, and inside Greta could see Daisy standing over the bed, stuffing an armful of clothes haphazardly into a valise. The inspector had left perhaps half an hour ago. After he'd gone, Daisy had been talkative, indignant. *Absurd! Too, too absurd*, she kept saying. She seemed to think the absurdity lay in the idea of Tom's taking sleeping pills at all. Of course, if one took that assertion to its natural conclusion, it led to a more alarming place still: the idea that Tom had taken them involuntarily.

That icy feeling passed over Greta again. It was the kind of thing one hesitated even to imagine, less still name. And yet they'd all been forced to hold the idea in their minds, at least for an instant, that something not just tragic but sinister had come to pass on the night of Tom's death. But it seemed that Daisy's mind had banished the thought again instantly.

"Daisy?" Greta knocked very gently. Daisy looked up from her task, her pretty face taut and drawn, her fine blonde hair askew.

"What is it?" she said, rather sharply for Daisy, who was always ladylike in her manners.

"May I come in?"

"No one's stopping you," Daisy said, still rather ungraciously.

Greta stepped inside and shut the door.

"Where are you going?" Newport could no longer be on the table, not when the inspector had just told them all to stay put.

Daisy's hands trembled; she stopped her packing, if you could even call it that. Greta saw the mess of jumbled garments inside her suitcase, which was as much an indicator as anything that the immaculate Daisy Buchanan was in a bad way.

"I don't *know*," Daisy said then, her voice cracking. "Edgar said he'd put me up in a hotel and Pammy can come to me there. He said he'd come for me in the morning. Only we can't go far, because that horrible inspector's got this absurd idea of foul play, and says we have to stick around this dreadful place!" She looked up. "I'm sorry. I didn't mean . . . It's just—oh, it's *everything*!" She flopped down on the bed then, abandoning the half-full valise, and covered her face with her hands. Greta had the sense that she was trying very hard not to burst out into ugly sobs.

Jordan's words ran through her head: *Daisy's not allowed to be ugly.*

"It's all right," Greta said as Daisy struggled not to cry, and took a seat on the bed beside her. "A change of scene sounds like a good idea. It must be very upsetting for you to be in this house."

To Greta's surprise, Daisy laughed. "Is that what I am, upset? I don't even know what I feel anymore." She was quiet for a moment, and then shook her head.

"I never thought there was very much *to* Tom, you know. His emotions always seemed so . . . simple." She winced. "I never dreamed he'd do something like this. I never thought he knew the meaning of despair."

Greta wished she could be as sure as Daisy that Tom's death was an open-and-shut case of suicide. And, as her tangle of conflicting thoughts reminded her, the inspector hadn't said it *wasn't* suicide. *Anomalies*, that was all he'd put forth. There was, after all, still the matter of the suicide note—a note that more than one of their number had confidently authenticated. But the tingling in Greta's scalp and on the nape of her neck whenever she thought of the inspector's visit signaled something that was hard to ignore.

Daisy looked down at her lap.

"Life is strange, isn't it? When I was a little girl, Mother was always reminding Daddy that she could have married any boy in town. I suppose she thought reminding him all the time would get him to stop chasing skirts, but it never did." Daisy paused. "My mother was a tremendous romantic, you see. She married Daddy because she fell for him; he was charming, she said, and sort of wistful, a dreamer. She never stopped telling us girls not to make her mistake. Ironic, don't you think?"

Greta considered that.

"So you chose someone who was the opposite?" No one could have accused Tom of being wistful or a dreamer—or charming.

Daisy sighed.

"Jay wanted me to wait for him but I couldn't. He was a dreamer. Poor. A hopeless romantic." She looked up. "I never wanted to marry a romantic. They're dangerous. They fall out of love with you the minute you turn out to be human, and then they blame you for being a disappointment."

"Jay's not like that," Greta said automatically, then stopped herself. After all, what did she know? Her brother *was* a romantic. And he could be easily dissatisfied, too, and quick to move on. Would he be like that in love?

"He said some rather uncalled-for things yesterday, you know—after the funeral." Daisy didn't seem angry now, only melancholic. "He was angry that all those men were making a fuss over me. And it's true, I do *like* being noticed." She shrugged. "Daddy would always tell me: 'Daisy Fay, you just swivel like a sunflower when someone shines some sun on you.' Mother always said I was a little flirt." Daisy sighed. "But I can't help liking attention. It makes me feel alive. And I need to feel alive." She shuddered, and half glanced at Greta. "I've always been horrifically afraid of dying, you know."

Greta studied her companion. It was a side of Daisy she'd never seen before: so self-aware, so quiet and detached.

"I'm sure we're all afraid of dying," she said gently.

Daisy looked up, her eyes wide blue pools.

"Do you know, I don't believe Jay is," she said after a pause. "I think he believes he'll live forever."

Greta contemplated that.

"Does he know you're planning to leave in the morning?" she said finally.

Daisy shook her head.

"I'll tell him at dinner."

"*G*oing?" Jay dropped his fork in the artichoke salad. "To a hotel? With *him?*"

Daisy flushed.

"Not *with* him, Jay. He just—Edgar offered to put me up somewhere."

"I'll just bet he did."

"Jay, stop."

"So he's to take care of you now, is that it? You're to live under Edgar Buchanan's protection? He'll certainly love that. I suppose he'll be buying all your clothes now, and perhaps he'll give you an allowance so long as you behave nicely for him."

"*Don't,* Jay." Daisy balled up her napkin. There was silence in the room.

"I just don't understand why you'd let him take care of you instead of me."

Jordan's sharp eyes moved between the two of them. No wonder she was suspicious. Jay's words, his tone, were the nearest to a public declaration Greta had heard. Perhaps he noticed it, too, as he seemed to catch himself.

"That is . . . we're your friends, Daisy. We're your true friends here. You know that."

Daisy bowed her head, and Greta thought she saw a tear fall onto the starched napkin.

"I'm sorry, Jay," was all she said before she left the table.

The *Marguerite* rocked gently, its white hull gleaming where it broke free of the water, and small wavelets lapped at the edge of the dock, bluish now in the twilight. Greta walked down the jetty, and stepped gingerly aboard the boat. She suppressed a shudder as she put her hand to the cabin door: memories flooded her of the last time she had opened it. But now it was almost as if nothing amiss had occurred here, except for the lingering smell of bleach that had not quite given way to briny air. Greta took a few breaths, clearing her mind of the images that threatened to resurface.

She'd *known* something wasn't quite right since that night. Not in her conscious mind, perhaps, but somewhere underneath that, she'd felt a whisper of unease that she had no logical answer for. She didn't want to believe in foul play any more than the others did, and yet she was here, searching for traces of some more sinister truth.

The cabin: she let her gaze rove over it carefully, methodically. From left to right, she took in its details, remembering back to that day and calling up in her mind's eye exactly how it had been. The chair had been almost where it was now—a little more to the left, pushed out from the desk, as though the ricochet had sent Tom backward toward the door. The little porthole windows had been closed, just as they were now. The hurricane lamp had been on the floor; now it was righted, and set back on the desk.

Anomalies, the inspector had said. And *anomalies* were exactly what Greta was looking for now.

She combed the cabin inch by inch. She examined the desk and its contents first, lifting each item—lamp, clock, inkwell—then carefully putting each one back. She wasn't sure exactly what she was looking for, but nothing seemed out of place. She did notice, though, that the ink in the inkwell was a different shade than the ink in Tom's letter. But it would have been natural enough, wouldn't it, to write it in his room?

And then, as she was pacing slowly over the floor—she was following the grid of the boards, up one way then down again—something in the gutter between two boards glinted and caught her eye. A small shard of glass—less than a fingernail in size—caught hard between two floorboards. Had she trod on it with her kid boots, she wouldn't have felt a thing.

Greta reached out and extracted it from where it was jammed. She had to pinch it a little to make it give way, and let out a small yelp as it nicked her under the thumbnail. She wrapped it in a handkerchief and stowed it in her pocket. It was only a small shard, after all, and it could have been there for some time. But then again, maybe not. She combed over the rest of the cabin, but found nothing except, to her dismay, a spot of blood on the wall that had escaped the cleaners' notice. The air felt close once more, and she hurried to the door, and outside she breathed deeply until her stomach settled.

Then she hurried back up the jetty, and went in search of Beecham.

"Well, certainly, Miss Gatsby, if you wish it." The butler blinked down at her. He looked his usual tidy self again this afternoon, his mustache neatly combed. "An inventory shall be made. I conducted the last one a mere two weeks ago, however, and found all in order. Do you suspect further, ahem, disappearances in the household?"

The meticulous Beecham took inventory of the household's china, glassware, and silverware every couple of months, and the staff were under strict instructions to alert him of any casualties—a shattered dish, a broken glass—so that these could be recorded in a ledger and, with Mr. Gatsby's approval, duly replaced.

Greta hesitated at his question.

"I have no concrete suspicions, Beecham. Likely you will find nothing missing at all. I would just be grateful if you would check."

"It shall be done." He gave a gracious nod, and held the door for her. But as she stepped out of his study, Greta couldn't help but notice the tremor in his hand as he did so. She'd never seen that before. Their inimitable Beecham was simply getting older, she decided. Because what else could cause such a stoic man to shake like that?

Chapter Eighteen

Greta was sealing a letter she'd penned to Nora when a knock came at her bedroom door: it was Ada, bearing fresh towels. But instead of just dropping them, she lingered. Greta could sense the nervous energy rolling off her, and waited for more. There was something, presumably, that Ada wanted to say. Usually, Ada was the most buoyant and spirited member of the household: she ran, rather than walked, down stairs, and was always humming or singing to herself as she went about the house no matter how many times Dantry told her to be *more unobtrusive*. But these past few days, she had been almost as quiet as mousy Molly.

Greta flashed back to that nighttime sighting of Ada out by the jetty—knowing what she knew now, any odd behavior had only come to seem odder. And then there had been Mrs. Dantry's anonymous letter . . . But Ada, pretty-featured and dewy-skinned, looked the picture of innocence as she turned to Greta.

"Miss Gatsby . . . the police officer who came by earlier . . ." She hesitated. "Was it about the necklace? Is there to be an investigation?"

Greta didn't want to lie to Ada, but nor did she particularly want to add to whatever rumor mills were churning downstairs by telling her the real reason for the inspector's visit.

"They're certainly looking into it, but I hope you won't trouble yourself about it, Ada."

Ada, looking uncomfortable, made her way back downstairs. Greta sat down on the bed.

After the inspector's visit, there had been no time to ring for Beecham to show the man out; instead, the inspector had turned on his heel and left the room abruptly, and as the door swung wide it had revealed Mrs. Dantry standing right outside.

But did it matter what the household knew? The staff deserved not to be kept in the dark—although, really, they were *all* in the dark right now.

Greta glanced down at the silver photo frame on the vanity. What a tangle they were in, what a thicket.

"Well, Mother? Father?" She searched their far-off stares. "What do you make of this strange business?"

She sighed. She could almost imagine them, sometimes, come to life once more: her father bright-eyed at the breakfast table, newspaper on his knee; her mother balancing the books for the week, her knowing glance as she looked up over the rims of her wire spectacles. Greta's mother had been a keenly intelligent woman, and one of those lucky, all-too-rare ones whose intelligence had been welcomed—cherished even—by her spouse. But she had never failed to remind her daughter that the world wasn't always so accommodating.

A woman's mind is her sword, she'd say to Greta—she'd been fond of aphorisms, especially ones carried over from the old country. *Keep it sharp,* she'd add, *and keep it hidden.*

Well, Greta would follow her mother's advice for now. She would keep her eyes and ears open, and she would bide her time. She hadn't told anybody of her trip out to the *Marguerite,* and she wasn't planning to. Though the others hadn't dismissed the barbiturates business quite so roundly as Daisy had, it was clear to Greta that they had chosen not to fully absorb its import. Jay and Nick still seemed to view the development as a quirk that would be cleared up soon enough, and Greta sensed that if she were to tell them where she'd been and what she'd been up to, they'd be disappointed in her, as though she'd somehow broken faith with them. As for Jordan, the whole business seemed to appeal to her sense of drama, but with no great onus to examine the consequences.

Greta sighed again. What a long, exhausting day it had been. Edgar's news of the bankruptcy, and then running into Nora on the street—and then *this*. Greta's brain pounded, but even so, she could barely keep her eyes open.

Lifting Ada's fresh towels from the bed, Greta felt something jostle in her blouse pocket: that funny little matchbook she'd picked up in the car. She put the towels down and opened it again. What use had Tom Buchanan had for an address in the Bowery?

Greta slipped the matchbook into the top drawer of her nightstand, and lay back, staring at the ceiling in the dark. She feared with all the swirling thoughts, sleep would be slow to come tonight, but she was wrong. The dreams were disquieting enough, though, in their own way. In them, she was bobbing in the water alongside the *Marguerite*, struggling to stay afloat in waterlogged clothes, and all around her was strange flotsam: spent matches, strings of broken pearls, and sheaves of sodden paper everywhere, scrawled with Tom's handwriting. In her dream, she was trying to rescue them, pulling sheet after sheet from the water's surface, but to no avail. The blue ink ran beyond recognition; whatever message they had held, never to be known.

After her troubled night's sleep, Greta had little appetite for breakfast— and so didn't begrudge the discreet cough that interrupted her on her way to the dining room the next morning.

"Miss Gatsby. I wonder if I might have a word . . . ?"

Following Beecham's lead, Greta moved to a corner of the hall, a prudent distance out of earshot from any adjoining doors.

"Miss Gatsby," he said in a low voice, "I did the full inventory as requested, and I'm afraid . . . well, as it happens, we're one glass short. I've asked the staff, but no one recalls having broken one."

Greta's neck prickled. She had been right, then.

"I see. Thank you for your efforts, Beecham. Can you tell me what sort of a glass it was?"

As she had known he would, Beecham answered precisely.

"A claret glass, Miss Gatsby. Crystal—from the Miramar set." He frowned. "It's most upsetting."

It was, Greta agreed, though perhaps not for the reasons he thought.

"Thank you, Beecham, I'm grateful for your close inspection."

He inclined his head, then left her to her thoughts, from which Jordan's voice momentarily roused her.

"What did that dour butler of yours have to say that has you so entranced?"

"Nothing," Greta said. "Nothing of importance."

She, too, could wear a mask when she chose.

"Anyone seen Daisy?" Nick asked as he stirred his coffee. The motion seemed to calm him; he'd been stirring much longer than that one spoon of sugar made necessary. Perhaps yesterday's visit from the inspector had got to him deeper than he let on.

"Not yet." Jordan shrugged. "I saw her from my window earlier, wandering around the gardens."

"Doesn't she want any breakfast?" Nick glanced at the doorway where Molly had appeared, waiting expectantly to take their orders. The girl's ponytail seemed pulled tighter than usual this morning, so that her eyebrows rode a half inch higher on her face and gave her more than ever the affect of a frightened rabbit. One wanted to be kind, but Greta had to admit, she had just a little bit of sympathy for Mrs. Smith's irritation with the girl.

Jordan shrugged. "S'pose not."

Jay stood and excused himself. "I've no appetite this morning myself, I'm afraid."

The exit was abrupt, and they watched him go, surprised.

"I'm beginning to think Mrs. Smith's talents are quite wasted in this household." Jordan helped herself to some stuffed tomatoes, a petite crab Benedict, and a second poached egg. "You're all in want of a little more hedonism."

"Hedonism has its time and place, Jord," Nick said, sounding weary.

"Yes, and I'd hate to miss it." Jordan pinched one of the croissants in the basket and made an approving noise. "Oh good, still warm."

Molly appeared with more coffee, changing out the urns on the sideboard.

"Is the other girl sick?" Jordan commented, once Molly had left again. She gestured with the tip of her fork. "You've got that shivery little one doing all the work."

Greta's mind was only half on breakfast; she was considerably more interested in the news Beecham had just imparted.

"Perhaps Ada is unwell," she offered.

"Well, that would be just what we need." Jordan shuddered. "A nice bit of influenza doing the rounds."

Nick made a wry face at Greta across the table, but when Molly came back in, Jordan asked her about it. The response was surprising.

"She's not unwell, I don't think, miss. It's only, she's gone off somewhere."

Greta felt a flicker of unease.

"Gone off somewhere?"

"Well, she's taken her bicycle. She must have started early." Molly gave a helpless shrug. She was out of her depth on this one, and clearly didn't want to be blamed for delivering bad news.

Jordan's eyes widened; the hint of gossip seemed to have buoyed her spirits a little.

"Oh, I say! She's done a bunk!"

Nick looked sharply at her.

"Stop it, Jord."

Greta frowned. Surely it was nothing like that.

"Are all her things still in the room, Molly?"

The other girl faltered.

"It all looked the same to me. I think."

Was she concerned, and just hiding it? Greta couldn't tell. Unlike Ada, Molly was the kind to keep her feelings private.

"Perhaps she's the necklace thief! Or else she's just had enough of this and run off." Jordan sighed. "Who *wouldn't* get spooked, living in a house of death?"

"Yes, *enough,* Jord, thank you!" Greta said, glancing toward Molly. "She's probably just fixing a flat tire as we speak. No doubt she'll show up with a perfectly good explanation soon enough."

Molly looked relieved. "Yes, I'm sure you're right, miss."

Jordan eyed the window with interest as Molly left the room: something just as compelling as an absent housemaid seemed to have captured her attention.

"Look at that, your brother's gone for a walk in the garden, too. He looks very purposeful, mind you. In a rush to track down Daisy, is he? I suppose she hasn't gone far."

"She really ought to have had some breakfast," Nick observed. "Poor old thing, she'll fade away if she goes on like this."

"Oh look, there they are now," Jordan said comfortably, ogling the window behind Greta. "He did catch up with her."

"And are you going to narrate *all* their movements for us, Jord?" Nick asked.

Jordan opened her mouth to retort, then froze, jaw agape.

"Oh my *word*," she said.

Greta turned around, craning to see what had so transfixed Jordan.

There was Daisy, walking hurriedly back toward the house, her distress obvious even from here. And there, left in the grass, was Jay, just pulling himself up to stand.

"I don't *believe* it," Jordan said. "He got *down on one knee!*"

Greta swallowed. *And it didn't go well, by the looks of it.*

"I *knew* it," Jordan said. "I just *knew* there was something going on with them. I can't believe she didn't tell me!"

The front door slammed, and from the hallway came the sound of Daisy's quick tread hurrying up the stairs—and then the slam of another door.

Jordan stood from the table.

"I'd better see how she is."

"I suppose you all think me a fool now." Jay sat half-up in bed, gray light streaming through the enormous room. Jay's bedroom was an Aladdin's cave of favored curios that he'd picked up, magpielike, over the years. There were collections of Vienna porcelain, the finest redware pottery from Mexico, and carved jade snuff bottles from China; a mantel clock of French bronze stood above the fireplace, and silk screen paintings adorned the walls. And there in the middle of it was Jay, looking strangely vulnerable in his enormous white bed. Vulnerable was not a way the world usually saw the great Jay Gatsby.

"We don't think you're a fool, Jay," Greta said.

"Well, maybe I am a fool, but not *that* sort of fool." His jaw jutted forward. "She told me many times . . . I wouldn't have thrown myself at her if I hadn't had the encouragement."

"But did she say she wanted to marry you?"

It would have been a very different thing for Daisy to tell Jay she loved him when marrying him was an impossibility. Sometimes, assuming what a person logically *ought* to feel got in the way of Jay's noticing what they really *did* feel. It wasn't arrogance, exactly. Greta's brother just often failed to understand that what seemed so clear to him could appear quite differently to others.

Who knew what Daisy was feeling? She had been battered by one unfathomable shock after another this past week. Perhaps the fantasy of how things might have been, of how happy Jay and she could have been in another life, was the one good thing she had left—and certain fantasies were too precious to risk putting to the test.

He glanced up at Greta.

"She acted . . . almost horrified, Gigi, when I asked her. As though I were out of my mind to even suggest it." He shook his head. "I know it was rushed, but I thought . . . well, dammit, now's the time! She has no *money*! She needs help."

Greta frowned.

"I should think it's to her credit, Jay, that the money wasn't an inducement."

He threw her a look.

"But now *Edgar's* supporting her—not exactly the picture of an independent woman." He scowled. "Daisy doesn't know *how* to be independent, Gigi. It's either me or him."

"He's Pammy's uncle. Perhaps she thinks it's appropriate that he should help them out."

Jay snorted.

Greta could sense underneath his indignation and wounded pride and bruised heart something else that worried her more. She now knew that for years, Daisy had been his great love, and he'd staked his future on her. She had become a goal, and Jay was someone who lived and breathed his goals. If you dropped him in a desert with no water, Greta's brother would make his way out of it just by sheer fixity of purpose. It was his great gift in many ways—that tirelessness, that inexhaustible devotion. Doubt was an irrelevance to him, just a thing that got in the way. But now, with that inner conviction cut off at the root, he would have to uncouple himself from the vision he had built himself around . . . Greta didn't know exactly how her brother would handle something like that.

"I'm very sorry, Jay . . ." Greta hesitated. "I am. But . . . do you think Daisy could ever truly be all you make her out to be?" She glanced at Jay's face, which was rather stormy now, and hurried on.

"I mean, I don't deny she's very beautiful and very charming. But perhaps . . . well, you do rather put her on a pedestal."

He put his head back against the white damask pillows and looked at the ceiling.

"All men have their gods, Gigi. All the happy ones, at least." He blinked. "I saw it in the war—we all need something purer than what we've got down here in the mud."

In the mud. Greta pictured him, then, in the trenches, the thought of Daisy keeping him going, just like the other men with photographs of sweethearts in their breast pockets. Only Jay's dream of Daisy had never dimmed an inch since then.

Was it foolish to insist on such an idyll when reality could hardly match up? Perhaps. But surely there was some beauty in it, too. Greta glanced out the bedroom window, out across the gardens, to where the *Marguerite* bobbed against the jetty. After all, Jay was right—the world was a sordid place. Perhaps more so than many of them were willing to countenance right now. Down here in the mud, sometimes we needed angels.

"I'm glad you're back, Gigi," Jay said then, just as she wondered if, in his exhaustion, he might have drifted off to sleep.

"Yes." She looked down at him. "I am, too." For all the grim events of the past days, she wouldn't choose to be back at the Academy for any price.

Jay hesitated.

"I know you never liked it there. I know you thought I wasn't listening to you when I insisted you go to all those schools."

A spark of pain flared in Greta. The pain of being sent away, of always being at arm's length. Something she tried not to dwell on, usually. Something she'd never expected Jay to bring up.

"Well, if you were listening, then why—"

"So that it could be different! Different for you than it was for me. I know how people talk about me; don't think I don't notice. And it seems I'm doomed to it no matter how fashionable my clothes are, or how successfully I leave the old accent behind. It's something else, the *je ne sais quoi*; something you only get by growing up around those people. By believing you're one of them. But it has to start when you're young." He looked up at her, his eyes bright in his wan face. "It was too late for me, but not for you."

Greta dropped her eyes from his. She wasn't sure she'd ever heard him so earnest, or heard his longing so clearly.

"But what if I don't?" she said at last. "What if I don't fit in?"

He propped himself up on his elbows.

"Don't you?" he said, as if he'd failed her.

She shook her head.

"I don't belong in a bubble, Jay. Nobody does."

He studied her awhile, and some sadness crossed his face.

"You're awfully brave, you know, Gigi. I suppose I never told you that?"

"No." Greta swallowed. "I don't think you have."

"Well then." He lay back on his pillows. "I'm telling you now."

Chapter Nineteen

The goodbyes were subdued. Jay sent his excuses via Beecham: he was suffering from a migraine, they were informed, which was too severe for him to leave his bed right now. Greta thought it might be true. He'd had migraines often enough after the war. In his absence, Nick and Jordan and Greta gathered in the hallway as they waited for the brown Studebaker to pull up. Daisy stood on the threshold, her face very pale.

"Tell him goodbye from me," she said to Greta.

"I will."

There was silence for a moment.

"You *are* sure, Daisy?" Nick said.

Daisy said nothing for a while, staring at her hands.

"I couldn't marry him, Nick. There's been too much speculation, too many rumors already—people would never stop talking; it would be unbearable. Besides," Daisy went on, a reckless edge to her voice; she was suddenly near tears. "What Jay feels for me . . . it's infatuation. A dream. I would only disappoint him were we ever to marry—once he realized who I really was. Jay likes having someone to adore—and adoration, you know, only works at a distance."

There was another moment's silence, and Greta wondered if, deep down, maybe such an idealized view of herself was something *Daisy* wasn't prepared to sacrifice.

Or maybe she was just trying to do the right thing.

Daisy glanced at her, the round blue eyes full of sadness and determination.

"I'm not a fool, and I won't let Jay become one, either."

The Studebaker appeared in the driveway then, and Daisy wiped her eyes and gathered herself. Soon her bags were in the car, and Edgar stood in a proprietary sort of way on the steps, waiting.

"You take care of yourself now, Daise." Jordan squeezed her before letting her go, and Nick kissed her on the cheek.

Daisy swallowed, then turned and let Edgar shepherd her away. Descending the front steps, Edgar looked back over his shoulder at the group of them, something cold and hard in his glance. Greta watched the car as it choked into life and circled the driveway, backlit against the waning afternoon. Beside her, Jordan gave a halfhearted sort of wave.

"Odious little man," she murmured. But Greta's gaze was on the small figure in the Studebaker's passenger seat and on that pinched white face in the window, its wide eyes fixed on the Gatsby house as the car pulled away.

An hour later, Greta sat in the gardens alone. The afternoon was on the cusp of evening now, a quiet hour that suited her mood. She had a lot to think about.

Edgar Buchanan, for one. What did *he* think of the whole barbiturates business? Rosemary Buchanan, too, was bound to have feelings about the *anomalies*. Jay and Nick might still be keeping faith that a rational explanation would present itself, but Greta knew well enough that "rational" did not invariably mean "benign."

She sighed, and closed her eyes, taking in the faint fragrance from the rose beds, listening to the sounds of the garden around her. Bill was washing the car again by the sound of it. The birds chirruped; the hiss of water from the garage continued, a soothing noise.

Greta sat up. Now *that* was odd.

She hadn't thought of it before, but abruptly now it hit her. Bill might be punctilious about hosing down the Phantom these days, but he certainly hadn't cleaned her before going out that day to pick up Greta. She'd noticed the crust of dry mud on the undercarriage that afternoon. But that wasn't the odd part. The odd part was that the car had been dirty in the first place. Hadn't Jay said they'd all been marooned indoors, with all that rain?

So why did the car have mud on the undercarriage, as though it had been driving around on rain-churned country roads? It hadn't been fresh from the drive down to the station, either. For one thing, it had been sunny all day, and the roads were dry by then; for another, the mud was caked and gray, not freshly spattered.

So it seemed that Bill had been out somewhere after all, while Jay and his party were cooped up at the house.

Or *supposedly* cooped up. It was always possible that Bill had gone off on an excursion of his own, rashly borrowing his employer's car . . . but Greta suspected that he hadn't taken the journey alone.

Bill was rubbing down the car with a rag when she reached the garage. He looked up at her, his freckles bright in the sun. His brow furrowed.

"Miss Gatsby. Do you need me to take you somewhere?"

"Actually, I had a question for you, Bill."

Though his face remained perfectly affable, she thought she saw some small shift in it.

"Well, then, I shall try my best to answer it." He looked at her expectantly.

"Mr. Buchanan," Greta said. "He didn't come here with a car."

"That's right."

"You picked them up from the train, I suppose?"

Bill nodded.

"And took them wherever they might need to go during their stay?"

"Indeed." His voice remained courteous but confused, and Greta did wonder if she might be barking up the wrong tree.

"Did Mr. Buchanan—" she began. "Did Mr. Buchanan ever ask you to take him anywhere . . . unusual?"

Bill's smile tightened. Gone was the bright-eyed fellow with an easy grin who'd joked with her on her arrival.

"Unusual, miss? I don't think so. I took him and the missus into town on a few occasions—I suppose you wouldn't consider that unusual?" He laughed a little, but Greta wondered if it didn't sound somewhat forced.

"I suppose not," she agreed. There was a moment's silence. Something in the air had changed. She felt surer now. She *was* on the right track.

"Bill, do you remember the day you came to get me from the station?" She waited for his nod before continuing. "I remember," she said, "the car was all muddied."

He flushed.

"I hadn't had time to clean her that morning, I'm afraid. I overslept." He spoke stiffly, but Greta shook her head.

"Please don't misunderstand me, Bill. It doesn't matter a jot to me if the car has a bit of mud on her. I'm just curious about where she went that got her so muddy."

Bill put his hands in his pockets.

"I can't say I remember all that clearly, miss. I just drive where I'm told."

"I understand. It's just, you see, my brother said he and his friends hadn't left the house in days because of the rain. He said they'd been all cooped up inside. So I'm wondering where the car went, you see."

She saw the flutter of a pulse in his left jaw.

"I needn't tell my brother if that's your concern," Greta said quietly. "I just want to know."

Bill hesitated, and for a moment, she thought he'd come clean, but then the guarded look came back down.

"Well, miss, now that I think about it, I do remember taking her out for a quick spin to check the brakes. They'd been giving a bit of trouble; I'd done a small repair and wanted to test the job."

He was a resourceful liar, Greta decided. He'd been almost convincing.

"I don't think that's true, Bill." She looked at him steadily. "I'm not trying to get you into trouble. But just tell me, will you—did you take him to other places, too? Or was it only the Bowery?"

She was gratified to see Bill's ears turn pink. Not such a shot in the dark after all. Bill blinked at her, opened his mouth, closed it.

Perhaps it was the thrill of being right that made Greta's back straighten, made her breath steady as she said the next thing. To get what she wanted—what she needed—it would be necessary to adopt a new sort of authority.

"You had better tell me everything," Greta said, in as stern a voice as she could muster.

And, somewhat to her surprise, he did.

Bill had taken Tom Buchanan to that address in the Bowery on three occasions, it transpired. Always at night, after the household had gone to bed, always on a Saturday. The address was some sort of a speakeasy. Bill didn't know what Tom did in there. His job was just to wait outside, try not to fall asleep, and be ready to drive Tom home when he stumbled out some hours later. Bill hadn't *wanted* the job, he made clear—but Mr. Buchanan had been quite insistent, and Bill had been afraid to cross him. The third of the three visits, he admitted when pressed, had been the night before Greta's return. In other words, the night before Tom died.

Greta's mind whirled. Tom certainly had not gone all the way to the Bowery just for the gin.

Women, then? Or something else? The Bowery was a part of Manhattan she knew by reputation only, rumored to be a hotbed of petty vices and some not-so-petty ones. Brothels, gambling dens, all sorts of way stations of ill repute. They said you couldn't throw a stone without hitting a pickpocket.

"And nobody heard or saw you go?" she said.

Bill shrugged.

"I didn't take the car up to the house. Mr. Buchanan walked down to the garage. He'd tell me in the afternoon, and that night I'd wait for his knock. I kept the car in a crawl until we got to the end of the driveway so as not to wake anyone."

"And you've no idea what he did in there? Whom he met? Anything like that?"

"None," Bill said, and Greta believed him.

She frowned. "What day is today, Bill?" With everything that had been going on, she had quite lost track; they all had.

He looked at her as though it might be a trick question.

"Why, Saturday, Miss Gatsby," he said, perplexed. "The Fourth."

A Saturday—the same day of the week as Tom's Bowery trips. Presumably, whatever had been going on those nights might very well be afoot tonight, too. A daring, somewhat daunting idea glided through Greta's mind. She didn't allow herself the time to deliberate: if she did, she might falter.

"I think, Bill, that you and I will have to take the Phantom for a spin tonight."

Bill eyed her, disbelieving.

"Tonight, miss? *You?* The Bowery is no place at all for a young lady."

"Nonetheless, I think we'd better go. And," she said, when he still looked determined against it, "not to put too fine a point on it, Bill, but I don't think you're in much position to refuse."

Bill stared at her.

"If your brother finds out, miss..."

"I don't see why he should," Greta said. "I mean, he's no likelier to find out about this than your trips with Tom Buchanan. And one might as well be hanged for a sheep as for a lamb—don't you think?"

Bill let out a low, reluctant laugh.

"You're more trouble than you look, Miss Gatsby. Anyone ever tell you that?"

She thought back to her school days, and the sorry days before that with Aunt Ida up in Winnipeg: the time she'd introduced the local kids to the stash of moonshine found in a neighbor's barn; the time she'd put a foot through Aunt Ida's roof after going up there to stargaze; the time she'd decided to try her rodeo skills on the new milk cow...

"Do you know, Bill, as a matter of fact, they have."

It was only as she reentered the house that it dawned on Greta: *The Fourth*, Bill had said, looking so bewildered by her question. Of course he'd looked bewildered! It was the Fourth of July.

She picked up a newspaper lying on the hall table just to be absolutely sure. Surely Jay had remembered, even if she hadn't.

"Jay?" She pushed open the library door, but it was empty. She tried the living room next, and found Jordan and Nick playing a desultory game of canasta.

"Did you know today's the Fourth?" She waved the paper at them. "The party—it's not still going ahead, is it?"

Jordan's eyes widened, saucerlike.

"Oh dear..." she murmured.

Nick turned on her.

"Jordan? You said you'd do it. *Jordan?*"

Jordan looked from Nick to Greta, sheepish.

"Well, I *meant* to."

Nick choked a little on his drink.

"Jay gave me the names." Jordan turned back to Greta. "I said I'd do the uninviting, so to speak. In the circumstances. Only, in the circumstances... well, I forgot."

"Oh hell." Nick was at the door in a few short strides, taking the stairs two at a time.

"Jay? *Jay?* We need a word with you!"

Jay closed his eyes and lay back on the pillows. The three of them were gathered around his bed, its occupant pale and disheveled in pajamas and morning robe.

"Let them come. What does it matter?"

"But, Jay..."

"Mrs. Smith will want to murder me, of course, but tell her I'll double her wages for the week and to just do what she can. She's got enough in that pantry to feed most of Long Island."

Greta knew her brother hated disappointing people. With friends and strangers alike, he seemed to feel this sense of responsibility to show everyone a good time, to offer something special.

"But, Jay, are you quite sure?"

He sighed, and tentatively rubbed his temples.

"I don't suppose it makes much difference, do you, Gigi?"

"I mean," Jordan chipped in, "they *have* come all this way . . ."

Nick exhaled, turned. "At the risk of stating the obvious: someone's just *died*, Jord."

"Well, *yes*. But all of us sitting around in widow's weeds is hardly going to help, is it? What's that saying, 'in the midst of death we are in life' . . . or thereabouts." She looked at Greta, as though supposing her the likeliest ally. "*You* know. Carpe diem and all that. I don't think Tom would mind. He loved a party." A note of relish was already creeping into her tone. "And we do all need rather a bit of cheering up."

Nick turned back to the putative host.

"I really don't think you're well enough for a party, Jay."

Jay glanced at him, then to the window out over the gardens.

"What does that matter? They can make themselves at home. They don't need me to be there."

Greta was torn between sympathy and frustration at her brother's full surrender to self-pity. Then again, she'd never had to suffer this particular brand of heartbreak. One could never be sure if reports were exaggerated, but it did sound quite terrible.

"Well, I think that's settled then," Jordan said brightly.

A respectful knock came at Jay's bedroom door.

"Pardon me, sir. Mr. Gatsby?"

Jay turned at Beecham's rumbling baritone.

"Sorry to disturb you, sir." Beecham stepped inside, looking only slightly taken aback to encounter such a bedside gathering. "But there appears to be, well, a *man* in the driveway with a carrier of . . . birds. *Live* birds, sir. He says he's making a delivery."

Jay blinked for a moment, then reclined back onto his pillows.

"Oh, yes. Yes, he is." He turned to the others.

"That, I expect, will be the peacocks."

"*P*eacocks?"

Dantry, predictably, was scandalized, and not only by the peacocks.

"I know, Mrs. Dantry, it's terribly unfortunate timing, but—"

"*Unfortunate* is one word for it," the housekeeper glared. "I don't suppose anyone considered the *propriety* of the situation? With Mr. Buchanan not dead a week?"

Greta closed her eyes briefly. Really, she thought, she ought to have sent Jordan down to break the news to Dantry. Jordan's unflappable complacency did have its uses.

"Indeed, Mrs. Dantry. And had my brother not been so distracted by his, I think you would agree, *very appropriate* shock and grief, he would most assuredly have remembered to cancel it."

"In all my days . . . ," the housekeeper said darkly, with a glance toward the garden windows. "First a dead man, and now *peacocks*."

Greta bit her tongue; she was on the cusp of asking whether the reverse order would have been preferable.

"Just open the door for them, will you, Dantry?" And with that, Greta steeled herself, and went to break the news to Mrs. Smith.

Chapter Twenty

Greta stood on the porch, her back to the wall—a reassuringly solid presence—as she stared out, dazed, across the lawns.

There were so *many* of them. They had arrived, first in small batches and then in droves, as dusk began to descend; in speedsters and phaetons and coupés, motorbikes and sidecars, hair and scarves streaming. There had even been one breathless pair on a tandem bicycle. Now the sky was purple and the bay behind it black, and everywhere in the gardens there were people.

Admittedly, Greta had missed the last two years of Jay's annual summer bash, but surely it had grown in size—tripled, quadrupled!—since she had last overlapped with it. How could he possibly know this many people? There must be hundreds of them here! And they all seemed to know one another, or else it was just the occasion of Jay's party that led them all to embrace one another so giddily, shouting and exclaiming, men twirling the women around in the air in greeting.

Everyone seemed dressed to the height of the latest fashions except for those who had apparently decided to treat the evening as a costume ball—she had already spotted two ex-presidents, one Henry the Eighth, one Lady

Macbeth, a number of Venetian carnivalgoers, a chimney sweep, an Uncle Sam on stilts, one Queen of Hearts, one Egyptian mummy, and the Three Blind Mice. In one corner was a small group of men in mobster costumes—at least, Greta *hoped* they were in costume. She'd also heard that there was a minor European count present and at least one disinherited Vanderbilt. Really, by the standards of this crowd, Jordan Baker had almost ceased to seem flamboyant. Back in her flapper dress, she was ambling through the crowd now with glee, intermittently catching Greta's eye and attempting to wave her over. Greta quickly averted her glance.

What did one even say to people like this?

The dining table had been lifted out onto the lawns—Bill and Beecham had handled that part—along with a variety of trestle tables Greta hadn't even known they owned. An army of candelabras had been rustled up from God knows where and were perched on every available surface. By the flashes of silver hip flasks that appeared from all sides, it seemed few guests had come to the party short of a drink, but nonetheless, the contents of Jay's extensive liquor cabinet lay variously placed on tables all about the garden, and some enterprising young fellow had found his way to the cellars, too—he had recently reemerged, in beaded slippers, a fez, and a kimono, with a stack of bottles under one arm, hallooing about a corkscrew. The peacocks were strutting loose about the garden, the only ones present who seemed to have a concern for dignity—and even so, they were forced to part with theirs frequently enough, as a few of the revelers seemed to delight in giving chase, scuttling the birds as though they were pigeons. Uproarious laughter followed the ensuing honks. Who knew that peacocks could be so *loud*?

"I believe"—Nick appeared at her side; she almost jumped—"someone has put goldfish in the fountain."

Greta glanced over at Jay's beautiful white fountain in scallop-shell design that stood in the middle of the garden. There could be worse homes, she supposed, if one were a goldfish.

"Who *are* all these people, Nick?"

He shrugged.

"Oh, some of them have been coming here for years." He sipped from a tall flute of champagne. When had that been opened?

"Your brother does have a knack for befriending people, certainly. But if we're honest, I think the real reason these parties started was Daisy." He glanced over. "Jay wanted to show her what he could do, the life he could create. The life he wanted to create for her."

The words weighed on Greta. All this merriment and high volume and glamour—all for someone else. As she looked around, it seemed to her that it was as Jay had said—few of the guests seemed to have noticed their host was not among them.

"Jay doesn't always come to his own parties," Nick said, as though reading her mind. "Sometimes, if Tom and Daisy weren't showing, he'd just tell me to come up to the balcony, and we'd sip on some whiskey up there and watch the crowds."

Greta supposed the revelers were used to thinking of their West Egg host as eccentric, even enigmatic. Jay already owned the party after all; there was nothing he needed to prove.

"That fellow over there"—Nick nodded to someone in a stovepipe hat, whom Greta had originally thought was costumed as Lincoln, but now saw was not—"is a magician; he always has a flock of doves with him. He'll unleash them soon enough, I'm sure. Last time, one of them ate the goldfish."

Greta eyed the magician, and the highly glamorous and scantily clad assistant who seemed to be accompanying him, and turned back to Nick.

"Do you think it's awful that we're doing this? With the funeral barely over?"

Nick's dark eyes held hers for a moment.

"Do *you*?"

Greta felt a warmth in her neck, and broke her eyes from his. The stars were out now, watching over this scene of giddy mania. She wondered what they made of it all.

"I don't know what to think," she admitted. It struck her for the first time that there was something oddly artificial about a party. About *deciding* to be happy; coordinating your inebriation with so many others; driving each other so determinedly, as part of a shared social contract, to this state of high exuberance. What had these people been doing just an hour or two ago—sitting in offices in the city? Reading the newspaper? Telephoning their mothers? She shook her head.

Jordan was right, in a way. Life—why we entered it, why we left it, why we did any of what we did in between—was a hard thing to fathom. And the look on people's faces . . . They seemed happy. Whatever had brought them here, whatever it was that united them . . . perhaps they need it, Greta thought. Perhaps we all do.

"I suppose," Nick said, "one might even think of it as a wake of sorts."

Greta looked out into the darkness, where the noise level only seemed to keep growing. The purpose of a wake was, after all, not to lionize or praise the dead. It was to usher them onward, bid them good passage into the unknown. Who knew what lay beyond all this? She looked out over the black water, the far shore, the green beacon of light from the Buchanans' distant dock. She reasoned if there was such a thing as a soul, there might be hope for Tom Buchanan yet. A man only had one life, but a soul might keep learning for infinitely longer than that.

"Penny for your thoughts," Nick said, and Greta found his gaze resting on her with a warmth that made her blink. Was it just the darkness, the velvety night around them, that made the exchange feel so intimate, so particularly meant for her?

"Oh." She flushed. "I don't know—life and death and parties." She wondered if she didn't look, as well as sound, rather foolish; Jordan had positively insisted on her donning a dress and some lipstick, and had even dug out an old ostrich-feather headpiece from somewhere, placing it on Greta's head with the air of a king bestowing a knighthood. Greta was of two minds about taking the damned thing off, but feared that this might bring Jordan to her side in speedy fashion.

But Nick only smiled that half smile of his.

"Life and parties principally, I hope," he said.

Suddenly, in a burst, the doves that Nick had spoken of soared upward from the dark lawn. For a moment, they hovered in the air like a spell, then coasted in a white shiver toward the trees, from where they began an agitated cooing. Somebody laughed uproariously, the sound traveling from near the water.

"You'll never get them down now!"

Before all the drama of the forgotten party, Greta had had a very particular plan for tonight—one that involved sneaking quietly out of the house after everyone retired for what would surely otherwise have been an early night. Bill's revelation had opened up a new path, and she owed it to herself—to her intuition and the sense of justice her mother had so dearly cultivated—to follow it. Greta thought she owed it to Tom, too, however repugnant the man might have been during his time on earth. Justice did not belong to individual men according to merit; it did not *belong* to anyone.

And yet . . . what Greta *wanted*, now, was to stay right here in the warm and glittering night, with Nick's dark eyes roving over hers. For a half second, she considered telling him about Bill's confession and the Bowery and asking whether he might come to investigate with her. But deep down, she knew he would not. In Jay's absence, he would feel obliged to step in, to constrain her and keep her safe. If she told him, she'd be giving up the only lead she had.

Jordan waltzed by then, a bottle of half-drunk champagne dangling from one slim wrist.

"Don't be so dry, you two!" She came over and tweaked Nick's elbow.

"You're missing all the fun. You must meet this Texan fellow I've been talking to. He tells me his people are cattle rustlers—isn't that enchanting? Do you suppose it's true? Oh, and he's brought a friend who's a *hypnotist!* Come on, you simply must let me introduce you."

Wake or no, Greta reflected, it was a very good thing Daisy wasn't here. She would have been mortally offended by all this.

"She knows how to enjoy life; you have to give her that." Nick's characteristic half smile pulled at his lips as he watched Jordan's retreating back; they had both begged off from meeting the hypnotist. Greta watched the smile, and wondered again, despite herself, what *exactly* had passed between Nick and Jordan, and whether it was quite extinct.

A couple cruised past her in full Harlequin costumes, their diamond-pattern tights shimmering in the moonlight, faces half-hidden behind black and gold masks. Around the poolside, five women were weaving about like trees in the wind, some sort of eurhythmic dancing spectacle, faintly Isadora Duncan–ish. A new batch of wine had been excavated from the cellar, and a dazed-looking Molly was making the rounds with trays of caviar-topped deviled eggs.

"Greta?"

Nick sounded hesitant, which was not like him.

"I wonder . . . should you like to go down to the waterfront for a bit?"

She glanced at him, feeling the blood rush to the tips of her ears, thankful for the dark night.

"I . . ."

I would.

I very, very much would.

But it would not be Saturday again for a whole week, and who knew what would have happened by then; Inspector Francis, she felt quite sure, was not sitting idle.

"I'd like to, but I . . . I'm not feeling all that well, I'm afraid." She didn't have to try hard to inject the right amount of regret.

"I think I'd better go to bed, in fact."

He looked . . . she *hoped* he looked disappointed. Or was he simply concerned?

"I'm sorry to hear it. Is there anything I can get you?"

She smiled at him.

"I'll be fine. An early night will put me to rights." She would go inside through the French doors and then slip out the front, she decided. The party, after all, would give her the cover she needed. Who would notice one car slipping down the driveway in the midst of all this?

Nick frowned.

"I'm afraid you won't get much sleep, not on a night like this."

Gales of laughter came from under a tree where a woman dressed as a panther, complete with tail, had handcuffed a man in silver face paint to the branches.

"No, I expect you're right."

Nick touched her arm very briefly.

"Well . . . I hope you feel better in the morning. Goodnight, Greta."

Turning her back on the party, and on Nick's dark gaze, Greta felt rather hard done by.

When she got to the hall, the view out the window informed her that Uncle Sam—now descended from his stilts—and the mobsters were sharing a bottle of champagne on the front doorstep, and Jordan Baker was getting a piggyback from a man in a cowboy hat only a few feet away. *That* wouldn't do.

Greta thought for a moment, then went upstairs to her bedroom and opened the window wide. Unlike Jay's bedroom, hers had no balcony, but she'd climbed out on the roof before on summer nights for the breeze and the view and the general frisson of it. She'd never climbed all the way *down*, though.

She sighed, and eased herself out onto the slate. She'd have to go round the side, too: if she climbed straight down from here, it would take her over the living room window and right back to the center of the party. At least the Dutch gable style meant she wouldn't have to go right over the center ridge, but could instead scoot around the more modest slope on the side. She offered up a moment of gratitude for Jay's idiosyncratic taste in architecture—and the fact that she hadn't been drinking tonight. The noise of the revelers, the peacocks, the pop of a champagne bottle, and the distant sound of the waves crashing on the bay drifted toward her as she edged around the eaves and over to the leeward side of the house where nothing faced her except darkness and trees. She descended cautiously, toehold by improvised toehold, and felt the blood beating in her ears as she looked up at last and judged herself a short-enough distance from the ground for a final leap. The earth met her with a muted thud, and Greta let her breathing settle for a few moments before she moved into the trees, and snuck down the hillside the last few hundred feet to the garage and Bill's apartment.

As she stepped over fallen leaves and snapping twigs, she took a last look back at the raucous scene behind her, and offered up a wish for whatever shred of soul the man called Tom Buchanan had once possessed. *Go well*, she thought, then turned back and rang the bell for Bill's upstairs apartment.

Chapter Twenty-One

The air was crisp. It was nearly midnight. They'd made good time and were already on the Queensboro Bridge: dark sky, dark water below, the city ahead full of lights. The night air seemed to crackle, something bright and dangerous and musky in it, like the tang of spent fireworks. Greta smiled to herself, remembering her route over the Gatsby gables. It *had* been a neat, rather daring exit, hadn't it?

She'd been acting out of character all day, really. And yet it was remarkable in the end, how easy it had been to step into the shoes of that other Greta: the one who demanded the truth and got it, who decided that Bill would drive them to the Bowery in the middle of the night and got her way. Greta had always had great trust in her instincts; that wasn't the problem. It just hadn't occurred to her that she might make others defer to those instincts, that her personal convictions might hold sway in the wider world, that they might have currency if she acted as though they did.

Authority wasn't something Greta had imagined for herself. It was for other people—parents and older brothers, prefects and headmistresses and traffic wardens. Where it came from—its origin, its source, who vested it—she had never much considered. She assumed a person just woke up with it one day, the new aura like a mantle about one's shoulders.

Well, if they did, then perhaps Greta's day was now.

She sighed, looking out at the bridge as they crossed into Manhattan. Despite the warm glow, her nerves were beginning to make themselves known. She decided to adopt the spirit of Jordan Baker—the kind of woman who surely wouldn't balk at venturing into a speakeasy unaccompanied.

But even Jordan wouldn't risk a seedy haunt in the middle of the Bowery.

They pulled off the bridge and began their descent downtown through the winding streets of Manhattan. Neighborhood by neighborhood, the scene changed: some brightly lit and humming with festive celebrations, some boarded up and shadowy and deserted.

The car began to slow at last.

"It's up ahead." Bill nodded. "On the left."

Greta peered out. They were on Dover Street, according to the sign. The speakeasy was on the bottom of a three-story building, a dusty brick structure with a fire escape clad in peeling black paint. The bottom floor was brightly lit, with small square windows behind iron bars, while one window glowed dimly on the second floor.

"Drive us around the block first, would you, Bill?"

As Bill cruised by, Greta saw a couple approach the doorway—dressed with every bit as much flair as Bill had described—and knock on the door. It opened, spilling yellow light across the street, and the couple quickly slipped inside.

"Can you park here, Bill?"

He pulled in across the street out of the glare of the lamppost. Jay's bright-yellow Phantom had never felt more distinctive. If anyone inside was watching, they'd surely remember the car—and in that case, Greta reminded herself, they'd be expecting someone very different to get out of it. She wondered if anyone would approach her, if they would ask about Tom. Would she dare tell them the truth if they did? Bill had told her that Tom had come out of here looking pleased on his first visit; the next two, not pleased at all. Greta had no particularly developed plan for tonight, but figured she would start with the bartender. With any luck, he would remember Tom, and if she tipped him well, perhaps he'd remember some more.

She put her hand on the door handle, and Bill turned in alarm.

"You're not—you're not planning to go *inside?*"

"Well, certainly." She met his wide-eyed stare. "How else am I to find out anything useful?" She reckoned she looked the part at least, and was rather grateful now for Jordan's intervention: judging by the clientele she'd seen going into the building, the establishment might not be "high class," but it certainly seemed to favor rakish dressers.

Bill's narrow, freckled face wore its most severe expression.

"I really don't think that's wise, Miss Gatsby. I'm saying this for your own good."

She looked apologetically at him.

"I'm sorry, Bill, but my only other option is to hand this information over to the police." Bill wouldn't like *that*, would he?

Neither, if she was honest, would Greta: instinct told her the inspector was liable to make a great mess of the whole thing.

Bill gave her a begrudging look.

"Have it your way, then. Just try not to get us both in trouble."

She nodded, and put her hand on the door, feeling a quiver of nerves now that she'd got her way. But she hadn't spent all those years cooped up in the Academy just to let an adventure pass her by when it came knocking. Besides, there was work to be done. With a quick breath, Greta stepped down from the car.

"I'll be back soon, Bill. Don't worry, I can handle my liquor."

Bill was unamused.

"That's not what I'm worried about, Miss Gatsby—"

But he was too late; she'd already shut the door.

"Yes?" A gruff voice came from inside as the door opened a mere crack.

Greta swallowed. All speakeasies had passwords, of course. A person couldn't just walk in off the street unless they were in the know. She thought fast.

"Swanee shore," she said, and the door swung wide. A heavyset man with a waxed mustache looked at her, annoyed.

"Keep your voice down, lady! You want the whole neighborhood to hear, pigs and all?"

"Sorry." She flushed, clasping the matchbook in her pocket like a talisman. There was a black velvet curtain behind the doorman, and from within came the sound of singing and the deep thrumming of a plucked double bass.

"G'on through." He nodded without another look in her direction, and Greta eased the curtain to one side, opened the door that lay behind it, then pushed through a second set of curtains. The place was bigger than she'd expected, and dim: two large rooms, the connecting doors pulled wide, and small tables everywhere lit with stubby red candles. It smelled of smoke and whiskey, orange rind and women's perfume. A singer and her small band took up one corner, commanding the attention of about half the room—the front half, which was mostly couples, the women dressed more daringly than Greta had ever seen. The half at the back was mostly men, drinking alone or in groups, ignoring the music. They sat in a row, too, at the bar that ran the far length of the room. Behind the bar, a bartender was polishing glasses, his black sleeve-garters gleaming against his white shirt, and it was his eye that Greta caught as she walked slowly to the back of the room. She wondered if the bar was always so full or whether the holiday was drawing out the crowds. More eyes were on her now as she moved. An unaccompanied woman.

There was one free seat at the bar and she took it, hoping the low light would hide her awkwardness and the flush she knew must be sweeping across her face.

"Happy Fourth, darlin'. Buy you a drink?" one of the men said. She shook her head.

"Thank you, no. I'm waiting for someone."

"Well, ain't he a lucky fella," the bartender said, turning her way. "But you don't sit at this bar for free, beautiful. If you're sittin', you're drinkin'. What'll it be?"

"A—a Tom Collins, please." The bartender smirked a little. They'd think her a novice now. She should have ordered something less like a lemonade; probably the other women here would be on their third or fourth gimlet. Greta tried to will the pinkness from her cheeks. It seemed to her that everyone was staring.

Well, let them look, she said sternly to herself. *You're here to do some looking of your own, remember?*

She sat a little straighter, and pushed her hair back from her face to get a good clear view of her surroundings and the people in it. There must be, oh, fifty bodies in the room—more, perhaps. And money, plenty of that, too—she could feel it, almost taste it. The way everyone was dressed, the flash of jewels and bright metal. It was a different kind of money, though—not just new money but risky money, money that still had the ring of violence in its ears. A highball glass landed on the bar in front of Greta, and she started.

"Thank you." She took a sip, and carefully extracted a bill from her purse.

Old money, she reflected, could be blood money, too—it was just that the blood no longer spoke so loudly. But had Tom Buchanan's fortune really been any cleaner than the money in this room? She doubted it.

Perhaps no fortune was entirely pure. There were certainly plenty who would look down on Greta's brother's methods of getting to where he'd got. He'd never been a racketeer, though—he'd earned people's respect with the rum-running business, had been scrupulous and courteous, always paid his debts, and kept out of trouble. He'd invested and scaled until he had enough to cash out and turn a profit on the stock market instead—generally thought to be a more salubrious place. Certainly, his money had grown faster there than it had any other way. But as far as Greta could see, the stock market was hardly any cleaner than rum-running: it was all buoyed on the backs of oil wells and railroads, which had no small amount of blood on *their* hands.

Still, she had never felt quite so much like prey as she did in this room. There was something so . . . *alert* . . . about the people here. Lazy on the surface, but beneath that, ears pricked and ready to pounce, like a pack of coyotes lounging in the sun.

Movement across the room caught her eye.

There was a spiral staircase in the far corner, and a man was climbing up it. She remembered the one lit window from outside: the speakeasy went up to the second floor, then.

"Excuse me," she said, and the barkeep sauntered over.

"I was wondering if you knew a friend of mine who comes here sometimes. Big fellow, looks like a quarterback, dark mustache. Name of Tom."

"Tom Collins?" The bartender smirked.

Greta flushed. "Tom *Buchanan*. He drinks at this bar."

The bartender shrugged. "A Tom is a Tom to me, lady. Stood you up tonight, did he?"

Revolting thought.

"I just wondered if you talked to him here. Or if you didn't, perhaps you saw who he *did* talk to . . ."

The bartender's eyebrows lowered sharply. "You workin' for someone?"

Greta stared. "Of course not. I just—I just thought you'd remember him. He was—is, I mean—a memorable sort of man."

The bartender narrowed his eyes.

"So you say. Well, perhaps he doesn't spend much time downstairs."

Greta glanced toward the spiral staircase.

"What's up there? Girls?" She kept her voice level.

The bartender's eyes narrowed further.

"I don't suppose it's much of your business. Now, why don't you sit and drink your drink like a good girl."

Behind them, a smattering of applause and wolf whistles broke out as the singer finished her number.

"Why, thank you," the singer cooed. "And God bless America."

The crowd chuckled at that, and though Greta couldn't fully decode it, she sensed the in-joke.

The next number was rowdier, and soon some of the couples at the front of the room were dancing. Greta kept her eyes on the staircase. Sometimes a man would walk into the bar, push aside the velvet curtain, and make straight for it without even stopping at the bar. If it wasn't a brothel, what was it?

The music was louder now, and when the barkeep gathered up a tray of dirty glasses and brought them out, rattling, through a kitchen doorway, it barely caused a disturbance. Greta hesitated just a moment as the door swung shut behind him, then dropped a tip onto the bar and stood. She kept to the back of the room as she made her way around to the staircase. Now she saw what she hadn't seen from the bar: a man seated by the bottom of the stairs, arms folded like a guard, watching her.

"Need somethin', doll?"

She glanced upward, hoping to make out something through the treads.

"I'd like to go upstairs," she said, giving him her most confident and womanly smile.

"I don't think that will be possible," a voice said, and suddenly the bartender with the garters was standing beside her—taller, somehow, than he'd seemed while at the bar. He seemed to tower over her, and Greta took an involuntary step backward.

"I think you'll be leaving now, won't you, little lady? And you'll be patronizing a different establishment in the future." He gestured for her to lead the way, and walked behind her until she reached the velvet curtain at the entryway.

"You have a nice evening now," he said, and though she didn't turn, she heard the smirk in his voice before the doorman pulled the door wide for her to leave, then slammed it behind her.

Greta stood on the sidewalk, heat pricking behind her eyes. *Stop it*, she told herself. She swallowed down the mix of disappointment and humiliation. Across the road, the yellow Phantom glowed in the street smog, faintly ghoulish. Bill mustn't have seen her; he made no move to start the car. Greta turned sharply as she heard a sound, but no one appeared—likely just a rat. She glanced at the garbage that lay against one wall of the building. It wasn't just the usual old bottles and cans: someone had thrown an old cot out on the sidewalk, too, its rusting frame glinting in the streetlight.

Greta moved her gaze up a floor: the light was still on in the second-story window. Right above the platform of that rusting fire escape . . .

She glanced back toward the Phantom, which still showed no sign of movement, and at the door to the speakeasy, which was windowless and quiet, no new patrons arriving. Then she eyed the metal bedframe once more, measuring the distance in her mind. The lowest rung of the fire escape—yes, surely, if she stood on that cot . . .

Once she'd knotted her skirts into place, it was not so hard, really, to hoist herself up and grab a foothold. She reached the first platform easily enough. It was a spindly little thing, with gaps between the treads she didn't want to look at too closely for fear of vertigo, but it would hold her weight. Worse was how the metal squeaked as she pulled herself up, then dinged beneath her boots as she moved across the narrow platform to the second ladder. She did her best to move quietly, and hoped the sounds of the night—and the sounds of the music from within—would cover her. The second-floor rooms must be vacant anyway: the windows were all dark except that brightly lit one at the far end.

She could see across to the water from here, out beyond the few blocks of city grid that separated her from the East River. Home, on the other side of that river, seemed suddenly very far.

Now wasn't the time to lose her nerve. Jay's car did look so *indiscreet* down there, though, glowing yellow like that. She wondered if Bill was dozing in the front seat or waiting anxiously for her return.

She moved quietly past the dark window of another room, edging closer to the light. Her eyes widened as she drew near. So *that* was what this was all about! Men sat around green baize tables, focused and intent. The baize was marked with white where players had chalked up their wagers. A gambling den.

And judging from the look of the people downstairs, this wasn't a small-money den, either. Places like this existed all over New York, Greta knew, as much a part of its unspoken underbelly as the speakeasies or opium dens. But while some gambling haunts were small-scale affairs, others were where the serious money came to change hands. And Greta was pretty sure which one she'd stumbled across: this was no back-alley cockfight.

A noise came from beside Greta and she stumbled, clinging to the railing. Peeling paint dug into her hand, but she barely noticed as the sound of a man's voice cut through the night.

"Well, well—what have we here?"

She just had time to take in a pale figure—his dark eyes, thin face like an anvil. "Having a little look around, are we?"

And a hand shot out from the open window, circling like a shackle around her wrist.

Chapter Twenty-Two

Greta stifled a scream. The people in the gambling room were the only ones in earshot; it would do no good to cry out and have *them* running to her aid. Who knew what men like that might do if they knew they were being spied upon?

To think he'd been sitting there in the dark! Watching her through those blank windows she'd passed by, unthinking.

"I'm sorry," she said. "I wasn't looking to bother anyone." Was it too late to play the innocent? He wasn't going to believe she'd climbed all the way up this ladder out of idle curiosity.

"Oh no? What *were* you looking for, then?" He gave her an unpleasant look. "Or is it *who*?"

Greta's mind spun. It wouldn't do to tell the truth. But perhaps a *version* of the truth . . .

"I—I admit, I was looking for someone," she said. *Meek*, she instructed herself, hanging her head low. *Meek and mild.* "A—a beau of mine. At least he used to be. He dropped me, I guess, and I just want him to tell me why. I know he comes here sometimes." She swallowed. Should she risk it? "Tom Buchanan—do you know him?"

She saw the flicker of surprise in the man's face. The grip on her wrist loosened momentarily, then tightened.

"I know the fella." His cold eyes quickened. "And if you see him, you better tell that son of a bitch to come back here and give me my money."

"He—he owes you money?" Perhaps bringing up Tom had been a poor choice.

"Damn right he does. Borrowed cash for a bad bet, and more fool me, I lent it to him. Haven't seen hide nor hair of that dog since. *Beau* of yours, you say?"

"I—I haven't seen him in some time, either." Greta tried not to picture the last sighting, Tom's body slumped in that chair. "But I'll certainly pass along your message if I do."

"I don't know what I was thinking," the man said disgustedly, and now Greta could see the gray hairs on his chin, silvery in the moonlight. Fear had sharpened her senses so that every line of him seemed to stand out, and the clammy weight of his hand made her feel sick. Why couldn't he just let go of her!

"Don't know what I was thinking, letting him borrow off me. That thickheaded son of a bitch was always thinking he was due for a win when he wasn't. Wanted *me* to put my money in that fool oil venture of his, and all they struck was dirt and worms. He kept saying it, though. *Any day now, Tucker, any day now they're gonna strike big! I just need a little something to tide me over till then.*"

The man let out a short laugh. "Then last week he loses my money along with his own, and out come the promises. Do I know how rich his family is, do I have any idea how much of Chicago they own? He'll sort it out, not to worry. He'll bite the bullet this time and write to Mother—the money will come, he says, never fear. Dear Mamma won't turn him down. Swore up and down he'd send her the letter the very next day." He snorted. "Well, was it a pack of lies, or has he another reason for not showing his face here since? Too busy with his fancy women, maybe?" He gave her another look up and down that made Greta's skin crawl. She tugged her arm back, but the awful man didn't budge.

"Let go of me!" she said. *Fancy woman!*

"You didn't seem in such a hurry to be gone five minutes ago," he said.

True enough. Greta took a breath, and tried a different tone.

"It's all very shocking, sir," she said. "But alas, I'm in no position to summon the scoundrel back." The words were truer than he could know. "So if you'll kindly unhand me—"

He cut her off.

"Oh, no need to act the lady with me now. We both know what kind of girls that man of yours runs with! Come on inside, why don't you?" His tone changed. "You might as well, now that you're here. You might enjoy it."

She tugged at her wrist again.

"Wouldn't you like to help settle your friend's debts?" he went on, his cold eyes bright with a new, ugly light. "I'm sure we could come to some arrangement."

Fear and revulsion roiled within her.

"I will *not* be entering your establishment, sir. Now let go of me!"

Just then a horn blared loudly on the street below, and Greta's heart jumped. Her captor started, too; his grip loosened, and as it did, she threw her weight against it, smashing his hand against the windowsill as hard as she could. He roared a curse, and Greta bolted across the narrow platform and down the ladder, hands and knees shaking as she climbed down. She didn't trust herself to look back and see if someone was following. The ground danced through the gaps in the treads, and as she felt the ladder shudder and clank beneath her, she wondered if it was shaking from her movement or someone else's. She reached the last step and dropped the remaining few feet, swinging free of the cot and landing with a thud on the pavement.

"Miss *Gatsby!*" It was Bill, pulled up to the curb, engine humming. "What in hell fire do you think you're *doing?*"

She jumped into the back seat, and Bill took off. A look out the rear window showed two men in the doorway of the bar, one of them pointing her way.

"I hope, Miss Gatsby," Bill said as they sped uptown toward the bridge, "that we won't be having any more moonlight trips. At least, if you do, I think you will have to find yourself another driver."

Greta's heart rate settled at last, and she leaned back against the seat, letting the cool leather cradle her head.

The way that awful man had described Tom had matched up quite well with what Greta would have expected of him: sure of his own good fortune, complacent about his bad investments, and confident, more to the point, that his mother would step in to fill the gap while he waited to cash out.

And that was not a description of a suicidal man.

So had Tom rung up his mother in the twenty-four hours before he died, and been turned down by her? With no hope left of being bailed out, had he turned to a different form of escape?

Greta didn't believe it had happened that way, not if Tom's place as favored child was as secure as it seemed. And moreover, Greta had seen Rosemary Buchanan only days ago, and what she had seen was a woman wracked by fury, perhaps bitterness and resentment, too, but not guilt.

She shivered, and turned from the window. *Anomalies*: that word was becoming truer and truer. Greta had sensed before now the thin layer of denial keeping everyone afloat—Daisy, Edgar, Jay, and even Nick and Jordan, none of them had seemed willing to consider these anomalies very grave at all.

But in Greta's case, at least, such optimism had run its course.

Midnight had been long ago, but the party wasn't yet over by the sounds of it. Greta paused on the driveway—she'd come on foot up the few hundred feet from the garage, not wanting to be heard, but by the inebriated spurts of laughter drifting her way, she didn't suppose anyone still up was in a position to notice her comings and goings. Greta glanced at her watch in the moonlight. It was gone four in the morning. A splashing sound and another burst of muffled, drunken laughter drifted from the lawns.

She *ought* to go straight to bed, but . . .

Padding softly onto the grass, Greta hugged the side of the house and turned the corner. She was met by a scene of merry ruin lit solely by the moon: all the candles had long since burned down, and inside the house, the lights were off. But auditory clues informed her of the couple rolling in the grass a few feet downhill, evidently engaged in a particularly passionate embrace. A few more horizontal figures dotted the lawns here and there, presumably sleeping off their recent excesses.

A hardier bunch were ensconced on the porch, smoking and laughing: a couple of European-looking men, one with a monocle and the other with an extraordinary curled mustache, and with them, a woman dressed head to toe as a white rabbit.

"Bonsoir, mademoiselle!" one of the men hailed her, and the white rabbit squealed with laughter. "It's hardly the *soir* anymore, Rémy! It's almost *dawn*!"

Empty wine bottles and spilled candle wax were everywhere, but the general impression of debauchery was focused on the swimming pool and its environs. A knotted trail of silk magician's scarves was wrapped around the diving board, and a solitary white dove was stalking its perimeter like a small, tufted lifeguard, hopping over champagne corks as it went. A woman's sequined dress lay to one side, and Greta tried not to wonder too much about the current state of undress of its owner.

In the pool itself, hundreds if not thousands of playing cards floated, waterlogged and scattered across its surface—and there, in the middle of it all, bobbing in what appeared to be an empty wine barrel, was Jordan, clutching a bottle of champagne.

"Greta! I'm shipwrecked! Come sing a sea shanty with me."

"I . . ." Greta began. But on this particular occasion, she had to admit, she simply could not find the words. Choosing to believe that the morning would present a more salubrious scene, she made her way toward the French doors, and carved a path through the dark rooms within. She almost tripped over the sofa and the long pair of legs hanging over one side; a groan of a familiar timbre stopped her in her tracks.

"Nick? Is that you?"

She squinted, her eyes having become more used to the darkness now. It *was* Nick—splayed on the sofa in a most ungainly manner. And was that—? She leaned a little closer. Yes, lipstick. All over his collar.

Greta stood back. Not that *she* cared. Nick Carraway had every right to collect as much lipstick as he might desire.

She swallowed. In that moment, she felt an unaccountable pull to reach for the light switch and determine if this particular lipstick was in Jordan Baker's trademark scarlet hue. But that was Nick's concern, she reminded herself, and she did have some pride.

Nick mumbled something incoherent just then, and opened one eye.

"Greta." He held out a hand, or perhaps *flung* was the right word—it lolled over the edge of the sofa now, the back of his fingers brushing her shin. "You're back. We missed you."

But his eyes had closed again, and he sighed comfortably, seemingly returned to his dreams.

"Well, you certainly didn't miss me *too* much," Greta muttered under her breath, before weaving her way out of the room and, in a most disgruntled manner, up the stairs to bed.

Chapter Twenty-Three

Greta rubbed her eyes. It was a relief, really, to hear Molly's knock; her dream had not been at all pleasant. She'd gone to sleep, admittedly, thinking mostly about a lipstick-stained collar, but once sleep had come for her, it had been nightmares of men climbing ladders behind her and chasing after her in cars. The door rattled now as Molly entered, coffee tray precariously balanced. It was a wonder the girl managed to find her way to a career in domestic service, Greta thought: the nervous creature seemed inches away from upsetting whatever she carried.

"Good morning, Molly. How are you?"

Molly gave her a guarded look, as though the question might have some hidden meaning.

"All right, miss. Busy. There's much to be done about the house after last night's party."

Greta remembered the state of disrepair of the pool and lawns last night, and winced.

"Yes, I should think that's an understatement. I expect Dantry's not very happy about it."

"I wouldn't presume to know what Mrs. Dantry thinks, miss."

Molly's words were all humility, but there seemed to be a hint of rebuke in there, too. Greta reminded herself once again that Molly was no Nora and was not interested in exchanging confidences or joking remarks.

"Of course. Thank you, Molly. You can leave it there on the table; that will be fine." Greta remembered the other thing she'd been meaning to ask.

"What news of Ada?" It seemed to her Ada hadn't been helping out at the party last night, but there had been so much chaos, it was hard to say. Did that mean she was still gone?

Molly looked reluctant.

"No word from her, miss."

A cold weight settled in Greta's stomach. It looked like Jordan might have been right after all. Perhaps Ada *had* done a bunk—but so hastily! Without giving notice, without collecting her last wages . . .

"Has my brother been told?"

Molly's agitation deepened.

"I didn't—we didn't like to disturb him."

Greta dressed quickly, gulped down some coffee, then went downstairs, through the hall, and along the service passage toward the kitchen. She pushed open the swinging door to Mrs. Smith's fiefdom, the pristine white tiles and whirring fans and scent of bacon. It was empty for a moment, and then the door of the pantry swung back and Mrs. Smith emerged, expertly navigating the enormous bowl of peeled potatoes cradled in her arms. She started when she saw Greta, and some of the water sloshed over the edge of the bowl.

"Miss Gatsby! Is everything all right?"

"I hope so. Molly has just been telling me that Ada may have left the household. There's been no sign of her since yesterday?"

Mrs. Smith plonked the potatoes on the counter and gave Greta a gloomy look.

"True enough. I thought Mrs. D would have her guts for garters when she wasn't home by dinnertime. We thought she'd just been delayed at first. But by now, we can only reckon she's taken off for good." Mrs. Smith shook her head. "Ada always was a flighty one, though it's downright bad manners, not to mention foolish, to take off without a word like that. Perhaps we'll get a letter when she's back in New Hampshire with her people, instructing us where she wants her things sent. Cheeky little madam, I wouldn't put it past her."

Greta frowned. "So you *do* think she's all right?"

"All right's one word for it," the cook huffed. "Mrs. D says she's sure to show up yet, tail between her legs. Perhaps she's right. Perhaps Ada ran off with some lad, and when it all goes pear-shaped in a day or two, she'll be back at our door."

Perhaps. Greta climbed the few stairs back up to the kitchen passage, and walked through to the hall. She very much wanted to speak to Beecham about this. It was sheer paranoia, surely, that was leading her even to imagine that something could have happened to Ada. Really, it was hardly surprising that a sensitive young woman would have decided it was all too much for her, working in a house touched by such a grim and violent death.

She walked back down the kitchen passage and soon heard Nick and Jordan squabbling lightly in the dining room, for all the world like a married couple. Greta felt an uncomfortable pang. She had half expected to see a roomful of stray delinquents from last night all joining them for breakfast, but the last of the partygoers must have taken themselves off at some point; Nick and Jordan were alone.

"Morning, Greta." Nick looked up. Sunlight beamed across him; he seemed perfectly at ease, no hint of embarrassment or apology in his voice.

And why should he be apologetic? an irritable voice inside her said. *He's a free man, isn't he?*

Jordan glanced up from her coffee.

"Greta, you look as if you haven't slept a wink."

The words, while not flattering, were truer than Jordan guessed.

Greta pulled her eyes from the lawns outside, where Bill was trawling the pool with a large net. The beautiful lawns still looked strangely flattened in parts, as though they, too, had been deprived of their nightly rest.

"Have either of you seen Jay?"

They shook their heads.

"Still touched by the migraine, I suppose. I'm sure last night didn't help."

Well, she'd have a word with her brother later.

"I was just down in the kitchen," she said, and filled them in on Ada's ongoing absence. "Should we be worried? The staff don't seem to be. I don't know what to think."

Jordan looked intrigued at the prospect of more gossip; Nick frowned, then gave a glance out the window. He'd done it unthinkingly, but Greta saw where his eyes went: over the lawns, down the jetty, to the *Marguerite*. Her stomach turned.

Good Lord. Surely, he didn't think—

"Forgive me," Nick said hurriedly, seeing her appalled face. "I don't know what I was thinking. Of course she's fine, Greta. I'm sure there's nothing to worry about."

Greta still felt nauseous at the thought. Surely, Ada was fine. *Surely*. But Nick was right . . . it was rather reminiscent of the last time someone had gone missing from the house.

"We should look," she said, though the idea filled her with dread. "I'm sure you're right, but . . . just to be sure."

"What, out *there*?" Jordan was catching on. "Oh, how grotesque. Don't be silly, you two, of course she's fine. The girl's not *dead*, for heaven's sake; she just got spooked and did a bolt."

Greta swallowed. "I'm going all the same."

Nick balled up his napkin. "Not by yourself, you're not."

The day was still fresh, the dew brushing their feet as they walked. The water ahead of them shone with morning light, the water swishing gently against the dock. The very prettiness of the day made her nervous.

"You two are being terribly overdramatic, you know," Jordan said, as they strode across the lawns. Greta couldn't bring herself to say anything much until they reached the jetty, when Nick glanced sideways at her.

"Jordan's right. Ada is bound to be just fine."

Even so, Greta heard in his voice the same fear as in her own; he was willing the words to be true.

But when they pushed open the door and found the cabin empty, suddenly it *did* seem absurd that they should ever have feared to find Ada here.

"You see?" Jordan said happily. "You're both going mad, I'm afraid."

Nick laughed a little. "On this occasion, I'm relieved to be mad, Jord. I suppose our imaginations *have* been getting a little overheated."

Greta agreed—if the girl *had* made off with the pearls, she caught herself thinking, good luck to her—but meanwhile, her eyes were roaming the cabin. Now that the relief had flooded in, something else had accompanied it. A very faint feeling of disquiet. Something, some small thing, was out of place. She had to close her eyes again to realize what. *Yes.* It had been on the floor the morning they'd found Tom; later, after the police had inspected the cabin, it had been returned to its place on the desk.

The little red hurricane lamp. Where was it?

She stepped deeper into the cabin, the others staring.

"Greta? What are you up to?"

"Just . . . looking for something." But there were very few places in the cabin that it could have been put away, and she checked them: it was not hanging on a wall hook, not inside or on top of the dresser in the corner. There were two other lamps, pewter-colored ones, gathering dust on the back of the shelf, but the red one from that morning was gone. Perhaps the police had taken it away? Though why, she couldn't fathom.

"Well, that was a bit of a damp squib, wasn't it?" Jordan said. "Let's go back inside. My coffee will be quite cold by now."

The lawns, as they walked back, smelled sweeter now that Greta had been relieved of those awful thoughts about Ada. There was still plenty to preoccupy her, though. What an odd little detail, that missing lamp.

"The poor old garden's the worse for wear, isn't it?" Jordan commented, mistaking Greta's frown. "Still, it *was* a hell of a night." She turned. "That magician's assistant took quite a shine to you, Nicky."

Greta's ears pricked up despite herself; she tried not to let her neck tense. She remembered the magician's assistant, a glamorous-looking individual with not much clothing on at all.

"Hm," Nick said, his tone ambiguous.

"Mad as a bag of frogs, though," Jordan continued. "When you passed out on the couch, she seemed quite determined to wake you up. Rather in the manner of Sleeping Beauty. Although," she said thoughtfully, "I can't say you *were* particularly beautiful, Nicky, all splayed out like that."

"Very funny, Jord," Nick said, although Greta noticed his mouth did twitch at her words.

Greta snuck a glance at Jordan, who winked back in a knowing sort of way. Greta flushed.

So the lipstick wasn't Jordan's after all. And from the sounds of it, Nick hadn't been a very active participant. Perhaps he hadn't even really liked the girl. . . .

But Greta had a responsibility to some far more important questions. Chiefly, those raised by her little excursion last night. That horrible man's account had made her think again of the incongruities around Tom's death, and as the thought circled again, Greta felt she must share it.

"There's something I've been wondering," she said, as they neared the house. "Doesn't it strike you as strange," she continued slowly, "that Tom would kill himself over *money?*" She looked at them; they glanced at each other.

"Of course it was a *lot* of money, but not when his mother was sitting on a fortune many times that," she went on. "And Tom was used to her getting him off the hook. It would have been embarrassing to ask, perhaps, but all he needed to do was write her a letter."

Nick absorbed her words in his usual contemplative way, but an extraordinary change came over Jordan, whose eyes became positively saucerlike.

"Jordan? What is it?"

"I had totally forgotten. How queer!" Jordan stared at Greta. "There *was* a letter. At least, I'm almost sure—no, I *am* sure."

"What letter, Jord? You're not making much sense, you know," Nick said, sounding anxious now.

"Well, the morning we"—Jordan cleared her throat—"The morning we found Tom. You remember, I'd brought in that parcel of yours to the breakfast table, Greta—you gave yourself a little nick opening the damn book." She paused. "Well, there was a letter waiting to go out, too. I didn't look at it—I mean, I didn't pick it up or anything. I just noticed it was there. And now that I think about it, it was certainly a letter of Tom's. It was that ink, you know, that royal-blue color he always used. Very distinctive."

Greta's heart beat faster. Nick frowned.

"You're sure? Who was it addressed to?"

"I don't know! I'm telling you, I didn't pick it up and inspect it. I just saw it, and then I took up the salver with last night's mail and brought it inside." She looked hopefully at Greta. "Perhaps the servants will remember? Who sends out the mail?"

Molly stood before them in the living room, eyeing them apprehensively. The mantel clock ticked behind her. *I didn't do it*, her fretful look seemed to say. *I didn't do it, whatever it is.*

"Molly, there's no need to worry," Greta said. "It's only that I have a question about something you might remember." She paused. "The day Mr. Buchanan was found dead—I wonder, do you remember anything about the morning mail? Not the incoming mail," she clarified. "Just any letters that left this house. Do you remember anything at all about those?"

Molly blinked. "Why, there were none, Miss Gatsby."

"No letters at all?" Greta felt the prickle across her skin. "In the outgoing mail? Are you sure?"

"Quite sure, Miss Gatsby." Molly looked at her, then toward the others. A pious note had crept into her voice now; she was offended, perhaps, at the idea that she might have misremembered.

"The mailman comes at ten thirty. Normally, I'd have the letters ready for him, only that day we were all, well." She stopped. "Mr. Buchanan had just been found on the boat."

"Yes, of course. Everyone was very distracted, naturally."

"Well, when he showed up, Mrs. Dantry told me to run and get the mail, and I did but there were no letters waiting." Her voice had grown stauncher in the telling. "I remember it quite clearly, miss."

Greta's skin prickled.

"Thank you, Molly." She forced a smile. "That's most helpful."

The girl disappeared from the room and the others exchanged looks.

"It could have fallen off the table . . ." Nick said dubiously.

Jordan snorted.

"Well, it's not on the floor *now*, is it, Nick? Somebody took it, is all I can think." She looked at Greta.

"Somebody decided that letter shouldn't be mailed after all—and that somebody wasn't Tom."

Chapter Twenty-Four

The inspector had evidently telephoned Edgar, too: the black Model T had barely pulled up before a familiar brown Studebaker followed it up the driveway. A groggy-headed Jay had been coaxed down from upstairs, and Greta groaned inwardly when she saw Daisy emerging from the Studebaker while Edgar held the door for her. But in the living room, the awkwardness between them was soon overwhelmed by the inspector's presence and the words that bounced back and forth.

"I don't understand," Jay was saying testily. "*What* missing letter?"

Jordan told her story again.

"It was Tom's handwriting. And no, I *don't* know whom it was addressed to; I didn't pick it up. I just saw enough to know that it was his script and his ink—I'd stake anything on it." She looked around as though daring anyone to contradict her. "He'd left it out for that morning's mail, but it was never sent. Your maid's account makes that very clear. Somebody pinched it before the mailman got here."

Edgar looked incredulous.

"Somebody *pinched* it?" He folded his arms. "I don't see how you can say it was his letter, anyway. You didn't even look at it. Anyone might have sent a letter; anyone might have used royal-blue ink."

"All right, then." Jordan looked around. "Did anyone else leave a letter to be mailed that day? Speak up now. Anyone?"

There was silence, and Jordan narrowed her eyes at Edgar.

Jordan had not been mistaken, Greta was sure of that. But was it possible . . . was it possible that she was lying? But why would she lie?

"There's one more thing," Greta said then. She had weighed whether to disclose this detail, but in light of the new developments, it seemed time. She told them about the glass shard she'd found on the boat and how Beecham's inventory had turned up one mysteriously absent glass that had vanished only in the last two weeks.

"I have it here, Inspector." Greta handed over the little shard she'd wrapped in a silk handkerchief. She wondered if under a microscope he'd be able to verify the pattern—or better yet, what exactly was in the glass.

"What were you even doing out on that damned boat?" Jay looked at her askance.

She shrugged. "I had a hunch, I suppose."

Jay's eyes were very bright, either the effect of the migraine or the grim conversation. He gave Greta an exasperated look.

"I shouldn't think it matters whether Tom drank his accursed barbiturates out of a crystal goblet or a copper tankard! What matters is he drank them, and sorry to say, that's that."

"Of course it doesn't matter what he drank them out of." Greta kept her voice even. "What matters," she said, "is that someone cleaned up the glass—and it's highly unlikely that someone was Tom."

"What your sister means," Jordan said, "is that it looks like somebody was trying to hide evidence."

Jay shook his head, then winced at the motion. "But see here . . . what you're saying—"

"What you're saying is perfectly abhorrent!"

They all turned. Daisy was pink-cheeked with rage.

"How—how *dare* you." Her lip trembled. "As if I haven't been through enough! As if all this isn't enough without being dragged through some sordid, repellent fantasy!" Tears brimmed in her eyes.

The inspector regarded her more curiously, then shifted his eyes back to Jordan, and then Greta, as though intuiting that she had somehow instigated all this.

"I suppose you know perfectly well what you *are* saying," he said.

There was a sort of hush in the room. Nobody could be in doubt of it, but nobody wanted to say the words aloud.

"I don't understand," Nick said flatly. "If we . . . if we really *are* supposed to consider this as foul play"—he stumbled over the words, but kept going—"then what about the suicide note? Are we really going to call that a forgery? We all saw it, you know, and we all swore up and down it was his writing."

"*I* believe it was foul play," Jordan said abruptly. "Even if the rest of you are too lily-livered. Tom simply wasn't a suicidal sort of fellow—and all this business with the barbiturates, it doesn't add up. It's *fishy*, that's all."

"But if it was a forgery"—Jay spoke, and everyone's eyes turned toward him, including the inspector's—"if it *was* a forgery, then . . . you know, we're not talking about some marauder, some vagrant who came at him out there in the dark. We're talking about—"

"Someone who knew him." Jordan cleared her throat, and Greta noticed how studiously everyone avoided eye contact.

"We're talking," Jordan continued, "about one of us."

A tremor seemed to go through the room.

Greta looked around at them all—Jordan defiant; Jay and Nick, who looked nauseous; and Daisy and Edgar, who looked angry. The inspector presided over it all, as cool as a spectator at a tennis match. With Jordan's words, the last thin branches they'd been clinging to had snapped, and they'd all hit the ground with a thump. But Greta had already been down here for a while; the fall was no great shock to her.

There *was* a problem, though, going around and around in her mind. Nick had been right to pinpoint the issue of the suicide note. If it was a forgery, how had it been done? Despite what Edgar said, Greta was sure Tom's particular flamboyant shade of ink was not very common at all. Had someone snuck into his room and stolen his fountain pen? And they would have had to be a very skilled forger, surely: Daisy, Jay, and Nick had all verified the writing as authentic.

Of course it *was* a very short note. Barely a couple of lines and not signed ...

Suddenly, she stood up straighter.

Wait a minute ...

The feeling was like being doused in cold water and coming up gasping. The idea she'd just had seemed outrageous—and yet it made sense. More sense than anything else, at least.

"Daisy." She turned. "In that note, Tom called you *old girl*. Remember?"

Daisy said nothing; if anything, her cheeks grew pinker.

"Did he call you that ordinarily?" Greta insisted. "I mean, was that a term he used for you?"

"Are you taking some kind of pleasure, Greta, in reminding me of all this?" Daisy's voice was choked with indignation, but Greta's thoughts were buzzing too fast to allow for compunction or embarrassment.

Greta shook her head.

"I don't believe he did call you that," she went on boldly. "I certainly never heard it." In fact, she'd never heard Tom call Daisy anything but *Daisy*, and on a few short-tempered occasions, a sarcastic *dear*. Tom and Daisy hadn't been much into terms of endearment.

That odd, short suicide note. So curt, so abrupt. *But so like Tom*, they'd thought. Well, they'd been wrong. It *was* his writing. But—

"What does it matter to *you*!" Daisy erupted. "What does any of it matter to you if he wanted to get one last dig at me before he—before . . ."

She buried her face in her hands. Jay moved to comfort her, then stopped himself.

Greta shook her head. "Daisy, I only meant . . . look"—she turned toward the rest of the group—"Tom's note, I don't believe it was meant for Daisy at all."

Jordan was the first to find words.

"I beg your pardon?"

"I don't think he wrote that note for Daisy," Greta insisted. "And I don't think it was a suicide note. I think he was writing to his mother. Edgar, tell us: he called your mother that, didn't he? *Old girl?*"

Edgar stared.

"But what's that got to do with anything?"

"So you're saying he was writing that note to his mother?" Nick glanced toward Daisy. "I don't see how—"

"Because it wasn't a suicide note, Nick," Greta interrupted. "It was a request for money." She took a breath. "I ran into an acquaintance of Tom's yesterday."

"You what?" Jay said, but she ignored him.

"And he told me Tom was writing to his mother for funds to tide him over while he waited for his investments to come good." She turned to Edgar, whose cold eyes slid first toward the inspector, then back to her.

"Mrs. Buchanan never got such a letter, did she, Edgar?"

Edgar shook his head, his eyes narrowing.

"Now we know what Jordan's missing letter was about," Greta went on. "It was a request for money, addressed to his mother. And it was meant to be posted that day. Tom wasn't about to kill himself over some bad debt, not when he had only to convince his mother to dip into her pockets for him." She looked around at them.

"And why did someone need to get rid of that letter? Well, it wasn't the only copy." A shiver went up her spine as she said it. The picture was becoming clearer in her mind.

"You can imagine, it was an awkward letter to write. Even for Tom, asking for money was a touch embarrassing. The kind of letter you might not get quite right the first time. You'd want to phrase it carefully. I suppose Tom made a false start—maybe a few false starts. But I can tell you more or less what the final letter sounded like." She glanced around to see if they were following. "*Old girl*," she said slowly. "*I'm terribly sorry about all this, but can you loan me a bit of cash?*"

She watched their faces as they took it in.

"The letter on the boat," she said, "was an abandoned draft. That's why it was so short. That's why it wasn't signed. It just, very conveniently for someone, *looked* like a suicide note."

The others all looked a little dazed except for Edgar and the inspector, whose faces were perfectly opaque. Nobody spoke, so she went on.

"Tom didn't know someone had stolen his draft, of course. So he finished the real letter, and left it out for the morning's mail on the hall table. And whoever had stolen the draft didn't know the real letter was there—not at first, anyway. Because it was there the next morning when Jordan picked up *her* mail from the night before." She looked around. "But an hour later, it had disappeared."

Her nerves were tingling as she stopped speaking; she felt short of breath. The others stared back at her.

"By Jove." Nick moved uncomfortably. "It's a hell of a lot to take in. It's just, do you *really* think . . ."

"It would make sense," Jordan said slowly. "It would explain why he didn't sign the letter, for starters."

Daisy let out a whimper.

"But who would do such a—such an evil thing?"

Greta saw the naked pain in her brother's eyes.

"I—I think I need some air," Jay said. He moved blindly toward the window, pushed up the sash, and drew down deep breaths. Jay never really could absorb horror, she reflected. Despite all he'd endured—loss, war, and all sorts of other man-made evils—there was that part of him that steadfastly refused to believe the worst of anybody. He had a purer soul, Greta thought, than she did—but she worried it would take its toll on him one day.

"But do you think it can *really* be true?" Nick turned back. "It's so . . ."

"*Clever*," Jordan finished. "It's so fiendishly clever. I can't think how anyone—any of *us* at least—would have the mind for it."

Greta glanced at the inspector. It *was* clever. And more than that: it was a curious combination of calculated planning and wild opportunism. There had been planning here, and yet the half-written letter as a suicide note, *that* could not have been planned. That had been a windfall, a curious piece of luck or inspiration that had been woven into the killer's plans, the finishing touch for what should already have been a perfectly convincing suicide.

But they had not counted on Mrs. Buchanan wanting an inquest.

And they had not thought that anyone would have noticed Tom's letter quietly awaiting the morning post.

Daisy, silent until now, flung herself violently onto the sofa.

"Why does everyone keep saying such terrible, horrible things? It's too gruesome—I can't bear it!" She banged a small fist against the silk upholstery. "Why can't he—oh, why can't he just be *dead* without all of this . . . this horridness!"

Edgar rose quietly from his chair.

"It's all conjecture on Miss Gatsby's part."

"Well, look," Nick said reasonably. "How about this? If there *was* a letter, and someone swiped it off the salver—to, well, to cover their tracks, as

Greta suggests—then I suppose it didn't simply disappear into thin air. It would have been burned, perhaps, or thrown away. Perhaps it—or traces of it—can be found. That way we'll know for certain."

He glanced around. It was a good point. After all, it was midsummer; no fires had been lit in the house for months, and traces of ash or embers in a grate would surely be noticeable. It was a slim chance, but not impossible, surely, that the letter had been disposed of in some other, less foolproof fashion.

And it seemed that finding it was the only way to prove Greta was right.

Jay turned from the window. His face looked heavy; he glanced at Daisy, then turned away, the moment too brief for anyone but Greta to notice.

"It seems like there's only one thing for it, then," Jordan said.

"I should think you'll want to bring in your squad, Inspector. The house will need to be searched."

Chapter Twenty-Five

"They're like ants, aren't they?" Nick observed, coming up to the dining-room window where Greta stood. Men in uniform were combing the gardens. From her vantage point, Greta could see the kitchen gardens and the lawns right down to the water and the jetty with the *Marguerite*. Edgar was outside with the inspector, and Jordan was in the next room, comforting Daisy. She wasn't sure where Jay had got to—coaxing Mrs. Smith down from a cliff, perhaps.

The policemen *were* like ants: a small colony discovering and circling areas of interest. Inspector Francis had six men out rummaging through everything. It was remarkable how quickly the house had felt taken over. They'd begun indoors before moving into the gardens, ransacking the living room first, then the library, billiards room, gun room, and dining room. Two more were searching upstairs now, having already covered the staff quarters. The whole process had felt even more unpleasant than Greta had thought it would. The Persian rugs were dirtied, the silk sofas rumpled, even the plants had been lifted from their pots to check for heaven knows what and the soil scattered across the floor. No wonder Beecham looked so unwell.

"It's awfully hard to get one's head around," Nick said quietly. "The idea that there really could have been some, well... foul play." He glanced up at her. "*You* seem to have digested it."

She knew what Nick meant; she'd been so consumed by the puzzle of it all, so focused on the inspector's *anomalies*, she had almost blocked out the awfulness of it: the fact that if this *was* murder, then a person—a real, breathing person—had done it. And as Jordan had pointed out, that person could be no stranger to them.

"I suppose"—she turned her eyes toward Nick—"I didn't really *believe* it was... you know..."

"Murder," Nick supplied. They both paused, hearing the word aloud.

"Murder," she acknowledged, "until today. But I think there was a feeling, you know. A sort of awful, dread feeling." She thought about it some more. "If I'm honest, Nick, I think it's almost a relief. To have it said and out in the open instead of seeping through my dreams."

His gray eyes were troubled. "But if there *is* a murder, Greta, there's a murderer. In which case, isn't having things out in the open the most dangerous place for them to be?"

She looked at his drawn, handsome face, and felt a shiver go through her. Fear, perhaps, at what he'd just adverted to—or something else entirely. She flushed, and moved her eyes away.

The barbiturates made more sense now than they had before, of course. It was how a killer could have got so close to a bear of a man like Tom— someone who would have been able to overpower most anyone with or without a gun. But with Tom drugged, they'd have been able to shoot him at close enough range to make it seem a by-the-book suicide. They wouldn't have thought they'd be risking a forensic report, not when the cause of death looked so clear.

But there was so much else that Greta couldn't find answers for. If there *was* an assignation arranged on the boat, how had it been planned? And when; by whom? *Did* it have something to do with Molly's man in the bushes?

And the gun—who had brought it to the boat, the killer? Or was it Tom himself; had he already been suspicious of the person he'd gone to meet?

Greta looked back out the window to where Edgar and the inspector stood under a large tree, deep in conversation. Edgar's gestures as he spoke were sharp and exacting, as though he were giving orders, and perhaps he was. Inspector Francis might look down on blow-ins like Jay, but he struck Greta as the type with a high regard for figures of the "establishment"—people like Tom and Edgar, whose grandfather in his day had held the status they held now. The inspector would consent to the Buchanans being placed above him; it was men like Jay who made the *sir* stick in his throat. He thought they'd cheated him, that "upstarts" like the Gatsbys had somehow jumped the line.

She supposed it was human instinct to want to identify one's enemy. But what a poor job we made of it.

She looked back out at Edgar under the tree: cold, hard Edgar Buchanan, who'd had such bad blood with Tom, who'd driven off in a fury that night. Whom she'd caught on the stairs when he was supposed to be outside; he'd given her some feeble excuse, but what had he been up to, really? And Edgar was the only one, Greta remembered, not at the dining table when Molly had had that sighting from the kitchen window.

Anyone, Greta supposed, could be a murderer, given the right circumstances. Given the right motivation and enough desperation. She glanced back out at Edgar. He was gesturing now to the inspector, his movements clipped and certain. The inspector was a big man, a head taller than Edgar; it was like watching a sheepdog in thrall to a whippet.

She could feel Nick breathing quietly beside her, closer than she had realized. It occurred to her that this was exactly where they had stood the night of her homecoming. He'd asked her to dance in just this spot.

"What about your work?" she said eventually. "Are you even allowed to go back to Manhattan?" She swallowed. She supposed they were all of them suspects now after these most recent developments. But perhaps she rather *wanted* Nick gone from the house after last night. She couldn't tell quite what she felt; she had been at ease with him before, but no longer.

"I don't think leaving is possible right now, Greta." He looked at her. "The thing is, if you're right about all this stuff—*if* you are—well, I can't just go off and leave you here, can I? If you're not . . ." He swallowed. "Not safe."

Oh, Nick.

But whatever that look had stirred she pushed away. It was not useful now.

"Jay will be here," she pointed out instead.

"Yes." Nick frowned. "And his safety, too, is my concern. I shall put Jordan on the train this afternoon if she wants—but I shall stay."

Greta looked at him soberly. "For all you know, *we're* the ones who aren't safe for *you* to be around."

He gave her a wry smile. "That's exactly what Jordan said."

A flurry of activity outside the window made them both look. The inspector seemed to have been called over by one of his men, and was in conversation with him for some time. Nick pushed up the window sash.

"Inspector!" he called. "Did you find something?"

The inspector looked toward the house as though he had forgotten anyone were there.

"Nothing to concern yourself with, Mr. Carraway," he said breezily. "Nothing of your concern at all."

The inspector's men stayed until the light started to fade, at which point the inspector came inside to take his leave. He seemed to have the bit between his teeth now, determined to be thorough. After searching through all the house trash, the officers were now loading up one of the police cars with the garden waste left out for composting, which they would sort through back at the station.

"I don't envy them *that*." Jordan eyed the bagged-up compost.

"Inspector." Greta remembered something she had meant to mention. It seemed unlikely the two things were connected, but all the same...

"One of our housemaids," she said. "Ada Prescott, the one who told you about seeing the light in the boat—she left the house yesterday on her bicycle and hasn't come back yet. No note was left. The staff seem to think she just got spooked and ran off. But I wondered if we ought to file a report for a missing person."

Daisy, silent in the corner until now, sat up straighter.

"*I'll* give you a reason why a maid disappears without notice. Theft, Inspector—a missing set of pearls, to be precise."

The inspector frowned.

"Have you wired her family to check if she's come home?"

Greta flushed.

"Well, no."

"Then I suggest you do so before allocating police time on some scullery girl," he said.

"We trust you'll exert your impeccable judgment, Inspector," Edgar said smoothly. He stood with Daisy on one side of the room, as though guarding her from the rest of them. "Meanwhile, I think we may take our leave."

Greta walked him out to the hall where he looked irritably for Beecham.

"Where's that man of yours? We need our coats."

But Greta saw how his eyes lingered on something else: the silver salver on the console where the letters for tomorrow's post lay. Edgar's jaw tightened and he looked away, but not before sparking Greta's intuition.

"You knew about the letter, didn't you?" she said. "You knew Tom was planning to write to your mother that night asking her for money."

Edgar glowered at her.

"That was what you were talking about out in the garden that night," Greta said slowly.

You may think you can cheat me, but you shan't.

He hadn't wanted Tom to ask their mother for money—to "cheat" Edgar, as he saw it, of his inheritance. She remembered Rosemary Buchanan's letter complaining about Edgar's fixation on those little jade heirlooms. The obsession that had seemed so petty made a different kind of sense now. He *knew* Tom was in money trouble; probably the snuffboxes had been sold or pawned the next day. He *knew*.

"Everything he 'borrowed' from your mother you knew she wasn't getting back. Which meant, all the while, the inheritance you could look forward to from her was shrinking."

Edgar folded his arms. They were alone in the hallway; Jay had gone off in search of Beecham.

"Pretty manners, haven't you, Miss Gatsby? Listening at doors."

"Pretty manners *you* have," she rejoined. "Snooping about our house. I saw you standing on the stairs that night. You'd been upstairs, hadn't you?"

Edgar folded his arms, looking at her with intense distaste. She watched his Adam's apple bob and settle.

"I didn't know," he said sharply, "whether to believe my brother about the letter; I thought perhaps he was just goading me. I came back inside with half a mind to go up to his room and search for it. But," he said pointedly, "I thought better of it. I never went upstairs that night."

Greta stared at him. He had lied about the letter already. What was to say he was telling the truth now? She thought about his mother's letter again and the "temper tantrums" she'd referred to. What kind of thing was this man capable of when he didn't get his way?

"Daisy!" Edgar called loudly over Greta's shoulder. "Come on, we must be going."

Daisy appeared in the doorway flanked by Jordan and Nick, and then the inspector. *Accuse me*, Edgar's eyes seemed to challenge Greta. *Accuse me of something, I dare you.* She wouldn't—but she'd certainly tell the others what she'd learned later.

Stiff goodbyes were said. The inspector doffed his hat in what Greta couldn't help but feel was a sneering sort of way, and when the front door closed behind them, she felt a brief jolt of relief.

Even Jordan had little appetite at dinner that night.

"Murder investigations aren't half so much fun as I thought they'd be," she said, pushing the duck confit morosely around her plate.

Jay still felt too ill to eat, and had retired to his room, so it was just the three of them. Greta had spoken to Beecham before they sat down about wiring Ada's people in New Hampshire. Perhaps Daisy was right about the pearls—Ada *had* seemed anxious about a police investigation, hadn't she? Greta almost hoped it was the reason she'd run off. It seemed better than any of the other reasons for a young woman to disappear.

"Edgar's rather taken to the whole thing, though, hasn't he?" Nick said.

So he, too, had noticed it—how suddenly Tom's brother seemed to be in command of everything, as though the inspector were working for him personally.

"He knew about the letter," she said, and proceeded to fill Nick and Jordan in on the brief exchange in the hall. Nick, she thought, looked particularly startled.

"Who's to say he didn't go upstairs, and find the letter?" she went on. "The draft was probably lying out there in his room—the draft that someone used as a suicide note."

"You think *he* . . ." Nick looked incredulous. "His own *brother*?"

Greta shrugged. They'd all seen Edgar leave, it was true. But what was to keep him from having parked his car a little way down the road, and come back on foot? It seemed risky, but perhaps it had been worth the risk to him. And what better cover than a house party where he alone was *not* one of the overnight guests?

Jordan stopped poking a duck leg and looked up.

"The letter, though. The *real* letter, the one I saw on the salver the next morning. It disappeared around ten in the morning. Edgar couldn't have stolen it; he wasn't here."

Greta frowned. It was true.

But was it possible Edgar hadn't been working alone?

Perhaps she was letting her imagination run too wild after all.

"Jord, if you're not going to eat that duck, I do wish you'd stop mauling it," Nick commented.

Jordan sighed, and put down her fork.

"Sorry, Nicky. Murder, you know. It does rather dull the appetite."

It was only after dinner that Greta noticed the letter for her on the salver. When she saw it was from Nora, she opened it quickly.

It is quite shocking, Nora had written in her cramped but neat hand, *to read your words. Regarding Mr. Buchanan, I cannot recall anything out of the ordinary—he was his usual rather lecherous self, nothing more. As to the supposed anonymous letter, I haven't a notion, but I wouldn't put it past the old biddy to be lying about it.*

She wrote that Silas's job at the garage was going well and that she herself had started selling some of her embroidery to a few nearby stores.

It will do for now, I suppose, and I intend to keep it going for as long as I can. I reckon it's better than signing over one's waking hours to work in service. (No offense intended.)

Greta pocketed the letter. She was glad at least that Nora had written back, but she had been hoping for a clue—for a little remembered something that would suddenly take on a new significance. But there had been nothing at all.

Greta tossed and turned for many hours in bed that night. The grandfather clock chimed, and she sighed and rolled over, counting the minutes until at last she fell into a dreamless sleep. After that, it seemed as though very little time passed before she woke to the sound of Molly's voice as she burst into Greta's bedroom in a remarkably animated manner.

"Oh, Miss Gatsby!" She panted. "You'd best come downstairs right away!"

Chapter Twenty-Six

Inspector Francis stood in the middle of the hallway with an officer flanking him on either side. The tremendous chandelier seemed to shiver above him as if from some disturbance. Beecham was in the hall, too, with Molly, who'd flown back downstairs having delivered her message; Jordan, in her morning robe, was just emerging from the library.

"Ah. Miss Gatsby. May I inquire," the inspector said crisply, "as to the whereabouts of your brother?"

Her heart began to beat faster. Why so much spectacle? Why these other two?

"He's recovering from rather a bad migraine." Nick appeared on the landing and walked toward them. "I can certainly go and have a word with him."

"That won't be necessary, Mr. Carraway." The inspector nodded to his men, and wordlessly, they left his side and began to climb the stairs.

"Inspector!" The words flew from Greta's chest. "What is the meaning of this?"

He looked from her to Nick, and she saw a kind of grim pleasure in his eyes. His subordinates had rounded the corner of the landing now and were out of sight, but she could hear the tramp of their boots.

"Your brother is advised, Miss Gatsby, to come and spend some time at the station. For questioning."

"But whatever *for*?" Nick demanded. "You can perfectly well ask him your questions here."

"We'd prefer"—the inspector drew himself up to his full height—"to do so at the station."

This man had never liked them, Greta saw, not one bit. He had suffered himself to behave courteously to them while he had to, that was all. Now he no longer felt the need—and *that*, she thought, was worrying.

"But you can't just—just drag him away," she said. "He didn't *do* anything."

"Quite right," Jordan piped up. "*I* should make a better suspect, frankly. Why not take me down to the station, Inspector? Jay's no use to you; he's incorrigibly pure of heart."

Inspector Francis gave her a withering look as Jay appeared at the top of the stairs, a navy-clad officer on either side. He was still in his silk pajamas and robe; the morning light shone full on his face, causing him to squint a little even as it lit up his golden hair. Greta's heart constricted. He knew full well what was happening, and in the circumstances, she thought he looked far too composed. His face was still, like a martyr going to meet his fate. He wasn't going to fight this at all.

Greta heard the hiss of Beecham's breath behind her.

"Inspector," Jay said from the top of the stairs. "My presence seems to be of particular interest to you."

The inspector grimaced.

"I trust my men have made it clear to you how much we'd"—he paused—"*appreciate* a conversation with you down at the station."

This couldn't be happening.

"Inspector." Nick was pale, his voice unsteady with anger. "Your manner would suggest that my friend is not being asked but rather compelled to accompany you. Are you suggesting that Mr. Gatsby is under arrest? You have no authority here without a warrant."

Inspector Francis looked annoyed.

"We hope it won't come to that. Those who have nothing to hide have nothing to fear, and Mr. Gatsby would be well-advised to cooperate." He cleared his throat. "An assessment of new evidence has brought questions to light, which we feel Mr. Gatsby may be well placed to answer."

"Damn it all, man, *what* new evidence?"

Nick was losing his cool now, and Greta silently urged him not to add fuel to the flames. Nick was not a pompous man, but he was still a man, and one protected by a certain status all his life. Of course it did not occur to him that someone like him or Jay could *really* be arrested. When you had the kind of social standing Jay had, the police were there to do your bidding, not to come for you like a dog with bared teeth.

But status was fickle. Power shifted.

"Among other things, this." The inspector produced something from his breast pocket. A mess of tissuey fragments that had been carefully glued back together like a jigsaw. It was stained and faintly malodorous; clearly it had been reconstructed from pieces carried off in yesterday's kitchen trash. So they *had* found it. For a moment, Greta was impressed. She had not thought they would be so thorough nor so successful.

"As you see," the inspector said, without giving them the chance to see anything at all, "it is a letter from the deceased Mr. Buchanan asking his mother for the loan of some one million dollars." He let his eyes drift over the group, enjoying their full attention. *One million.* The sum, indeed, was startling. "The first few lines are a perfect match for the note found with the body. So there can be now no question. We were duped—and by someone who knew the deceased intimately, and had every opportunity and motive to wish him ill."

Greta's heart quickened.

"In addition," the inspector continued, "we found this." He nodded to one of his goons, who opened a bag and drew out a cylindrical object, something like a tall metal pepper pot.

"What *is* that?" Jordan wrinkled her nose.

"That, Miss Baker, is a suppressor. Used to dampen the noise of the fatal shot the night Mr. Buchanan was killed. It was found by one of my men combing the shore yesterday, some hundred yards north of here—washed back up by the tides. The killer seems to have imagined they would get rid of it by throwing it overboard."

So that was why no one had woken. Not even Ada and Molly, staring out the window as the lamp was overturned, had heard a shot. Greta pulled her gaze from the sinister object.

"But it could have been anyone," she said, glaring at the man's obtuse, smug face. "You can't drag off my brother, Inspector, without due cause!"

He glared back at her.

"Well, Miss Gatsby, if the fact that Mr. Buchanan was murdered with your brother's gun counted for nothing," he began, "*and* the fact that the gun was kept in a room to which he held the keys, *and* the fact that your brother was the only one who had a stash of barbiturates in his possession... then what inference would you expect us to draw from the fact that he declared his love to the deceased's widow only days ago, demanding her hand in marriage and reiterating that"—he made a show of consulting his notes—"he would do *anything to marry her?*"

Greta felt her blood boil.

Daisy! That treacherous little—

"Inspector!" Nick looked aghast. "What you're saying is simply—"

"That was a private matter," Jay said. His voice was quiet now but steady. "Do you understand, Inspector? Whatever was said between Daisy and myself on that subject—that was *private*."

"Well, clearly it wasn't," Greta snapped. "Since Daisy's doing her best to incriminate you." She turned. "Inspector, I hope it's as clear to you as it is to me that a person in Daisy's position might have ulterior motives for throwing around allegations like this."

"Greta!" Jay said in warning tones. "You're not to accuse Daisy of anything, do you hear?"

The inspector's cheeks meanwhile had turned an angry pink.

"*You* are the one making assumptions, Miss Gatsby," he barked. "I never suggested I had heard this from Mrs. Buchanan. It was reported to me from a different source."

Greta saw the relief on Jay's face. *Oh, Jay!* Even now, it was as though Daisy's good opinion was all that mattered. Was he blind to what was happening to him? Did he not see that this man meant him ill? She remembered how, when Jay was a boy, he'd seemed strangely unable to detect the overtures of bullying, mistaking them for a friendlier sort of outreach. Greta had a memory of their mother, chagrined, mending patches on a shirt torn in yet another street fight. *Can't you see what they're like, Jimmy? Can't you tell good friends from bad?* Greta felt a quiver of foreboding go through her.

"Now, Mr. Gatsby." Inspector Francis looked toward Jay. "Are you ready to come with us? I see my men"—he glanced at one of the hulking figures to Jay's right—"have procured a spare set of clothing for you; I suggest we delay things no longer."

"This is absurd!" Nick exploded, as Jay said, "Very well, Inspector."

Nick wheeled on him.

"Jay, are you really going to just let them lead you away?"

Jay looked soberly at him, then at Greta.

"I don't see that I have a lot of options, old sport. I'm sorry about all this, Gigi—hold the fort while I'm gone, won't you?"

The inspector looked satisfied.

"At least someone here is seeing reason."

"Inspector Francis, sir." Beecham, who had quietly joined them again, cleared his throat. He looked as ill as Greta felt.

"Allow me at least to collect some of Mr. Gatsby's things—his wash bag . . . we must ensure his comfort while in your care."

"No need, my good man," the inspector said without turning his head. "Mr. Gatsby will have access to everything he needs. And if he is cooperative, as no doubt he will be"—he gave Jay a look—"he will not be with us very long at all. Isn't that right, Mr. Gatsby?"

"I shall be all right, Beecham," Jay said. "No need for anyone to worry."

"I still say it's all hogwash," Jordan said.

"You said he's not under arrest," Greta insisted. "So he can decide to leave the station if he wants?"

The inspector hesitated.

"For now, I am classing your brother's participation as voluntary." He looked at Jay. "Which I can assure you is in everybody's interest. For the rest . . . well, we must see how the case progresses."

The two junior officers began to escort Jay across the hall.

"If he's not under arrest, there's no reason he can't be accompanied, is there?" Greta stepped forward, and the inspector's eyes narrowed.

"Our vehicle is at capacity, Miss Gatsby. And if you'll forgive my saying so, I fear you would be a quite . . . *disruptive* presence at the station."

Jordan looked at Greta appraisingly. "Disruptive, indeed?"

"Well, he's damn well entitled to a lawyer," Nick retorted, "whether you let us into your little inquisition room or not. And you can be sure he'll be getting one."

The inspector flicked his eyes toward Jay and then back.

"If Mr. Gatsby feels his conduct necessitates a lawyer's involvement, he is, of course, entitled to procure one."

"Don't twist my words, damn you," said Nick, but the inspector merely flashed him a cold look as he moved toward the door. He swung it wide, then looked over his shoulder.

"Mr. Gatsby." He doffed his hat. "After you."

Chapter Twenty-Seven

Greta watched the small figures walk out to the car and the glossy black vehicle pull away.

I've failed him, she thought as she watched it dwindle. Jay had been her guardian, but they were supposed to be each other's—the only family either had left. And while Jay had seen far more of the world and knew many things she didn't, Greta feared he suffered from a certain myopia, a naivete even, of his own—he never seemed to quite believe that people could truly wish him harm, that a person he trusted might turn on him and hurt him. Despite having fought in a war, despite all he'd seen, somehow her brother did not really seem to believe in true evil or malice. This insistent belief of his in the good intentions of others! Perhaps it was not naivete, exactly. It was simply what he chose to believe even when it was exhausting, even when it meant swimming against the current to do so.

"I can't believe this." Nick sank into a chair, shaking his head. "How could such a thing happen—to *Jay?*"

It wasn't only that Nick believed Jay's innocence, Greta realized. Nor was it injustice alone that distressed him. It was the shock, the profound sense of affront—that *men like them* could get in trouble in any serious way.

It wasn't just the men, of course. It was all of them in their wealthy, self-satisfied little world—but it was the men most of all.

Meanwhile, the police had swung like a weather vane since yesterday.

And if the police were a weathervane, Rosemary Buchanan was surely the wind.

She ought to have seen it in the hush-hush way Edgar had cozied up with the inspector to talk beneath the trees. The officers had obviously found the silencer at some point in the afternoon and said nothing about it to the Gatsbys. Had Jay been the suspect even then? She ought to have been on her guard sooner.

Greta sank into a chair opposite Nick. The inspector had said that if everything got "resolved," Jay could be home with them in a few hours. And yet, she felt quite certain he would not be. The phrase had been too blithely delivered.

"It's all just circumstantial," she said aloud. "They'd need more evidence or a confession to keep him there."

Nick nodded.

"And he won't confess. That is, I mean . . . he can't, because he didn't do it." His voice was resolute, but did he sound just a little too determined?

"Of *course* he didn't do it, Nick!"

"Well, whether he did or not"—Jordan looked up from her seat at the window, where she sat examining her nails—"you want him home, don't you? Better get a good lawyer on it right away if you ask me."

Nick said he knew a man, and went out to give him a call. When he came back, he had his hat in hand.

"I'm going down to the station. Our inspector mayn't want to feel us breathing down his neck, but feel it he shall."

Minutes later, Greta watched the yellow Phantom putter down the driveway, then turned and rang the bell for Beecham.

"Thank you, everybody." Greta scanned the faces of the assembled staff and the different emotions written there: bewilderment, mistrust, concern. They would all know of Jay's ignominious exit by now, no doubt.

Be of use, Greta reminded herself somewhat sternly. The sternness was useful—it kept her from trembling, and someone needed to steer this ship. As their eyes met hers, Greta realized that ever since Jay had acquired this household of staff, these people had been taking care of her. Now, it seemed, it was her job to take care of them.

She cleared her throat.

"I'm afraid I'm behindhand in acknowledging your fortitude over these past days. It's been a grueling time, and you've all pulled through with tremendous presence of mind. My brother and I have been very grateful. I'm only sorry he's not here at the moment to say as much himself." She took a steadying breath.

"On which note, I need to make you all aware of what has just happened, though I expect you've heard or seen some version of it already. Police Inspector Francis has just been here at the house and removed Jay to the station for questioning. He has somehow been put under the horrifically incorrect impression that my brother bears some sort of responsibility for the death of Mr. Buchanan."

There was a rustling and a faint, unpleasant murmuring, as if a foul breeze moved through the room. Beecham and Molly had seen the whole thing themselves, of course; Dantry was tighter-lipped than Greta had yet seen her, and Mrs. Smith looked downright mutinous. Only Bill Richardson, summoned from the privacy of the garage apartment, looked untroubled by the news. Surely he hadn't been *expecting* this?

"This idea, needless to say, is wholly incorrect." Greta exerted herself to keep her voice firm. "I know the disquieting circumstances of Mr. Buchanan's death have been most upsetting for everyone here over the past week and not something any of us wish to revisit, but I implore you all now: if you have information, *any* information, that might help reverse the inspector's terrible misapprehension, I implore you to make that known to me as soon as you possibly can." She hesitated. "And please be assured that if there are any . . . aspects that might present you or another member of this household in an unflattering light, you can count on my discretion. Nothing will be revealed to the police force that is not utterly and completely necessary."

There was more murmuring. She had made her plea; the rest was in their hands. She cleared her throat once more.

"Furthermore, if in light of these events, anybody here does not wish to continue their employment at this house, they may submit their resignation to me and I will see that their wages are paid up until the end of the month and that they are furnished with excellent references." She paused. "Of course, I very much hope that you will all want to remain, but I would not wish for any of you to do so in an atmosphere of discomfort. We will always be grateful for the service you have given us. That is all. Thank you."

They filed out without a backward glance; only Beecham hung back, and asked gravely if he might have some tea brought up.

The small kindness made Greta's throat constrict. No doubt he'd seen how, despite her level voice, her hands had been shaking. She sighed.

"Thank you, Beecham. That would be most kind."

He nodded, then closed the door and left her alone with her thoughts—and Jordan's.

"That was wise of you. Getting the staff on your side. The police will be trying to get to them, too, I should think."

It was not comforting, but it was surely true. If the inspector was hellbent on making Jay his man, no doubt he'd try and winkle some incriminating words out of the rest of the household soon. Getting Jay safely home meant they'd all have to rally around him. But—as Nora or Silas might have pointed out—loyalty was a privilege, not a right. Greta hoped Jay had done enough for his staff to earn it.

Beecham would never say a word against Jay, she knew. Mrs. Dantry always had a bee in her bonnet, and there was no knowing whom it would choose to sting. Mrs. Smith was clearly in a stew and resentful about being put through such an experience. Bill Richardson's chief concern would be not to get himself in trouble. And then there was Molly, who, in a way, Greta worried most about. One had the sense she would be easy to intimidate. If the police harangued her enough, what awful thing might she start to agree she had seen or overheard?

"Do you think Edgar actually supposes Jay did it?" Jordan said then. "I mean, if it wasn't Daisy, it must have been Edgar, mustn't it—telling that odious inspector all about Jay's proposal?"

Did Edgar *really* believe Jay was their man?

Greta stared out at the empty driveway, the breeze, and the waving trees.

"I suppose so," she said. There was an alternative, of course. Perhaps all this was a piece of misdirection to serve interests of Edgar's own.

As Greta had pessimistically predicted, Jay was not home in a matter of hours. They postponed dinner until ten o'clock, at which point Fielding, the lawyer, telephoned to say that Jay would be staying overnight in the station—still "voluntarily"—but that he was quite all right and they were not to worry.

"Not to worry!" Greta exclaimed.

It was with a half-hearted attempt at preserving normality that they sat down to the dinner Molly brought up.

"Fielding says"—Nick forked the salmon rillettes glumly around his plate—"that they *can* hold Jay without charging him, perhaps even a second night if they want to. But he says it shall be all right as long as Jay keeps a clear head and doesn't say anything silly."

Say anything silly. Greta shivered.

Was it possible that . . . ?

No. Not Jay. She couldn't allow it.

And yet, Tom had been such an abominable man . . . and who knew what Daisy had said to Jay over the past weeks and months . . . if Jay had thought she *wanted* to be rid of him—

No. Greta put down her knife and fork, and under the table pushed her palms against her thighs to stop the tremor in them. She must pull herself together.

Nick shook his head. "It's a humiliation for Jay, of course, but with any luck, he'll be home in the morning."

Greta thought of her brother spending the night in a police cell. He had been used to adversity once upon a time, but he'd worked so hard to escape all that. He'd wrapped his wealth around him like a shield. She was afraid an experience like this would be quite severe on him. He had always dealt with hardship so much better than humiliation.

The table felt much too large, their little party strangely shrunken. It wasn't just Jay's absence, either. Opposite Greta was the place where Daisy used to sit, and there, the chair Tom had sat in on his last night. She shivered again. Even for the sake of Mrs. Smith's dignity, she did not think she could manage another bite tonight.

After dinner, no one seemed eager to retire to their rooms in a house that suddenly felt alien and too large. Nick poured them all a drink. Greta stared out the window at the darkness. Just yesterday she'd been bothering about Nick's collar and the lipstick. What did any of that matter now? She was glad, inordinately glad after all, that he was still here—still on hand to be the friend Jay needed at a time like this.

"Do you think Daisy knows?" Greta said. "That Jay's been carted off by the police, I mean?"

Nick's jaw set grimly.

"If she doesn't, she very soon will."

Jordan turned from where she had been walking aimlessly around the room, touching things, picking up this and that. She set down a blanc de chine figurine and folded her arms.

"I do think it's rather unfair, you know, how that dreadful inspector still thinks Jay was the only one with a sedative. I suppose Jay's keeping mum so as not to throw any sort of suspicion on Daisy, but he should probably tell the odious man everything at this point, don't you think?"

Greta blinked. "Tell him everything? What do you mean?"

Jordan's eyes widened. "You didn't know? Why, Jay lent his barbiturates to Daisy—the night before Tom died."

Chapter Twenty-Eight

"I suppose Daisy *could* have done it." Jordan squinted, considering. "I mean, I can't say I'd terribly blame her, you know. Tom was quite a rotter, really."

Greta stared. "Jordan . . . what barbiturates?"

"Jay gave some to her." Jordan perched on a chair arm, and began to swing her foot restlessly. "Daisy had been sleeping rather poorly, you see, and he suggested she borrow some of his. So she had her own little stash. I understand why she didn't tell the inspector, of course—it was all rather unnerving. Or she might have forgotten, I suppose."

"So the police don't know the half of it," Greta said slowly. "Well, it won't stay that way for long. Nick, we'll telephone your lawyer right now—and Daisy can think twice about playing my brother for a fool!"

She marched to the door and flung it open to find Beecham standing nearby, a little flushed. Had he been listening? How unlike him.

"Beecham—is everything all right?"

He inclined his head.

"I came to see if you needed anything else for the evening, Miss Gatsby, before retiring for the night."

"Thank you, we are quite well."

He left, but Greta's march to the telephone had been interrupted. Nick stood behind her, and put his hand gently on her arm.

"I don't say you're not right about this, Greta." He frowned. "But if you tell the inspector about all this—and *especially* about the affair—Daisy's reputation will be dragged through the mud, and Jay's, perhaps worse than it has been already. But if we sit tight, Fielding assured me it's a waiting game—Jay's bound to be out of there soon."

But they couldn't count on that, could they? As far as Greta was concerned, Jay was protecting Daisy and hurting himself—and that had to stop. If Daisy's reputation went down like a sinking ship, so be it.

"It's awfully late," Nick continued. "I should think the inspector's asleep in his bed by now. Why not leave it until morning? Perhaps Jay will be home by then."

She exhaled, and let her hand drop from the door.

"All right," she said. "First thing tomorrow."

Greta dreamed she was down on the jetty with Jay, gazing across the sound toward the Buchanans' house and the shimmering green light at the end of their dock. It was something they had often done of a summer evening in the past. But now in the dream, Jay reached out for the light as if he could grab it, moving blindly forward as though he could not see the water's edge. She tried to call his name but her voice was gone, her limbs immobile, and she could do nothing but watch as Jay sleepwalked forward, mesmerized, and was swallowed into darkness.

She woke up sweating, and saw it was already light—not long after dawn by the looks of it. But there was no point attempting to go back to sleep. Her mind wouldn't let her, and as soon as it was a reasonable hour, she'd ask Bill to run her down to the police station.

A thought came to her then, and she rose from bed, dug her feet into the Turkish slippers that lay waiting, and shuffled across the corridor to Daisy's room—no longer locked now. Greta made straight for the en suite bathroom, carefully opening all the cabinets in turn. It would be an awful lot better if she could *prove* Daisy had had a stash of barbiturates in there. Nothing in the bathroom. Back in the bedroom, she opened the chest of drawers and then the wardrobe.

And froze.

It was right there on the shelf: Daisy's pearl necklace. Exactly where it ought to have been, nestled comfortably in the blue-velvet box that lay wide open, inviting Greta's stare: lustrous, majestic, each pearl the size of a thumbnail, as clear as a mirror but as warm and rich as ivory. A small fortune in a blue-velvet box.

And someone had put it back.

Greta's head pounded. *Why?*

If the thief had got away with it thus far, why put it back at all? It made no sense. And how long had it been lying here, anyway?

Greta blinked down at the necklace, its soft white glow and the shimmering clasp of diamonds . . . She reached out and touched it, running a finger over the small orbs, which felt almost warm to the touch. The faintest smell of Daisy's fragrance—jasmine, spring blossoms—still lingered.

She simply didn't know what to make of this one.

Was it something to do with Ada? Beecham was to have wired her parents yesterday; Greta assumed he hadn't forgotten. Downstairs, she rang the bell and waited impatiently for him, but it was Dantry who appeared.

"Mrs. Dantry. Have we had any word from Ada's people yet?"

"Not that I'm aware, miss."

Greta frowned. "Where's Beecham?" It would usually be him who answered this bell.

"Mr. Beecham is not on the premises, it would appear," Dantry said, clearly revisiting a grievance. "His bicycle is gone; evidently, he has decided to absent himself unannounced."

That was odd. Beecham was committed to a household that ran like clockwork. Then again, he'd probably expected to be back in plenty of time before breakfast; normally, upstairs wouldn't be awake for another hour.

"Well, in that case, Mrs. Dantry, could *you* ask Bill to bring the car around? I need to go into town rather urgently."

She was putting on her gloves as the sound of footsteps came from the stairs and Nick appeared in the hall.

"I thought I heard you up and about. I couldn't sleep much, either. Are you headed for the station?"

She nodded. "There's a *real* murderer somewhere in this whole sorry business, and the inspector had better start trying to find them."

Nick looked at her squarely.

"Very well. I shall get my hat."

In the car, she told Nick about Daisy's pearls, and he was suitably startled. Greta lowered her voice then, seeing that Bill in the front was clearly intrigued, too.

"Are you really going to tell them about Jay and Daisy's affair?" Nick fixed his dark eyes on hers. "I'm not sure it'll help Jay, you know."

Greta didn't *want* to drag anyone's name through the mud, but the way things were, the police thought Jay's proposal had been the work of an obsessive who'd never received encouragement from Daisy at all—and, of course, that looked suspicious. But Daisy had been unhappy enough in her marriage to fall for someone else . . . which gave *her* a motive for wanting Tom out of the picture at least as much as it gave Jay one.

But it could make things harder for Jay, too. Knowing about the affair might lead the police to double down on him. Greta shook her head.

"The barbiturates in Daisy's room, at least. They have to hear about that."

Nick studied her face for a moment, and then put his hand over hers on the leather seat.

"Greta . . . do you really think Daisy could have had something to do with this?"

Greta looked down at his hand on hers. It was warm; she could feel it through the mesh lace of her glove.

"I don't know. But you said it yourself, Nick—Daisy's an actress. A talented actress. And someone here is giving us a very good performance."

Nick frowned, and looked away. The street corners rolled by. After a while, he turned back.

"Look . . . I know the timing may be a bit off, but all the same, I did want to ask you: When all this is over—because it *will* be over, you know, despite how it feels right now—when it's all over, might you like to go out for lunch sometime? The two of us?"

Greta's gaze, averted, had landed on the rearview mirror, and she saw Bill's eyebrows zoom upward. He'd make gossip of her quick enough—to Dantry and Molly, even Beecham. And it would be embarrassing gossip, too, when Nick dropped her for some glamorous girl-about-town. He would, wouldn't he? He might be a nice man, but he was still a man.

"I . . . I don't know, Nick."

Did her words sound as strangled as they felt? Any woman with her head on straight knew to be cautious about such things—so why did she feel like she'd just made a mistake?

Nick nodded briskly, decisively.

"I quite understand," he said, and his eyes were on the window again, and all she had to look at was the back of his head. Greta opened her mouth, closed it again.

Wasn't he even going to *try* to persuade her just a little?

It seemed not.

A young officer was smoking outside the Great Neck precinct as the Phantom pulled into the yard; he quickly threw down the butt and stamped it out.

"Can I help you, sir? Miss?"

"We have some new information for the inspector. About the Buchanan case." Greta mustered all the authority she could. "We need to speak with him urgently."

Wary now, the young officer opened the door for them.

"Stanhope," he called to another fellow at a desk. "Er . . . more visitors."

More visitors?

Sergeant Stanhope—Greta recognized the young man who'd taken the report of Daisy's missing pearls—turned from the desk inside the door. So did a coiffed, blonde figure in a navy dress.

"Daisy!" Nick exclaimed.

She stepped toward them, her eyes red-rimmed.

"I heard what happened. I couldn't believe it. Poor Jay. It's too awful!"

Greta was momentarily lost for words.

"By gad, Daisy!" Nick said, clearly not suffering from the same affliction. "Don't you realize the hand you've had in all this?"

Daisy's cheeks were pink, her eyes wide.

"I?"

"All that stuff about poor old Jay being so madly in love with you and how he'd do 'anything' for you to be together. Telling them he proposed to you. What the deuce did you go and say all that for? They've been having a field day with it."

Daisy opened and shut her mouth.

"I . . . well, I *did* mention it to Edgar, but I didn't . . . I'm sure *he* didn't mean . . ." She seemed to compose herself. "Look, it was all true, about the proposal. What was I supposed to say?" She looked down at the floor. "I *did* tell Jay I wouldn't leave Tom. I told him that many times."

Sergeant Stanhope cleared his throat.

"Er, sir? Madam . . ." His gaze bobbed between them. "If you're here about Mr. Gatsby, he'll, er, be out in a minute."

They all turned to stare.

"You mean he's . . ."

Stanhope nodded. "His presence is, er, no longer required, the inspector says. Mr. Gatsby is warmly thanked for his participation in our inquiries. A great, er, service to the community."

Nick turned and stared at Greta and Daisy.

"Of *course* he's been released." Daisy brightened, smiling gratefully at Stanhope now. "We all knew he couldn't have had a hand in this."

"The inspector asked us to try calling your residence, miss." Stanhope addressed Greta now. "A message was left, but perhaps you were already on your way here."

A tired voice came from behind them. "Hello, chaps."

"Jay!"

He looked a little unkempt after his day and night in the cell, a little pale and whiskery, but otherwise unharmed. Walking alongside him was a tidy little man with a briefcase whom Greta assumed was Fielding, the lawyer. She threw herself on Jay, and he squeezed back with a weary smile as Nick clapped him on the shoulder. Daisy, though, hung behind, for once not in the vanguard.

"Thank God they're through with this nonsensical business," Nick said. "It's an outrage, really. At least everyone seems to have finally come to their senses."

Jay's stare had strayed to Daisy. His lips tightened; he looked away, reaching a hand out to the lawyer instead.

"I'm most indebted, sir."

"Pleasure." Fielding tipped his hat. "Strange sort of a case, isn't it? One wonders where it shall all lead."

"I'm ever so glad you're out of this nasty place, Jay," Daisy said.

Jay nodded, but didn't let his eyes meet hers.

"Your necklace." Nick turned to Daisy. "It reappeared—oddest thing. Greta found it this morning in your bedroom."

Daisy turned.

"You did? How strange," she murmured, her hand touching her throat as though the necklace lay there now.

But now that the relief had had a moment to settle, Greta was thinking about the other strange thing. The police had practically fallen over themselves this morning in their haste to get Jay out of here. She hadn't had to say a word about Daisy and the barbiturates; no new evidence, so far as she knew, had come to light. So what did they know that she didn't? The inspector wanted someone's head on a plate—why would he let his favorite candidate go? And so abruptly. The more she thought about it, the surer she was. The inspector's suspicion had fallen elsewhere.

"Did he say anything about a new suspect, Jay?"

He shook his head.

"Let's just get out of here, shall we?"

Outside, the Phantom was idling. There was a pause; the four of them stood awkwardly.

Daisy hesitated.

"May I come for the necklace tomorrow?"

Jay looked away.

"Do as you please," he said finally, and Daisy swallowed, nodded, turned to go.

"I'll get that for you, sir." Bill had hopped out from the driver's seat and was opening the door when something else caught Greta's eye. There was a bicycle leaning up against the wall of the police station, and she rather thought she recognized it.

"Bill, isn't that the bicycle belonging to Mr. Beecham?"

He looked to where she was pointing.

"Might be, miss."

She turned on her heel, and all but ran back to the station.

When the question was put to him, Sergeant Stanhope looked at her helplessly.

"I'm sorry, Miss Gatsby. I can't answer that."

Greta looked around at her surroundings. She had missed it before, but now it seemed unmistakable: the tension, almost a giddiness, in the air. The men in the precinct were excited about something, and it wasn't Jay's release.

But really, what could Beecham be doing here? Had he remembered something worth reporting, and chosen to take it straight to the inspector's ears?

A faint cold shiver ran down her back. *Or what if—*

"Here, Stanhope!" Another officer ducked his head out of one of the rooms, then tossed a fountain pen toward Stanhope's desk. "This is out of ink. Get us another, will you? The mad butler's about to sign his confession."

Chapter Twenty-Nine

"You can't be *serious*."

"Look, miss—"

"You're not seriously telling me you're trying to pin this on Beecham!"

Behind her, the door swung open.

"Greta," Nick said. "Is everything all right? I think we really ought to get your brother—"

"They've got Beecham in there, Nick, and they're trying to make him confess to murder!"

Moments later, Jay was back in the station, looking at Sergeant Stanhope with the same expression of disbelief.

"This is *absurd*."

"Beg your pardon, sir, but"—Stanhope leaned across his desk, glancing over his shoulder at the empty corridor—"the chap confessed already. Every last detail. I don't see that *he'd* have made an error about it, do you? Walked in off the street first thing this morning, and made a full confession right at this desk, out of the blue."

His words stunned them into a moment's silence. It didn't make any *sense*.

"It's all another ruddy mistake," Jay said. "It must be." But the confusion was evident in his voice.

"He can't have done it," Greta said. "No matter what he's telling you." She looked to her brother. "Honestly—*Beecham?*"

"I don't know what to tell you, miss." The sergeant shrugged.

Nick cleared his throat.

"I realize that Beecham is a well-loved member of your household. But speaking plainly, I don't see that that makes him incapable of the crime. Is it really so impossible that he's telling the truth?"

"*Yes,*" Greta said, glaring at him.

"It does seem *unlikely,*" offered Jay. Nick looked between the two of them.

"Name me a likely suspect, then," he said gently. "Name me one of our number you *would* find credible." He shook his head, his eyes turning from Jay to his sister. "It's a devil of a case, Greta, just like Fielding said. I should love to think it was the work of an outsider, but it simply can't have been. Every candidate's as unlikely as the next, in my view, yet someone *must* have done it."

"Indeed, sir," Stanhope chimed in.

"What about Edgar?" Greta blurted. "I'm sure he could have done it somehow."

"Miss Gatsby," the sergeant said carefully. "Are you really suggesting that a gentleman like Mr. Edgar killed his own brother? With all due respect, I heard the butler's confession myself. I agree he seems a mild-mannered sort of man, not the type one would imagine, but it takes all sorts, miss."

"You'd better call Fielding back, Jay," Greta said. "I should think Beecham needs him more than you ever did."

B ack at the house, Jordan crowed to see Jay back safely, but once they broke the news of Beecham, it displaced every other thought.

"No!" she exclaimed, agog. "No, but *really*? Mr. Pomp and Circumstance? He *confessed*?"

"I don't think he did it," Greta said firmly. "And nor does Jay."

Jordan looked shrewdly at Nick.

"But *you* do."

"I didn't say that," Nick said hesitantly. "But I don't know why a man would confess to a crime he didn't commit."

Greta turned to glare at him.

"Honestly! Have you no loyalty at all?"

Nick stared at her, and Greta took an unpleasant sort of satisfaction in it.

"Look, I like the old fellow myself. I'm just being *rational*."

"Yes, you never know," Jordan chimed in. "People can become madmen overnight, you know. An imbalance in the brain. They're perfectly normal one day and then the next . . ."

"Whoever did this"—Greta spoke quietly; she had gained control of herself once more—"was no madman. Not *unhinged* anyway. Tom's death was carefully planned. The victim wasn't random, and it wasn't an act of impulse."

For a moment, no one spoke.

"Well, and what about the pearls?" Jay said finally.

Jordan still hadn't heard of the discovery, and Greta quickly briefed them all and took them upstairs to see. The pearls were right where Greta had left them, as luminous and beautiful as ever. Jay took the string in his hands, and stared. Draped between his fingers, they seemed to glow with some inner light. One could almost hear the sound of the sea they had come from, the siren song that lured unsuspecting men.

"Well, I had better keep these under lock and key for now, I suppose." Jay sighed. "And I had better go downstairs and tell the staff about Beecham."

The kitchen still smelled of breakfast, and the air was hot and damp. Greta felt her blouse sticking to her back. When Jay broke the bad news, a ripple of shock went through the air, and at first, there was only silence.

"Mr. Beecham!" Molly's hands were trembling. "Surely not. Oh heavens. Mr. *Beecham?*"

"I don't believe it," Mrs. Smith said staunchly.

Dantry was silent, as was Bill Richardson. With his keen ears, Greta thought, he'd most likely picked up on the news already on the drive home. But if he had, he'd kept it to himself, judging by the looks on everyone else's faces.

"I don't think we can believe it, either, Mrs. Smith," Greta said. "Though nor can I think what would provoke him into a false confession. Jay has engaged a lawyer to assist him; I hope that in due course the police will admit us to speak with him ourselves."

The words seemed to offer little consolation.

"And is he to be convicted, then?" Molly asked finally.

"We hope not," Jay said.

Mrs. Smith dropped heavily into a kitchen chair.

"Convicted . . . but it's unthinkable, just unthinkable . . ." She looked up. "He wouldn't do such a thing! He has a soft heart underneath all those buttoned-up airs." She shook her head. "He was ever so anxious about Ada, you know."

Greta caught Jay's frown.

"Ada's still missing," she explained—another state of affairs that was becoming more worrisome by the day.

Mrs. Smith sniffed. "Yes, and poor Mr. Beecham was very fretful. Wasn't he, Molly? He quizzed us no end on when we'd last seen her, and were we sure, and had she said anything before she left."

Greta saw Molly's quick glance. What Mrs. Smith was choosing to interpret as concern could very well be seen differently. To the police, it could certainly sound like a man with a guilty secret. But the idea of Beecham hurting Ada...

Jay sighed.

"I would encourage you all to take the rest of today and tomorrow off," he said. "We all need a rest, I think, after news such as this."

When Fielding called sometime later, it was not good news. Beecham had already confessed, and signed his statement, too. He'd turned Fielding away, telling him he had no need of a lawyer or desire to meet one. He'd been entered into remand now, and unless his confession was somehow found to be false, Fielding explained, due to his uncontested guilt, he would be sentenced without trial.

Greta's stomach sank. It seemed too grim to countenance. And yet Nick's point returned: Why would Beecham confess unless it was true?

"But *why*?" she said again, as Jay stood there with the telephone receiver still in his hand, the call finished. "What motive could he possibly have had to kill Tom?"

Jay shook his head, eyeing the receiver as though it might hold some remaining clue.

"Apparently, he's saying it wasn't premeditated. He saw a light on the boat, and went out thinking it might be some intruder. Found Tom out there, belligerent and drunk, and when he tried to get him to go indoors, there was a scuffle. Tom had the gun with him and it went off."

Greta shook her head.

"And the note written in Tom's hand?"

"Fell out of Tom's pocket."

Greta scoffed. "And I suppose the barbiturates somehow fell into Tom's mouth, too."

Jay sighed.

"It seems the inspector's rowing back on their importance."

Climbing the stairs back to her room, Greta mulled it over. Beecham was lying. But why?

She had reached the landing now, where Jordan's bedroom door stood wide open. Greta paused. Despite her distraction, something inside the room had caught her eye: a faint black staining on the carpet around the fireplace. Or perhaps not staining, exactly—just the dark and slightly shimmering residue of coal dust imperfectly swept up.

Which was particularly odd, given that it was a hot June and no fires had been lit in months.

Greta had a flash of a long-ago childhood in a small house in North Dakota; of watching round-eyed as her father took down a dirty handkerchief-wrapped brick from inside the fireplace, and unwrapped it slowly to reveal a glistening gold bar. Her parents had inherited from their own parents certain fears, certain ways of mitigating them. It had been second nature to them to hide what small wealth they had, and that chimney had been their treasure vault.

"All right there, Greta?"

Greta started as Jordan came to the door.

"The pearls," Greta said slowly. "It was you, wasn't it?"

Chapter Thirty

She waited to see whether Jordan would deny the whole thing.

The other woman sighed, eyeing Greta sidelong.

"I suppose," she said, "you're not going to give me any credit for returning them?"

Was that—could it be—a hint of *amusement*? There really wasn't much, Greta reflected, that could shame Jordan Baker.

"But why'd you do it in the first place?"

"Oh, I don't know—silly impulse. I was heaven knows how many martinis in, and I wasn't thinking, just feeling rather snippy and spiteful."

Jordan's mouth twisted to the side in a tired, ironic way.

"Daisy was being insufferable that night. You remember, Tom had said those nasty things to her downstairs, and I suppose she'd felt rather humiliated although, of course, she didn't want to let it show in front of all of you. Instead, *I* sat in her room while she stamped around in a fury, then lashed out at me instead."

"You were angry with her, you mean?"

Jordan nodded. "She can be a bit of a shrew when she's upset like that. It's only because she was feeling so wounded, of course, and spoiling for a quarrel. And usually, I give as good as I get, you know. Normally, we'd go back and forth for a few rounds until it was out of our systems and we were ready to laugh about it."

"But not this time?" Greta said, privately thinking that a friendship like Jordan and Daisy's sounded more turbulent than most marriages.

Jordan sighed. "Not this time. That night it just got under my skin so. I don't know what to tell you, really. It was an evil night, perhaps; there was something unhealthy in the air." She shrugged. "I waited until she was in the bathroom, and I opened the box where she'd just put them." She flashed a look at Greta. "I stashed them in my girdle."

Greta stared. Even now, Jordan looked only mildly repentant.

"I mean, I didn't have any plan about what to do with them. I just dropped them on the floor of my room and went to sleep on martinis and spite." She paused. "In the morning, I felt a bit of an idiot. I hid them under some clothes so the maids wouldn't see, and thought I'd sneak them back into Daisy's room later." Jordan grimaced. "And then, of course, we found Tom. The pearls just went clean out of my head after that—until Daisy noticed they were missing and there was such a hullaballoo. And *then* I didn't know how to put them back. I knew I ought to, but I didn't have time before the funeral, and then she started keeping that bloody door locked. Besides, she was playing the role of grieving widow so intently, she barely left her room."

Greta shook her head. "But you let Ada and Molly take the rap for it."

Jordan grimaced.

"Yes, well, there was nothing I could do right then. I *would* have tried to put them back if I'd had the chance. I couldn't think what else to do with them that wasn't likely to incriminate *someone*. So I thought I'd just stash them away and wait it out. When that maid of yours did a runner, it seemed an ideal time to return them. She was gone, after all, and if everyone assumed it was her, we could put the whole silly business to bed." She sighed again. "Well, turn me in to Daisy if you want to, Greta—I daresay she's known me to do worse."

A little more repentance would certainly have been becoming, Greta thought. But she didn't feel compelled to tell Daisy about this, nor Jay and Nick—not unless it became necessary. Jordan was right in a way: a string of pearls, no matter how prized, mattered little in light of all the rest that had happened. *And might yet happen*, a small voice inside said.

"They were Tom's wedding gift," Jordan said. "Did she ever tell you that?" She sighed. "I sometimes think that wedding day was the last happy day of Daisy's life. She was so thrilled to put them around her neck, you know—but it seems to me they've been strangling her ever since."

She shook herself.

"Do you know, Greta, I think this past week has been making me terribly morbid. I wonder if anything shall ever feel the way it used to again."

Greta had wondered that, too.

"Jay?" Greta tapped on the door, and received a tired "come in."

She had supposed he would be in bed after such a sleepless night, but instead, she found Jay sitting in the window seat, his eyes fixed on the view over the bay—or perhaps, she realized, to the house beyond it, Daisy's house, just about visible in the distance.

"Were they awful to you in there?"

He turned.

"When we were at the front, you know, we'd often talk about what it would be like to get captured by the Boche—what an interrogation would be like." He gave her a wry smile. "I'm glad to say, last night is as close as I came."

Greta looked at him.

"Did you tell them about Daisy's barbiturates?"

His face turned pale.

"How did you hear about that?"

"Jordan told me." Greta searched her brother's eyes. "Jay... you can't put yourself in harm's way for her. Especially considering she—"

"I can," he said curtly. "And I must."

Greta felt a coolness against her skin.

"Do you mean because... because you think she had something to do with it?"

He looked away.

"I mean, Gigi, because I told Daisy long ago I'd always take care of her. I would never do anything to hurt her. If I could have sheltered her from all of this, I would have. If I could have sheltered *you* from this, I would have."

Greta shook her head.

"But I don't need sheltering."

"It's my job, and evidently you *do* need it—playing the detective, combing the *Marguerite* for God knows what, talking to God knows whom; this *acquaintance* of Tom's you say you met. Don't you realize, Gigi? If there is a killer, you can't be running your mouth to every Tom, Dick, and Harry. You think this is a game? That you're still in school, and someone is going to give you top marks and a diploma every time you sniff out some little clue? It doesn't work like that. You know nothing of the world, Greta, and you can't go around playing with fire."

"So what, I should do nothing? After what happened to you? After what's happening to Beecham?" She glared at him. "I'm not a fool, Jay, nor a child, and I'd be terribly glad if you'd stop treating me like one."

"When you were a child, you looked up to me. You *believed* in me; you trusted what I said."

"And I believe in you still. But would you have the blind loyalty of a spaniel?"

Jay shook his head. "Innocence is precious—you should not be so willing to lose it, Greta. This world has a way of tainting people."

Who was he talking about—Daisy? Himself? His words unnerved her, and in the end, they failed. No one else's lost innocence could be recovered by preserving hers. No such exchange existed, but how very like Jay to think it did.

"You trifle with your own safety because you don't understand how much there is to lose." Jay turned, looking out the window again. "Do you know what it was like for me at the front? Watching other men take a bullet whenever they made a mistake and put their heads above the trench? Knowing that if you don't make it home, your little sister will have no one left in the world? Knowing that she'll never see her parents again, that she'll never have that because of you?"

Greta stared.

"What do you mean by that?"

He turned and looked at her, his eyes red rimmed.

"Jay, what are you talking about? They didn't die because of you."

He squeezed his hands into fists, and released them.

"I was supposed to be at the store that day." His voice was quiet, lost in the past. "Daddy was starting to train me up in those days, don't you remember? Wanted me to take over from Momma; her back had started giving her too much trouble. But the army was recruiting in town that day, and I cycled in to sign up. They'd forbidden me to—didn't want any child of theirs in some European skirmish going back to a continent of wars and persecution, that was how they saw it. I don't think there was anything so heroic in my wanting to go off to war, either. But the uniforms were so smart, the buttons just *shone*." He gave a short, sour laugh. "It all seemed quite romantic, I suppose, being a soldier.

"If they hadn't been shorthanded that day, who knows what might have happened. Momma was napping in the back room, and Daddy's sense of smell was shot. I suppose by the time he realized there was a fire spreading and went to get Momma, it was too late."

Greta swallowed.

She had never known, never guessed. And hearing him talk about it . . . she always tried not to picture her parents' last moments, the fear. She liked to hope that the smoke inhalation and lack of oxygen had dulled things a little, dulled the panic they would otherwise have surely felt.

"Why did you never tell me any of this?" she said.

He stared as if she were stupid.

"Because I never wanted to think about it. And I never wanted you to know. You looked up to me; I was all you had left. I didn't want you to know how hollow that was. That if I'd showed up to work like I'd promised, I could have saved them, and instead, I was in town, looking to fight the Boche because of some shiny buttons."

She thought about it for a minute.

"You're right, Jay." She looked over at him. "Who knows what would have happened had you been there. You might have died in the fire, too."

He turned again toward the bay. "Maybe I was supposed to," he said, sullen.

"You're *supposed* to be here," Greta said. "Right here, right now. With me—and you know they'd both agree."

He sighed, and shrugged a little.

"Well, I wish they could be here to tell me that."

Greta went to the window, and stood behind him, staring out at the water. "I do, too," she said.

The ghosts of the past seemed to move with her as Greta went slowly downstairs, made her way to the service corridor, and knocked on the housemaids' door. A nervous voice said, "Come in."

Molly was sitting on her bed, and sat up straighter when she saw Greta.

"Miss? Is everything all right?"

What a question. Greta hardly knew whom to worry about more—Beecham, who seemed so determined to get himself locked up, or Ada, who with any luck was safely back in New Hampshire by now, but who might very well not be. It was Beecham, after all, who'd been supposed to contact her people. Had he even sent the letter?

"Molly..." Greta hesitated. "I know that what I'm asking is rather intrusive, but I wondered if I might be able to have a look through Ada's things? I don't mean to alarm you," she said hurriedly. "But I just wonder if she might have left something behind that would tell us where she went."

Molly's pale eyes found Greta's.

"You think she's in trouble, Miss Gatsby?"

"I think it's possible." Greta hesitated. "And I think it's possible there's something about Mr. Buchanan's death that she knows and no one else does."

Molly's eyes widened further, and Greta reproached herself for having said anything.

"What do you expect to find, miss?" the girl said, dubious now.

"I don't know," Greta admitted. Perhaps an address of where Ada had left for. A train timetable or a ticket receipt. Anything.

Molly nodded, but looked unconvinced. On the bedside locker that had been Ada's, a skin of dust had formed on the half-drunk water glass. How unpleasant, to share a room with this ghostly absence. She glanced over at Molly's side, at the frayed books and the family photograph in its cheap frame. It was a humbling reminder, Greta thought, of how much she didn't know about the other people who lived in this house.

"Are those your people?" she said, indicating the frame on the nightstand.

Molly nodded.

"You must miss them."

Molly's face grew stonier then, as though she were forbidding it to show emotion.

"I just want to do right by them, miss."

Greta nodded, and averted her eyes. Ada from New Hampshire; Molly from out west; Nora, who had spent those grueling weeks on a wind-tossed ship, all the way from that distant Atlantic isle. Nora, Ada, Molly—these young women traveled such distances to create a life for themselves, to support their families. It was not easy.

They, and others like them, deserved protection—from exploitation and mistreatment, from the cruelties and whims of employers. But here they were without their families, without husbands or anyone with more status to stand for them. How was such protection to be secured?

"Miss?"

Molly was frowning at her.

"Aren't you going to search her things?"

Greta flushed.

She started with Ada's nightstand, pulling out the drawer and combing through its contents. But there was no note, no bundle of hidden letters, just some hairpins, an empty cloth purse, and a stubby old pencil. On the floor of the wardrobe, there was a rather moth-eaten carpetbag and, when Greta moved it aside, something stranger.

A red hurricane lamp.

Almost certainly, it was the lamp from the boat—the missing one. The police might have come across it when they searched the rooms before, but they wouldn't have known there was anything odd about it—only Greta knew where it usually belonged, and she hadn't mentioned anything to them about the odd little disappearance.

But why on earth would Ada have it among her things?

"Molly." She paused. "Have you any idea what this is doing here?"

Molly craned her neck to see, then made a face.

"Not the faintest, miss. We have our stock of candles for the evening. What would she need one of those for?"

Greta closed the door slowly. Frowning, she moved on to the dresser. Molly had told her the top two drawers were Ada's. She felt like an intruder as she opened the first one, where Ada's underthings lay neatly folded in rows. But something had rattled—jangled—as she pulled the drawer open, and now her eye caught a metal glimmer amid the fabric. Ah, yes: it was the locket Dantry had been suspicious of back when they'd conducted that unpleasant search for Daisy's pearls. But now the locket was open.

Greta picked it up.

The right half of the locket showed a picture of a woman, clearly Ada's mother—same nose, wide-set eyes, and heart-shaped face—but it was the portrait on the left that made Greta stare. She knew that face. Even as a much younger man, the resemblance was overwhelming. The thick eyebrows, the deep hooded eyes; even in his youth, a certain cragginess of the features.

Beecham.

"Did you find something, miss?" Molly's voice came distantly from across the room.

Could it really be?

"Afraid not," Greta said, her voice thick with the lie. She was still trying to absorb what she had seen. Everyone knew Beecham as an old bachelor—there had never been any word of a family, of a divorce or tragic widowhood—and besides, Greta knew Ada's mother to be very much alive. So what did it mean that apparently—so far as the locket indicated at least—Beecham was Ada's father? Greta pushed the dresser drawer shut again, thinking fast.

It certainly wasn't coincidence that they'd both been working in the same household. Had Beecham helped Ada get the job, and joined with her in keeping her parentage a secret? Or had it been a ploy of Ada's, tracking down an absent father who had abandoned her? Greta shook her head. One thing she felt sure of, though: if it had been a secret at first, it was a secret no longer. Beecham knew perfectly well who Ada was now.

She was starting to put together a theory. Beecham's false confession:

the only way it really made sense was if he was lying to protect someone. But whom in this house would he have been willing to fall on his sword for? Until this moment, Greta wouldn't have imagined there was any such person. But a father might well lie to protect his daughter. A daughter whom he believed had done something terrible.

He thought Ada was the killer.

Things slipped into place now: how ill Beecham had looked from the very day of Tom's murder. Greta had thought it was just the burden of scandal, a violent death on his employer's grounds. But now she was sure: he'd known something from the start. Perhaps he was the one who'd told Ada to run.

The bed creaked behind her as Molly nervously shifted her weight.

Greta arranged her face before she turned around.

"Forgive me for bothering you, Molly." She forced an apologetic smile. "A bit of a wild goose chase after all."

The precinct was humming with activity; there was the clatter of a telegraph machine in the corner and the sound of men's voices talking loudly over it. Greta had been surreptitious about her departure from the house. Though part of her had been dying to share the discovery of the locket with Jay, she just didn't know what he'd make of it. *Hand it over to me,* he'd probably have said, and that would be that. She understood his anxieties better now, his need to protect her, and it pained her to think of yet another secret he'd kept from her all these years—but what he wanted from her, she could not give. He could not keep her in a bubble. He could not convince her to let sleeping dogs lie—not at a time like this.

Sergeant Stanhope was still at his desk. His face wore a faint air of excitement in keeping with the general mood in the precinct, but it ebbed a little when he saw Greta.

"Miss Gatsby," he said cautiously. "You've returned."

"Sergeant, I've been informed that Mr. Beecham's guilty plea has been entered and that he is now in remand."

"That's correct." Stanhope eyed her.

"So as a prisoner in remand," Greta continued, "he is now legally entitled to receive visits, is he not?"

The sergeant stared at her.

"Surely *you're* not wanting to visit him, miss?"

Greta raised her eyebrows.

"I thought society was rather keen on ladies undertaking charitable works, Sergeant."

"Well, but not usually with murderers."

"I should have thought their souls the most in need of salvation."

Sergeant Stanhope looked at her sidelong.

"You—you honestly want to visit him, Miss Gatsby? No joke?"

There was no wryness in Greta's tone now.

"I'm very much in earnest. I appeal to you, please—let me have just five minutes with him. After all, Sergeant"—she looked him full in the eye—"your interrogation is concluded and the guilty plea entered; I don't see that there's anything I could disrupt, do you?"

Greta had money in her bag, and it occurred to her that slipping a crisp bill to the police officer might be a way to achieve her goal. But her intuition told her that Sergeant Stanhope wasn't the type.

The young man hesitated, glanced over his shoulder, then turned back, his voice low.

"The inspector's on lunch. You'd better make it quick."

Chapter Thirty-One

The room was dim, small, and cold. Beecham's bushy eyebrows rose higher at the sight of her than she had yet seen them do. She felt a pang: even in here, in such surroundings, he managed to retain his usual dignity.

His chair made a screeching noise as he stood abruptly.

"Miss Gatsby."

"Beecham, I'm so glad to see you—although far from glad to see you *here*."

Beneath his immense composure, she detected a struggle. She was sure it galled him to be seen like this.

"Beecham," she said quietly, "whatever you've said to the officers, I don't believe you did it. And nor do the others, you know."

"That's very kind, Miss Gatsby," Beecham said stiffly. "But I must disabuse you of any illusions. I have already made the truth known to the inspector, as his men have no doubt informed you."

"Yes." Greta put her hand on the chair opposite. "May I sit?"

He inclined his head.

Greta settled herself, then folded her hands in her lap. She might as well get straight to the point. "Beecham"—she looked him right in the eye—"I know about Ada."

She waited for her words to take effect, but the man's poker face was inscrutable. If he knew or suspected what her words meant, he showed no sign.

"Ada—she's your daughter, isn't she?"

The effect this time was marked; she'd never imagined Beecham could flush so deeply. Why, the man was beetroot.

"My . . ." he wheezed. "Miss Gatsby, Ada is not . . . Ada is . . ." He gave her a strangled sort of look, caught between what he wanted to say and what he feared he should not. There seemed to be a war of sorts waging inside him.

"Ada is what?"

Beecham shifted his eyes away from hers. The man looked to be in a kind of agony, and she wondered if she had made a mistake coming here, asking him these questions. He stared at the floor as though it might offer means of escape.

"My niece," he choked out at last. "She's my niece, Miss Gatsby. My brother's child."

Niece! So Greta had not been quite right after all—but she had been close.

"Forgive me, Beecham. I did not mean to impugn anyone. I found a locket of hers, you see, and the photograph of the man inside—well, the likeness is considerable." She looked at him; his eyes were still averted. "But there's nothing shameful in being the girl's uncle," she said gently. "Why keep it secret?"

Beecham still kept his gaze away from her. Did he think she had betrayed him? She had undone something, that was certain: she could feel an unraveling in the room even now.

"No shame of mine," he said eventually, "but shame of my brother's." He licked his lips, then made himself continue. "He disappeared from home when he was seventeen. Ran off, married a girl, though the rest of us knew nothing of that. Left the wife and child before the babe could walk, it seems. In the end, he was killed in France. I knew nothing of the family—none of us did." He cleared his throat. "But Ada's mother knew the name of the town he was from, and when Ada was old enough, she tried to track his people down. She'd gone into service as a girl, and when she found out where I was working, she applied to the same household.

"I didn't know at first," he went on. "Ada didn't want me to think she was after money. Despite how my brother had treated her, she wanted no restitution."

"But you found out eventually?" Greta said.

Beecham gave a faint nod.

"She told me." He paused. "We did not disclose it to the rest of the household," he said. "I am ashamed of that now. The secret was kept at my behest. I said it would save her embarrassment, but I suspect it was my own embarrassment that concerned me more. I did not want the household to know how shamefully my brother had acted." He stopped again, as if mastering some difficult emotion, and finally turned to look Greta in the eye.

"You see, Miss Gatsby, I was one of three children, all boys. I never married, and both my brothers perished in the war—both childless as far as anyone knew. So you see, the idea that, after all, there was a *child*—"

He stopped, his hand pressed to his mouth. Greta understood.

"She is all that remains of your family—and fatherless as she is, and having suffered the abandonment of your delinquent brother, you consider it your duty to protect her at all costs," Greta said, her voice quiet. "No matter what she did; even if she had done something terrible."

Beecham's gaze snapped back to hers.

"But she did not," he said carefully, and his eyes spoke a message for Greta alone. *I will not say it. No matter what you put to me. You cannot make me say it.*

It was all the confirmation she needed. Beecham suspected Ada of Tom Buchanan's murder, and aimed to offer himself in Ada's stead. Misguided, even dangerous though it was, Greta couldn't help marveling at such strength of purpose, such devotion to what was left of his family. The look in his eyes made clear that he had one purpose above all others now, and it was to guard Ada from harm. Greta thought briefly of her own childhood, those cold years at Aunt Ida's in Winnipeg. What wouldn't she have given then for someone to care for her so fiercely. Jay had, she knew that, but he hadn't been *there*—and, really, he'd been only a boy himself.

"I see," she said quietly. "And so tell me," she continued, as if to change the subject, "why exactly did you shoot Mr. Buchanan, Beecham? The police haven't really been able to answer our questions on that point. What was it he said that offended you so?"

Beecham looked at her slowly. He knew she was trying to catch him out. Motive: it was perhaps the greatest gap in the case he was trying to build against himself.

"Very well," he said eventually. "I admit it, Miss Gatsby, you were right. I *was* trying to protect Ada."

Greta's heart beat faster. Beecham cleared his throat, his eyes on hers, and it seemed to her there was a sort of dance taking place between them now.

"You see," he went on, "that night wasn't quite as I described. It's true that I woke, and saw a light on in the boat. But that wasn't all I saw." Greta saw a flash of real pain cross his face. What he was speaking now was a half-truth perhaps, but the essence of it, surely, was real.

"I saw Ada. In her red cloak."

Greta nodded. She knew the one. A rather daring shade; Ada had been quite a vision, cycling off to market in it.

"I saw her go down the lawns toward the jetty, and go onto the boat." He took a breath, blinked hard. "And because it was so odd, and because I felt it might be dangerous, I followed her. I took the gun on impulse," he added hurriedly.

"When I looked through the window, I—I saw her and Mr. Buchanan in a . . . compromising situation. I had stumbled upon some kind of tryst, it seemed. I was so outraged on behalf of my niece's virtue . . . I was simply overcome with rage," he carried on, but his voice was less convincing now. The depth, the haunted quality, had gone out of it. Greta suspected they had come to a part that was fabricated.

"I threw open the door and told Ada to get out, and she ran. I fought with Mr. Buchanan. And then I shot him."

Greta regarded Beecham as he finished his story, his hands shaking. Parts of it had the ring of truth. But only parts.

"And how *did* you shoot Mr. Buchanan?" she said. "I mean, where were you standing? Where was *he* standing?"

Beecham looked at her steadily, knowing he was on dangerous ground. He had not been there when it happened, Greta surmised, therefore the more detail he gave, the more likely he was to be caught out.

"As I told the inspector," he said, "I remember very little of those fatal moments. I was in a blind rage, I suppose. All I remember is coming to afterward and looking around me. And I suppose that's when I noticed the letter, and in my desperation, I decided to make it serve as a suicide note." He delivered himself of this last part neatly, with a kind of grim satisfaction, as though remembering a cue.

A neat dodge, Greta thought. Beecham's new "confession" was a strategic one. If any other witness came forward suggesting that Ada had left the house that night, or had been glimpsed where she oughtn't to have been, that was now accounted for. Beecham had told just enough of the truth to safeguard Ada against any inconvenient accounts that might surface. And meanwhile, he was further from freedom than ever.

I can't catch him out, Greta decided. *But I can make a last appeal.*

"Murder is a very dreadful thing, isn't it, Beecham?" she said. "An act that corrodes the soul, they say. Even a good soul—or a soul that *means* to be good—must start to disintegrate after a thing like that. The person we once were is . . . well, irrecoverable. Don't you think?"

He gave her a heavy look.

"And a person, having once crossed such a line, might find themselves in terrible desperation. They might act in any number of ways. Having already done the unthinkable once, they might well do the unthinkable again." She looked at him, refusing to break the stare. "It would be imperative, wouldn't it, to protect anyone else who might get hurt?"

Beecham held her gaze.

"No one else will get hurt, Miss Gatsby."

He was unshaken. Greta did not imagine he would shield the girl if he thought her still dangerous. But he might be wrong; he might be very wrong indeed. Whatever had driven Ada to the grim deed, whatever fear or rage or other demons had prompted her to act, there was no guarantee of their lying quiet and sated now. Murder could not purge a soul; it could only harm it, distort it further.

"Miss Gatsby," Beecham said eventually, "I don't believe there's anything more I can tell you. The police have my record of events—you can verify my account with them."

Greta looked at his pained face—she could not torment the man further. She reached out and pressed his hand.

"I shall come and visit you again, Beecham." She tried to smile. "I shall come again soon."

A flicker passed over his face, the ghost of an expression, as if he were attempting a smile but had already forgotten how.

"Very good, Miss Gatsby." His voice was as courteous as ever, but the words pierced Greta as she turned and left.

"Did you see him, Miss Gatsby? What did he say?"

Greta met Bill's sharp gaze in the mirror.

"D'you reckon they'll send him to the chair?"

The bile rose in Greta's throat.

"I don't know what they'll do."

She thought back to what she did know. Beecham's story was plausible enough on the face of it. Greta might even believe it if she hadn't seen his eyes, if she hadn't heard his voice, as he told it.

But Ada—what could have provoked her to such a deed?

Jordan had said once, hadn't she, how the female staff at the Buchanans' had to be vetted by Daisy to ensure they weren't too "tempting." Tom had been the kind of man, then, who not only philandered but also chose to do so with girls of no power and little means. Did he get his way by impressing them with cheap compliments and cheaper gifts? Or was it worse? Might he have . . . forced himself on Ada? That would be reason enough for her to have wanted him dead.

Then Greta thought of something else. It was Ada who'd reported that story about the light on the boat. How could it possibly be true, then—if *she* had been out on the boat when Tom was shot dead? She'd made it up, presumably, to place herself firmly in the house at the critical moment. Had she got Molly to lie for her, too? Molly was certainly the sort who might be pressured into such a thing. Ada had probably convinced her it would protect them both.

"Damn!" Bill said, as the tires crunched beneath them. They were already motoring up the Gatsbys' driveway.

"Everything all right?" Greta leaned forward.

"Suppose so. Sounds like I drove over something."

But the car moved forward uninterrupted, and moments later, they were pulling up in the forecourt. Greta dismounted, wishing now Jay hadn't suggested a day off for everyone; it would be most inconvenient if Molly was gone. Greta really needed to interrogate her about that night and Ada's story.

Mrs. Dantry opened the front door; *she* hadn't left, then.

"Are the others still around, Dantry? I want to speak to Molly."

The housekeeper frowned.

"Molly? She's gone into town, I believe. And Mrs. Smith's gone to visit her sister for the night."

How frustrating.

"Do we know if Molly will be back tonight?"

Dantry frowned.

"I didn't make it my business to ask, miss," she said reprovingly. "By the by, there's a letter for you on the salver. Been there since this morning."

Greta glanced over as Dantry left the hall and departed down the service passage. Frowning, she moved the letter knife and plucked the envelope from where it lay on the salver. *Nora.* What could Nora be writing to her for?

"Is that you, Greta?" Nick's voice called from the living room. She went to the doorway; Nick and Jordan were there, Jordan with her feet up on the chaise longue, half-hidden behind a large potted palm, and Nick at the window, sunlight falling in bars across his pale linen suit as he turned toward her.

"Where have you been? We didn't know you'd been out."

"Back to the police station." Greta reported on her findings, and they stared in astonishment.

"It sounds like you may have been right, then, about old Beecham being put up to that confession," Nick said. "But if he's hell-bent on sticking to it—"

"What *I* wonder," Jordan said, "is what cause your pretty housemaid had to do away with Tom? A tumble in the hay gone wrong, I suppose." She paused. "Poor girl. Nice-looking, wasn't she? She'll turn up in a ditch somewhere, I shouldn't wonder. A man might stand a chance on the run like that, but not a girl like her."

Greta's stomach turned. She hoped very much indeed that Jordan was wrong.

Nick glanced down at Greta's hand. She was still carrying that letter of Nora's.

"What's that? Anything important?"

"I don't know yet," she admitted, turning it over.

That was odd—the envelope was open, and yet she didn't remember opening it just now. She supposed she must have. She reached in, and unfolded the single sheaf inside.

Miss Gatsby, it read.

Please can you pay us a visit at your earliest convenience—there has been a development that I think you should know about.

I count upon your discretion.

Your friend,

Nora

Chapter Thirty-Two

E*arliest convenience?* What could be so urgent? Greta's heart quickened. Nora was a truly levelheaded sort. She would not write for nothing.

Had she remembered something, perhaps—back from her time here in the household? Something that could shed a new light . . .

Greta hadn't thought of it before. But that letter delivered so mysteriously to Dantry: What if it wasn't mere spite or prejudice after all? What if someone had wanted to get rid of Nora for other, more strategic reasons?

"It seems I have a friend to visit."

Nick and Jordan glanced at each other, then back at Greta.

"Ought I to come with you?" Nick rose, but Greta waved him back to the sofa. Nora had asked for her utmost discretion after all.

"Stay. I shan't be long."

Greta grabbed her hat, and ran down the driveway, but when she got to the garage, she was greeted with the sight of Jay's Phantom hoisted up on a riser with one of its tires off.

Bill gave her a grim look.

"Got glass in both front tires, it seems, and I only have one spare. I can patch the other, but it'll take a while."

Glass. That must be what they'd run over on the driveway.

"Yes, shredded up the tires nicely, I'm afraid. She won't be taking anyone for a spin anytime soon."

The sun beat down hard, and sweat had broken out on Greta's neck; she wasn't much in the habit of bicycling. It was hillier than she'd remembered, this road through the wealthy outskirts of Great Neck, and its views of the sea offered her no pleasure now. She pedaled harder, and finally came to busier streets and wove her way along them to the train station. She dismounted, panting, and looked about, trying to jog her memory. There was a return address on the envelope, sure enough, but that wasn't much good when one didn't know the route.

Memory failed her at first as she took a wrong turn, and then another one. But then she found it: a short block with an alley in the middle, and that construction site at the far end, piled high with limestone bricks, a coating of chalk-dust everywhere. And there, yes, there was the yellow door. Greta hurried down the street, leaned her bicycle against the wall in the fine white dust, and knocked hard.

She was dismayed when there was no answer. Nora had made it sound important...

"Miss Gatsby!"

She turned. It was Nora, coming down the street toward her. Greta felt the release of tension down her back.

"You got my letter, so?"

Greta nodded.

"What is it? What's wrong?"

"Not out here, all right?" Nora put down her basket and fished keys from her pocket. They climbed the dark stairway to the second floor, and stepped inside the apartment.

"Close the door." Nora waved. "I'll go and get her."

Greta stared. Get whom? But in moments, Nora was back in the room, looking perplexed.

"I don't know where she's gone," she said. "She said she'd wait here."

"*Who* did?" Greta said at last, and Nora looked back at her anxiously.

"Ada."

"*Ada?*" There was a bolt on the door and Greta drew it. "Nora, do you mean to tell me Ada has been staying here with you this whole time?"

"Why, yes."

"But we . . ." Greta swallowed, her heart battering in her ribs. "I think Ada—I think she may be the one who did it. Who killed Tom Buchanan."

Nora's eyes widened incredulously.

"*Ada?* You must be joking."

"Beecham saw her."

"Oh, Beecham," Nora scoffed. She had always had her criticisms of Beecham, Greta remembered. *A pompous blowhard*, she'd called him on one occasion.

"Ada told me everything." Nora stood her ground. "If Beecham saw someone, it certainly wasn't her."

"Beecham's in jail, Nora." Greta suspected the news hadn't traveled far yet. "He's trying to take the rap for this, and he's doing it to protect Ada. He saw her out the window that night in her red cloak."

Nora looked taken aback at the mention of jail, but rallied quickly.

"I don't know what he saw, but Ada didn't leave her room that night. He must have been mistaken."

Greta frowned.

Now that she thought of it, it was the cloak, the red cloak, that Beecham had spoken of. Not of Ada's face, or hair, or any features that might have identified her. To him, the red cloak had been synonymous with the girl. But what if someone else had been wearing it?

It had been dark that night, and raining, and that could play tricks on the eyes; Beecham was not a young man.

Greta thought again of the lurker Molly had seen earlier that day hovering outside the kitchen. Could they have anything to do with the figure Beecham had seen? Greta wished she knew just how much of Beecham's story was true. *Had* he seen Ada on the boat that night? Or had he only seen her cloak?

"So what did she tell you?" Greta sank into a chair, her limbs feeling rather weak from all the surprises of the day.

"I gather there was something about a necklace," Nora said. "Ada thought you meant to have her put in the clink over it. That happened to a friend of hers, you know—some high-society lady's jewels went missing, and the poor girl got hauled off to jail. Ada saw those policemen pulling up to the house and just lost her sense." She sighed. "She showed up here, and I took her in for a cup of tea and a talking-to. I told her she'd been a fool, that running away like that would make everyone think the worst of her, but then the more she told me about the goings-on there . . . I thought perhaps she *would* be safer not going back. I mean, if there really *was* a murderer at that house . . . they'd be suspicious of her now, wouldn't they? Running off like that. They'd think she knew something."

"And *does* she?" Greta said.

Nora hesitated.

"She might. I can't make sense of it, mind you." She glanced at the door, clearly expecting Ada's return. It made Greta edgy.

"That's why I asked you to come," Nora went on. "It sounds silly I suppose, but it's about a lantern."

Lantern.

"There was one found on the boat the morning of Mr. Buchanan's death, I gather," Nora went on, and Greta nodded, bewildered by the turn the conversation had taken. It was one of her clearest memories of that morning, strangely enough. There had been something at once mesmerizing and macabre about it, the way the lamp rolled so rhythmically back and forth with the bobbing of the boat.

"Yes, I suppose it must have been knocked over in the struggle. Or," Greta amended, "we thought at the time, with the force of the ricochet."

Nora nodded.

"That's what's been troubling Ada. She started thinking about it more, and she felt something wasn't right." She looked at Greta. "It was a hurricane lamp, you see, and the thing about hurricane lamps is they're built for storms. If they get knocked over, they go out right away—it's what's so particular about them."

"All right," Greta said slowly.

"But Ada says that's not what she saw." Nora looked pointedly at Greta. "She says the light *she* saw didn't go out suddenly. She says it faded before it died—like a lamp that was running out of oil or needed the wick trimmed."

"She means it went out of its own accord," Greta said slowly, "instead of someone tipping it over."

Nora nodded.

"She took the lamp away to try it herself. To check what happened once it was tipped over. It went out in an instant."

So that was why Ada had removed the lamp from the boat.

"I can't see that it matters so much, really," Nora said. "But it's been troubling Ada."

Greta frowned.

If the lamp *had* gone out of its own accord—burning low on kerosene, say—and Tom was sitting there, alive, then surely he'd have simply lit another. There were matches and candles and lanterns all to hand. So she considered the obvious inference: Tom hadn't lit another because by then he was dead. Which meant the time of death would be considerably earlier than they had thought, for one thing. Greta saw it in her mind's eye—that lamp burning lower and lower in the room, Tom's corpse splayed in the chair beside it, light and dark all the same to him now.

But in that case, how had the lamp made it onto the floor at all? It hadn't been a windy night, certainly not choppy enough for things to tumble to the cabin floor of their own accord. So who had put it there—and put it there *after* Tom was murdered? Greta was beginning to think the small detail had been staged. But why?

Nora got up from the table, looking restlessly toward the window.

"It is *odd* that she wasn't here when you arrived," she murmured.

A flicker of discomfort surfaced in Greta. Nora turned from the window.

"I didn't notice if her bicycle was outside, perhaps I'll just check."

They went downstairs; Ada's bicycle was still there. She hadn't gone far, then.

"Perhaps to post a letter," Nora said.

But Greta's eye was on something else. All that chalk dust from the construction site that had settled on the road like the very faintest snow—there were marks in it. Footsteps, a good deal of footsteps from the many comings and goings, but something else besides. The dusting was fine so the marks weren't deep, but they were there. The harder Greta looked, the clearer they were. An ill feeling turned her stomach. Unless she was reading it wrong, something had recently been dragged past these very steps. Dragged—she followed the trail with her eyes—down the mouth of that narrow alley.

It's nothing, she told herself. The construction workers storing bags of cement, perhaps. There might be a dozen explanations. But her heart was beating far too fast.

"Miss Gatsby?" Nora's voice seemed to come from far away. "Miss Gatsby, where are you going?"

But Greta was already in the alley, her eyes adjusting to its dimmer light. And as they did, she saw something that made her cry out in horror. There, behind a wheelbarrow, a foot was sticking out.

A woman's brown boot covered in chalk.

Chapter Thirty-Three

She'd been gagged, her hands and legs trussed and tied to a metal brace on the wall—but, thank heavens, Ada was alive and breathing. Greta dropped to her knees, squeezing into the small space of the alley to get closer. Ada's eyelids flickered heavily. Greta couldn't tell if the girl registered her presence. There was a bloodied brick lying beside her; it was clear enough how this had all come about.

"Oh, *Ada!*" Nora gulped. "What kind of—what kind of *monster* . . ."

She squatted beside Ada, next to Greta, who was busy checking the pulse. It was too slow, but it was there. Next, she checked the head wound, which was a distressing sight, but at least there wasn't too much blood on the ground—Ada hadn't lost an excessive amount. Greta swallowed, wiped her hand, and began to unpick the girl's bindings.

"She's alive. At least she's alive," Nora was saying.

Yes—and let's pray she stays that way.

"It must have happened before I got here," Greta said. But how long before; how long had Ada been lying like this? Gagged and weak and dazed, she hadn't even been able to call for help. Had Greta and Nora not come looking, how long might it have been until somebody found her? It didn't bear thinking about.

"I only left the house an hour ago," Nora said, tearful now.

So sometime between sixty and thirty minutes ago, someone had lured Ada downstairs and attacked her. Greta's head spun. This morning, she had thought she knew who Tom's killer was. Now she was sure of nothing but this: someone very dangerous, someone with murder on their mind, was on the loose.

Between them, they carried Ada out of the alley. She groaned softly, her eyes flickering then closing.

"Ada?" The girl opened them again, trying to focus.

"Ada? Ada, can you hear me?" Nora was supporting the legs; Greta had her arms.

"Should we take her upstairs?"

"I don't want to jostle her around."

They managed to get her inside, propped against the stairwell. Greta went back to the door and scanned the street, where a boy of twelve or thereabouts was playing with a baseball.

"Here!" she called. "You! I have a dollar for you if you'll go and fetch a medic as fast as your legs will take you."

She pulled the silver coin from her purse to show she was in earnest, and with only a moment's hesitation, he ran.

"I'll bring down water." Nora ran upstairs while Greta stayed with Ada, who was slumped now against the stairs, her eyes open but frowning sleepily.

"Ada?"

The girl tried to shake her head, then leaned over and retched onto the ground. When she was finished, she looked dizzily at Greta.

"What happened?" she said in a thick voice.

Greta squeezed her hand.

"We were hoping you could tell us that, Ada. We found you here. Somebody attacked you. They hit you on the back of the head. You're at Nora's house, remember?"

Ada closed her eyes again.

"Can you tell us anything about what happened?" Greta pressed.

The girl began to shake her head again, but stopped with a groan. Nora reappeared with a jug of cold water and some clean rags, and they sluiced some of the water over the head wound, parting the matted hair as they did so. Ada whimpered, and Nora looked ill at the sight. At least it looked shallow, Greta thought, although she understood just enough to know that the real injury could be below the surface if the impact of the brick had been hard enough.

They wiped cool water over Ada's face then and her throat and the back of her neck. She was growing more alert, and soon her mouth opened in a little gasp.

"Can you take a sip of water, Ada?"

Nora tipped a small amount into her mouth, and for a moment, Ada looked as though she might be sick again. Nora and Greta exchanged glances. Now that the first few minutes of horror had passed, the awfulness of it—the bloodthirsty, vicious nature of the deed—was coming home to Greta, and she found herself shivering.

Tom's death had been horrific, of course, but all the same, a part of her could understand how a person like him, who reveled in provoking others, was more apt to meet with violence.

But what had Ada ever done to invite a horror such as this? Gently, Greta squeezed the girl's hand.

"Can you tell us anything about what happened to you? Do you know who did this?"

She blinked at Greta, and gasped out a *no*.

"Bell rang . . . came downstairs . . . there was no one."

"You didn't see anybody?"

Ada grunted.

"Had my head turned . . . must have come at me."

Greta looked at Nora and saw her own feelings mirrored there. It was sickening to imagine. The attacker had been hiding behind the corner of the alley—and when Ada had come out to look, they'd waited until her head was turned, then sprung at her.

"A medic is coming, all right, Ada? They'll take care of you."

"Ada, is there anyone you suspect of doing this?" Nora said, leaning close. "Please tell us. If there's someone you think might have had reason to do this to you . . ."

Ada said nothing. A tear rolled down her face from underneath her closed lids.

"No," she whispered.

"Oh, Ada." Nora squeezed her hand, and Greta saw there were tears in Nora's eyes, too. "You're going to be all right. I promise."

It was a dangerous promise to make. *Let it be so*, Greta thought grimly, holding the water glass to Ada's lips again. As she did so, her mind sifted urgently through what she knew. If only there were more pieces of the puzzle. If only she had more clues to make it all fit.

"There, sir—that's them." A boy's voice sounded, and Greta looked up to see a bewhiskered man in a tweed suit and gladstone bag marching their way. The young lad she'd sent off was scampering behind him like a puppy.

"Now then, what's all this?" The doctor crouched beside Ada, and took in the situation. "Fall down the stairs, did we? That's a nasty one."

"She was attacked, Doctor," Greta said. "She was hit with a brick in the back of the head."

She watched the doctor's face grow a shade paler.

"The blackguard." He looked at Ada. "Husband, was it?"

Greta wondered what the doctor must have seen in his many years to make this his first thought.

"We don't know who the assailant was, Doctor," she said. "Ada didn't get a chance to see."

Silently, Ada started to cry.

"I just opened the door," she managed to say. "I just opened the door and turned around..."

The doctor nodded grimly, took Ada's wrist in his, and briefly checked her pulse. Then he examined the head wound.

"Any signs of..." He cleared his throat. "Of an assault? That is to say, of an intimate—"

"It wasn't that kind of an attack, Doctor."

"Some mercy," he said, evidently relieved. "An attempt at burglary then, no doubt." He jerked his chin to where the boy stood watching, eyes agog. "You, lad. Have you seen anyone here lurking about? Anyone out of place?"

"No, sir." The boy craned for a better look at the blood.

The doctor pressed the pads of his fingers carefully against Ada's head, and she gave a feeble cry.

"It's all right," he said gently. "Now, miss, can you tell me your name?"

Ada gave it, and verified the date. But Greta's thoughts had wheeled off in another direction. That remark the doctor had made—*anyone lurking about*—it had reminded her of something. The man—or the shadow of a man—Molly had seen that day by the kitchen window...

Greta drew a breath, trying to marshal the thoughts that were exploding now like fireworks in her brain.

It was such a small detail, such a very small detail. And perhaps because it was so very small, she hadn't paid it as much attention as she ought. But suddenly she was thinking about it in a whole new way. She'd had such trouble reconciling that account, that mystery figure who'd vanished into thin air...

Surely not...

And yet the more she thought about it...

The doctor sat back on his heels. "We'll take her to the hospital for a proper examination. I should think there's some contusion, but if we're lucky, it will resolve itself. You may have been rather a lucky girl after all, my dear."

Greta, dazed though she was by the flood of thoughts that had just burst open, returned to the moment.

Lucky didn't seem the right word. But was the doctor really saying Ada would be all right?

"There, now." Nora brushed the sweat-matted hair back from Ada's face. "Did you hear that?" She turned around. "May we come with you to the hospital, Doctor? We ought to be there with her."

"I can transport you," he conceded. "You'll have to stay in the waiting room. I can't say how long it shall take."

Greta's heart was racing. She looked down at Ada, pale and groggy, and then to Nora, whose sharp face was full of emotion, and then toward the doctor, who was now eyeing Greta curiously, wondering no doubt how she fit into all this. She didn't look like she was from around here.

Greta brushed down her skirts and stood.

"Doctor." She rifled in her purse for a calling card. "Ada is under the care of our household—the Gatsbys of West Egg. Please, take the very best care of her, and send the bill to this address." She handed it over, and gave the promised coin to the boy. Nora stared at her.

"You're not coming?" she said, incredulous. "You're leaving *now*?"

Greta swallowed.

"I'm sorry." She turned. "I shall come as soon as I can. But there's something I must do first."

Nora's frown deepened, then her eyes grew wide with understanding.

"Greta—"

"I'm sorry," Greta said, already stepping toward her bicycle. "I must go."

"Greta!" The voice rang in the street behind her as Greta hurried away. "For heaven's sake, be *careful*!"

Back on the main road, the sight of a taxicab made Greta abandon her bicycle, and sprint across the street.

"Excuse me! Hello? Can you take me to West Egg, please? As fast as you can."

The cabbie looked at her askance, but slowly cranked the engine into gear.

"What's all the rush, miss?" he said, weaving out of the town center. "Late for a lawn party?"

"Something like that," Greta mumbled. He gave her a look in the rearview mirror, but she was busy organizing her own frenzied thoughts. She was starting to look at everything differently now. All the little details, the way they added up.

That lurking man outside the window.

The disappearing glass. *The Miramar pattern*, Beecham had said.

Ada's red cloak.

Yes, it all added up. Strangely and horribly, it added up.

It hadn't occurred to Greta that the killer would have made *two* trips to the boat that night, but now she saw that this was exactly what they'd done. And she thought she knew why. She cursed herself for looking in the wrong direction for so long.

She should have been more cautious. Because of her, Ada had nearly died. No doubt it was as Nora had said: the killer had been spooked when Ada ran away. They thought her disappearance meant that she knew too much. And then Nora's letter had led them to her! Had they gone to Nora's house already suspecting Ada's presence, or simply thought, as Greta had, that Nora had remembered something important?

Greta shook her head. What mattered now was getting home—to quietly alert the others and make an urgent telephone call to the police. She'd make that inspector listen even if he didn't want to. He'd *have* to: the attack on Ada was proof enough the killer was getting reckless now. They'd think they'd bought themselves some time by getting rid of the poor girl, but surely, they wouldn't stick around long after such an attack. Even now, Greta thought, they might be making preparations to leave.

She felt a strange mixture of relief and utter dread as the car turned sharply up the drive of the Gatsby estate, and those high mullioned windows rose up ahead. And then they rounded the corner onto the forecourt, and Greta's stomach turned over. There was a car in the driveway, but it wasn't Jay's Phantom. It was a brown Studebaker she knew only too well.

Edgar was here.

"Stop, please," Greta said hurriedly. She had the fare in her hand.

"Can you do something for me?" She met the driver's expectant eyes in the mirror. "I need you to go to the police precinct in Great Neck. Find Inspector Francis, or the next in command if he's not there—tell them it's urgent, all right? Tell them we need them to come out here, as many officers as they can spare." She held his startled gaze. "The Gatsby house on West Egg, they'll know the one."

The driver stared at her, jaw open.

"Miss, are you . . . are you all right?"

"I will be," she said, "if you pass along the message."

The driver stared back at her in the rearview mirror. He didn't look at all inclined to accept the request. He probably didn't like the police much himself.

"We'll pay you," she said. "Handsomely. A week's wages. Just get them over here, soon as you can, you understand? They mightn't listen to you at first. You'll have to make them." She pushed an extra five dollars into his hand. She'd place the call as soon as she could get safely to the telephone, but that depended on the hallway being empty enough that she could make the call without raising attention.

He looked at her a little longer, then sighed, and put the car back into gear.

"All right, lady. I'll see what I can do."

She watched him speed back down the driveway, and sent up a little prayer that he was going in the direction she'd asked. Then she turned back toward the house. She darted up the steps, thinking how quiet it seemed suddenly, as though the garden, the birdsong, the distant sound of the bay had all been wound to a stop. She pushed open the front door and stood in the empty hallway, listening. Voices: Nick's and Jordan's. They were in the library by the sounds of it. She waited a moment longer to see if anyone else was with them.

"I don't see why she had to bring *him* along," Jordan said.

"I'm beginning to doubt Daisy's judgment altogether," Nick agreed.

Greta exhaled. First things first, then: she stepped softly across the hall to the nook where the telephone stood, and lifted the receiver. She backed into the corner to keep her voice from traveling, and asked the operator to get her the police. But no response followed—the line was dead.

A sick feeling crept through Greta's veins. There could be a fault on the line or a downed tree somewhere. But deep down, she was sure it was none of those things. Someone had cut the cable. Greta swallowed. If they knew the game was up . . . well then, they'd be more dangerous than ever.

She gripped the receiver, unsure if she'd imagined a noise just now. *Had she heard something?* Barely breathing, she waited a few more moments but heard only the distant drift of the library conversation. She crossed the hallway with a last glance over her shoulder, then opened the door.

"Greta!" Nick looked up. "Are you all right? You look like you've seen a ghost!"

She put a finger to her lips.

"Where's Jay?" she said in an undertone. "Is Daisy here?"

The others' expressions wavered between bafflement and concern.

"She's come back for the pearls. With *Edgar*," Jordan added. "Your brother's out pacing the garden, trying not to explode."

In the garden! If Greta had only approached from the other side of the house, she'd have seen him.

"Look, you two," she said. "I want you to get outside, find Jay, and stay there. I—I think we're in danger."

Nick was out of his seat instantly.

"Greta? What danger?"

She cracked the door to the hallway, and looked out. Still deserted.

"I don't have time to explain now." She turned back. "But you'd better trust me. Get a rifle from the gun room if you can. Just go—I'll follow."

"Don't be absurd," Nick said. "I'm staying with you."

She glanced at him and then at Jordan, who looked equal parts alarmed and excited. There was no time to argue. When she tried the door of the gun room, she found it locked. Damn the thing! Why had Jay started being so careful about it *now*? She rattled the handle, and Nick and Jordan stared.

"Is that Ada girl coming back here?" Jordan said. "What's going on?"

"It's not Ada," Greta said. "It was never Ada." She abandoned the attempts to get the door open, then froze at the sound of a voice on the second floor.

"Fine then," Edgar was saying tersely. "In that case, I shall wait in the car."

There was the clack of shoes on marble as he started down the staircase, and then he swept around its bend and found the three of them staring at him.

"What is it?" he snapped. "Why are you all looking at me like that?"

"Edgar," Greta hissed. "Please go back upstairs and get Daisy. We all need to leave this house. Now."

"Greta says we're in some sort of danger," Jordan volunteered.

"Don't pay Miss Gatsby any mind," a voice said from behind them; a voice that made Greta's skin crawl. "No one's in any danger—unless they're planning to be very, very stupid. And no one's planning on *that*. Are we, Mr. Gatsby?"

Chapter Thirty-Four

All the blood drained from Greta's head. *No,* she thought. But she forced herself to turn around.

There, a few feet away, was Jay, pale and sweating, with a gun against his temple. And behind him, the slight figure holding the gun steady.

"Molly?" Nick said, astonished. "Good god, girl, have you lost your senses?"

"Far from it, Mr. Carraway," the housemaid said. Her voice sent a chill through Greta. It was Molly's voice, but gone was the timid, whispery delivery, replaced by something cool and hard.

"And now," she carried on, "since you've all assembled here so conveniently, I'll just ask you to line up there against the wall." She gestured without moving the gun from Jay's temple.

For a moment, no one spoke; not one of them moved.

"I don't believe it," Jordan said, folding her arms. "I don't believe you *could* kill anyone, and I don't believe you did. Look at you! You're just a little shrimp of a thing."

Molly's eyes seemed to sharpen, the pupils darkening.

"Miss Baker, I have killed before and I will kill again if need be. I don't *want* to—but if you get in my way, you'll pay for it."

Nick put a hand on Jordan's shoulder.

"Molly . . . I don't know why you're doing this, but why don't you just let go of Jay and then we can all talk? Keep the gun. Just let Jay come over here and stand next to me. Everyone will feel ever so much calmer, then."

He sounded so steady, Greta could almost believe his heart wasn't battering like hers was. But Molly only grimaced.

"Mr. Carraway, you're wasting your breath. I know how negotiating works and you're not in a position to do it. Now"—she gestured again, more sharply—"over there, please."

Greta stole a glance at Jay. His eyes were stretched wide, his face stiff; he seemed to be trying not to breathe.

Molly's voice was flinty. "I haven't got all day."

Too late. She'd figured it out too late. Greta could do nothing but follow the others. Slowly, with Nick leading, they moved into a line with their backs against the wall.

"I've seen to Mrs. Dantry," Molly said. "Don't worry." She smiled sourly, catching Greta's look of alarm. "She's not hurt. And, of course, Mrs. Smith and Bill have left by now—so don't rely on either of *them* helping you." She eyed the small line-up. "By the way, don't think it's escaped me that one of your number is still upstairs."

Greta saw Jay turn a shade paler.

Daisy.

"Mr. Gatsby"—Molly gave him a nudge with the gun, and Jay winced—"call her down, please."

"I don't know what you're talking about," Jay panted, eyes darting toward his temple where the gun rested.

"You and your friends had better stop treating me like an imbecile, Mr. Gatsby. Call your lady friend downstairs now if you know what's good for you."

A beat passed.

"No."

Greta stared at her brother, her heart contracting. *Her stubborn, foolish, noble brother.* Even now, he was in love with Daisy; even now, he would endanger everything to protect her.

"Mr. Gatsby, I'm warning you." Molly adjusted the barrel against his head.

"Jay, don't be a martyr," Greta burst out. "Just do what Molly says."

The housemaid's sharp eyes met hers for a moment.

"That's a change of tune, Miss Gatsby." She leveled her gaze back toward Jay. "But at least someone is seeing sense. Don't try my patience any longer, Mr. Gatsby, I'm a woman of my word." She nudged the gun tighter. "I'm going to count down from three. Three." She paused. "Two."

Jay said nothing, there was just his shallow breathing.

Molly clicked off the safety.

"*Daisy!*"

The shout seemed to ripple across the great hall; it was as if the whole house stopped breathing.

"Damn you, Nick, *damn* you!" Jay spat out the words furiously, for it was Nick who had yelled. Greta thought her brother would have hurled himself bodily toward his friend but for Molly, who gripped his arm harder and wrenched it behind his back.

There were footsteps overhead on the landing.

Daisy's voice drifted down. "Nick?"

"Daisy, don't come downstairs! Don't listen to him!"

Molly hissed, and smacked Jay on the temple with the revolver. Greta cried out and moved toward him, but Molly gave her a look and pressed the gun hard against Jay's skull so that Greta froze again.

"What on *earth* is going on down there?" Footsteps on marble: Daisy was on the staircase. Greta turned her head. In a few more moments, Daisy saw them, and when she did, her scream echoed through the hall, reverberating off the walls.

"What are—what do you think you're doing, you?" she cried. "Put that *away*. Put that awful thing away!"

Molly stared, then looked over the rest of them with the same cold incredulity.

"You all seem to believe," she said, "that you're the ones in charge. Are you really so used to power that you can't recognize when it's deserted you? Mrs. Buchanan"—she turned toward the stairs, the gun's muzzle never leaving Jay's skull—"come down and join your party. Unless you want me to put a bullet through Mr. Gatsby's brains."

Daisy hesitated, but only for a moment. She took one slow step down, and then another. Jay called to her to stop, and earned another bash on the temple.

"Keep going, Mrs. Buchanan," Molly said.

Greta spared a glance at Edgar, who simply stared, his face blank of all emotion as Daisy descended the final steps. Daisy's chin trembled, but she looked at Molly head-on.

"I suppose I am to understand that *you* are the monster who murdered my husband?"

Molly's eyes narrowed.

"You call *me* the monster?"

Daisy's cheeks turned pink with fury.

"He was not a *murderer!*"

"Are you quite sure about that, Mrs. Buchanan?"

"Damn you, of course he wasn't!" Molly's words had finally stirred the poker-faced Edgar to speech. "The Buchanans don't go around murdering people!"

Molly studied him now, as though his face held some special, unpleasant interest, but Edgar didn't flinch under the weight of the sudden attention.

"You don't remember me at all, do you, Mr. Buchanan?" she said.

Chapter Thirty-Five

Edgar blinked.

"Remember you? Why the devil should I remember you?"

The corner of Molly's lip rose in bitterness. "Why indeed? I shouldn't think you remember any of us farmhands. We were little more than cattle to you, I suppose."

Farm hands. Greta's mind was spinning. She thought of the photo she'd seen on Molly's nightstand, that serious-looking family—mother, father, boy, and girl—outside a humble brick house.

"My parents," Molly said, "worked on your father's estate. They came to this country dreaming of a life they could build with their own hands. There wasn't a day they didn't work till sundown. They gave everything."

Edgar looked at her blankly. How many thousands of acres had the Buchanans' land stretched to? How many workers, servants, laborers had passed through his childhood years?

The gun was unwavering in Molly's hand, but Greta could see part of her thoughts were no longer in this room. She was looking backward through the years, although nothing in her face softened.

"Of course you wouldn't remember Kristof, either. He was five years older than me," she continued. "He was not quite like other boys. You wouldn't notice the differences at first, but they were there. He was clumsy with his arms and legs, easily flustered. He was slow to follow directions; loud noises paralyzed him. It's just the way he was. He could work fine with my father, but that was because Father understood him. I think it embarrassed Kristof sometimes, that he was not quite the same as the other boys were. He was shy—but so sweet natured. Everybody said it. There was nobody sweeter." Molly's eyes roved over them one by one, then moved once more to Edgar.

"We prayed the doctors would grant him an exemption when the draft came in—and they did." Molly paused. She seemed to be taking some grim pleasure in this captive audience.

"But he was supposed to carry his exemption papers with him whenever he went to town, and he forgot. Kristof was always forgetful." She paused again. "Not that it would have mattered that day, from what we heard. 'Raid' was what they called it; I say it was just sport."

Greta felt a chill down her spine. The look Molly was giving Edgar dispatched any lingering doubt: Molly would not hesitate to pull that trigger.

"They said they only came for the draft dodgers, for any fellows who looked the wrong age to be walking around town. But later, we heard they went for boys as young as fourteen and men of fifty. They hauled them into paddy wagons," she went on. "Knocked around anyone who talked back or tried to run, or whose faces they didn't like. Some of them had whips. One boy was tarred and feathered. There was no rhyme or reason to it. They went for anyone they had a fancy to humiliate." She stopped for a moment, and Greta saw Jay swallow hard, his eyes glassy.

"Kristof had been running errands for our mother." Molly's eyes traveled over them all, daring any of them not to give her their full attention. "The shopkeeper told us later how Kristof got kicked to the ground, how he'd been all but trampled under Master Buchanan's horse. How he'd been frantic and crying, and how, when he tried to get out of the paddy wagon, Master Buchanan had struck him about the head until he hit the floor." She looked steadily at Edgar.

"My father took him home from jail the next day, but Kristof couldn't keep down food. Something wasn't right; he was afraid, disoriented. We thought he was just upset . . ." Molly stopped, blinked. "He was terribly sleepy, and Mother put him to bed early."

Greta waited, already knowing what came next.

"He never woke up. The physician told us later that there must have been some bleeding inside the brain." She looked at them. "We didn't know. How were we to know? He'd only gone into town to buy bread."

There was a moment's silence when she stopped, and Greta heard Jay's shallow, slow breathing.

"There were many men involved that day," Edgar said finally. "And in such moments, regrettable things can happen."

"*Regrettable?*" Molly laughed. "Yes, Mr. Buchanan, my brother's death was *regrettable*. You Buchanans are cut from the same cloth, I see."

Greta didn't doubt it was so. That awful League Tom had been so proud of, such vile things done in its name.

"But, Molly—" Greta's words burst from her. "Molly, even so! Even though Tom had such blood on his hands—you would risk your life, this one and the next, all for vengeance?"

Perhaps jail meant nothing to Molly; perhaps even the electric chair did not frighten her. But to give up one's very soul . . .

Molly turned a clear gaze toward her. "I would hardly expect you to understand, Miss Gatsby. I see you do not have the love for your brother that I did for mine." She half smiled. "Perhaps you are the one to be pitied in the end."

The words cut like a knife. But she must not let Molly throw her off. *Just keep her talking*, Greta told herself. It was the best she could do for now. It was the only thing.

"Your brother was lucky, indeed, to have your devotion." Greta set her jaw. "Though he might not approve of how you have applied it. I suppose," she said, "you were the one who got Nora fired?"

Molly half smiled.

"I would have preferred a position in the Buchanan house, of course," she said, "but since Mr. Buchanan's last *indiscretion*, they were no longer hiring young unmarried women. I came to Great Neck with only my forged references and the aim of befriending staff at houses on the Buchanans' circuit, anywhere that I would come face-to-face with the man who destroyed my family. I joined the church and a sewing group; I talked to everyone." She paused. "It was my great fortune to meet Nora so shortly after I arrived. She took an interest in me, said she'd help me find a position somewhere. But soon I realized it was *her* position I needed. The Buchanans spent more time at the Gatsby house than anywhere else; during the summer, they would be there for weeks! I knew I would have ample opportunity. Of course, there were no available openings." She glanced at Greta. "But as luck would have it, Nora had confided in me about her romance with a fellow member of staff, which would be poorly viewed if it was to come to light. So I sent your housekeeper a letter, and made sure to be first in line when Nora was dismissed." She gave a half shrug. "I was using a different name then. Even if Nora heard of a new girl at the Gatsby house, I knew she'd never realize it was me."

Greta swallowed. How carefully the plans had been laid. Molly's brother must have been dead six years at the least—had she been dreaming of revenge all that time?

"That is all quite ingenious," she said.

"Oh, you need not patronize me, Miss Gatsby. I assure you I'm not dependent on your approval."

"I did not believe you were."

Greta looked at Jay, whose steady eyes met hers. *Don't worry about me,* they seemed to be saying. *Save yourself. Save the rest of them.*

If only she could. Had that cabbie gone to the police as she'd asked? Perhaps he'd merely taken the extra dollars and considered it a good day's work. What did her concerns matter to him?

"So tell us how you managed the rest," Greta went on. "Had you picked that particular night in advance?"

Molly narrowed her eyes. Perhaps she knew what Greta's aim was, drawing her out like this, but she didn't seem to mind. Perhaps she even wanted her careful planning recognized.

"I am ashamed to say, I had been losing my nerve," she admitted. "Days passed, and I knew that the Buchanans were soon to leave; I had to act, or lose my chance. I had procured the gun some days prior and hidden it. It was simple enough to borrow the key to the gun room from Mr. Gatsby's bedroom. And the night of your return"—she looked coolly at Greta—"seemed the night to do it, since there were to be three extra people in the house. More commotion, more distraction." She paused. "And if suspicion was ever to fall on the household, which, of course, I hoped it wouldn't, there would be three more suspects."

"Why, you—" Daisy bit back the rest with visible effort. She seemed to be swinging between fear and rage.

"Of course, at that stage," Greta pushed on, "you hadn't yet seen Tom's discarded letter, had you? You hadn't planned to frame it as a suicide but as an intruder's random act of violence. *That* was why you made up the story about the man at the window. You knew we would remember it the next day, and would give credence to it then. Poor Tom had gone for a wander in the garden and been shot by a burglar."

Molly looked at her.

"I didn't see how else to do it. Not then," she said with a tight smile. "Not yet."

Greta's heart beat fast. In the end, that had been the one thing that, no matter how she'd tried to square it, simply wouldn't add up. The mystery man at the window: it was the one detail that didn't make sense, didn't fit. Greta had *wanted* that lurking shadow to have been Edgar, but out there on the street with Ada and Nora, she'd realized there was only one logical answer: it didn't fit, because Molly had made the whole thing up. Not from an overactive imagination, not from nerves or jitters, but strategically, oh so deliberately.

Greta forced herself to look Molly square in the eye. "But then you switched course. You decided to frame it as a suicide instead, even though you'd already laid a trail in a different direction. Switching tack like that, with your plan already in motion. Didn't you think it riskier?"

"On the contrary," Molly said, "it was the most wonderful piece of luck. After I'd tried Mrs. Smith's patience so sorely, she said I'd better get out of her hair and do the turndowns upstairs. So I did . . . and I saw the note. It was staring up at me in the garbage basket when I went to empty it. A little creased, but I was able to iron that out easily enough. I saw at once that it would be perfect for my purposes." A peaceful look spread across her features for a moment.

"It seemed meant to be. I almost wondered if the hands of some higher power weren't working through me. Because what could be more convenient than suicide? It was the only means of death that wouldn't result in a police investigation. Far better than being shot in the garden by some mysterious vagrant. And to have such a perfect letter in his own hand! It was foolproof. Ironclad." She paused.

"I didn't know there was a finished letter. There was nothing on his desk to suggest it. It was only the next morning that I spotted it on the salver and understood. I got rid of it immediately—I knew if I didn't, everyone would see the trick at once. I just had to pray that in the uproar, no one would have noticed or remembered seeing it."

"*I* did," Jordan spat.

Molly turned.

"Indeed, Miss Baker. Your eyesight is to be commended, then, if not your powers of logic."

"You managed it very well, Molly," Greta said smoothly. She thought, again, of the cab driver and her plea. If he *did* go to the station, she reckoned, he ought to be there by now. She pushed herself to continue.

"Once you had changed the plan, though, you needed things to be a little different. You needed to shoot your victim at close range for one thing. It needed to be very carefully staged for the suicide to be convincing. So how did you get Tom to meet you on the boat at such an hour?"

Molly smiled stiffly.

"He'd been making... *overtures* to Ada, almost since he'd arrived in this house. Unwelcome ones, I might add; it was quite revolting. But earlier that evening, I told him I had a message from Ada, that she would meet him later that night out in the garden." She seemed pleased with the recollection. "He came up with the idea of the boat. It was perfect, really."

Daisy exploded. "You vile, vile *beast*."

Molly gave her a look of distaste.

"Had he been a different sort of man—one who refrained from pawing at servants at least—I suppose I would have had to come up with a different sort of ruse. But really, it was quite easy." She stopped, and looked back to Greta. "You seem to think you're serving some purpose, Miss Gatsby, by pretending to be captivated by all my little strategies. Your hopes are misguided though—as I told you, the rest of the staff aren't due back until tomorrow. As for myself"—she glanced at the clock in the hall—"I shall be leaving for the station soon. But I may satisfy your curiosity a little longer. I suppose you've figured out where I got the barbiturates from? I knew there was a whole store of them in your room, Mr. Gatsby," she said, addressing Jay almost conversationally; Jay kept his head very still, unblinking.

"Once we had the rendezvous in place, the rest was easy. I knew the drugs would knock him out enough for me to stage a convincing shot. I knew perfectly well the effect such drugs could have. My mother started to take them every night after Kristof. They made her like a rag doll."

But Greta could spare no thought for the family Molly described, broken by Tom Buchanan. Jay was what she had to focus on. Getting him—getting all of them—safely out of here. Jay had been on the wrong end of the gun barrel all this time, and though he was holding himself together, he looked terribly pale. Molly, Greta was sure, wasn't used to holding a gun. What if she made a mistake; what if she got worked up and let it off accidentally?

"So you crushed the pills in a glass of claret, and left it in the boat for him," she prompted.

Molly frowned.

"How did you know it was claret?"

"You cleaned up the broken glass," Greta said, "but you left a shard behind. Beecham verified the missing item with his inventory. I didn't realize the significance then, though I ought to have. The Miramar hasn't been used in months."

Molly raised an eyebrow.

"Well, bravo, Miss Gatsby. I admit, I didn't see the mistake at first. When it broke, my first thought was to leave it there, as if it had been shattered in the ricochet. A broken glass in and of itself would not have raised concerns. But then I realized someone might wonder how Tom, not knowing the service areas at all, had procured a glass from the back of the butler's pantry."

"Cleaning all that up must have cost you a pretty piece of time," Greta observed. "But I suppose you weren't concerned about Ada waking up—presumably you'd drugged her, too."

"Only a little—a very little. I had to be sure she wouldn't wake up and find me out of the room, but I *did* need to rouse her later."

"When you pretended to have a nightmare."

Molly nodded. "As I soon as I got in, I jumped back into bed and started tossing and calling out. It was a devil of a job to wake her though—I practically had to scream in her ear. Then, when she was awake, I 'noticed' the light, and that got her attention."

Greta nodded. She willed her eyes not to drift toward the window—Molly must not suspect she was waiting for anyone—and fixed her gaze on Molly. They were coming to the second trip of the night, the trip that had thrown Greta so off course.

"So when the light on the boat went out, did that cause difficulties?"

Molly gave her a sharp look.

"You've put a good bit together, haven't you, Miss Gatsby? At first, I was concerned, since it seemed to get Ada more worked up. Nobody *left* the boat after the light went out, you see, which spooked her. I thought at first she was going to rouse Dantry or old Mr. Beecham. But I talked her down soon enough. A few minutes later, she was back asleep." Molly stopped. "It was hours yet before anyone would be awake, and the barbiturates were still in Ada's system—I said her name quite loudly just to be sure—and then I thought for a while, and saw how I could turn things even further to my advantage. If I went out there and tipped over the lamp, everyone would conclude Mr. Buchanan had knocked it over himself, presumably in his last flailing moments. That would give me as perfect an alibi as I could hope for, as I'd have been in the room with Ada at the exact moment he died."

Greta caught Jordan's agitated glance. *What do you think you're doing*, it seemed to say. *You're making conversation with a murderer!* Greta forced her eyes back to Molly.

"Yes, it was very well done. Only, of course, someone *did* see you."

Molly blinked.

"Who?"

"Beecham. He watched you from upstairs. You were wearing Ada's cloak, so he thought you were Ada."

Molly looked amused. "How perfect."

"You weren't intending to frame her on purpose, then?"

Molly shook her head. "Ada's cloak was simply nearest the door. Beecham's mistake was just my good fortune, I suppose."

Greta's head was throbbing now. The others' faces had receded into the background, all of them but Jay's, frozen and pale, his eyes locked on her. Greta forced herself to focus. She didn't know how much longer she could keep this up.

"Yes, it would have worked out well for you; Beecham would have kept your secret. Everything would have been fine had there not been the autopsy."

A vein began to throb in Molly's temple.

"The staging of the suicide seemed to me quite foolproof; I hadn't imagined the coroner would take it further." Her self-control was waning. "Even when the police got involved, I was sure it would all blow over. And it *would* have," she said, "if everyone had kept their cool. I couldn't have predicted old Beecham would go and turn himself in."

"You felt bad about that?" Greta probed. If Molly felt guilt, she could use that.

The housemaid's eyes narrowed.

"He was an innocent man, of course I didn't want him thrown in jail. But no one told him to do it."

"And Ada?" Greta said quietly.

She saw Molly's face tighten then; the vein pulsed harder. *That distresses her*, Greta noted. Molly hadn't wanted to harm Ada.

"I had hoped," Molly said, "initially at least, I really had hoped that we could all go back to normal. But when I saw the letter from Nora today, I knew something odd must be afoot. What on earth could she be writing to *you* about? I had a dreadful thought it might be about Ada, though I hoped it wasn't. You'd shown me the lamp from the boat that she'd hidden, so I was well aware she must have suspicions—I just hoped she'd taken those suspicions back up to New Hampshire with her." She blinked fast.

"I wanted to destroy the letter altogether, but that old shrew Dantry saw me with it, so I couldn't, but I knew I needed to get to Nora's house. I made sure the Phantom was out of commission for a few hours, then I bicycled into town as fast as I could. It would all depend, I told myself, on who opened the door." Her voice grew heavy. "And it was Ada, and then I knew. If she and Nora wanted to meet with you, I was in trouble. I didn't want to knock her out, but I had to. I couldn't risk it. All I needed was an hour or two. Just enough time to get back here, take the little money I had, and be back at Great Neck for the afternoon train. That was all." She eyed Greta. "I'd cut the telephone just in case, but I hadn't thought it would come to that. But then you had to rush back here, charging about, wanting the police..."

So Molly *had* been in the passageway, listening. Greta shivered. She had the sense that Molly's storytelling was coming to an end; she'd said her piece, and soon she'd have to figure out what to do with them.

"I knew the jig was up then," Molly said. "Slipping out the back and quietly catching the train wouldn't be an option. Too short of a lead time if you set the cops on me now. Hence all this." She gestured. "Which is really not what I wanted. But we must carry on." She turned to Edgar. "So, Mr. Buchanan, I shall be needing the keys to your car, since Mr. Gatsby's is not operational—besides being far too conspicuous."

"Don't give them to her, Edgar," Jordan burst out.

"Hush, Jord—" Nick turned.

"There's five of us and only one of her!"

Molly's mouth twisted.

"Yes, Miss Baker. And that makes a bullet for each of you."

Greta swallowed. Jordan was right, but so was Molly. If they charged her now, there was no way she could shoot all five of them. But she could shoot one of them; she could *kill* one of them.

Five bullets. Greta made a mental note. Most likely the gun in Molly's hands was the one she'd used before: a six-shooter minus the bullet that had killed Tom.

"Now, the keys, please," Molly repeated. "And Mrs. Buchanan"—she gestured—"I shall be needing that necklace of yours."

The pearls hung once more around Daisy's neck, and Daisy looked at Molly now with helpless rage.

"Come," Molly said. "Let's not make a fuss."

"They're not yours," Daisy said, choked with fury.

Daisy, Greta could tell, was barely containing herself. She looked almost as though, despite the gun, she was really contemplating making a run at Molly. Edgar, on the other hand, took the keys from his pocket without blinking. Greta detected in the younger Buchanan brother a finely honed sense of survival. And he would risk nothing on behalf of the others, she was sure; he would be operating only for himself even if it meant endangering everyone else.

It was then that Jay seemed to go into shock. Though his eyes remained steady, a long shudder wracked his body, and then another. Daisy went pale; her eyes widened. She trembled as she dipped her head forward and unclasped the necklace.

"Here. Take it—take it!"

"Put it on the floor," Molly said. "And your keys, Mr. Buchanan."

The keys and necklace were laid on the marble floor.

"Now push them across to me. Good."

Molly did not stoop to pick them up; she could not without losing her hold on Jay; another deep shudder went through his body.

"Let him go!" Daisy burst out. "Just let him go; he's done nothing to you!"

Molly narrowed her eyes.

"As Miss Baker has so eloquently pointed out, I am outnumbered. You know I need one of you as my hostage. Are you volunteering yourself in his place, Mrs. Buchanan?"

There was only the briefest pause.

"Yes. Only let Jay go." Daisy breathed, steadfast. Greta stared, hardly believing what she heard. Self-centered Daisy Buchanan? Molly seemed surprised, too, but then her eyes narrowed, and she shook her head.

"No, I shall retain Mr. Gatsby, I think, a little longer. What I need now is to get the six of you out of the way. I shall put you in the pantry. It is windowless and it locks, which is the best I can do, and Dantry is there already. I suppose Mrs. Smith will find you there in the morning when she returns." She looked them over. "Miss Baker, you're nearest—you may lead the way."

Jordan didn't move.

"*Now*, please, Miss Baker."

But instead of moving toward the kitchen passage, Jordan turned for the front door.

Molly's voice rang out. "*Miss Baker!*"

Jordan stopped but did not turn around.

"*Where* are you going?"

Jordan swiveled, fists balled at her sides, dark eyes flashing.

"I've no intention of letting you march me into some windowless room to do God knows what with us," she retorted. "For all I know, you're planning to massacre us in there one by one."

"I'm afraid," Molly said stiffly, "you don't have the luxury of choice."

"Oh, don't I?" Jordan's face was alight with anger. "Shoot me, then, if you're going to. I'd rather you do it right here than in some dank little cubby hole."

The words were barely out of her mouth when there was the sound of a gun firing, and Daisy screamed. But the shot had been a warning shot, fired at the ceiling. There was a moment's pulsing silence, and Greta felt her heart pound in her chest. The chandelier swung gently above them, its crystals jangling from the disturbance.

"Miss Baker," Molly said slowly. "That was a demonstration. You ought not to doubt by now that I am capable of shooting you if I say I will."

Greta saw the emotions flickering across Jordan's face, now drained of color. Then she seemed to come to a decision.

She folded her arms. "Do it, then, if you must. I tell you, I'm not afraid of death. But I won't die like a fox in a hole."

There was a terrible pause.

"Jordan, *please!*" Daisy cried.

"So be it, Miss Baker," Molly said grimly, and Greta saw her adjust her grip on the gun. *She was really going to do it.* Pushing Jay wide of her now, Molly aimed—

There was another scream, and the air rang with the aftershock.

Greta blinked, and saw a body on the ground. But it wasn't Jordan.

It was Nick.

Chapter Thirty-Six

"Nobody move!" Molly barked, but Jordan had already dropped to her knees.

"Oh, *Nick!*"

He was sprawled on the ground, eyes open, face stunned. There was blood on his shirt: a stain the size of a dime.

It's only his shoulder, Greta thought desperately. If they could just get him medical attention . . .

"Nicky." Jordan let out a choked sob. "I'm so terribly sorry. What were you thinking?"

"What were *you* thinking?" Daisy snapped.

"Everyone, move *away* from him," Molly said, louder now. She was white-faced; the gun trembled a little. She was as thrown by this as they were. But that wasn't good; if Molly panicked, she might do anything.

Nick exhaled, air whistling between his teeth as he fought with the pain. Jordan still knelt by his side as though she hadn't heard Molly's command.

"Mr. Carraway." Molly turned. "Can you stand?"

"No doubt," he exhaled. "Momentarily."

Jordan took the handkerchief from his pocket and pressed it to the wound, staunching it until Nick took it from her and waved her away. He maneuvered himself to a seated position, and winced.

"I don't suppose someone could give me a hand?"

Grudgingly, Molly nodded to Daisy, and in a few moments Nick was on his feet, pale but steady.

"Good," Molly said. "Now, after that unfortunate incident, I trust there will be no more such events." But her voice was shaking.

"He needs a doctor, Molly," Greta said. Molly wheeled on her.

"And whose fault is that? Mr. Gatsby—can you lead us toward the kitchen?"

Greta felt her heart pounding in her skull as she followed the others down the service passage. If Mrs. Smith didn't return until tomorrow . . .

In single file, they reached the kitchen, and Molly indicated the heavy door that opened into the pantry.

"Now walk on through. Mrs. Dantry will surely be glad of the company."

Jay opened the door.

"Please, Molly—" Greta began.

"All the way to the back," Molly ordered.

There was Dantry at the back of the pantry, gagged and furious, her hands tied to one of the iron racks that ran the length of the long, narrow room. The pantry shelves had always been a sight of abundance, heavy with meats and cheeses, with peeled vegetables in bowls of ice water. But now, with its lone light bulb dangling from a thin cord above them, it reminded Greta of nothing so much as a morgue. Daisy began to whimper.

And then came the sound of the doorbell.

Greta's heart missed a beat; it was almost impossible to keep the hope from showing in her face. Was it the police at last?

"I'll be damned," Edgar muttered. Everyone stood frozen, waiting for Molly's decision. If no one answered the door, would it be suspicious?

"Shut up!" Molly hissed. "Shut up, all of you." The panic was obvious as her eyes darted between them, finally landing on Greta, who was at the rear of their single-file line and nearest the pantry door.

"You, come with me. The rest of you, stay exactly where you are. Not that you'll have any choice."

Daisy's whimpering had turned to dry, rhythmic sobs.

Molly stood outside the pantry, gun aimed squarely on Greta.

"Slowly walk out of there. Then turn around and lock the door," Molly instructed.

Everything in Greta resisted, but she forced herself to do it. The key turned; the bolt shot across. She couldn't hear Daisy's whimpering anymore. In that moment, it was hard not to despair.

"Good. Now walk in front of me—nice and steady—until we get to the hallway. If you try to make a break for it, Miss Gatsby, I'll shoot."

Greta swallowed.

"I won't run."

They made a slow march back along the service passage into the hall. As they passed the living room doorway, Molly hissed. She'd seen the Black Maria through the living-room window; now she knew.

"I suppose *you're* responsible for this." She prodded Greta sharply in the back with the gun. "I suppose you thought you were being very clever. Well, now, you're going to go to the door, and you're going to tell them that everything is fine here, perfectly fine and that you're terribly, *terribly* sorry to have wasted their time."

The doorbell rang again, echoing through the hall. Greta thought it had never before been so loud.

"Is that quite clear, Miss Gatsby? If you try to do anything clever, here's what I'll do. I won't shoot you: I'll push you out the door, let the police take care of you. And then I'll go back inside and put a bullet in your brother's head. Do you understand?"

Greta's heart was beating so fast, she felt sure she would be sick. It wasn't a bluff she could afford to call.

"Yes," Greta said softly. "I understand."

She heard her own hollow footsteps as she walked the last paces toward the door. She felt the cold, smooth shape of the gun nesting between her shoulder blades.

"That's it," Molly said. "Easy, now. Don't be foolish, Miss Gatsby."

Greta turned the key and released the latch. Inspector Francis stood there, skepticism writ plainly on his face. Beside him was Sergeant Stanhope.

"Well?" the inspector said brusquely. "What's all this, then? Are you all being murdered in your beds?"

Oh, the stupid, odious man!

"Of course not, Inspector," she said stiffly. "What made you imagine such a thing?"

The inspector folded his arms.

"Well, I suppose it would be the fellow who came barreling into the precinct not thirty minutes ago, rabbiting on about a young lady who had told him there was some sort of grave trouble afoot at this particular address. Said we'd best get out here at once." He narrowed his eyes. "I suppose that young lady wouldn't be you?"

"Oh . . ." She forced an appropriate expression onto her face. "How unfortunate. I—I'm afraid when I returned here in a cab earlier, there was quite an argument going on inside—Mrs. Buchanan, you see, had come back to collect her things, and a dreadful row had broken out. They were all screaming bloody murder. The cabbie must have got quite the wrong idea." She cleared her throat. "As you see, I'm quite well; we are all quite well."

Didn't the man have any instinct at all? She wanted desperately to wink or make a sign, anything to let him know that this was all a horrible charade, but she didn't dare. The stupid fellow probably wouldn't understand—he'd likely ask what she was winking at him for, and then it would all be over.

The inspector stared narrowly at her.

"Are you sure you don't want us to come in, Miss Gatsby?"

The gun pressed deeper into her back.

"I really am sorry," she stuttered. "It was just a silly mistake."

"Bloody nuisance," the inspector mumbled under his breath. "Look, Sergeant, you go wait in the car."

The young man hesitated, then did as he was bidden. As he walked away, the sun winking off the gold trim on his uniform, it was all Greta could do to keep the tears from springing to her eyes. *Come back,* she wanted to cry out. *Help us.*

"It's a serious matter, you know, Miss Gatsby—the wasting of police time." The inspector leaned in. "We were doing our job, taking your brother in for a chat. This little hoax had better not be anyone's idea of a tit for tat."

Greta swallowed. The tears threatened to spring up again—the frustration was unbearable.

"Certainly not, Inspector."

He tipped his hat with a sardonic look. She could have hit him, truly.

"All right, then," he said, and she watched his retreating back until the door was pushed closed from behind her.

"Well done, Miss Gatsby," Molly said. "I'm glad to see you've kept some sense." She steered Greta back around, but stopped by the living room door, waiting to be sure the officers really left. There was the sound of an engine starting.

"That's it," Molly said with satisfaction.

Greta looked down.

She was standing beside the credenza, where the letter salver lay—and on top of it, the letter knife, that little jade-handled dagger that had been sharp enough to slice into her thumb that fateful morning. It was just a hair's breadth from her little finger. Greta didn't think twice; she couldn't afford to. Her hand simply closed over the knife, lifting it soundlessly from its tray.

Outside, the tires crunched over gravel, and Molly gave a satisfied sound. "All right. Come on."

The dagger was stuffed in the front of Greta's waistband so that Molly, behind her, had no view of it—but Greta had to move carefully now, to be sure she didn't dislodge it. If it got loose, and clattered to the ground . . . But she stepped forward, and it held. She felt the thin piece of metal against her stomach as she walked. Only it was no good to her now, with Molly behind her. She needed a distraction, something to give her an advantage.

"Hurry up." Molly nudged the gun again against Greta's back. "If I am delayed, you will answer for it."

Drawing breath to keep from shaking, Greta moved slowly. As they walked down the kitchen passage, she tried a last appeal.

"Nick," she said, "he's bleeding—he might bleed out before tomorrow."

There was silence behind her.

"He'll be all right," Molly said finally, but there was discomfort in her voice. This wasn't what she wanted; Greta had heard the same unease in Molly's voice when she spoke of Ada earlier. For Molly, killing Tom had been simple justice—but Ada and Nick, she hadn't wanted to hurt them. Greta remembered how white-faced she had been after firing that shot; how her hand had trembled on the gun. Molly was not a monster, or at least she was not one yet. Her humanity was still there, and it was being tormented. She was afraid, but not of Greta; she was afraid of the person she was becoming.

They stopped outside the pantry door.

"All right, you lot." Molly rammed the door with her left hand, never taking her right from the gun at Greta's back. "Listen to me. Miss Gatsby will be opening this door and joining you. All of you, stand back by the far wall."

Greta swallowed, and the flat of the knife pressed against her stomach. Her mind was spinning. If she could only seize the advantage somehow, even for a moment; if she could wrong-foot Molly . . .

"All right," Molly addressed her. "Go on in."

Greta steeled herself and moved to the door, turned the key. The bolt slid back. She gripped the doorknob and twisted. She made a show of it, twisting and pushing to no avail.

"It won't open," she lied. Her palms were sweating; she hoped her voice was convincing. "I—I think it's stuck."

"Rot." Molly scowled. "Open it!"

Greta repeated the performance—her desperation, surely, was believable. She made another deep turn of the knob and a show of leaning in toward the door, as though it were withstanding her weight.

"I can't get it to budge."

Molly snarled.

"The rest of you in there! If you're up to any tricks, you'd better think again. I told you to stand back!"

She waited a moment, then nodded to Greta to try again. Greta rattled the handle, turned it. She was sweating terribly; she hoped Molly would think it was from exertion.

"Damn you, move over," Molly said impatiently. She moved next to Greta, but kept her gun trained on her even as she edged her aside. Then she put her hand on the doorknob and twisted hard.

It was only a second, but a second was all Greta needed. The door gave way instantly; Molly tottered, and locked together, the two women stumbled through the doorway. The knife was already in Greta's hand, and then, faster than she'd thought herself able, at Molly's throat.

Chapter Thirty-Seven

Across the room, somebody gasped, but Greta didn't dare take her eyes from Molly's face, the blade at Molly's neck. Molly was panting; so was she. Their eyes locked.

"Did you think you'd got one over on me, Miss Gatsby? I can end this as quickly as you can, you know."

As Molly spoke, Greta became conscious of the cold touch of the gun against her belly. She kept her eyes on the gleam of the blade in front of her. Her heart thundered. They might look evenly matched, but there was a difference: Molly had proved she could pull a trigger, but Greta had no such confidence about striking a fatal blow. Yet at all costs she must convince Molly of her mettle.

"Stay *back*," Molly snarled, as across the room they sensed someone step closer. From the corner of her eye, Greta saw Nick.

"We'd all have been just fine, you know," Molly said through gritted teeth, "if you hadn't tried to play the sleuth in all this."

Greta kept her hand steady on the knife. She saw that it had grazed Molly already; the tiniest bead of blood had formed on the girl's throat.

"You really thought we'd all just carry on as before," Greta retorted, "after Tom died?"

"We would have," Molly said. "We almost did."

In the corner of her eye, Greta saw more movement. It was Nick again: he had inched a little farther in their direction. He wanted her—and only her—to see him. What was he up to?

"You don't have the nerve to kill me, Miss Gatsby. Give it up."

The gun burrowed deeper into Greta's stomach. Her mind raced. Physically, they were evenly matched. The upper hand she needed she'd have to get some other way. She thought again how Molly had trembled on seeing Nick's injury; her insistence about not wanting to hurt Ada. The girl was split in two, her conscience tormented.

Greta could make use of that.

Behind Molly, there was movement again. Nick, something with his foot—he reached it toward the lowest pantry shelf. A small movement—he was tipping something. Tipping something over?

It was one of those bowls where Mrs. Smith kept the peeled vegetables. Bowls full of ice water. Nick was tipping water onto the floor.

Nerves sparked down Greta's back. *Now* she knew something Molly didn't . . . and in her whirling thoughts, a strategy of sorts came to her.

This stalemate could not be won through brute strength or speed. It was Molly's mind, her strength of purpose, that Greta would have to overpower first.

"You're proud of being a killer, are you, Molly?"

Greta locked her eyes on Molly's to keep her gaze from traveling, but even so, she saw the gleam from the corner of her eye: the yellow glare of the light bulb overhead, mirrored now in a puddle of water that was forming, edging toward them.

"Not proud," Molly hissed. "I did what justice demanded."

"With Tom, perhaps." Greta readied herself. "But killing Ada? Was that justice?"

Instantly, Molly's face changed.

I've hit home, Greta thought.

"I didn't kill her! I knocked her out, that's all!"

Greta pressed the knife closer against Molly's skin.

"She's dead, Molly. She died in that alley in a pool of her own blood. Thanks to you." The words came easily, and Greta's voice shook as she delivered them. They didn't feel like a lie; it was all too easy to envision how it might have gone. Through grace alone, Ada's fate had taken a different path.

"No!" Molly shook her head. "I just had to keep her quiet! Just for a few hours! I just needed a little time!"

Greta looked into her eyes.

"You cracked her skull. You killed her."

"No." Molly's voice was high and pinched. "You're lying!"

Slowly, Greta pressed her advantage, her weight shifting forward ever so slightly, forcing Molly to take a step back.

"How could I lie," she said, "about a thing like that?"

"No," Molly murmured. She backed up another half step; it was enough. Her eyes widened; her foot skidded through water.

Greta dropped the knife as Molly lurched backward, wrenching the barrel of the gun toward the ceiling. There was a shot, and as Molly wrestled with the gun, another, and the sound of glass exploding, and then darkness. As the ricochet rattled through Greta, she heard the screams and felt the gun drop and clatter to the ground.

The light bulb: a bullet had shattered it, and in the windowless room, all was pitch dark. *Where was the gun?* If Molly found it first . . . Greta did a rushed tally. Five bullets: one in the hall ceiling, one in Nick's shoulder, two in the pantry just now. That left one bullet.

In the chaos of bodies and shouting, Greta saw a crack of light: the pantry door was opening. Someone was escaping. *Molly.* Gun or not, all she'd need to do was turn that key and they'd be locked in here in the darkness, just as she'd planned all along.

Greta charged toward the door, yanking it back before it could close. Then Molly let go abruptly, causing Greta to tumble backward, but she caught herself, scrambled to her feet, and bolted out the pantry door in Molly's wake. The light in the kitchen was blinding for a moment. Then she saw Molly halfway to the back door, the one that led out to the kitchen garden. She wasn't holding the gun. But at the sound of Greta's footsteps, she stopped, grabbed a cleaver from the counter, and spun around.

"I warn you, I'm getting out of here, whatever it takes."

"Oh no you're not." Edgar's voice rang out from behind them. He'd emerged from the pantry behind Greta, and he was holding the gun. Its barrel was trained squarely on Molly.

"Stay right where you are," he said.

Molly hesitated.

"Now drop that." He nodded to the cleaver Molly held.

Molly didn't move, and Edgar cocked the gun.

"I'm as ruthless as you are."

Greta saw the endgame play out on Molly's face. The bitterness, the rage. For a moment, Greta thought Molly would charge Edgar, would *make* him shoot her, but it seemed Molly preferred to live. Slowly, she unclenched her grip. The cleaver clanged to the floor.

Edgar laughed, took a step closer.

"You knew you couldn't get away with it, didn't you? A filthy little wench like you. You thought you could kill my brother, a Buchanan—and get away with it? You thought *that* was how the world works?"

He hadn't lowered the gun; its barrel was still trained on Molly's chest.

"Nobody will miss you," Edgar said softly. "When you're gone, nobody will even notice. A miserable thing like you. You're nothing in this world. You're the dirt under my boot."

He raised the gun higher and advanced a step.

"Edgar, *no!*" Greta cried out.

He sneered. "Not to worry, Miss Gatsby. Nobody will question that I shot the bitch in self-defense."

Molly was defenseless, unarmed—and he meant to shoot her in cold blood. "Edgar, *put down the gun*. Don't doubt I'll tell the police the truth!"

"My word against yours, Miss Gatsby," he said smugly, and pulled the trigger.

Chapter Thirty-Eight

Time seemed to freeze for a moment. When it began again, Molly stood where she had stood before, stunned and seemingly uninjured. Edgar could not possibly have missed her, not from that distance. But there had been no scream, no deafening aftershock. The gun had fired, but with a thin, rattling sort of sound this time.

There was no fifth bullet.

"Fool," Molly said quietly—and then she wheeled around and was out the door, knocking the garden ladder across the path behind her. With a scream of rage, Edgar threw the gun to the ground and gave chase. Greta raced behind, her head spinning. She was still reeling from the moment that had not come to pass: a vision of Molly on the kitchen floor; Edgar standing over her, pleased with his handiwork. *My word against yours.* The vile man. And yet it was Molly they now must chase down, Molly who must not get away. Did she still have the keys to Edgar's Studebaker? She was certainly running in that direction.

As she raced through the grass, Greta heard the shouts of the others bursting through the kitchen door behind her, but there were voices ahead, too. Dashing around the side of the house, Greta stumbled—

And when she righted herself, stopped and stared.

There stood Sergeant Stanhope, uniform aglow in the sun, looking exceptionally pleased with himself. He was pinning Molly's arms behind her back as Molly writhed and shouted while Inspector Francis brandished a pair of handcuffs. Edgar stood near them, bent over to draw breath.

The sergeant saw Greta and grinned. She gaped back at him, and stood, dazed, as the others caught up with shouts and exclamations. There was Nick, his face still much too bloodless, and Jay, supporting him. There was Jordan, looking thoroughly stunned for once, and Daisy behind her, helping Mrs. Dantry.

"We were right on time by the looks of it," Sergeant Stanhope said.

"You weren't so very convincing, you know, Miss Gatsby," the inspector said gruffly, as he fastened the handcuffs. "I shouldn't take up acting if I were you. We parked at the bottom of the driveway and walked back up through the tree cover. Just in time to meet *this* young lass on her way out."

Greta shook her head, marveling. So they hadn't believed her story after all.

Molly snarled, "You think you're something special, don't you. You think you're so very fine. Well, anyone would have done what I did. Anyone would have if they'd had the courage. If they'd had any honor."

Edgar marched up to her and drew his head back, but Jay, who must have sensed what was coming, quickly stepped between them, receiving a gob of Edgar's saliva in his face for the trouble.

"Now, then," said Inspector Francis, as Jay slowly wiped the liquid from his face.

"Edgar," Jay said in a clear, commanding voice, "get the hell off my lawn."

Edgar turned, fuming.

"Believe me, it will be my pleasure." He looked to where the women were standing. "Come, Daisy."

Daisy shook her head. Her fine blonde hair danced in the breeze.

"I'm not going anywhere with you, Edgar. And if I ever see you again, it will be too soon."

"Inspector," Greta interjected. "Mr. Carraway's shoulder is wounded, and he needs to be seen by a medic."

Inspector Francis looked him over.

"Shot you, did she, the vixen? We can take you to the hospital right now, if you can stomach sharing the back seat for a few minutes."

Nick flinched.

"I think I'd rather wait for the ambulance, Inspector."

"We'll have one out with the utmost urgency," Inspector Francis assured him. "As for the rest of you, we'll need a full statement from each of those present," he said gravely. "But I daresay it can wait until you feel a little more . . . recovered. Stanhope and I shall be back shortly. Stanhope, get the car, would you?"

"I should like a ride with you to the station, Inspector," Mrs. Dantry broke in, then turned around. "Mr. Gatsby, I am tendering my resignation as of this moment."

"Well, all right, Dantry," Jay said dryly. "We'll struggle on somehow, I'm sure."

Mrs. Dantry narrowed her eyes, then marched down the driveway after Stanhope and Molly.

As her ringing footsteps faded, a strange kind of silence descended over the small group: a mixture of grim exhaustion and a strange, shivery euphoria.

"I feel a little faint," Daisy said at last.

"So do I," Jordan confessed.

"So do I," said Nick and Jay together, and Daisy gave a hiccup of laughter.

"Well, you're the hero of the hour, Greta." Nick shaded his eyes from the sun with his good hand as Stanhope pulled the police vehicle into the forecourt. The inspector was already leading Molly away; Greta watched her as she went, stiff-backed and somehow smaller looking again.

"Hear, hear," Jordan said. "Greta the Great."

Jay put an arm around her shoulder.

"The very greatest of Gatsbys." He paused. "Although very reckless, too. Please promise me you'll never get up to anything like this again."

"I hope I shan't have to promise *that*, Jay." Despite herself, Greta laughed. "I'm hardly likely to be facing down more murderers in the future, am I?"

Behind them, the late afternoon sun shone over the bay. The water twinkled. Sunset would be here soon.

"Well, I don't know about the rest of you," Jordan said as the black Model T receded into the distance. "But I, for one, could really use a drink."

Epilogue

"All aboard! All aboard!"

The conductor strode along the platform, and already passengers were leaning out of windows, making their goodbyes. Nick had the tickets tucked into his sling; the wound was healing very well, the doctor said, but since Nick was right-handed, the office would have to wait a little longer for his return.

"Still, I don't suppose they'll fire me now," he said. "Considering the circumstances."

His dry sense of humor was back, but Greta still felt a dart of guilt every time she looked at the sling. After the initial euphoria of their escape, things had felt quite dark for a few days as they each absorbed the shock of recent events at their own pace. Jordan had been ministering to Nick quite devotedly since his injury—whether out of a sense of culpability or from more tender feelings, Greta couldn't tell. Greta herself had been almost too shy to venture into his room. She wondered if Molly had not been at least a little bit right: were it not for Greta's interference, that shot would never have been fired. If Greta hadn't been so determined to find the killer, perhaps Ada would never have been injured, and Molly would have simply slipped away on some train or another, and no blood would have been spilled besides Tom Buchanan's.

At the same time, thanks to Greta, Beecham's life had been restored to him, and Molly was behind bars. And Ada and Nick both seemed to be recovering well.

Although Ada had decided against returning to her former position at the house, she had called by to visit Mrs. Smith and Bill, who had been positively agog with all the extraordinary events recounted to them upon their return to work. Molly, a murderer! And Ada was Beecham's niece! It was unclear which piece of information Mrs. Smith had found more stupefying.

Beecham had come back to work, and was much his inscrutable self. Jay would be advertising for Mrs. Dantry's replacement after the summer—meanwhile, as far as Greta was concerned, her absence was a considerable improvement.

The day after Molly's arrest, Daisy had come into Greta's room and sat at the foot of the bed.

"I keep asking myself," she'd said, "whether deep down, I *did* know the truth—that Tom's death was unnatural, I mean. You always did rather suspect foul play, didn't you? I think perhaps, deep down, I heard a little voice, too. I just didn't want to believe it."

Greta had a flash of her mother then, imparting one of her favorite adages many years ago. *Always listen to the still, small voice.* Was it intuition she had meant, or one's conscience?

Both, perhaps.

"I suppose if *I'd* had any intuition in my life," Daisy had said then, "I wouldn't have married Tom, for a start."

Daisy, Greta thought, seemed different; older, perhaps. Not *aged* exactly, or at least not on the outside; her skin was as fresh as ever, her hair as lustrous. It was something else. Before, Daisy had been one of those people always somehow in movement, excited or agitated—even her woes were exuberant. But now she was quieter. Sun filtered thinly through the bay window. Daisy's hands stayed folded as she talked. Her eyelids didn't flutter, nor did her gaze dart about.

"You meant it, about her taking you instead," Greta had said, looking Daisy in the eye. "Didn't you? For Molly to take you as a hostage in Jay's place. It was a very brave thing."

Jordan had once said that Daisy Buchanan was cleverer than most people. Certainly, Daisy was skilled; she could hide her true feelings perhaps better than anyone Greta knew. So *did* she love Jay? Or if she didn't now, then had she once?

"I did mean it," Daisy said quietly. She looked away. "Jay reminds me of who I could have been. Who I almost was." She ran her fingertips over the bedspread, her voice quiet. "As long as he's alive, I think a part of me will live, too."

"And yet you will not marry him?"

"I cannot."

Now Greta glanced up at Daisy, who was already seated inside the train car. She'd been the first to board, leaving the others to make their long-drawn-out goodbyes. *The heat*, she'd offered as an excuse. It was, indeed, a hot day and plenty of the ladies on the train had their fans out, but Greta knew it wasn't that. She could see Daisy through the window now, applying lavender water with a handkerchief, dabbing delicately behind her ears. The handkerchief itself was a square of jaunty green silk that seemed to belong to the other Daisy, the old Daisy, at odds with her sober navy dress. Jay's eyes kept darting toward the window, too, and Greta knew the deep fear he held in his heart: that he would not see Daisy Buchanan ever again.

Daisy, Jordan, and Nick were all traveling back to Grand Central Station, from where they would go their separate ways: Nick, to recuperate at a wealthy aunt's pied-à-terre in France; Jordan, to the golf championship that awaited her in Florida, and Daisy, to recover her daughter from Rosemary Buchanan. Where Daisy would live long-term was not yet certain, but there was a new sturdiness in Daisy that she hadn't noticed before—though perhaps it had always been there, covered over. Perhaps, when she'd wondered who brought out the best in Daisy Buchanan, she'd been asking the wrong question. Perhaps the best in Daisy was right there, and all it needed was space and solitude, and a little sunlight, to bloom.

A whistle blew, and the activity on the train platform seemed to redouble.

"I suppose this is our cue," Nick said. He had his valise in his good hand; Jay had put Jordan's and Daisy's cases on the train already.

"Take care of yourself, old sport," Jay said now, laying a hand on Nick's good shoulder. Greta saw him struggling for the words to encompass what they'd all endured.

"We'll miss you, you know. Won't we, Gigi?"

She flushed.

"Of course," she said quickly.

Nick gave a dry laugh. "Will you? I should think I'd just be a bad reminder for you now."

"You could never be that," Greta said, and immediately regretted it. There'd been too much warmth in her voice, she knew from Jordan's curious glance. Nick seemed to study Greta's face for a moment.

I suppose what he really means is that we'll *be a bad reminder,* Greta thought. She couldn't blame Nick, or Jordan or Daisy, if they never wanted to see the Gatsbys again. Sometimes moving forward meant purging the past—and the people in it. Would that be the case here?

I suppose it depends how desperate each of us is to forget.

The events of last week would not leave Greta anytime soon. She had thought of Molly many times in the past few days—more than she let on to anyone. Molly, too, had only made it out alive by the skin of her teeth, though whether she felt lucky about that now was another matter. Had she picked out a six-shooter from the gun room as she believed, rather than a five-shooter, she'd probably have died at Edgar's hand that day. But Greta suspected Molly would have done it all again, given the chance. She'd followed Tom Buchanan halfway across the country, renouncing her future, her freedom, even the family she had left, not to mention the sanctity of her own soul, in order to mete out the justice she believed was deserved. That had been Molly's gambit, and the Gatsbys had been at the center of it. They'd been the price of entry, the first pawn in the game.

Greta had thought often since that day of the similarities between Molly and herself. Molly, too, had been the child of immigrants; like Greta, she'd had just one sibling, a brother she'd looked up to. Like Greta, her family had suffered a great tragedy when she was still young.

Most of all, it was Molly's parents that Greta thought of: what fears they must have had, braving this new country alone, and what tremendous hopes. But whatever hopes they'd held for their children had been so cruelly dashed—first they'd lost their son, and now, in an arguably worse way, they'd lost their daughter.

"Many dreams get poisoned in this land," Nora had observed, when Greta called by to tell the story.

The art of the gambit: a tactical sacrifice. But even a tactical sacrifice was a privilege of sorts, she reflected now. Not everyone got to choose what was lost; what was taken from them.

And what, Greta wondered, had her parents hoped for her and Jay? She remembered her mother's favorite aphorism of all: *Money is good; love is better.*

Greta and Jay were taking a trip of their own, too; they were shutting down the house for a month, and going north to the Cape—not to the fashionable parts, just a small hamlet on the south side where there would be no high society, no one but locals and fishermen. Their father had enjoyed fishing; maybe Jay would try it. It was going to be a strange time, just the two of them, no guests, no staff. It was bound to be awkward at first. But she wondered what they would find on the other side of that awkwardness. She hoped, perhaps, to find that shopkeeper's son once more, the starry-eyed boy who'd brought flowers to their mother's table.

Greta's parents had raised their children to believe in this new land and its great meritocracy, and they had. But while Jay had worked hard for the life they now possessed, perhaps their relief at escaping those dark early years had obscured another truth: that Greta's brother was not uniquely brilliant, not uniquely lucky or deserving. Rather, he had risen on a fast and reckless tide, the same one that had filled the halls of Congress with railway tycoons and oilmen with plump white hands that held a whole nation in their grip. The newspapers seemed trapped in a state of awe at new advances, at innovation and progress and gain. But there seemed to be another trajectory in full swing, too, harsher and more accelerated than before, where the rich got richer and the poor got ever poorer. Where wealth flowed ever upward, and the chasm between haves and have-nots widened every day. Greta looked down the platform. There were signs of wealth everywhere, and other signs, too: the grimy faces of the engine boys calling, "Yes, sir," as they scurried across the platform, harried and overworked.

Had her parents been wrong all along, or had something changed? Sped up, perhaps, before anyone could check it. For surely this state of affairs was nothing new—but it seemed faster, more extreme than before; how markedly the scales had tipped. Was there something peculiarly American in it or was it just the wild, propulsive pace of the times, this prized second decade of the new century?

Silas said a change was coming, that the poets of Harlem were speaking it on the wind. *Change would be a good thing*, Greta thought. It would be a good thing for a person to be part of.

It had come to Greta as she cycled home from Nora's apartment: evidently one did not have to travel the world like Nellie Bly to find things worth changing. Things worth insisting about. And another thought came to her, too: she'd been anticipating only one kind of remedy for the injustice she kept seeing, and perhaps she'd been wrong about that as well. It wasn't *protection* that the likes of Nora and Ada, or even Silas, needed most. It was community. The strength that came from banding together, not the borrowed patronage of the elite.

And in theory, every American might have it. That was the whole point of the Constitution after all, was it not? Freedom of association, freedom of speech; it was the freedom to unite, to draw strength from numbers. But what good was freedom of the press if you couldn't read or afford a twopenny paper? What good was freedom of association if you had no place to convene, no free hour to do it in? *Speech might be free*, Greta thought, *but to be heard cost money.*

She, Greta, had money.

And perhaps, instead of being the one to chronicle the injustices she saw, as she had once thought she would, Greta might find a way to help others lift the pen. To speak their own words. To come together.

The conductor gave another whistle.

"All right, Nicky." Beside her, Jordan gave Nick's shirt a tweak. "We'd better not miss our train."

Nick put his good arm around Jay's shoulders, and they walked together to the train door. Jordan hung back with Greta, and as they walked, Greta felt her sideways glance. It was a little sardonic but perhaps less so than usual.

"He's not in love with me, you know."

Greta kept her eyes on the train.

"What—who do you mean?" she said.

"Oh, *you* know." Jordan turned fully now. "He's not in love with me, even if he *did* try to take a bullet for me." Her mouth twisted. "Lovely Nicky. He always did have an overdeveloped sense of chivalry."

Greta flushed. She knew what Jordan was telling her; she supposed it was an invitation of sorts. But an invitation to what? Nick was boarding his train and on his way to France, and after that ... after that, who knew?

"You're incorrigible, Jordan," Greta said at last, and Jordan smiled.

"I *am*, aren't I?" she said, and sauntered up the steps of the train.

"Goodbye, Jay, darling." Jordan gave him a peck on the cheek. "Do be careful, now. No more adventures for a while, I think." She turned. "Greta, till next time." She gave a quick wink before disappearing inside the train.

Nick hovered on the bottom step, his straw boater dazzling in the sun. He reached for Jay's hand and shook it. He looked Greta's way then, the full force of his gaze like a shock.

"Goodbye, Greta," he said.

She nodded. She was supposed to say it back, but for some reason, the word was stuck in her throat.

"You know," he said then, "you do owe me a dance."

Greta blinked—he remembered that?—and Nick gave her one of those quiet smiles she'd come to know and appreciate very much. But there wasn't time for her to say anything; the conductor was passing in front of them, hollering, "All aboard."

"Goodbye," she said, as he bounded up the steps, but the commotion was too intense by then and her voice too quiet. Moments later, the train rattled to life. Greta looked toward the window of the compartment. On one side, Daisy looked out at them, pale-faced and watchful, as though she were impressing the image upon her mind. Jordan had the other window seat, and gave a jaunty wave as she caught Greta's eye. Nick leaned over her, struggling with the window, which flung open at last, and his face leaned out over Jordan's.

"Arrivederci!" Jordan called, and Nick held a handkerchief aloft in farewell. It was Daisy's: as the train chugged out of the station, the green silk square caught the wind and billowed, a shimmering emerald flag. Greta felt a squeeze in her chest as the train gathered speed. She kept her eyes on the small bright square of green. There was something dreamlike about it, something sad even. She realized then what it reminded her of: the Buchanans' green beacon across the sound, the one Jay had used to watch for at night. It had always looked so magical, so beautiful, the otherworldly flicker of some ever-receding dream.

The Buchanans.

They had been a part of Jay's life for so many years; they had consumed him. What would he do now without them?

As if in response, Greta felt Jay's arm wrap around her shoulder. She glanced up at his face, careworn yet boyish still. He smiled a small smile, then looked away, squinting into the distance, the crow's-feet crinkling at the corners of his green eyes. He wasn't looking in the direction of the disappearing train, though, but rather the other way, out toward the horizon—as though he were waiting for something. As though something tremendous and new might be coming down the track at any minute.

And who knew? Greta closed her eyes for a moment, and tilted her head toward the sun. Maybe, just maybe, it was.

Author Note

Thank you so much for reading *The Gatsby Gambit*. I'm honored that you did, and I really hope you enjoyed it. There are many reasons why I wanted to write this story—because I love a good mystery, for one thing, and because I am a huge fan of *The Great Gatsby*, for another. It was an absolute treat to spend so much time immersed in a world that gave me both. While writing, I also found myself thinking a lot about the way we see the world today compared to how Fitzgerald and his readers would have seen it. Fitzgerald's concern about the harm that careless wealthy people can inflict on those around them is a central aspect of *The Great Gatsby*. But it's also true that its characters only interacted with a tiny portion of what would have been American society at the time. As we would say now, they lived in a bubble, and a very small one. In *The Gatsby Gambit*, I tried to spend a bit more time outside that particular bubble, and to bring Greta into a world beyond it. I trust that she will learn to navigate it well!

Even though I'm sure to have made some inadvertent mistakes, I tried to be as faithful to historical detail as I could—for example, East and West Egg's likely real-life location in Long Island, and which train lines and bridges would have been in place; what a likely haute cuisine menu from the

AUTHOR NOTE

1920s might have featured; or specific clothing choices that might have been in vogue. (How disappointing to learn that those wonderful tasseled fringes were not part of 1920s fashion at all! In fact, this is a misconception brought about by the 1960s revival of flapper fashion!)

It occurred to me that, while most of the book can very easily be separated into fact and fiction, some readers may wonder about references to the "American Protective League" of which Tom Buchanan was supposedly a part, and out of whose actions the violence of the novel ultimately arises: Was this League a real phenomenon? Yes, it very much was.

The APL was founded in 1917, when fears of German espionage in the US were running high. A Chicago businessman pitched his idea to the Department of Justice for a volunteer force to "enforce patriotism and stifle dissent," which was approved by President Wilson. By that fall, the privately funded group would have an estimated two hundred fifty thousand to three hundred thousand members in over six hundred cities, in time inspiring multiple copycat organizations (including Knights of Liberty, American Rights League, Boy Spies of America, American Defense Society, and Sedition Slammers).

Once dues of seventy-five cents were paid, Leaguers could wear a badge that read AMERICAN PROTECTIVE LEAGUE–SECRET SERVICE, and investigate anyone they deemed a threat. They gathered information on neighbors, friends, and strangers; raided homes and offices; and held "slacker raids"—stopping men in streets, saloons, ballparks, and movie theaters and seizing any who weren't carrying draft papers. (In New York alone, more than sixty thousand men were detained, of which only thirteen hundred—by some estimates fewer—were determined to be draft dodgers.) Citizens identified as having German descent, or accused of being pro-German or antiwar, might be detained for much longer.

The specific fate of Molly's brother in *The Gatsby Gambit* is entirely invented. However, it was not unusual for the Leaguers' vigilantism to devolve

AUTHOR NOTE

into assaults. Reports include attempted lynchings and tarring and feathering their targets. But APL vigilantes were rarely arrested or tried, and very rarely convicted. Although the organization was officially dissolved by the Justice Department after the war (along with copycat organizations), the APL and its copycats had stirred an appetite that was not so easily disbanded. In the years that followed the official end of the APL, the KKK would undergo a dramatic nationwide revival, and America saw a stark increase in the number of racial lynchings and attacks on various "undesirables."

As with many political organizations, evaluating the APL today can give rise to different opinions. Some people still view the APL as an example of patriotic heroism. But I believe the historical record leads most of us today to think otherwise.

I hope this little footnote will be clarifying for those readers eager to weed out fact from fiction, as I always am when I read stories based in a historical setting. Be assured, the rest is very much fiction . . . although I still hope to get cocktails with Jordan Baker one of these days! Perhaps you'd care to join us?

Thank you again, reader, for taking this journey with me, and I so hope you enjoyed the ride.

Acknowledgments

So, so much behind-the-scenes work goes into the making of any book, and I am wildly grateful to the people who helped to make this one a reality. Gráinne Fox has the patience of a saint but even more stamina, and definitely a way better sense of humor. Laura Tisdel, I will be forever grateful for your leap of faith, your editorial insight, and your warm common sense. In the UK, I couldn't ask for a more inspiring editor/agent combo than Christina Demosthenous and Sue Armstrong. (Our festive lunch at the Ivy is a memory I continue to relish.) Thanks also to the inspiring marketing genius of Emily Moran at Dialogue Books, and to Madison Hernick and Carlos Zayas-Pons for staying on top of everything.

This book didn't leap onto the page by itself, either. Like any good story, the journey that got me to this point has all sorts of pivots, and I owe a debt of gratitude to a whole host of people from many chapters. Throughout many of those chapters features Natalie Kwan Butlin, who knows so much and shares it so generously, and is also a superlative friend. Going backwards in time: Markus Hoffmann, Joe Regal, Stephanie Steiker, and Elianna Kan, from whom I learned so much about the art and science of publishing (and not a little about perseverance); the University of East Anglia and the many wonderful people I met and learned from there (in class

ACKNOWLEDGMENTS

and out of); and Trinity College Dublin for its undergraduate creative writing seminar, a beacon amid the sometime drudgery of a law degree, and in retrospect, the first stepping stone to a wonderful new adventure. And while I'm here, I should probably also thank Maureen Catt and Shelley Price-Cardinal, two of the best English teachers a middle or high schooler could hope to have.

Meanwhile, dear friends have patiently let me turn them into periodic focus groups for covers, titles, and anything else I could think of, and have consistently offered the most nuanced of insights as well as the kind of friendship and support that could make a person giddy. Thanks to Réachbha Fitzgerald, Margaret Gales and Matt Mullin, Caroline Shoesmith and Robin Theakston, Danie and Lil Cherubin, Nadine Ravaud, Kyra Hild, Marion Siebold, Alma Kelliher and Shane O'Brian, Mary Deane and Nick Leonard, Eleanor Kearon, Liadhan Coakley, Halle and Stephanie Amore-Bauer, Grace Ross and Aaron Kavanaugh, Sarah Dickman and Justin Kilkenny, Kevin Frick and Lea Tsao, and Ilka Ritter.

And finally, the people without whom nothing would be possible: my family. First and last thanks to my parents, Anne Anderson and Martin Wheeler, who inspired not only a lifelong love of reading but every other quality I have worth mentioning. In word and deed, they taught me that books are precious, and that people are, too. Thanks also to their partners, my stepfathers Franklin Lowe and Manuel Dudli Bertrán, two of my most stalwart supporters and unpaid publicists, whom I am so lucky to have in my life. And finally to Pavol Roskovensky, a gentleman to beat all gentlemen (take that, Nick Carroway), and the love of my life: Thank you for your absolutely excessive belief in me, and for more joy than I could ever have imagined.

Bringing a book from manuscript to what you are reading is a team effort.

Renegade Books would like to thank everyone who helped to publish *The Gatsby Gambit* in the UK.

Editorial
Christina Demosthenous
Eleanor Gaffney

Contracts
Stephanie Evans
Sasha Duszynska Lewis
Isabel Camara

Sales
Megan Schaffer
Kyla Dean
Dominic Smith
Sinead White
Georgina Cutler-Ross
Kerri Hood
Jess Harvey
Natasha Weninger Kong

Design
Hannah Wood
Sara Mahon
Sasha Egonu

Production
Narges Nojoumi

Publicity
Annabel Robinson
Sophie Goodfellow
Antara Patel

Marketing
Emily Moran

Operations
Rosie Stevens

Finance
Chris Vale
Jonathan Gant

Audio
Rabeeah Moeen